To Teri -
To writing
To reading

Gray Fox Connection

To not bombing -
and thanks for all the help -

by Barbara K. Freeman

Barbara -

This book is a work of fiction. Names, characters, places and incidents are products of the author's imagination or are used fictitiously. Any resemblance to actual events or locales or persons, living or dead, is entirely coincidental.

Cover art by Mark Allison

Creative concept: Cindie Vinson

ISBN-13: 978-1478359227

ISBN-10: 1478359226

With thanks to so many who read this book and critiqued it so well, especially to writers extraordinaire Linda and Gary Hamner, Marisa Silver, Greg Verret and to all of the Monmouth Writers.

And with special recognition to Carol Cortner.
Peace be with you, my friend.

"Humankind has not woven the web of life. We are but one thread within it. Whatever we do to the web, we do to ourselves. All things are bound together. All things connect."
Chief Seattle

"Our ancient experience confirms at every point that everything is linked together, everything is inseparable."
Dalai Lama XIV

Storm

Have you ever been so pissed off you just had to do something? Anything, right or wrong, blowing something up maybe, to get the attention of the bastards who have been ignoring you?

Probably not. It takes a perfect storm of pissed-off-ness. It must be rare. You have to be mad enough to take action but not so mad to be stupid about it. If it's happened to anybody else, they're in jail now. Or, like me, not talking about it. Only this supposed work of fiction explains what might have happened a decade ago, why someone destroyed those Mormon temples and then disappeared. Me and D.B. Cooper.

I don't suppose I'd do it now, even without the hindsight that shows how badly it would work out. Back in that other millennium when they couldn't be heard otherwise, people burned buildings sometimes, a forestry building, for example, to try to protect old-growth forests. Those protesters were considered over the edge, rude. They got put in jail for a while if they were caught. But the word *terrorist* hadn't entered the common lexicon of this country in those days.

Of course it takes more than a can of gas and a match to bring down a big marble temple.

People assumed it was bigotry. I should have paid better attention to that. I was so sure they'd get it: no attacks on Sunday-go-to-meetin' houses. Just on big, self-righteous, exclusionary monstrosities. Assaults only when no one would be there to get hurt.

I thought.

PART I. Losing Andrea

Echo Lake

December 2000. Midnight. The worst part now, can't breathe, my fear thickening the air. I want to tug at my bloody sports bra, tight so my pudgy body could be a man's, not that I intend to be seen. Tugging won't help: it's fear suffocating me, not bra.

My lungs wheeze and rattle. Despite the fine snow drifting down in the night, I'm sweating under the black ski mask, as I try to thread a metal-fiber rope through a metal temple gate without metal-metal shrieks that could bring people running. One person, or two, or a horde, it doesn't matter. There I stand, inside the fence. Exposed at the gate across the broad drive thirty feet from the street. My sixty-year-old legs unlikely to outrun anyone, even with a head start, even if I abandon the plastic explosives, even though I know where the rope ladder is, the way out. A good 200 yards away. Might as well be 200 miles.

Skreeetch.

Shit. I leave the gate, crouch in shadows, wait. Uncover the luminous dial of my watch, let ten minutes creep by.

Quiet.

I go back to the gate. Carefully, carefully thread metal rope through links in the fence. Carefully, carefully pull the other end through the gate. Snap on the padlock, go back to shadows, survey my handiwork. The lock hangs against the gatepost, invisible even from my side; the metal rope is visible if you know to look for it.

I pull the sleeve of my black sweater over my latex glove and stretch the ski mask to dry my face. Cold kisses my skin. I can breathe again, because now anyone checking on my middle-of-the-night activity will punch the key code into the gate box, wait while the rope keeps the gate from opening, get out of the car to see what the problem is, and have to go find a hacksaw to get through. Enough time, even for me. I hope.

Keeping to the shadows, I retrieve the bomb bag which I left by the back fence after I climbed in. Bring it to the base of the building. Safe enough, the mixing of the last ingredient to create explosive potential, the mixture stable enough.

Quiet.

But tamping the plastic into the foundation vents—shit. Too much noise. This is the worst part. Tap tap. Chink. So loud.

I connect the last wire of the first electronic firing device and go to the next vent. Movement? I shrink behind bushes. There's movement all right. Me. Shaking. Dam Sam. I wait, take deep breaths. I want this damn rotten marble polemic gone. Can't proceed with shakes like this. I listen to whispering snow. I calm down.

Again I mix, again I tamp into foundation vent and connect wires. Again I move on. This third one is under the angel Moroni, the last one I'll do in front. Two to go, in the back.

Lights.

I find shrubbery. Shadows. My breathing. Loud. This is the

worst part. Another ten minutes pass. Quiet. Car was just turning around, I guess.

Finally the last vent I mix, tamp. I also stuff into the vent the backpack and plastic bags I'd used to carry materiel. Blowing them to shreds seems a nice idea.

I connect the final wire.

The rope ladder still hangs where I left it, on the back fence by the woods. I fight the bloody thing getting out as much as I had getting in. Rung is up against the fence, can't get my toe in. The step tilts as I try to pull my poor old round body up it. Tilts the other way when I counterbalance. Have the same trouble every time. I should practice. Somewhere unseen; that's the problem. I throw my upper half over the top of the six-foot chain link and more-or-less fall in a heap. Dam Sam. At least I'm on the outside. I want away from there. I lift the ladder off using a branch I had stashed nearby. Before I leave the woods I ditch my hammer in a nice ugly brush pile.

I'm panting by the time I reach the car, parked half a mile away in forest-edged suburbs. I was panting to start; let's not fool ourselves. I'd have been a lot better at this thirty years ago, but I wasn't pissed at temples then.

My ski mask, gloves, sweater, shoes, and the rope ladder all go into a garbage bag in the front seat. I sit on plastic drop cloths, too, because I suppose there would be some telltale bits on me.

My heart pounds; my chest labors, but my rental car sedately passes dark homes and silent woods. Past the temple, gate in my lock's thrall, yards motionless and hushed. Not quite one a.m. I roll down the window. In my flushed state, I welcome the freezing air. And the lovely deep rumble comes clearly to me after I hit the detonator and merge onto the freeway.

With that rumble my anger rises, explodes and falls to rubble like the frikken building itself. Those self-righteous s.o.b.s wouldn't listen to me: let them hear the rumble. One less haughty excluding wall on the planet. My urge satisfied, the itch scratched. Maybe I can give up the midnight forays now. But I thought that twice before.

An hour later, my adrenaline dissipated, I turn on the car radio to stay awake.

"Temple bombers kill two."

WHAT??!

"Bombers struck again …"

Rental car, rudderless, drifts as I stare at its radio trying to understand.

"Two elders, temple workers, were killed …"

"No. No no no no. You have to be wrong."

Death. Destruction. Natter natter.

"Wrong. You are wrong. I'm no killer." I loathe Mormon temples. But my most beloved are Mormons. I don't hurt people, my loved ones or their comrades or anyone else. I have to screw up my courage to step on a large spider. People killed. It is not possible. No one is EVER in a Mormon temple on Sunday. Or at midnight.

I get the car lined up in its lane again. My gawd. The damned radio keeps repeating: "Bombers … destruction … two dead …" Instinct keeps me pointed toward my motorhome waiting at the Provo campground.

My mind has that synapse-buzz of nightmares and tough exams. People killed. Think about it later. Go. Don't speed. Where's cruise control in this car? Run! Normally I'd fight panic by rethinking a trig proof. Lovely cool rationality. Not now. My feet take charge.

Twenty minutes later, briefly on plan, I drive directly to the showers at the RV camp and force myself to take care to wash away all bomb residue and Echo Lake mud. As planned, I wrap dirty clothing in the painter's drape that covered the car seat. But then, instead of parking rental car beside Winnie Winnebago and calming myself with chamomile tea, I hurry to return the car to the rental agency. Even in panic I see I shouldn't leave it at the RV camp. Or steal it. I toss clothing and everything bomber into a dumpster at the back of some strip mall.

Soon my chaste bomber car sits at the side of the rental car lot, keys gone through the chute beside the office door. My nerves snap and pop as I pace in the dim light. The cab seems to take hours, but by the clock only another ten minutes elapse before a lone car approaches down the dark street then swings in, its "taxi 375-625-2575" light glowing welcome yellow. A lovely number, a good omen? Please god, something good. Reporter error. Let it be reporter error.

In an instant I'm climbing into the cab's back seat. The driver says, "Mrs. Bennett? I'm Henri," and I nearly bail out because I'm Andrea Glass, not Mrs. Bennett. I remember in time the name I gave the dispatcher, fall back into the seat, glance at the driver to see if he noticed, then double my double-take. Quadri-take? Henri is Caribbean brown. In Provo. Men here are white, pink cheeks, short fine fair hair.

"Doan know aboot returnen a cahr in these bitty hours," he comments in the blessed darkness, my door now shut, dome light off.

I flop around to secure seatbelt and senses. "Doan know aboot a guy with dreadknots in Provo."

"DreadLOCKS, ma'am."

"Oh, geez I'm such an idiot." I feel so white, so like a person who never left Yoder, Oregon. "A dreadnought is the kind of guitar my friend plays. A Martin Dreadnought."

"A Martin. Mighty fine guitar. I guess youah mistake be a bit of a compliment. I take it that way." He pulls onto the deserted street. "You got a destination or you just wanna drive around? At three in the morning."

I give him the address of the RV camp. "You have a Caribbean lilt, a Jamaican style, Henri. In Provo, Utah." Was this hysteria or just regression to natural nosiness?

"Yes ma'am. Gonna split though, soon's I get this car paid for. Can't even get a decent cuppa java in this town."

"I travel with my own coffee but drank too much tonight." My wits are still jumping and galloping, but I'm catching up to them. Need some reason for my predawn activity. "Couldn't sleep, read for a while, figured I might as well head south. Planned to leave in a couple of hours anyway, beat the traffic."

"Well, ma'am, you sure as shootin beatin the traffic now."

We pull up to my RV. "Nice little guy. I thought maybe you be one those people drive a hotel down the road."

"This has everything I need in 25 feet. Bed, bath, fridge, stove, four wheels. Good luck to you; I enjoyed talking to you." Aghast now at my verbosity, I run up the steps—well, Henri would see a rotund waddle, but it's dash to me—into Winnie the Brave.

Shoot, Newt. I should have just said good morning; pleasant morning for travel. He'll remember about dreadnoughts. Stupid me. I'm a statement/reason kind of person. I don't think well on my feet. Which I'm still trying to do.

I race through the RV departure checklist: coffee brewed for the road, dishes stashed, potential flying objects stowed, lights off, shades up, Winnie unplugged in shivering flash-light. I climb into the driver's seat, and if six-ton vehicles can tiptoe, that's what Winnie does, a scant hour after my post-bomb shower.

But I made big mistakes. Returning a rental car and taking a cab in the middle of the night, and then being chatty on top of it. Might as well just go buy a T-shirt with a big target and *Shoot a Bomber Here.*

Maybe it would help some that I'm headed west, not south like I told Henri. I want to go home to Oregon. Like a fox driven—or soon to be driven—by hounds, I want my den. Maybe en route I'll figure out what to do next.

* * * *

The next hours have few landmarks in my mind. Like a fox spooked by lightning, Winnie tucked her tailpipe and fled. A nightmare in black and lime-green technicolor.

I remember a spirited discussion—you might say squabble—with the silver coffee carafe on my console. It winked and wavered at me, reflecting light and fear. I had suggested that this mad dash was, well, … mad.

"Are you kidding," she said. "You get your butt out of here."

"Why not go with the original plan? Back to Idaho. Tell everybody I've been camping in McCall since last week when I paid for the campsite there, right where I told my family I was."

"Forget it. People were killed in that temple."

"Yeah. I noticed."

"You're in deep shit, Sweetie. Provo is not a healthy distance from that temple anymore. Not with people dead. They'll be looking that far now. And you registered at the Provo campground, hundreds of miles from McCall. You rented a car in Provo."

I drove along, appalled.

"And then, galloping-mouth disease. Dreadnoughts. Good gawd."

Good gawd, what a rude carafe.

I remember that exhaustion struck me at about six that morning, just after I crossed the Utah border into Idaho. Surrounded by nothingness, I managed to find a place in an old gravel pit to park Winnie. Maybe I was safe there. Certainly safer than on the highway, drifting all over the road. I turned furnace on and lights off, doffed my shoes, and crawled into bed in Winnie's back corner. My brain took a firm grasp of my mind and reviewed that neat proof of the Pythagorean Theorem, the one in which you imbed four right triangles in a square and compare areas. Lovely algebraic argument. Lovely oblivious sleep.

I remember waking that Monday afternoon to fear, the dream of falling, the ground gone, wind whistling about my ears. Making cheese sandwiches and brewing coffee for the road, I watched the TV in the console above the passenger seat. Maybe those reports yesterday were wrong. How could people have been there?

"Two killed in the Echo Lake temple bombing …"

I remember resting my head on my arms at Winnie's little dining table. My eyes burned. I turned toward the window. Bleak as my heart out there. Wind rocked Winnie even in her shelter behind boulders. Desolation. Long shadows, gray gravel pit within brown brushland. December cold, barren, nothing moving but a scrap of paper in the wind. Fitting.

We started driving.

"You think this rig will go far on empty?" Karinne Carafe, back at it.

Oh. Mygawd. The gauge's needle hovered at E. And then dropped below. Thirty miles, no exits. Fugitive out of gas—pretty dumb.

A sign. Sinclair. Yes! Winnie guzzled happily, oblivious to the chill air breathing down my neck. In line in the station's store I kept my big mouth shut while travelers talked about the day's news.

"...shrine a complete loss, two people dead," one woman was saying. Glasses in colorless frames, no chin, brown hair that clumped like overcooked spaghetti.

"Damn extremists, killing people now." Red-faced guy with a belly hanging over jeans that stayed up by the invisible magic beefy guys sometimes possess.

"I don't think they meant to kill anyone, middle of the night that way."

"Oh, they wanted maximum damage. Ya better believe it. People who mess with explosives know. Somebody'll get hurt. They knew."

I should have overheard Red Face years ago. Too late. His lecture was too late for me.

Time—and miles—passed. Karinne and I argued incessantly, about what to do, how safe I was, whether I should go home or go hide. Her silver sides flickered and gleamed at me in the night, and she pretty well freaked me out. Her tone sounded like Dad after one of my typical childish protests. My father, but in a higher pitch. Shrill.

Midnight. I wanted to keep going, but Winnie was again weaving from fast lane to margin and back. I pulled into an abandoned gas station on a side road and crawled into bed. But the mind that had been fading dangerously began to sputter and snap like a downed electric line. So sorry. Scared. Sad. Sad, sad. Gotta run. Sorry ... I thought about sum-of-angle proofs. Cosine first?

I dreamed. Auditory dreams, doors clanging shut. Soft thuds, dirt clods on casket. Whose casket? Theirs, the two people of the temple? Or mine?

And then, early the next morning, I looked down Meacham Hill. Again.

Heading Down

Meacham Hill, westward bound. It's a pivot-point. Like a Sedona vortex, but you touch a pivot point, and you don't even know it at the time, but later you look back and see you've headed in a whole new direction, and you say, *yep, I got whipped around and it happened right there at Meacham Hill.* Only a westerner would call this collision of Blue and Wallowa Mountains a hill, so high above the patchwork of the valley floor that you think maybe that roll of white at the horizon is the Cascade Range, though it's over a hundred miles west. You can feel the burly Columbia, out of sight on your right, joining forces with the Snake to muscle its way through two mountain ranges to the Pacific.

And your life lies before you there, too, in that same blue haze, and you see too much, but you don't see yourself whirling around the pivot point. Until later.

* * * *

When I reached the overlook that Tuesday morning, the power of the place pulled me to the side of the road. I shut off Winnie's motor and gazed from snowy slope to gray-brown prairie, fallow now but in summer converted by force of human will to waving wheat. Gray-brown turns blue with distance, formidable distance, distance that must have made pioneers weep. They'd crossed prairie, they'd crossed mountains, they'd crossed desert. And now this, the season getting late and it all to do again. Knowing the Cascades were there at the far edge, they'd have loathed the thought of my beautiful Mt. Hood, symbol, not of nature's grandeur, but of nature's perverse intractability. A hundred miles across that prairie-desert, two thousand weary steps for every mile, then one more stupendous barrier, and all they wanted was a fertile valley where they could make their homes and live in peace. Pioneers quit and settled on the brown prairie. Pioneers kept tromping, their shoes and their souls worn down to fibrous strands. Pioneers lost their lives trying to get around Mt. Hood on the raging river or trying to go over the mountains, winching wagons down cliffs, trees bearing the scars a century later. Some got through and prospered in the lush Willamette Valley. Meacham, a pivot point they'd have said, where I understood how tough I'd have to be.

* * * *

Even Karinne was silent in the face of this vast power. And I. I shared that helpless no-not-more—not-again grief.

* * * *

The swoosh of an occasional car seemed to bounce off essential silence, which brought my thoughts to Holly. Nearly a decade ago, a few miles east, terrible endless crashing followed a long climb, a single lane of traffic because of snow, then the logjam of cars caught beside or behind the plywood truck as it jackknifed. A pivot point for Holly and a close call for Winnie and Neil and me, ahead of that wreck by seconds. All the clanging banging screeching noise had been engulfed by silence when Neil and I walked back past the truck and the plywood splayed all over the freeway and entered a scene I hope someday to forget, a tormented wrecking yard of car bodies scattered and heaped, the silence so profound it was as though noise had never been. Though tatters of sound drifted through—airplane droning, voices thinly asking or deciding, the muffled rat-ta-tat of a loose car part in uneasy air—silence engulfed sound here, like cold that denies fire's warmth.

When we had come to the little girl, alone, sobbing in a Cinderella pumpkin coach once a red car, Neil raised an eyebrow, I nodded and stopped while he continued on. Between her sobs I learned that Holly was ten, that two people had carried her barely-conscious mother away, that her father was there and then he wasn't amid all the twisting noise. I wrapped the shaking child in a blanket after cutting her loose from her seatbelt, talking all the while as to a horse in a thunderstorm, filling the space with quiet words—I was the real me then, more than an angry shell. I splinted her crooked leg, and moved her from her precarious perch atop detritus, not far because I could see the pain in her face with the least jostle.

My butt froze as we sat wrapped in blankets on a piece of plywood in the snow, waiting for real help to arrive. Holly's favorite subject was math, I learned, and they were studying fractions, so I improvised, a silly song about fractious fractions and their disputes over who they really were. "Said fraction Half to fraction Two-thirds, 'Are you a part, are you a ratio, or are you just some dang division prob-ob-oblem?'" Her look of mock-horror emboldened me to expand into geometry, my forte. I sang about obtuse isosceles triangles who weren't very smart and acute triangles with sharp minds and pointed remarks. I was, at least, a distraction.

Neil checked back—he'd been helping carry the injured to a triage area, where he saw Holly's mother, concussed, helpless, worried about Holly, wondering if I'd be Substitute Grandma Em, the grandma they were on their way to see for Christmas, and I was Grandma Em for another hour there in the snow, and we told Holly maybe her dad had already been transported to the hospital, though nobody, probably not even Holly, believed it.

* * * *

Karinne was silent, Winnie was silent. Silent snow obliterated the view, but my mind's eye saw the long valley ahead. And there too was fact: I faced not so much a pivot point as the recognition of pivot point, somewhere, Echo Lake maybe, or maybe a consequence of that other pivot point four years ago, right here, for that other person, me / not me, becoming the now-me. Neil must have seen in that far vista the short vista of his own life after so many strokes so young, because he said, "A good life. We've had a good life together, Andy. I just regret that I didn't get to walk with our girl, down the aisle toward her future. I'll never understand why we had to miss that wedding."

"It's a sorrowful thing," I'd said, and I kept driving down that long hill past inert fields and idle irrigation pipes, right into the angry me, present tense. Because Neil was right and it had hurt ever since we first knew it was going to happen that way, a temple wedding excluding us because we weren't Mormons even though she was our only child but now it hurt even worse, unbearably worse because Neil's strokes had begun shortly after and, though we didn't know, we did know, that he would soon be gone from me, too.

* * * *

And so this person, this smoldering pile of rubble who had been that other person, arrives here alone. And repeats Neil's words in the silence: A good life. We had a good life together. I just regret, oh Neil, regret flows from me like some artesian well, I couldn't not do this, I couldn't let them destroy us like that. But … what have I done?" I saw the pivot-consequence, my last cherished things about to be ripped away. My home, my daughter, my grandchildren, oh especially my family which I'd tended and adored, the ties, breached by Mormon policy a decade ago, now entirely undone by my own hand. Because I'd made myself a fugitive, about to hide from family as I hid from whatever hounds would be chasing the temple-bomber. I looked at Karinne who shimmered silently now as through clouds, and I wiped my eyes and drove on down that long hill.

* * * *

That other time I, the Andrea Rubble Heap had driven steadily, all the anger buried deep because Neil needed grace in his last days. This time I drove steadily, too, but all my emotions were seeping out around the edges. I'd have to vanish. Without a trace? No word to my daughter? How long was I safe? How soon would they start looking for me? What about my grandchildren? How was I going to access money? What about my daughter?

That other time I got home ten hours later and made sure Neil was resting comfortably. Then I went to the den and searched the net for bomb recipes: just finding something would assuage my anger, I thought. This time, if I dared go home, it would be to gather. What does a fugitive need to survive? That time I ended in burying my husband. This time I would bury everything else, everything I loved, as if losing a daughter to a foreign faith and a husband to premature disintegration weren't enough. How did our forebears stand it, this moving on, this losing everything?

* * * *

Neil's last stroke assaulted him four days after we got home that time. He couldn't talk but spoke to me with his eyes. I'm ready, they said.

I'm not, I thought. Oh, I'm so not ready to lose you.

We held hands. It grew late. Lamplight and regret.

Dreaming.

"No," he said.

I started upright and looked at him. He couldn't talk. He couldn't have just said no. "Are you eavesdropping on my dreams now, Neil?" I said.

His dark eyes had regained their luster, and I hoped life was regenerating in him. But he shook his head. No, he had to go. No, no more joint adventures. No, I mustn't follow that dream.

I'd been in the dark, setting the charge when he woke me. But dream would never become reality, I thought then.

* * * *

He died.

I grieved. Hollow emptiness consumed me. I turned up the CD to try to fill the void. Shostakovich, angry, dissonant, Neil's requiem. The sounds of my grieving so ugly, those gnashing chords almost melodic by comparison.

I packed up Winnie and drove. Fleeing grief, overtaken by fury, I went shopping. A little here, a little there. Enough for a bomb—just a test. I thought.

Now I was fleeing from fury, overtaken by grief.

Karinne was shrill again. "You've got to figure out what you're going to do."

"I know. I know. But how . . ."

"Leave Neil alone. He's gone, buried. Let him rest."

"I know. But how do I bury Sabrina? And the kids?"

"They're not dead. Don't bury them." Karinne's flicker had turned to bright-sunlit glare on that eastern Oregon prairie.

"Oh, Karinne. They are dead to me. I ..."

"Get over it, woman. Maybe later you'll find a way back. Right now you concentrate on where to run, and how."

"Somehow I've got to say good-bye."

* * * *

I took the exit for Echo. Echos of Echo Lake but oh well. I had to walk. I pulled over in one of the wide spots you find along country roads and got the hell away from Karinne.

Was I giving everything up? Forever? What about money? What do fugitives use for ID? Run how? Hide where? How long? Questions arose faster than Mormons erect shrines. Remember that really bad guy? Fugitive, came out of hiding and authorities arrested him as he came out of a store where he had gone to purchase rope. *Rope.* Will I do something that foolish?

It only took half a mile, the sound of the Umatilla River swishing beside me, and I found a bit of balance. I ignored Karinne when I got back to Winnie and started a list. Pages of lists, each page a different problem, the top two *get money* and *talk to Sabrina.*

Get money: wanting no more tracks linking me to Provo, I'd been paying cash for gas, but now I was out of cash and getting low on gas. I looked at the map. And smiled. I actually smiled. The intersection just behind me led to I-82 and Umatilla, where I might stop if I were returning home from McCall. Only ten miles out of my way, a place to find an ATM, get groceries and gas. Karinne was mercifully quiet as we got on the road again.

* * * *

Talk to Sabrina: I wanted to stop by, see her and the kids.

Karinne laughed. More of a bark, if carafes can bark. "This is different. People dead, your face would betray you."

Yeah, the other times I'd nodded and looked sad. It was like bowing my head when they prayed, respecting their feelings. I'd had no guilt to hide because I'd done only minor conversion—sprawling marble edifice to collapsed marble heap.

"Then Sabrina knew you wouldn't be involved. Now she'd see your face and think you might be." Damn superior carafe, always right.

As Winnie was approaching the green and blue westerly part

of the Columbia River, I did call. I had to at least talk to her. Karinne thought my story was plausible.

"I'm on my way to New Mexico," I told my daughter. "I'm going to be gone a while. Maybe through the winter. Albuquerque desert or Chama snow."

"Mom. I'm glad you're enjoying yourself, but all winter? What about Christmas? What about the kids?"

Ahh. The worst part, Christmas without grandchildren. "Well," I said, "don't read too much into this, but I've met an interesting fellow, RV traveler with canoe and motorcycle. Sings. Plays guitar."

"Mom. A boyfriend?"

"No. Just a likable guy, 'sing in the sunshine,' you know."

"Mom." She always moms me when she thinks I'm daft. "Christmas? Sure, you go for a while, but you always come back for the holidays. For the kids–and Mark and me."

"It'll be fine. We've had holidays apart before." *But not since the one just before Neil died, us traveling because they'd been with his folks. Oh crap. Say something. Fast.* "Sabrina, I love our traditions. I may hate myself Christmas morning without all the excitement. But I'm ready for a change, and David is interesting. We tried my flute with his guitar last night," *I don't have my flute with me; gotta get it* "and it wasn't bad. I'll miss you and the kids, but I ought to indulge in a little adventure. Maybe even head for Norway later, or the French Alps, or New Zealand. The travel bug is like malaria. Fever just comes on you from time to time." *Shut up, Andy. You're protesting too much.*

"So is it a travel bug or a … what's his name? David-bug?"

"Yep."

"Oh, Mom. We'll miss you, and I don't know what Christmas will be like without you."

"I'll miss you, too, but you'll be fine. I'll call. Or e-mail. And I'll miss you. Guess I said that. I'm not sure how long I'll be gone." Week or two? Month or two? Decade or two?

"But, Mom … "

The sound of a crying child saved me from more of this. Five-year-old Josh, high in curiosity, low in caution; Sabrina needed to go.

I thought about getting a new carafe. One without the metallic surface. Because the lecturer started right up again when I hit END. "Thought you couldn't lie, Andy."

New life, new skills, I supposed. I'd pulled Dagaz, rune of transformation, before I left home, but I thought it was about transforming temples.

For now I just had a splitting heartache. A future without Sabrina and those gorgeous grandkids? I'd miss them like I'd miss my own thumb or my right eye.

Improv

A day later, Wednesday, I was putting stuff in rural mailboxes near Eugene, when a big guy in a bigger SUV cut me off. Splotchy face, downturned mouth, jowls. If this sounds bad, it felt worse. I was doing illegal things. In broad daylight with little planning. Worse than putting unstamped stuff IN the boxes, I was also taking stuff OUT. I didn't think the guy knew about the taking out part, but I didn't want him looking through the brown bag on my front seat either.

I had bypassed my western Oregon home the night before—I was wanting to hide, not go driving the RV up the driveway—cleaned Winnie up at a KOA campground, and sold her earlier this very same morning. Ah, you should never name an inanimate object; as it was I felt I'd betrayed Winnie the Brave. Though her bones were steel and her heart polyester, she had been a faithful longtime friend. And I sold her. At half her value, with dishes and folding chairs and snow chains and towels, at the same dealership where Neil and I bought her a decade before. I hoped a deserving family would adopt her.

So now, with the next thing on my list being *new identity* I was searching for information. Scary, this whole procedure. Worse than planting bombs, conspicuous, legs shaking so hard I'd have fallen if I'd been standing on them. In yet another rental car I was opening country mailboxes and looking for likely items with women's names—social security numbers were often on correspondence then. It wasn't stealing. Not really. I intended to give it back. But tell that to the judge. Or to the big beefy guy whose great, tall black vehicle had me trapped against the bank of five mailboxes I'd been riffling through.

His name must've been Eddie Bauer: As I looked through my passenger-side window, militant gold fender-trim and *Eddie Bauer* assaulted my eyes. To see the guy himself, I had to duck my head down and look back and up. My thought processes were nonexistent, just a *bzaap bzaap* coming from somewhere inside my skull, just awareness of my heart jarring my body, some dim wondering if Mr. BigAndBeefy Eddie Bauer could hear all the heart-pounding brain-zapping noise in here, sure signs I was guilty of more than handing out flyers.

Where had he come from? I'd been watching my back, nobody there until suddenly he was there, passing me, stopping, backing up. Before I had time to react he cut me off like a cop car might, slanting in diagonally from my right bumper. My left side was inches from the mailbox, his left side inches from my car. His mouth was moving in what sure looked like a shout.

I rolled down my passenger-side window, smiled and waved a flyer at him, an appealing green one I'd created at a Eugene print shop from a newspaper ad for Christmas crafts, my cover story for stopping at all those mailboxes. Not stamped, not legal—*but sir it's for the community, local artisans, proceeds to the needy, ...*

I still couldn't hear Mr. BigAndBeefy over the fear roaring in my ears, but it sure didn't feel friendly. He didn't take the flyer. I rolled my window back up, nodding in accordance with whatever-the-deuce he was shouting.

A moment of clarity broke through my fog. Really, what was he going to do? He couldn't jump out and punch me in the nose or anything: his maneuver had trapped him in his car too. I looked in my review mirror. He didn't have me blocked from the back. I smiled and nodded at him one more time, shifted into reverse, zipped backwards beneath the big O of his eyes, and did a Uey in the driveway opposite the mailboxes. As I left him in the dust of that graveled country road, I saw him backing, turning, backing, turning to follow me. His car was an intimidating herky behemoth, but mine was agile. I went around a bend, took a right onto a paved highway, went over a hill, took a left, didn't see any sign of him. Enough. I had enough mail! When I could lose myself in a Safeway parking lot, I stopped and performed some Lamaze pant-puffs until the world lost its purple tinge.

What a waste of adrenaline. Steaming envelopes open that night—handy, those motel steam irons—I didn't find much. One woman's date of birth from a medical bill. Canceled checks in another person's bank statement: driver's license number. Some retirement payments: social security numbers. Several pre-approvals for credit cards. That was it.

"You need one complete identity. Not a lousy bunch of partials." Karinne Carafe, out in the car in a plastic bag, seemed to have passed the baton to the motel room coffee pot.

Here's a theorem for you, Karinne: Once things start going bad, they keep going bad. We'll call it the Going Bad Domino

Effect Theorem. And Corollary One: Any problem you solve is immediately replaced by a more difficult unsolved one. In this case, the problem is that I need a different identity. The solution was to get one from a mailbox. The worse problem is that I now have a bunch of incriminating mail and little ID.

It might help somehow. I copied information then used a gluestick to reseal envelopes. On each envelope I wrote *delivered to wrong address*, or *wrong box*, or *delivery error* with pencil, blue ink, or black ink; left hand or right hand; loopy or angular; tilted left, right or straight; cursive or printed or all caps. With 324 possible combinations, maybe all the “mis-deliveries” would look more curious than suspicious. Certainly I was *not* going to risk redelivering everything myself.

"The Echo Lake temple is a total loss," the TV news guy said. "It’s dangerous. No one can go in yet. Workers are proceeding piece by piece. The death toll remains two, an elderly couple whose remains wait in temple debris until it is safe to retrieve them."

How can they report deaths without bodies? How do they know there was really anybody there?

Don’t think about it, Andy. You’ve got major problems to solve.

Problem: Need a false identity.

Solution: No clue. Maybe try using some of the incomplete stuff from the mailbox raid.

Problem: Hide where?

Solution: Not the city. I know too little about cities. Not the country. No crowds to lose myself in. Answer: the wilderness.

Next problem: "What wilderness? You're not exactly Mountain Woman."

Solution: Arizona?

Problem: "Ari*zona*? It's warm, but it's full of poisonous things and drought and flash floods and problems a fugitive couldn't go ask an expert Arizonan about.

Solution: Go with familiar hazards, bears and cougars, maybe. They're shy. The northwest.

Problem: "You'll never survive the cold.

Solution: Maybe that banana belt north of Vancouver, sheltered by Vancouver Island? I've heard palm trees grow there. Gulf-stream warm, without poisonous slithery stinging things. Plenty of water. Literally the end-of-the-road, no people.

Problem: "You're still no Mountain Woman. I suppose you plan to build your own shelter and eat worms? "

Solution: Get supplies from home.

Problem: "You're hiding, remember?"

Solution: Sneak home.

Problem: "You can't keep driving a car rented to Andrea Glass."

Solution: Buy a motorcycle. Always wanted a big bike. It would be easy to hide, too.

Problem: "How much stuff does an out-of-shape senior need to survive in the wilderness?"

After I dumped the pile of contraband mail in four drive-through slots, I sighed in relief and went to Kinkos for web access to answer some of those questions.

But I left Kinkos stymied. No motorcycle, no hiker biking.

Har har. Not even a Harley Hog could carry everything I'd need. Tent. Sleeping bag. Clothing, rain gear. Dehydrated food alone weighed fifty pounds, given that this un-Mountain-Woman was no huntress and felt sorry even for poor bloody flopping fish. And the balmy place was on Vancouver Island. The ferry, no ID, nope. What was I thinking, considering Canada anywhere, without ID?

The hounds would be nipping my heels soon. I'd made zero progress, the plans I'd begun to sketch blown apart like my temples. Lots of fear, though. And frustration.

Bad dreams count as things going bad. Mine was a short film clip circling through my brain. Little motorcycle, big passenger, bigger backpack, all picking up speed until air resistance swept pack and me away like a dirigible in a hurricane. Tumbling, Andy over backpack, backpack over Andy. Then the film sequence replayed itself: I fly-floated off the bike, tumbling, tumbling. Then again. Recycling on the cycle. Har har. Tiresome bloody cartoon.

I awoke to find myself in the motel's big easy chair, TV tuned to the Peter Howard news show which featured me, sort of. Howard talked to a governmental investigator, FBI, I think, and led off with, "So how many bombings have there been? They've been going on a long time now. Five years isn't it?"

"Three years, three bombings. Three too many. Started in October of 1997."

Howard did a medium job of skewering the G-man for failing to catch the bombers. And the G-man did a medium job of evading barbs. He thought there might be more than one "gang," he carefully avoided specifics, and he hinted they'd learned a lot about bomb materiel and other "crime characteristics."

Well whoop teedoo, Stu. Forensics labs can all decipher that kind of stuff these days.

"Oh, come on, George," Howard was saying. "What have you done to track down these gangsters? Another temple bombed. Idaho Falls, L.A., and now Echo Lake, with two dead. Why can't you catch these guys?"

"Well, Peter, we have widened our search."

Dam Sam.

"It's a big country," George continued. "No one goes around with a blinking 'bomber' sign on their head. With these deaths we've again added agents.

"We are checking all flights into the Salt Lake area; we're checking motel registrations and car rentals. We're checking information across 5000 square miles. We've utilized new computer programs to cross check similar records for Idaho Falls in 1997 and L.A. in 1999."

Ohgod, ohgod. Rental cars. Similar records. Expanded search. Cross checking. Here came fear again, flooding right over the top of flippant. I'd been merely sitting there watching TV, but I couldn't catch my breath.

"A huge data base," George continued. "ongoing from before the Utah bombing. We're contacting B&Bs, campgrounds, anywhere a gang might go."

Frigate frigate, frigate! I'd still hoped to hear tch-tching over reporting errors, hoped to hear they'd found those people happily vacationing in Palm Springs. Nope. TWO DEAD, Two Dead, two dead, words reverberating in my head like reflections in the mirrors of the upper temple rooms, a vision of a reflected image of a reflected image of a reflected image, a chandelier, say, or your own face, approximating infinity.

"Peter, surely you understand—thousands of visitors pass through those areas in the time frame of the bombings…"

With panic growling in my gut, fear gnawing at my bones, I jumped up and thumped the *off* button on the TV.

A little time. A little time. Thousands of visitors in Utah. At least George didn't claim to have promising leads. Calm down. They were looking for a gang. I was one small, lone RV. Amid thousands of travelers. I had some time.

But no plan. I had no plan, except an unworkable one. I stormed out, my devils trailing behind, and walked a brisk mile in cold rain. Math. Think math. Nice rational orderly abstractions. Blessed dark night, hiding my mutters: Law of Cosines …a^2… substitute for h …cosine alpha …

* * * *

The next morning I awoke thinking about that 5000 square mile search area. Got up, got pen and paper, divided by pi. A forty mile radius, missing Provo by five or ten miles. I was still safe.

Umm, unless the search centered in Salt Lake City, not Echo Lake. Or unless you discounted the area that was salt lake.

I couldn't dawdle.

But Eugene would require another day. I was leaving many tracks: selling Winnie, renting the car, staying in a motel, but Karinne and I had decided that I couldn't avoid making a trail right now. Hurry, gather then disappear. *Hurry.*

A motorcycle wouldn't work. Karinne was right. I'm no Mountain Woman, able to live off the land. I needed stuff. Finnegan, the Chevy Prism at home, wouldn't work. If they were looking for me, they'd be looking for my car. Taking the bus wouldn't work. I could see myself boarding a bus with a mountain of supplies and a ticket to Wilderness. Har har.

My best hope from my abortive mailbox adventures was Beverly Thomas, with a social security number, a driver's license number—and an offer of a pre-approved credit card, for what that was worth. But maybe Beverly could buy a car. Could I get my picture on her driver's license?

I called Oregon's Department of Motor Vehicles. It doesn't matter if you know your license number. To replace a "lost" one requires a social security card—card, not just number—*and* birth certificate. Or a whole slew of other things like a bank card, vehicle registration, voter registration card, or parole card.

Parole card? Parole card! Go to jail to stay out of jail? Do not pass GO?

I had none of those documents, and one needs several.

Forget a driver's license. Forget a motorcycle. Forget Canada, every road leading to an ID checkpoint. Dam Sam.

Solution: I, Beverly was going to try to be like one of Andy's fringy friends and drive without a license. In the USA. No tickets, no warnings, under the radar. Scary.

At breakfast I grabbed a newspaper and started looking at used car ads. By private owners. Maybe they wouldn't pay much attention to who was buying the car. As long as I had cash.

* * * *

Problem: "You need to cash that Winnie check. And you'd better get an un-Andy checking account."

Things got bad. I, Andrea Glass, went to a branch of my regular bank, cashed the check for Winnie and got more cash from the ATM, then drove a mile to another bank. There, I, Beverly Thomas, tried to open a checking account. But I needed picture ID. I tried to buy cashiers checks. But I needed picture ID. The teller looked over her glasses at me, and I heard her think, "Why doesn't this woman have ID?"

"Shoot." My mind raced. "Didn't need ID for the bus, didn't think about needing ID to *give* you cash. I'll have to come back tomorrow, I guess."

As I left the bank, I turned, as if looking for a clock. The teller was helping the next customer. Not watching me. Not calling the cops. Didn't seem to be hitting a panic button. I skittered out and away, unwilling to press my luck.

Wouldn't I ever have a calm, boring day again? All this adrenaline. All this cash in my pocket. Every day some kind of scare.

* * * *

And then I found a car. For once things didn't get bad. I even got to have a friendly, non-carafe conversation. After an hour with the newspaper and numerous phone calls trying to find something cheaper, I looked at Nan Evans's Subaru Forester. Nancy and her husband had bought a Volvo and then realized they couldn't afford both cars. The three-year-old Forester had 20 thousand miles on it. Clean. Okay tires. A haphazard collection of quick-lube receipts implied reasonable maintenance. Deep blue was unlikely to catch the eye of thieves or police and would hide well in a shadowy forest. All-wheel drive and high clearance —helpful where ever the heck I was headed.

Thirtysomething Nan Evans had a soft voice, a random arm wave, a red checkered shirt half-tucked into blue jeans, children in elementary school. Her fine brown hair blew in her eyes as we discussed details.

"Could you meet me at the car rental place?" I asked. "It's ten minutes away."

"Well, gosh." She pushed hair out of her eyes. It flopped right back. "I've got to be here when the kids get home from school."

Lost in time, perhaps? School didn't get out for another hour. I started counting hundred dollar bills. "I like the Forester, can't drive two cars at once." I held onto the bills. "There should be time for you to go deposit this while I return my rental. You can meet me, then I'll bring you back here."

"Okay. I guess. Gee. What time is it?" She pushed at her hair again then signed the title over to me, Beverly Thomas. With the PO box I'd obtained earlier that morning I now had two things in Beverly's name. "I'll leave a note for the kids. In case. Which rental agency again?"

I drew a map and she met me twenty minutes later. On the way back, we talked about war—Viet Nam and Bosnia and Rwanda. And we beat her kids home.

I wished I could have gotten to know her. She resembled a

younger version of a social science teacher I once worked with. Bright, concerned about peace and environment and poverty.

And perhaps Nan was the last real person, this the last real conversation, before wilderness doors thumped closed behind me.

* * * *

Problem: "Where the heck in the wilderness are you headed? B.C. is out. "

Solution: The southern Oregon coast? Another banana belt there, I'd heard. I glanced out at the somber December day and felt damp coldness seep into my bones. Fear? Premonition? Even camping in better seasons I'd experienced pervasive chill and the sometimes-comfort of a sleeping bag that wicks moisture from the air.

Problem: "How the heck will you get all the stuff you'll need to this wilderness place?"

Solution: Subaruth, the new Forester, then carry in one load at a time, I supposed.

* * * *

I began completing owner transfer information for the Forester. With Beverly's name on the title, I'd have one little piece in place to get her identity. And the car couldn't be traced to Andrea Glass.

Oh damn. I needed proof of insurance. Beverly's, not Andrea's. Gollygeewhillakers. I gave up.

You'd think everybody would live a straight life. Crime is just too complicated.

"Still no leads," the radio said. "Progress slow … reward for information … bombers were elusive. Services tomorrow for the husband and wife who were killed."

A deep breath, with a hitch in it. They must have gotten the bodies out. No explanation about what that couple found to do there at midnight.

A little cafe served a decadent hot roast beef sandwich with mashed potatoes, the gravy swamping everything. And wonderful hot coffee, some for Karinne Carafe, too.

No car registration, no driver's license. Maybe it didn't matter. Or maybe this problem would get me in the end. For now, I just wanted to seriously apply myself to those mashed potatoes.

Tomorrow I'd sneak home to collect my things. Tonight I registered as Beverly Thomas in a Woodburn motel, close to my Silver Creek home, but far enough to escape recognition. The second place I tried accepted cash, no ID required. Andrea Glass had vanished. For a while.

I pounded the pillow flat, sprawled on my back, breathed deep. Eau de Febreez. Essence de la Lysol. Destination unresolved, I thought. Turned on my side. Car resolved, identity unresolved. I flipped on my back. How to cart all my stuff to and from the car? Not a clue. Knew I should hurry. Felt like I was swinging in slow circles, head and feet pivoting about some central point in the bed. Tired.

Terrible tragedy in Utah.

If you've got the sum of angles formula for cosines, how does the argument for sines work again?

I dreamed I was trying to catch up with my family, which

kept vanishing over the next hill. "Wait, wait," I cried.

"Come on, Gramma Em. It's just ahead." We were going to picnic together, in a special place under shade trees by the creek. But when I got to the spot where they had been, they were far ahead at the top of the next hill.

"Wait, wait," I cried.

"Come on, Stand-in Gramma Em. It's just ahead." Again they were gone. Again I glimpsed them on the next hill.

"Wait, wait!"

"Come on Gramma …"

Home

By four on Friday morning I was driving home. Twenty minutes later I parked at Silver Creek's 24-hour grocery and started walking, five more miles. A few cars passed, but I ducked into trees or down beside a culvert before their headlights reached me.

At 6:30 I entered the forest behind my house. Darkness made slow going of that last half mile through tangled vines. Cold and wet, I got home at about 7:30. A shower and hot coffee helped. But I worried. Would anyone show up asking questions?

Four days had elapsed since I bombed the temple. They'd search first in Salt Lake for clues, then Ogden, another busy city forty miles northwest of Echo Lake. Then maybe Evanston, Wyoming, thirty-five miles east of Echo Lake. Finally Provo. Maybe. Lots in Provo to keep agents busy asking questions.

But I returned a car in Provo very early. Before dawn. Just after the bombing. Talked to Henri. Dum-de-dum-dumb.

A week? Two weeks, before my name came up? Maybe more. I'm a social fibber, not an accomplished liar: I sure didn't want anyone to stumble into me here. I'd be wary.

I donned rain gear, grabbed another cup of instant coffee, and abandoned the house in favor of the larger hiding space outdoors. On the way in I'd left groceries—and some electronic surveillance stuff I'd bought in Eugene— in an old goat shed. Picnic breakfast consisted of cereal, milk, fruit and coffee.

What if I needed out of here in a hurry? The front way was too obvious. This morning's route had been much too slow. So I improved it, cutting away brush and brambles just enough to create a quick, nearly invisible "deer trail."

My home naturally invited people to the back door, so I cut another trail from the rarely-used front. Above the driveway, hidden by a shrub-lined bank, I could dodge into the brush on the uphill side and around to the goat shed. I put my new parabolic sound detector in a black garbage bag and hid it by the house trail.

In the early evening darkness I walked a mile, the front way down my lane, around the hill, past the one other house that shares the drive. The night felt friendly, shadows welcoming, bushes protective. I needed no flashlight, no moon, because I knew every bump and pothole by heart. I moved quietly through quiet dark, fearing only discovery by neighbors Ann and David. What an upside-down universe, having to avoid them. Their house, set well back from the lane, told me through its glowing lights that they were home. A good thing: no headlights would turn in and surprise me.

The calm night, the rain whispering on the hood of my jacket, the winter creek talking to itself—balms to nerves so jangled for the last few days.

I used brown string to tie my first seeing eye to a tree at the base of the lane near the main road. This deck-of-cards sized detector would sound a buzzer at home if anything moved. I placed the second gadget, with a doorbell ringtone, half a mile closer to the house, on my side of the neighbor's turn off. Deer often move through the field here, but I hoped the monitor's range was too short to be affected.

* * * *

At home I placed shoes and clothing strategically. If an alarm sounded, I'd grab my things as I ran out. Pluck and run. Har har. Plucky me.

I got a stir-fry dinner from the freezer and ate from the frying pan. My carryout meal if I fled. But quiet enfolded me, for a while.

Now, how did I proceed to gather clothes and supplies? Enough to last months. Little enough to carry. Maybe cache and carry. Har har.

In the basement I found a good fold-up shovel, clothespins, a collapsible water bottle, duffel bag, a folding saw, and a small hatchet. And rope.

Quiet reigned there, far from the road in my home nestled in hills. From the basement not even the sound of the winter creek or the rain on evergreens was audible. Only my sips of coffee and my clanking brain interrupted the stillness. I'd solved many problems as a math teacher, but this—what to take, what to leave—challenged my mind and my emotions.

And then the buzzer erupted into the silence.

Frigate. Frigate, frigate! Even before my heart resumed its beat, I ran, turning off lights as I took the other route to the front yard, through the garage and up the steps into darkness. I raced to the place I had hidden the parabolic ear. Fear squeezed my throat and made me pant. I couldn't catch my breath; my lungs whistled for air. Even exhaling required enormous effort as I pushed carbon dioxide past the dam in my throat. My head claimed I was out of sight and beyond hearing, but my heart knew the noise of my wheezing carried past the woods, through the yard, down the drive, halfway to Nebraska.

* * * *

Gradually my breathing calmed. The listening gadget was hard to find in the dark off the trail in its black bag. After serious battle with briars, I finally retrieved it and settled watchfully in the brush.

My rationality returned slowly. Damn, I'd left hot coffee. I watched and listened and got wet. And colder. The icy sizzle of rain on leaves provided the only sound. Nobody came.

In stealth mode except for my rebellious clanging heart, I crept into the yard and peered down the steps then around the corner to my driveway. No one. I went in the front door. Silence. I took a deep breath and turned on the lights. No one. Coast was clear.

I have battled blackberries many times in my life, but never to so much detriment. Bloody scratches marked my face, arms, back and knees. The shower's warmth on the back of my neck helped stop my shakes; but after hitting my frozen butt, the water cascaded icy cold to my feet. I'd felt warmer sitting in the snow with Holly. I rotated, as before a hot bonfire on a freezing mountain night. Slowly I warmed.

As the shower washed away residues of panic, evidence of stupidity emerged. Andy — um, Beverly — you put up both a far buzzer and a near bell, you dope. You *dope*. Dam-Sam.

Only the buzzer had sounded. That meant "get ready, someone—or something—has entered the lane." A mile away. Could have been a deer. Or someone visiting the neighbors.

Geez Louise. Plot and plan and then pull a stupid stunt.

Scratches. Damn deep bloody ones. For no bloody reason. I treated them with cortisone cream, not ointment. I had been off the trail, probably in poison oak, a bigger threat than infection. I put wet clothes in the dryer and kept hot coffee close to a drain. Don't want to compound my stupidity by leaving anything wet or hot.

In the basement I came across a fishing kit with a telescoping pole. Small. Light. I'd take it. I might become Mountain Woman yet. Especially if I got hungry. My shopping list was getting long: warmer sleeping bag, lighter tarps, maybe a tent.

Upstairs again, I found my confrontation with brambles put me in a good frame of mind for constructing a medicine kit. I gathered items from bathroom medicine cabinet and mudroom vet supplies left over from dog, goat, and horse days with Neil and Sabrina. Blade, my pocketknife already in Subaruth, had gotten all sorts of critters out of all sorts of tangles over the years. Likely he'd save me from Messes of the Future.

I dumped instant coffee, dehydrated mashed potatoes, and powdered milk into plastic zipper bags. On my bookshelf I found a paperback on wild herbs and edible plants. Yes.

At the next false alarm I carried my full duffel bag with me to the porch and left it there when I went back in. Duffel to go.

The bell went off twice more that evening, the far buzzer once, but separately. No one came. At midnight, visitors unlikely, I did laundry and took the duffel, wrapped in a protective garbage bag up beside my listening gadget. This time I took a flashlight and worried less about hiding things. Why would anyone else come up here?

What about clothes? Finally in nightgown and slippers, I stood gazing at my bedroom closet in despair. How does one select few enough clothes to carry, but a sufficient amount to stay warm and dry? How was I supposed to think after that news report?

The eleven o'clock news had extensively covered memorial services for the couple I now termed *collateral damage*, the Whitesons. A pleasant-looking pair of faces peered out of photos as news reporters described forty-six years of marriage, six children, and thirty-two grandchildren. Hundreds of weeping people streamed out of the church and gathered around the gravesite. Awful.

No one understood why the couple was there in the middle of a Sunday night. Maybe cleaning up after a Saturday wedding, what with another scheduled for Monday afternoon?

Where was their car? Unbelievable. I was so careful.

* * * *

No matter which way I turned that night, I saw Whiteson mourners. Angry hordes chased me down the road, through a rutted field, into a forest. I fell into a pit that became a grave and the bell sounded. My actual near bell; someone in the driveway, maybe. I careened from bed, grabbed clothing, and streaked to the porch. Had there been a buzz? No one came. Must've been deer. It was four a.m. I groaned back to bed and buried my head under the pillow. My knees and shoulders and legs ached from yesterday's exertions. My arm throbbed where a vicious briar had gouged me. A microwaved heating pad was beginning to help and sweet slumber wafted near, when the bell sounded again. Geez-Louise. Ran, waited. No visitor.

And at 6:00, the bell again. When I came back in, half-dressed and grumpy, I gave up on sleep. I wanted decent brewed coffee. I shrugged into my shirt and filled the coffeemaker.

"Coffee's a giveaway if anybody comes."

Dam-Sam. I don't care, Karinne. I'm sick of instant microwave caffeine. Do they have decent coffee in jail? Geez-Louise. Too cross for caution, I fixed lovely hot oatmeal and drank half a pot of good coffee.

Nobody came to take me away, and finally my inner flame arose. I figured out clothing: a big old navy wool sweater, jeans, turtlenecks, work shirts. Stuff I'd need for cold wet days like today. Walking shoes. Galoshes? Warm gloves and leather work gloves.

Needle and thread. Safety pins. Flannel sheet. Towels, the super-absorbent ones.

There's a quiet spot in my woods like a child's secret place, mature trees and moss and ferns. I hauled the duffel bag past the goat shed to that space, and the big garbage bag full of my morning's gather. I slung a rope over a limb as high as I could throw, and dangled my parcels out of rodent reach. I got the tent I'd found in the basement and set it up next to a mossy log under my dangling bundles. Usable, I thought, but heavy. Bulky. Ill-suited to Fleeing Woman.

But in the misty dappled light the old tent put me in mind of old times and all the useful things we took camping. Back to the basement for plastic milk jugs, emergency survival blankets. A small flashlight and a headlamp. Batteries. Candles. Poncho and stocking cap. I saw with new eyes my wonderful warm polyester fleece blanket and grabbed it. Then little things: sketchpad, pencils. Picture of Sabrina's family. My flute: I'd told Sabrina I had it with me.

I retrieved a little packet from my sock drawer and sat on the bed, unwrapping white tissue to expose the carved wooden box, flowers etched across its top and sides. Its tiny hinges opened to reveal the pin, a silver bird, flower stem in its beak, a tiny pearl atop the flower's six flawless petals. Created by Grandma's papa for her wedding, it perched on the shoulder of her gown. And on my mother's. And mine.

Picking the bird up, I fastened it to my tee shirt. I sat, right hand exploring the contours of bird and flower on my left shoulder. It should be Sabrina's now. I should have secured it to the shimmering white of her gown.

I unpinned it, returned it to its box and tissue. I added bubble wrap and fit it into my flute case. One more item for a plastic bag heavy with afterthoughts, which I lugged to the woods.

Heavy duffel, two more heavy bags, maybe a tent. It was going to be a long haul to the top of the trail. I wished I could use a shopping cart like other bag ladies. Hee hee.

That burgundy fleece blanket looked so cozy. Despite nips of coffee from the thermos in the goat shed, I sagged. Terrible night. A hundred awakenings. I'd test the tent all right, from inside. I stashed my additional stuff under a fallen tree, crawled into the tent, flopped onto a survival blanket, pulled Burgundy Blanket over me, and made my jacket into a pillow.

I awoke in mid afternoon, warm but hungry. Dang dried fruit is up the tree. Tent leaked, one corner saturated. Then I realized I had awakened because of the voices. *Voices! Here?*

Outsider

Kids' voices. Sabrina's voice, and Mark's. What were they doing here?

"Mom, come take a look at this one. It's gorgeous. I like this one, Mom. I think we should take it. Mom? Can we get this one? Can we cut it down now?"

Oh, they're looking for a Christmas tree. The annual ritual. I forgot.

"Joshua, that tree is taller than our house!"

By now I had my shoes on and my rain jacket. The voices came from the other side of the creek, where the main trail went up into younger growth. Good Christmas trees were most likely there. They might circle around to here, though. No little trees in this area. Lucky. They'll walk on through if they come by.

The tent collapsed easily when I pulled the poles loose, and I wadded it up with its contents and stuffed it under the downed tree beside the garbage bag. Invisible there.

No worries about making noise; my family's clamor certainly surpassed my rustlings. I moved away from the group, came to the fence line, found a low spot, and crawled over. They'd be careful to stay on my property: I wouldn't be seen here.

I didn't see them either, but they painted themselves in a warm wash across the canvas of my mind. Their voices came to me in bright echoing tones, with Mark's deep timbre balancing the sound, and I understood the context, if not the content, of their dialogue. Five noisy kids with McKenzie still in a backpack on her mom's back, Mark probably carrying three-year old Emma on his shoulders until he needed to haul the tree. Poor Laurie, the eldest at eight, always wanting to be mother-hen to Brian, who felt hen-*pecked* at age seven. Even on a tree expedition, they were at it, Laurie's voice rising in frustration and her best attempt at command. Sabrina and Mark were good parents, but they were busy with the two littlest ones. And Josh. Sweet five year-old Josh, stubbornly investigating, everything fascinating, until he got lost or tangled up. The kind of kid who begs for a thirty-foot Christmas tree.

They needed a grandma. Someone to pay attention to Josh, poking into mysteries with him. Someone to tell Laurie she's a good kid to worry about her brother, but maybe for today she could let him be his own responsibility. Someone to whisper to Brian to just say, "Okay, Laurie" a lot. Someone to tell Sabrina what a fine bunch of kids she's raising, and wasn't it great how Joshua investigates, and how Brian perseveres, and how Laurie looks out for her siblings. And to tell Mark how lucky we are to have him, tromping in the woods after a week full of woods-tromping as a surveyor. I should be headed to the house to fix them all hot chocolate. Who will tell them what a marvelous job they did, picking just the right tree?

One thing about rain. If anyone had seen me that afternoon, they would think the wetness on my face came from the sky. Because I don't cry.

* * * *

They found their tree. I followed them toward the house, went around to my listening spot and eavesdropped on their conversation: tying the tree onto the car and drying off in the house and going potty. I savored their voices like chocolate torte drizzled with raspberry sauce. I couldn't have ached any more, even if I had known three years would pass before I heard them again.

When they left, I wilted for a while. I dragged myself back to the goat shelter for fruit and my thermos of coffee. I had been hungry once, a very long time ago. Then I took my crumpled self up to my crumpled tent. I sat on a crumpled mossy log, lifted my face to the sky and there, where no human could hear me, I howled like a coyote.

* * * *

Howling does not help. Rocking, back and forth, back and forth, does not help. It does not relieve the pressure to wrap your arms across your body and push in with your elbows.

As my storm blew over, I raised my cheek from the mossy log where it had rested. My butt hurt, I realized, and I rearranged myself there on the ground beside the log, too weary yet to rise. I stroked soft gray-green moss. Then both hands absorbed its cool dampness, and I brought them to my eyes to soothe their fire. Leaves and grasses fluttered at the edge of the clearing, and I watched for the bird that must be there, but caught only flashes—small and gray. Rain whispered, and an occasional *plop* landed near my foot. I counted seconds between *plops*, but if there was a pattern, I wasn't finding it.

Time will pass, I thought, and pain won't cut so deep. Maybe I could survive until agony became ache. I was chilled, I realized, and my leg had gone numb. I rose in the encroaching twilight and paced the length of the log until the pins and needles in my foot subsided and I could trust my legs to take me down the hill out of the woods. Hauled the tent with me, shook it, hung it to dry. Went down the lane. Tied the bloody bell-ringing monitor to a fence post on the other side so it wouldn't see all the deer. Got it dirty first, to look like it had been there a long time protecting widow Andrea.

Wandered back to the house, distracted myself surfing the web to look for camping stuff. And a false identity.

Did I have to do this? Provo, so far from the bombed temple.

The consequences so great if I popped up on their radar.

All the same arguments. Over and over. I thought about just getting into Finnegan the Chevy Prism and driving to Sabrina's house. Could help set up the tree. Couldn't avoid the stares at my swollen eyes. And at the blackberry gashes. Maybe tomorrow.

Crying always makes you feel better, friends once claimed over coffee. How could they say that? Fiery eyes, swollen brain, stuffy nose; how do they make you feel better?

Real life nightmares but no dreams. Long hours of oblivion.

* * * *

Why was I out on the porch, shivering? Oh, yeah. Far buzzer. Why did my eyes burn, my head hurt? Why had my heart and my stomach switched places?

Oh. Yeah.

Seven a.m. No near bell. Neighbors going out. Or deer browsing by the road.

On a comfortable heap of old straw in the goat shed, I sipped my coffee and thought about going to see Sabrina. Giving up this whole ridiculous run and hide thing.

I knew better. The family would be getting ready for church anyway. Maybe I could call Sabrina in a few weeks, ask anything-happenin' questions. Come back home, maybe.

I plodded up my trail with the duffel, stashing it in another tree just off a wide shoulder of the road where I could park-and-pack Subaruth.

Seven hundred eighty yards. One thousand, five hundred sixty steps, not counting the little half-steps I took to keep my balance on the slippery uphill trail. Bulky bag kept swinging off my back, banging against my legs.

There's a wide strap that horse campers use for high lines to tie horses without damaging trees. Before the next trip up, I put the garbage bag in a hay net, secured the hay net to my back using high-line straps. Found some bamboo poles in the gardening shed to use as walking sticks. Again, fifteen hundred sixty gasping breaths, plus rest stops. My load balanced better, though.

Maybe I could sneak back in a few months, see if I had any we-want-to-talk-to-you mail. Maybe feel safe enough to stay. Or maybe I'd need to hide for a long time; maybe figure out the false identity thing, maybe move from a tent to an apartment, someplace like Omaha.

The house was due to be painted this summer. How would I pay taxes? Do yard work?

For sure I faced a really. Crappy. Christmas.

I thought about Holly. My stupid stupid suggestion that she find the good in change. In the face of her terrible tragedy. Why hadn't I tried to contact her again?

The woods kept ringing with children's voices, auditory afterimages. I detoured to visit Pi Tree, the Douglas Fir who requires 3.14 people to reach around her for a hug. I admired the ferns, babbled back at the winter creek, spoke to the trees we'd raised from babies, Pi Tree's offspring. Regretted my inattention here these last few years.

I even visited my bomb-building enclave, now clean and quiet.

I left the last garbage bag, the afterthoughts bag, to haul up the hill later and took my rubber legs into the house to the computer. My property was in a trust. I wrote a document handing trust management to longtime colleague Bruce Douglas. Bruce expected that role anyway if I died or was disabled. This good friend understood my temple sore spot and would perhaps guess what had happened, though he had no information to give or withhold if asked.

I wrote another letter enabling my neighbor to sell Finnegan Prism for 15% commission. Mike would get a good price, and he'd faithfully deposit the proceeds into my account.

And I wrote a letter to Sabrina. What could I say? But I knew she'd worry if evidence came up about my being in Oregon, selling Winnie. Probably she'd think the David character I'd invented had kidnaped me. So to assure her it was me, I mentioned a runaway horse incident that only she and I would know about. I told her that David had to go back to South Carolina, a death in the family, and that he had been only a symptom anyway. I was in emotional crisis, just couldn't face normal life for a while, wanted to travel.

A feeble excuse. I'm not the emotional-crisis type. But maybe she'd worry a little less, not report me missing; wonder but not be frantic.

My eyes burned.

I went out again, came across a piece of chicken wire. A potential cooktop. I took it, nails, and my last bag of stuff up the trail to my collection spot. Too many things. And not enough.

Then I spent the evening online, still trying to figure out false identities. I just didn't get it. Insufficient criminal mind, I guess. Everything required two other things first, just like getting Beverly's driver's license. And what if I went to DMV, posing as Beverly to replace her "lost license," and it turned out she's 16? Or black?

In a funk, I tried searching "false ID." Wow. Hundreds of listings. One, www.espionage-store.com, claimed they'd provide a whole new identity. These guys wanted money up front, of course. I folded the hundred dollars into a page of printer paper, listing Beverly's P.O. box.

Was I sending this straight to the FBI? Or did some guy have a good scam going?

I fiddled with social security death lists. You enter name and year of birth and it returns social security numbers, state where the person got her social security card, and where she died. A dead person's ID seems to work on TV, so maybe it would in real life. Only … I kept picturing a DMV clerk, computer right there, looking at me with raised eyebrow and asking how I'd died.

Dam-Sam. No driver's license, no car registration, so many little ways to break the law. I'd better not speed, better not miss a stop sign, better not have an accident.

While I watched the news—"investigation is ongoing"—I took out the computer's hard drive. I used a heavy hammer to beat it into pieces. Sad. I just felt so sad. Everything was broken.

* * * *

Tuesday I'd leave. Disappear. Monday was shopping day. When the alarm clock rang at five, I had trouble turning it off. I had trouble moving. My arms hurt from all the lifting. My legs hurt from all the hiking. My back from carrying. My fingers hurt, from no fathomable reason. The night's inactivity, bell and buzzer free, contributed to my woes, joints and muscles and tendons frozen.

I steamed some pain away in the shower. Coffee helped. My eyes still felt swollen and raw, and I wondered if repressed sorrow could do that. Then as I dressed I saw blisters along the inside of my wrist where I had been absently scratching. Poison oak. On my wrist, in my eyes. In the blackberry gashes. Society doesn't need prisons. Punishment happens.

The long walk to my car in Silver Creek further loosened

aching muscles, and I was too cold to itch. I drove through an espresso place in Salem, and the day brightened.

The pieces of my computer hard drive now reside in a landfill somewhere, sent there from a trash bin in a rest area halfway to Eugene. Left a hard drive in a rest area. Har har.

At Fred Meyer Grocery, I was surprised at how many bulk packaged dehydrated, dried, vacuum-packed foods abounded: two heaping carts full. I knew that coffee might keep me sane, didn't realize how much solace my whimsical purchases of cinnamon, cocoa, and artificial sweetener would later provide.

Essential survival items from Camper Place included maps, sleeping bag, tent, hiker meals. Two more heaping carts full. Things I hadn't planned to buy—waterproof pants, wool socks, long johns—might save sanity. Heck, they might save my life.

I risked attracting attention to ask for advice on back packs. Balance, load, height of backpack seemed important; I couldn't make a gazillion trips to tote all the home stuff plus all the new stuff, some unknown distance to some unknown destination, without an efficient system.

"A bunch of crones looking to find Right Stuff in Leftover Years," I said. "We're going to pack in together and camp, just to prove we can do it."

"Beats staying home and baking cookies." Young, enthusiastic outdoorsman Randy seemed to believe my yarn and suggested a backpack that carried a medium load. "Anything bigger and you'll collapse."

My aches confirmed that. I picked a deep green pack, good size, with a dozen special features according to Randy. Mostly I liked its handy water bottle and detachable fanny pack. And how invisible it would be in the forest.

At the bank Andrea Glass had to discard anonymity to get documents notarized for Bruce Douglas to become my trustee. Fear-and-skedaddle again there.

At the Eye Place I found three un-Andrea frames: rhinestone-retro, round grannies, and rectangular black. A bit of fun, finally. Goodwill had great wigs. And a ridiculous ruffled blouse, broomstick skirt, and paisley capris two sizes too small, part of my plan for changed appearance. Couldn't cheat on a diet in the wilderness.

I drove through Silver Creek and parked by my woods to load the things from home, lingering in shadows with each burden to look and listen for traffic before dashing with it to the car. Subaruth became *very* loaded down. Subrafull Subaruth.

That morning I had found an alternate route from home to Silver Creek, over fences, through orchards, along a swale, but now after I parked again in town, I felt safe enough in the dark to use my original strategy, walking along the road and ducking when I saw lights.

I carried the new maps, which I'd left at the top of the trail, home with me. Arrived at nine, studied maps (southern Oregon coast), took heart when TV had nothing to say about bombs or temples. By eleven I had zipped maps into an attaché case to take with me, made up my runaway pile of clothing, and stumbled off to bed. Bell and buzzer were blissfully quiet. Everything had gone right on this day.

Then came Tuesday.

Yonder

I got up late Tuesday morning, which was okay, because I planned to merely take a look around and leave that afternoon. The far buzzer rang once at about 5 a.m., the near bell kept quiet, and I slept until 7:30. Breakfast was uneventful. But the buzzer sounded again when I was in the shower. I dried my feet, wrapped one dark blue towel around soapy hair and another around wet body. Gotta take the bloody thing seriously, despite its false alarms. Then the near bell rang, too. I grabbed clothes and attaché case and streaked out as a car drove up.

My race into the woods could have been a slapstick comedy routine. One towel unraveled from my head, the other from my body. I needed several extra hands to hold clothes, shoes, attaché case, and towels. My bare feet churned in muck. My heart and stomach were churning in muck, too. As I crouched gasping in my hiding place, I heard a knock at the back door.

As for all the false alarms, I had gone out the front, across the yard and uphill into the brush. I was still close, perhaps a distance equal to that across a wide boulevard, looking down toward the side of the house opposite the driveway. My position felt vulnerable and exposed, but I had hung a bright beach towel here and been unable to see it from the house. Would they hear my gasping breaths? Would they follow my tracks? It felt like I was standing up there waving red flags and sounding sirens. But I thought it better to remain, hidden, quiet, listening, than to crash, bare, barefoot, dripping possessions, along the trail.

Somehow calm descended and my breathing steadied. The ridiculous scene, maybe? The shock of cold rain after hot shower? The practice from the false alarms?

I wrapped one dark blue towel around my body, dumped out the listening gadget—hooray-Renee, no digging in vines this time; naked in the rain is bad enough—and sat on the garbage bag. I draped the second towel over my head and shoulders then froze in place. Froze is the right word. Geez-Louise it was cold.

"Seems quiet. The daughter was probably right. Nobody's here."

They had talked to Sabrina.

"Door's unlocked like she said, but we need a warrant." Same voice again. Nasal-whine tones.

What's *he* nervous about? Thank gawd they're not going in. The house is still warm. Still wet in the bathroom. I didn't get my look around; hope they'll go. Soon, before hypothermia gets me.

A lower, deeper voice said, "I think I'll take a walk around the house. We don't need a warrant for that."

Oh, oh. I scooched down lower, behind the underbrush. My tracks? I hoped not: my trips earlier had only made shapeless rearrangements of mud. What was my plan B if he started up this way? Wrap in the black bag and role into the briars? Ohmygawd.

"Okay. I'll look around back here, maybe see what's in the garage."

Be my guest, Mr. Nervous Voice. Car's in the garage. Amazing.

Low Voice said, "Don't touch anything. Just look around." I peered between branches and saw him heading toward my side of the house. I shrank lower. He looked in windows; only a glance in my direction. So far so good.

Was the bathroom window steamy? Oh. Thank gawd for frosted glass.

Low Voice seemed too blond and too slim for such a baritone. I observed him obliquely, afraid a direct gaze would pull his attention my way. He seemed young, about Sabrina's age. From my vantage point he looked pressed and polished, though mud on his shoes and rain on his bare head didn't appear to concern him. Sharply defined creases in his trousers showed beneath a carefully belted black raincoat. His stride had authority and athleticism. Not football. Maybe military. Maybe basketball. He's tall. Even Neil couldn't look straight into that high window like that.

They're talking about a warrant. Guess this is it. I was half expecting it. Not this soon. Not ready. Frigate.

"I'd like to meet the person who'd feel ready, dressed only in soap and mud and soggy towels." My lecturer, still with me.

Shivers ran along my spine in spasms. I don't like having Low Voice as my adversary, I thought. Will he notice my path? Will he come up here? Shh shhh, don't move, trust your plan, it's just a deer trail.

Mr. Low Voice may not have considered the possibility of a naked sixtysomething grandma sitting in the woods. His focus stayed on the house.

Does he think Bonnie and Clyde are in there? At least he didn't have his gun drawn like on some crime show. More shiver spasms. Cold. Naked. Wet. *Naked in the Rain.* Good movie title. Sure beats *April in Paris.*

Low Voice went out of sight, down the steps toward the garage. I kept the listening device to my ear, but used my other hand to dry my hair. The two were talking again, back by their car, I thought.

"I'll go for the warrant." Low Voice seemed to be in charge. "I think it would be a good idea for you to stay here, just keep an eye on things; don't touch anything."

Frigate. Ship. I'll not see inside again.

"I know, I know. I can't imagine what could happen here, on this dead-end lane, but I'll keep watch. Okay with you if I bring that chair out from the basement?"

I heard the snap as a camp chair opened up.

"Put it here by the garage. You have an umbrella?" Low Voice said.

Nervous Voice muttered something I didn't catch.

"Here's mine," Low Voice said. "I'd like you to keep watch." Low Voice's voice got lower, "I don't know why; the place just doesn't feel empty."

Yeah, I definitely didn't like having Low Voice as an adversary. I caught another glimpse of him as he drove down the lane, the front way out.

I wiped muddy feet on soapy towel, then stood on it to fight sticky underwear over wet behind. Like trying to dress in the shower. With the shower still running. Rain got me wet as fast as I dried off. Clothes stuck. Heart thumped. Fingers froze. I put my bra in my pants pocket. No way I'd get it on. Maybe draping my jacket over my head. . .? Nope. I just kept getting wetter. I got stuck in shirt sleeves like an algebra student in a story problem, finally got the bloody shirt up my arms onto my shoulders, gave up on buttons, zipped the jacket over the top. Life imitates art again: Scene two of the great comedy, *Naked in the Rain.* Too bad I can't charge admission. Then again, thank gawd nobody's watching.

I did better with my feet, sitting again on the plastic bag, wiping with a dry spot on the corner of a towel before putting on socks and shoes.

Listening again, I heard only creek and rain. No movement, Mr. Nervous Voice was watching house and lane, I guessed. Time for me to go up my trail and out of here.

I watched myself acting calm. I had panicked for no reason a few days ago, but now, faced with real jeopardy, I kept my cool. Har har, so cool I was freezing. Roiling fear in my depths, though.

Gathering my stuff, I moved deeper into the woods. Got towels into plastic bag, clean side out, folded everything into attaché case except the awkward sound detector hidden again in brambles. I detoured to the goat shed, safely tucked behind the barn out of view of the house, picked up the milk jug and an orange and saw nothing else left there to give me away.

Goodbye house. I had expected to walk around and touch things. Goodbye piano. Goodbye Prius Prudence. I really have to stop anthropomorphizing everything. Goodbye, anyway. After looping the strap of the attaché through the handle of the milk jug, I slung it over my shoulder and across my chest like a Miss America banner—or a guerilla bandolier—so both hands were free on my walk uphill, the back way out.

I detoured briefly to pat Pi Tree on her broad trunk, her rough bark a comfort somehow. Didn't spend enough time appreciating my home these last years.

My trek took me over fences and through the orchard like yesterday morning, but in the swale I felt naked again, exposed. Too many cars, too close. Wait for shelter of darkness? No. Walking had warmed me, but chill—and fear—overtook me when I paused. So I backtracked to the forest, crossed the road at a gallop into more forest, and went south for about a mile before turning back west toward Silver Creek. I crossed one last field into a new housing development. Midday Tuesday, kids in school, parents at work; it was quieter in town than on the road to my house. Disoriented, I figured streets had to lead to a place I recognized. Small town, after all. Sure enough, I came down the hill to Main Street from the south, walked to Subaruth and drove off.

Shaking again, I stopped at the first rest area. Despite the blasting heater, warmth bounced against me and rolled off like geometry facts off a sophomore. I remained untouched, shivering, cold. The aftermath of tension. Like when Sabrina took that bad fall going full tilt on horseback—my nerves were steel until we got to the ER, then the little dots in my vision ballooned, filling blackness into my sight. I didn't quite faint then, and I didn't quite shake to death now.

Finally my freeze relented enough for me to fetch coffee and junk food from the rest area vending machines, coins dropping from my numb fingers to the ground as often as they jangled down the coin slot.

When I returned to the car, its motor still running, heater still blasting, I realized how hot it had gotten, maybe 100 degrees. I didn't care, got back in, kept the heater going, drank my coffee, and ate a breakfast of Fritos, oatmeal cookies, milk, and the orange.

A car pulled up beside me, and I was alarmed until I saw they were oblivious to my presence. And why would they care? They didn't know I was Bomber Woman; they didn't know about naked dashes into the woods; they didn't know about search warrants. They just wanted to use the restroom and then dig out the cooler with sandwiches from under the pile of brightly wrapped Christmas gifts in the cargo space.

I went from freezing to suffocating in thirty seconds flat. Turned off the motor, jumped out of the car, grabbed the cleaner towel, went into the restroom and dressed properly in one of the stalls. People came and went, no one paying much attention, until a woman came in as I was washing soap out of my hair.

"Wow. You must have been on the road a while."

"Well, yes." It seemed like a good idea for people to think the opposite of what was true. "The real problem, though, is that my grandkids managed to spill milkshake in my hair."

"Grandkids." she said. "How can such sweet critters be so exasperating?"

"Obviously you know about grandkids."

"Yes. Yes, yes. They stay with me during the summer, the oldest ones. I age about ten years per summer, and I wouldn't trade for an instant. Well, give yours a hug. Forgive the milkshake. Have a good trip." And she was out the door.

Wait, wait, I thought. Such a warm person, and who knew when I'll talk to anyone else. Couldn't we just brag about grandkids a bit longer?

With a second cup of coffee I drove to the far end of the rest area, away from other travelers. Put cortisone on poison oak—aggravated by heat and itching—then sorted my belongings as my heart gradually quit stuttering and banging.

I measured potato flakes, powdered milk and baking mix into zipper bags then into big drawstring plastic bags in the back seat. I put clothing in the passenger seat, camping equipment in the cargo area, and armsful of detritus—wrappers, empty boxes, bags—in the garbage cans on the way out of the rest area.

I drove south. My heart hurt again when I posted the letters to Sabrina and my trustee. Today it was clear enough. I really had to send that mail. Depart that life.

Leaving those last traces, postmarks from Eugene, I fled south on I-5 past Cottage Grove and then west at Drain. Gloom gathered around me as I drove. From Reedsport I went south again, Highway 101 now. By Coos Bay, rainy day became saturated, bottomless night beyond the glare of headlights. Ocean's roar was impotent in the timpani of rain on the windshield and the allegro "thwap, thwap" of the wipers. I found myself in an untethered capsule, warm, dry, lit by the glow of dashboard lights, besieged outside by gusty, driving rain that opposed the Forester's steady momentum.

The depressing obscurity provided one benefit: I felt safe getting gas in this state where you can stay in the car, tell the attendant "fill it, regular," and slip payment through a window rolled almost closed against the rain. I bought drive-through dinner, too, eighteen pieces of chicken, beans, coleslaw, biscuits, and macaroni and cheese, pulling everything into my sanctuary like bringing in firewood during a blizzard. Enough for days.

When I neared Gold Beach, my radio said, "In a new development in the Utah temple bombing case, a local woman is wanted for questioning. Police say Andrea Glass, of Silver Creek, Oregon, is a 'person of interest' in the case. The sixty-two year old former teacher is described as a white woman, five feet five inches tall weighing..."

Not my weight. Don't give my weight! But they did, of course, the lie on my driver's license still much too big a number.

So it had really begun. Andrea on the lam. No shakes now, but I fell deep into the night's blackness, the rain, the wind, the howling obscurity. Darkness snatched my headlight beams and threw them back at me as I moved through space in my capsule. Unreal day; surreal night.

I found a beach wayside, pulled in. Put on my slicker and rainpants. Staying close to the car, my sanctuary, I walked. Around and around. Terra firma. Sand, not space. Reality, not fiction.

When I got back in, I turned on the map light, retrieved dice from my purse, and rolled them. Tallied results. Mindlessly I rolled dice and rolled dice. Three. Eight. Six. You think you're prepared for it. For Sabrina's wedding, for Neil's death, for becoming a fugitive. But it's like preparing for a squall that turns out to be a hurricane. Blows everything away.

Half an hour? An hour? After a while my tallies looked like the kind of distribution that probability predicts. Lots of sevens, quite a few sixes and eights, only a couple of twos, a couple of twelves. You never know how a single roll of the dice will turn up, but a pattern eventually emerges from the chaos.

I put the dice away and drove a while longer.

Matt

The minute Matthew Sheridan stepped into that house he was sure. He had suspected it before he left to get the warrant.

"Someone is here," he told Wayne. "or has been. Not long ago." His FBI partner had kidded him about turning into a coonhound at night, "I think your ears are beginning to flop; when do you start baying" jokes, but sometimes the feeling of someone present was as tangible to Matt as tracks in snow.

"Well, like I said, nobody came or went while I was waiting out there," Wayne told him. "Nobody broke the seals we put on the doors. You think they're still in here?"

"I don't know. Let's look."

They came up empty-handed after a thorough search—closets, basement, attic. "Maybe she crawled out a window," Matt said.

"Maybe nobody was here." Wayne was a little huffy. "I was right out there watching the whole time. Over two hours in the rain. I'm telling you, nobody came or went."

"It's too warm in here, Wayne. There's a dampness to the bathroom. It doesn't feel like a house that's been sitting empty for weeks."

Kind of funny, Wayne's glare. Matt was six foot four, Wayne six even. The need to glare upward didn't stop Wayne. Occasionally his inner tiger revealed itself, and that was on the verge of happening now. Because Matt had an M.S. and a couple of lucky guesses behind him, he was making the decisions at the moment. Wayne had the years of experience. He'd spent the hours in the rain. No need to aggravate the guy.

"Okay, Wayne, you don't need to say it. Nobody is here. Nobody was in the house when we got here, or the seals on the doors would be broken." Unless she crawled out a window. "I'm going to play my hunch far enough to ask the local guys to keep a lookout."

"Yeah, sure, no harm there." Wayne nodded, his glare receding. "I want to start on the computer and desk. Okay with you?"

When Matt called the local sheriff's office, they told him it was a quiet day, no problem cruising, keeping an eye out, always happy to help out the feds.

"I really appreciate that," Matt told them. "A small Winnebago, or maybe a rental car." They had a copy of Andrea Glass's photo from her driver's license. "Just the next hour or two," Matt said, "though I suspect she's long gone."

Wayne looked at Matt a little more soberly after discovering the computer was missing its hard drive, more soberly still when the buzzer-bell combination went off just before the sheriff pulled in. "Whataya got, Matt, some damn Mormon telepathy thing going here?"

"Yeah, I kept trying to tell the chief that he needed to play the Mormon ESP card in these bombings. Finally got him to listen." To tell the truth, Matt had a hard time joking about it. He had asked to work this case ever since the first temple was destroyed in Idaho three years ago, arguing that his deep understanding of all things Mormon would get them a break.

"Deep understanding, my ass," Fred had replied. "You've got deep pissed-off-ness. You know the policy: keep agents off gut-grinding cases." The chief's fist pounded like feet on a basketball court. "You won't stay logical; and madder 'n hell just gets our guys hurt."

Matt had protested, of course, but the chief had a point. It galled Matt that people destroyed a sacred place, destroyed beauty and holiness, in an instant destroyed years of labor and devotion. They got away with it, and did it again.

It took those two deaths to make Fred relent. The press had turned up the heat, and the chief would fry unless he did something, like put his most successful sleuth on the job.

What bad timing. Wayne had brought it up as they were combing through bank records. "When's that baby due?"

"Any day now," Matt said, "and the other two are already a handful, into everything."

"Your wife got any help?"

"Yes, Danai's mother is there for as long as she's needed. Sally, Danai's sister will help through winter break. They'll be okay." Matt had hoped to be there for Danai this time.

He felt so uneasy about this bombing. Finally he was involved and something smelled rotten. What was that couple doing in the temple? "Mormons don't work on Sundays," he'd told Wayne, "except hospital workers, EMTs, people who sustain life." Middle-of-the-night Sunday? Absurd. Then after the funeral, all the Whiteson family disappeared. What was going on there?

Matt had gone to talk to his bishop about the Sunday temple dilemma. His bishop was puzzled, too. "I'm in Maryland; the Whitesons were in Utah. Maybe you should go talk to their bishop," he suggested.

Matt acted on that suggestion, but the resulting conversation only increased his unease. Was the man always this vague? He didn't know much about the Whitesons, who their friends were, or where family members lived. Matt had been planning to pursue the Whiteson connections when the information from the cab company came through, leading him here to Oregon.

The only thing that had felt right so far was when he'd walked into this house. And when he'd talked to Henri in Provo.

"She be a nice ole lady, jus' wantin' to get goin' south. Said she drank too much java, couldna sleep," Henri LeDoux had said. "She not gonna be able to tell you a thing. I di'n know about no temple bombin' at the time, don' think she did either. She jus' ask aboot my dreds, what I be doin' in Provo. Think she figured I don' exactly fit here."

Matt had acted fast. After talking to LeDoux yesterday, he called Mrs. Glass but only got the answering machine. He hung up, and he and Wayne caught the next flight into Portland. After several tries to phone Mrs. Glass, he talked to Mrs. Severson, the daughter, last night. Now here they were. Not fast enough.

After a couple of hours in the house, Matt observed that the temperature inside had dropped by five degrees. They hadn't touched the thermostat. Mrs. Glass was supposed to be in New Mexico.

"Okay, Boss," Wayne said. "It's strictly, 'yes, sir,' and 'no, sir' from now on. I dunno if you've got Heavenly Father or a damn good nose on your side, but you keep getting it right."

Neither Heavenly Father nor his nose led Matt to talk again to Mrs. Severson. Simple protocol called for face-to-face conversation. Mrs. Severson served him hot cider at her kitchen table. The way Matt read it, she wanted to help; property destroyed and people killed. She wondered why he wanted to talk to Mrs. Glass. She was a little angry with her mother for taking off, but not too surprised. When he described the bell-buzzer setup, though, her flying eyebrows told Matt how surprising *that* was.

"Mom never mentioned it," she said, "but I suppose it could have been there a while. She was alone. Security makes sense ..."

"Not typical of your mother," Matt suggested.

Mrs. Severson hesitated then nodded. "My mother and *security* just don't go together in the same sentence," she admitted.

Mentioning Mrs. Glass's presence in Provo provoked a small scowl then one of those "I'm-thinking" eye-slides. Then she said, "I guess it makes sense. She was in McCall on vacation, met someone she liked, decided to go to New Mexico for a while with him. Probably they stopped in Provo on the way. His name was David ... I don't know if she told me his last name."

Matt wondered about a several-day stop that ended abruptly hours after the bombing. He didn't bring it up. He was learning more from Mrs. Severson's honest reactions than he could by starting a debate. Her response was similar when he mentioned the missing hard drive on the computer—surprised but not astonished. The independent mom thing again.

"She was irritated because her computer was slow, but I thought that had to do with the telephone connection to the internet. Maybe she took the hard drive to the computer store? To have somebody check it out?"

"The house was warm today, Mrs. Severson," Matt told her. "Would anyone have been there? The place is unlocked; do people just stop in?"

"Down that lane—it's secure—she's never locked it. No, people don't go in, except us. I told you we were there on Saturday, to get a Christmas tree."

When Matt had called, she assured him no one was home and described being there, seeing no one, and going in to warm up.

Again, Matt nodded. If Andrea Glass knew anything about bombs—and his heart was ready to bet on it, even if his head never allowed betting—the daughter had no idea. How did it make sense to have unlocked doors and an alarm setup?

Then Sabrina Severson answered a question Matt never would have thought to ask. He hated the way surprises made him feel like a kid unprepared for class.

"We teased Mom about being gone when those other two

temples were bombed," she said. "Just because we knew she didn't like temples."

"Why doesn't she like temples?"

"I don't know exactly. She says all that money spent on them should go to the hungry or homeless, but she doesn't pay much attention to other elegant buildings. I think it's because she couldn't go when Mark and I married in the Atlanta temple."

"You're LDS, too?"

"You're a Mormon?"

Matt nodded. This was something to chew on. "You and your mother are close?"

"Oh, yes, very. I depend on her to be there if the kids are sick, and on holidays, and we just hang out together a lot."

"She didn't mention the electronic monitors?"

"No, but that isn't so unusual. Mom goes ahead and does things then forgets to mention them. She had her Toyota—for weeks, I think, before she came driving up in it one day and said, 'oh, yeah, I've been researching, thought it'd be a good car, thought I should do what I could for the environment.' 'Mom!' I said. I was so surprised, but it was typical, really."

Then the conversation abruptly changed tone. Two little ones were underfoot, the two biggest were squabbling, and Mrs. Severson clearly decided she'd talked to Matt long enough.

"Really, Mr. Sheridan," she said. "you're spending time on things like why Mom's house is warm. She's in her sixties, retired, travels, and she isn't going to know anything about bombs. Surely you'd be using your time better if you follow up on some of your other leads."

"Yes, ma'am, you're right," Matt said, unfolding his long legs and standing. "I didn't expect to take so much of your time. There aren't many leads, and I hoped your mother might have seen something. Maybe something she didn't recognize as significant. Maybe she talked to someone who scared her into dropping off her rental car at that oddball hour. We've put her name out there as a person of interest, because she just may have that key bit of information. So don't be surprised if it's on the news. Let her know, if she gets in touch, that I'm hoping she might be able to help me solve my case and get these destructive people behind bars."

"I'll do that," Mrs. Severson said, "but I don't think Mom will be able to help you any. She's just a Little Old Lady in Tennis Shoes, kind of absent-minded and oblivious, at that."

Little Old Lady in Tennis Shoes, indeed. Matt thought. Not so little, from what Henri LeDoux said. Maybe her tennis shoes came with cleats.

Searching

After a night in my new sleeping bag in the cargo area of the Forester, I could face neither cold chicken nor a coffeeless day. So I donned a longhaired black wig with black-framed glasses and a floppy hat, to visit a busy drive-through for an egg sandwich and two big coffees. Fearing a "Hey, didn't I see you on TV last night?" from the clerk, I was glad he was too rushed to look beyond his hand exchanging food and cash with my hand.

And then I drove.

I hadn't seen my picture on TV, but they always show some picture. Probably driver's license. Ohgawd.

Judging from radio reports last night and this morning, they didn't know much about my whereabouts, just "...last seen en route to Idaho on November 23. Records show her presence in Provo, near the site at the time of the bombing." Provo. Henri, I figured, or the cab company. The rental car, the RV camp.

At least they didn't mention my presence at home — or even Eugene, where I left all the tracks. They were a ways behind me, and I was heading into oblivion.

The so-called banana belt of Oregon's southwest coast didn't even meet iceberg-lettuce belt standards at the moment. Cold, windy, wet, not a bit better than the previous day. Maybe I could dissolve instead of fading away. Sure wasn't going to evaporate.

Campers go to designated sites with toilets and safe water.

Hikers travel along forest service trails. Hunters take their RVs to remote but accessible sites. The place I sought was off all those paths but on public lands, so I wouldn't be trespassing. I wanted an unpopulated place where I could walk to a reasonably level campsite near water at a low, warmer elevation.

From the map a promising road led inland near Oregon's southwest corner. No luck. I found myself driving along a blue and silver meandering river with too many homes on its banks, and then up into impossibly steep National Forest. I went back to Highway 101 northbound to the next road leading east into the forest. No luck. The day passed. One iteration preceded another, of serene, pastoral, populated scenery followed by catastrophic cliffs and chasms.

Roads wound up and up. Creeks boiled into waterfalls. No hiking along them. I was appalled at how I felt here, as though I were living *King Lear* or Ibsen's *Brand* or *The Book of Job.* When we rose above the shelter of lower hills, wind-driven rain again thrashed against Subaruth's windows, her wipers thrashing back. Gray day and dark forest cowed me, and mountains squeezed in and pushed me down toward the bowels of the earth. I drove through deep ravines, ducking to glimpse scraps of dim sky above dark ridges. The climb from each canyon floor only led me over a ridge to the next dismal gulch.

As I retraced one dead-end unproductive route, a newly fallen tree blocked my way out of the oppressive wilderness. The winds had toppled a vine maple after I passed on the way up. Six inch diameter, twenty-foot height. Too heavy to drag, too bushy to drive over.

The claustrophobia clawing at my throat brought a childhood memory: Seeing how far I could swim underwater, I'd reached my limit of breath-holding and with lungs screaming for air, kicked upward to the surface. And my head bumped into a log raft. Through an eternity of fear I kept holding my breath as I felt my way from under the raft. That fear resonated now. I wanted out of the suffocating forest as badly as I had wanted out of the muddy water under the raft.

Unfolding my camp saw, I decided to work on the top part of the tree, with smaller, lighter branches. If I could drag those limbs away, I'd have about half the oncoming lane clear. Enough, if barely.

The wind. The exertion. My panic. All pulled the breath from my throat as I fought the springy, leafless limbs. Jumpin Jupiter. I searched for something positive, some small bit of light. Well—I was sweaty but otherwise dry. The new rain pants worked.

Finally I drove through, branches brushing Subaruth, her wheels on the shoulder, awfully close to the ditch. When we again wound toward the valley's calm, I reconsidered surrender as an option. Or flinging myself over the side of the cliffs I was passing, to perhaps awaken from the nightmare. I'd encountered ... who? Charybdis? One of the Odyssey horrors.

The next road, though, followed a broader river valley that extended farther east; its wind and rain felt diminished. I found a trail that, while steep, was passable. It might do; there was hope. But it was a designated Forest Service trail only half a mile from a hosted campground. Risky. I'd keep searching tomorrow. Maybe I'd find gentler wilderness if I returned north a bit.

In Brookings I bought an *Oregonian* at a newsstand in an unlit strip mall. There I was. Front page. Nope. Not going to awaken from this bad dream. Maybe I should have left the state. An Oregonian "of interest" is big news here. Picture was DMV terrible. On the positive side, I'd enjoy not looking like this after wilderness vanquished chubby cheeks.

No news in the article that I hadn't already heard on the radio. In darkness and black wig, I bought gas and four more cups of coffee for Karinne and me, to chase the chill from my interior.

Another night in the car, more pouring rain and gloomy drives in the morning. Thursday afternoon I studied the contour map some more. After having been there, I could now see contours, distinguish hills from mountains from valleys. I thought so; mountains were steepest in the south, and I was wasting time here. So I headed toward Port Orford and the Sixes River, fifty miles north.

I listened to the radio whenever I was out of the canyons and kept hearing my name. On a talk show one fellow called in to curse the women's lib movement. "First the damn women burned their bras, and now they're turning into *gangsters."*

"She had nothing to do with it," the next caller said. "A 'person of interest' isn't 'the culprit.' A sixty year old schoolteacher wouldn't be planting bombs in the middle of the night."

"Why?" High pitched quavering woman's voice. Sounded

about ninety-five. "Why would anyone attack a place of worship?"

"Well, maybe because they hate Mormons," the talk show host said. "You have to wonder, though. Why temples, which are only for special events, and not churches where Mormons gather at least weekly?"

I thought about calling in myself. "Because they hate how people are excluded from those special events!" Was it so hard to understand?

"Is it so hard to understand that a fugitive shouldn't betray herself with a traceable phone call?" Yep. Karinne Carafe again, the Annoying One continuing to save me from myself.

OK. No calling. Maybe I'd write a letter, mail it someday from across the country. Or put up a web page. Have to learn how.

By Thursday evening, I knew I was getting close. The sense of menace dissipated, despite rain dumping from the sky. I'd thought of mountains as places of refuge, but up higher, not in chasms. I didn't want higher now, though, because *higher* meant *colder.*

"Maybe it's colder here anyway," Karinne wondered. "Does the Brookings banana belt extend this far?"

Is there such a thing as a Brookings banana belt?

I was now at the north end of the Siskiyou National Forest, and I'd spent two nights—and three days—in the car. My map showed a BLM campground nearby and several streams that flowed into the Sixes River.

The campground was empty: I thought I could risk using a

site on its upper loop, farthest from the river and least desirable to other visitors. In late December in miserable weather, no one else was likely to come, but I put on the black wig and matching black-rimmed glasses anyway. With a newspaper picture—and probably one on TV—I felt very vulnerable.

A limp tent soaks up water rather than repelling it, so I kept mine in the car, working from Subaruth's open hatchback, while I studied how to set it up. It turned out to be a simple process, though the vestibules flopped and leaked because I couldn't see what I was doing. My smokey fire heated water enough to try a hiker meal. Bleah.

The river sighed in the background, and the rain sighed too, as it whispered through trees. Their soft melody repeated, "You're all alone now; you're so alone."

It will feel good to wash up, change clothes, stretch out in the tent, I shouted silently, to override nature's refrain. Using leftover warm water from dinner, I managed a fair bath in the privy: out of the rain, not too smelly, very cold. I entertained thoughts of a river bath or a rain shower, but I'd had enough December alfresco bathing.

This bath didn't end in naked flight. Or naked fear. And no mud chaser this time.

Then, lonely murmur of wind and rain still in my ears, I again used the car's upraised back hatch to stay dry as I opened my sleeping bag, pinned the flannel sheet in, and cut off the excess. Luckily, as it turned out, I kept the trimmed-off piece. I came across Burgundy Blanket, and carried it, sleeping bag, and foam mattress across lonesome darkness to the tent. I scrunched up B.B. and curled around her in the sleeping bag. Her warmth mediated the realities on the other side of my tent's zipper, and my curl shifted to a stretch.

* * * *

The road crossed several streams within five miles of the campground. I checked them out from the car and found three creeks that held some '90s-style Republican promise—kinder and gentler. Here it was at least possible to walk alongside a cheery stream, not a raging near-waterfall. Rain, softer, but still cold, dictated the day's apparel: slicker and rainpants again, with galoshes over my walking shoes. As I investigated, "kinder and gentler" quickly became "steep and impassible," littered with dense underbrush and jumbles of rock. By Friday night I was again fed up with political promises. That evening I studied my maps, deciding to go east to Powers if the one unexplored creek here wasn't an improvement.

On Saturday, however, I found my spot. With overcast but no rain, the day began auspiciously and got better. I began with good hot coffee and decent oatmeal, thanks to drier firewood. Then I walked a mile north along the third creek. The terrain was gentle, so I continued around or through undergrowth. When another small stream entered from the east, I followed it for another half mile. Galoshes allowed me to wade when brush blocked the way alongside the stream or I might have quit, fearing I'd get lost if I left the little brook.

The brook made a bend to my left, and I saw light coming through trees to my right. I found the light's source, a lovely clearing nearly an acre in size. Yes. An ideal tent site, with trees and stream behind me to the north, trees to my left, and the meadow opening up ahead and to the right. Afraid to trust my luck, I walked around and through the meadow, looking for marshy spots, but it was perfect. Of course there were a few puddles after all the recent rain, but the meadow drained well, rolling downward from trees on the east and tilting toward the northwest corner where water seeped into Little Brook. Hooray LeeJay. This was really fine.

"Maybe it's good you went through all those awful places. Makes this meadow seem purely elegant." I didn't care how Karinne Carafe managed to talk at me here. I picked up my rain jacket from the bush where I had tossed it, blew a kiss to sun making a passable effort at shining through clouds, and headed back to my previous campsite for my gear.

Camp

Sunday morning, frosty and clear, made it hard to leave the warmth of sleeping bag and Burgundy Blanket at the BLM campground. But my new home beckoned. Today I would pack in most camping gear with enough food for a couple of days.

I parked Subaruth half a mile from my trail up Big Creek. She was well hidden, on a bank above normal eye-level and behind thick evergreen branches, but in case someone found her, I left a forest pass—purchased at the Eugene camper store—on her dash.

In two trips I got enough camp basics up to the meadow to make a good start. Two exhausting trips, tough going through the brushy undergrowth with bulky loads, over gullies and through the creek. Longer than the portage at home. Probably steeper, too. I was a sweaty, shaky, gasping wreck by midday. My gear lay in a heap by trees at meadow's edge. The tent went up fast now that I knew how to do it. I tossed in my sleeping bag and mattress, kicked off my shoes and took a nap.

When I awoke in mid-afternoon, through my open screen I saw clouds forming high in the western sky. "You got lucky with a couple of dry days. Better get ready for rain," Karinne's voice told me.

I created a canopy using two tarps placed end-to-end, looping ropes from tarps over tree branches on the east and north sides. On the west side, with no trees, I decided to hook tips of bamboo poles into tarp grommets, and run ropes like guy wires from tarp to ground, using tent stakes to hold the base of each rope. I needed to set two poles at the same time to keep one from flopping down while I secured the other. Since I didn't have four arms, much less a reach of ten feet, the neighborhood birds learned some new words. Ones that surprised me. Eventually I managed, by propping the poles a foot off the ground and then running back and forth to raise them a foot at a time.

I ended with a covered area as long as a medium living room but half its width, the canopy sloping from eight feet high on the eastern side to six feet on the west. I'd hunt for tree limbs later to support the sagging west side and maybe replace bamboo, too.

Neil and I had created similar shelters dozens of times when we camped. This was just a little bigger and a lot more lonely.

Moving my tent to the shelter's north edge, I kept its entrance beneath my tarp canopy, staked down two tent corners and—with clouds rolling in—put on its rain fly.

Night was coming. I got out dried fruit and jerky, and swung a bag with more food into a tree. Bears should be hibernating, but no point in pushing my luck. The forest floor had twigs, cones, and branches for a fire, but it got too dark to gather much. My smokey flame warmed neither me nor the tent behind me, but I balanced a pot in its embers, netting a cup of lukewarm coffee with my cold supper.

A taxing day, but a good one. Until now, anyway, when

darkness grew, and I had no real fire for comfort, no real dinner to fill my hollows. The meadow had seemed so benevolent that afternoon, but now gremlins lurked on its edges. Did I see critters moving in the shadows? Shadows moving in the wind?

This wasn't just solitude. This was that awful feeling of being little, in a strange place, and you can't find your mom.

I took refuge with Burgundy Blanket in the tent and thought about how to build my fire pit.

Monday morning. Two weeks since my life turned on end. After hauling another load up from the car, I dug a rectangular hole about a foot deep where my fire had been. On three sides around the hole, I mounded dirt and stones. I put big branches outside the mounds and nailed my wire fencing to the branches, across the fire pit. A few more rocks and some dirt on top of the branches held my wire grate firm. Not bad for a pilgrim. Before nightfall I gathered an enormous pile of firewood, bark, and moss, and started sorting it by size and flammability.

Now I used newspaper, a part without my picture, and the driest kindling to build a truly fine fire. By its light I kept working for a while, breaking and sawing my firewood into usable lengths. I got two pots of water going, one for coffee and one for a camp stew. My china was the fry pan, and my silverware was a spoon/fork camp utensil, but dinner felt elegant after the lukewarm entrees of the past few days. Cleanup was tricky in the dark, but necessary.

"You can't forget about food smells and wild animals just because you're tired, Andy. Um. Bev." Karinne looked much less elegant these days, a smoke-blackened aluminum coffeepot, not a silver carafe. "A bit of soap and some gravel will do. Dump away from camp and away from the creek."

My headband flashlight helped in the cleanup, lighting my way and leaving hands free. The evening's last project was a small hole beside the fire pit, in which I planted a branch to act as my coat rack and dryer. Dampness from the light afternoon rain was better left outside the tent.

On Tuesday, Thursday and Saturday, I made trips from car to camp, trekking one day and building camp the next. I'd had my only respite from rain, though there was one day of mere heavy fog. I strengthened my tarp-shelter with tree-branch supports. I dug a latrine, and even put sitting-branches across it, with a supply of moss toilet paper in a zipper bag nearby. Some of my most miserable time in the rain was spent there, until I remembered my poncho and hung it at the edge of the shelter to take along as my "privy roof."

In the tent, designed to sleep four, my spare clothing was on the right, in its garbage bag. Flute, books and sketchpad were in a "second drawer," another garbage bag beneath the clothing. The sleeping bag was on its foam pad to the left. I kept the headband flashlight, candle, and matches at the foot of the bed near the vestibule and door. A second flashlight was at the head of my sleeping bag, by the picture of Sabrina and her family.

My stomach tightened when I looked at that portrait. How were they? When would I see them? What were they thinking about me? Sabrina must be so worried. I was a "person of interest." I'd disappeared. Low Voice must be asking questions. My letter would be scant comfort. But what could I do?

Eventually food bundles hung from several trees. A good plan even if accidental. A critter might get one bundle; two would be unlikely. Each bag contained a little of every kind of food, so pulling down one sufficed.

I kept my fire going and coffee water hot. A few pieces of drying firewood and my cooking utensils were by the fire. I put jugs of brook water by the trees, along with a collapsible bottle full of previously boiled water and a jug of reconstituted milk. Perhaps my best meals were breakfasts of oatmeal and milk sprinkled with sweetener and cinnamon.

At the far end of my canopied living area, I had a stack of firewood, protected from windblown rain by an extra tarp. A clothesline ran between two trees, partially above the tent and under the northeast corner of the canopy.

I seemed to have forgotten no ropes. If I met my downfall, at least it would be for some other reason.

I noticed with pride that my shelter was working well. Rain ran off on the west side and drained down slope from there. Smoke blew the opposite direction, up the slope of the tarps and into trees on the east side where it dissipated. Not much sign of my presence here.

I had forgotten my fear of discovery. I felt safe. And for a week, I was too busy to notice the loneliness. Many times I had camped with Neil for no reason except the joy of it. Now I appreciated the prior experience and recaptured a bit of the pleasure. It took me longer than I expected to get camp set up, and my aches overrode exhaustion and kept me awake when I first went to bed. But I'd done it. I'd be able to manage this.

On Saturday, I made my ninth and last trip to Subaruth. Some detritus remained, mostly my go-to-town clothing and wigs.

That evening, December 23, I went to bed with my camp complete, with my last load from the car, everything in place; and my money, Andrea Glass credit cards and ID in plastic bags and buried. I awoke the next morning full of the knowledge that it was the day before Christmas.

Winter

Christmas Misery 2000 felt a lot like Wedding Misery 1991. Isolation and the need for distraction had marked Sabrina's day, too. Something to get past. Neil and I went the opposite direction from the Atlanta wedding, on a two week camping trip in the Canadian Rockies, the day one of many in high mountain fresh air. Now here I was: coast not mountains, Christmas not a wedding. But camping again, miserable again, needing distraction again.

I decided to spend the day building a windbreak on the breezy west side of my canopy. On Christmas Eve day I cut five sturdy seven-foot branches, trimmed them, dragged them back to camp, then planted them like posts along the western edge of my shelter. To lend greater stability, I made the windbreak footprint a broad V, with the point of the V facing west into the wind. Then I cut willowy branches along Little Brook, trimming and stacking them for the wall of the windbreak. I worked doggedly to avoid thinking. I don't cry. Tree branches, wet from previous rains, showered me effusively. Sufficient lament.

By evening I was too tired and cold to think about Christmas. It sure didn't feel like Christmas. I skipped the preceding days' meals of gourmet mashed potatoes with chicken gravy in favor of hiker's stew, quicker to fix, hotter than my first cooking effort and therefore almost palatable. Dried fruit and coffee made a decent dessert. As I crawled into my sleeping bag, I held aches and anguish at bay, somewhere in the depths of awareness.

Pearl gray light surrounded my tent. My bladder screamed for relief and my stomach growled. Christmas day. No tinsel, no sparkling lights. No brimming stockings by the fire. No fire, in fact. With luck, some good coals outside in the pit. My jeans felt damp and cold despite spending the night in the sleeping bag with me. Everything felt damp and cold. It hurt to move. Muscles ached. Bones ached, joints ached. I thrashed myself dressed, crawled to the door, zipped it open and crawled out. The rain had returned, not as a patter on my tarp but as mist on my face.

By the time I'd trekked to the latrine and stirred up the fire, an hour passed. Activity had warmed me. A double batch of oatmeal, two Tylenols, and very hot coffee brightened the day a notch. Pearl gray to stainless steel maybe.

I got to work. Between each two upright posts of the windscreen, I planted a light branch, also upright. Then I wove branches horizontally around three uprights: in-out-in and out-in-out. Rain clothes protected me from the steady drizzle, but not from sweaty dampness. Cutting and dragging branches made me hot; standing still to weave them made me cold.

I built the entire fence two feet high and then three feet high, and then one section fell over, dragging a second section with it. One half of the V sprung loose across the ground. Cold, wet. Alone. Undone. Christmas. Numb fingers. Santa brought me—pickup sticks.

Unruly sobs jerked at my gut but I refused them, fighting the unwilling earth, whacking away with the hatchet, shoveling away loosened soil, setting posts deep, then ramming soil down again against them. Rewove the downed section. Went back a buzillion times for more branches. I don't cry. Damn branches. Damn fence. Damn family. Forget kids, tree, packages. In-out-in. Out-in-out. Weaving boughs for a wall instead of a wreath.

Finally the windbreak was nearly five feet high. Enough to deflect most of the breeze and enhance the heat from my campfire. Low enough to see over. For support I used five Y-shaped branches, bases dug into the ground, notches hooked into uprights. No wobble when I pushed. Just enough air flowed through to maybe prevent wind from knocking it over.

Late winter afternoon augmented by drizzle. Encroaching darkness. Horrid day almost done. I built up the fire. Sloughed my rainsuit.

The wind screen helped. My back felt cool, not cold, when my front was to the fire. With dry longjohns and wool sweater, my wet clothing of the day hanging on the line, I felt almost comfortable.

One gift, the windscreen, provoked another: a four-course supper of vegetable soup, mashed potatoes with beef gravy and a side of teriyaki jerky, nuts with dried apricots, and a cup of hot chocolate. With an extravagant second cup, cinnamon-cocoa-coffee this time, I toasted my day's labor. "To a really fine windbreak. Viva le windbreak!"

It seemed shallow, though, my joy, layered atop mourning. Over a downright decadent third cup, I let my mind drift in the direction it had been slanting all day, to the now finished ritual at Sabrina's, gifts opened, rubbish collected, tired kids succumbing to bath and story time. Were they thinking about me? Worried about me? Did they believe I'd gone to New Mexico, to Chama?

Investigators had probably tracked my sale of Winnie in Oregon by now. And I imagine Bruce Douglas had contacted Sabrina to let her know he was managing the property at my request. What could they be thinking of me? I imagined them guessing. Was I in a hotel somewhere? On a train? I'd bet they'd never guess this, in the woods fighting tree limbs.

Sorrow lapped at my edges like little lake waves lapping at toes. Thought about Meacham hill, about Holly, that terrible accident. Thought about Neil. And about the Whitesons, the couple somehow in the wrong place, dying in the Echo Lake temple. Because I'd bombed it. An entire ocean of sorrow, huge breakers crashing down.

* * * *

Once I had Christmas behind me, I thought I had gotten past the hard part. Maybe so, but I'd planned for Christmas. I had not foreseen day upon unremitting gray dreary day. Weather varied from steady rain to intermittent rain to something northwesterners call heavy fog. More like rain without downward motion, fine water particles suspended in air, saturating everything. Canopies, tents, wind screens, rain flies—all are ineffectual against this insidious wetness.

They overwhelmed me, those days. I was so alone. I ached for Sabrina and Mark and the kids. My home. Pi Tree and

Winnie the Brave. Grieved for Neil, for the wedding we'd missed, for Holly, even for the wonderful family dog now buried behind my home. For my family oh for my family. And for the Whitesons.

I have often been alone, rarely lonely. Now I didn't know how to save myself. The light was awful. Came late, left early, sulked in between. Everything matched. Gray days. Bleak existence. Barren meadow. Dismal cold dampness seeped through my windbreak, into the tent, infiltrating sleeping bag and Burgundy Blanket, past my heart into bone marrow.

For weeks I lived in longjohns and wool sweater in my bed sack, trying to sleep the days away. Liquid weather occasionally became solid, freezing rain glazing tent and tarps and the sitting-poles of my latrine. Sometimes a bit of snow laced the trees. On drier days morning frost often lay on the meadow. Clear days were colder yet, ice stretching my plastic water containers, ice overflowing my coffeepot, ice lining Little Brook, icy hands and icy feet cohabiting the sleeping bag and spreading the chill.

I never quit being cold. I felt no joy now in the resilience of my wind screen even against hard gusts. Where were the sturdy Y posts to prop *myself* up? I crawled out of my sleeping bag on command of my bladder, then crawled right back in. I managed, on most days, to stir up the fire and have coffee and one hot meal. December left, January rolled along.

The pearl mist on the meadow provided a screen for the theater of my mind. It showed the last time I saw my grandchildren as I hid in the woods at home. It portrayed news clips of the Whitesons' funeral. It even went back to old classics like Neil's funeral and imaginary scenes from Sabrina's wedding. Where were the comedies? The musicals? Not here; it was all Tolstoy. Or Ibsen. Grieg accompaniment. Creations from frozen places. I'd left my rune stones behind, but I didn't need them. I'd be drawing Isa: ice, winter. No life, no growth.

I picked at the scabs left from my berry vine battles. The trouble with suicide, I thought as I watched my reopened wounds bleed, is that it's so much trouble. Sawing at my wrists with my pocket knife? Dangling from a tree at the end of a noose? Black actions, requiring more energy than I could find in the chill pewter fog of my existence.

Kindling

Eventually there came a morning when my bladder pulled me from bed, and then the scritching from my caffeine-deprived brain pushed me to use the last of my woodpile to heat water. No wood, no coffee. I had gathered all the dead branches in sight. The thought of losing my one remaining comfort spurred me to action, but gave me pause, too, when I discovered I didn't want to get lost as I searched for more firewood.

So. Suicide, maybe; blundering and lost, no. No, no. *Lost* implied becoming colder, wetter, more forlorn. If I died in this miserable place, it would be deliberate—and well caffeinated.

I had a problem to solve. Find wood, find the way back to camp. Mountain Woman was not thriving here, but Problem Solver? Well, maybe. The sluggish flow of blood in my veins quickened an infinitesimal amount.

I followed Little Brook along its bend north; easy enough to follow it back again. The going became too rough after a quarter of a mile, but half a dozen big armloads of burnable debris rewarded my effort.

Tying a rope from tree to tree worked, too. I could gather in sight of the rope, which in turn was in sight of camp. Landmarks provided a third strategy: the big cedar tree to the east, a bluff to the south.

Gathering required mindfulness, staying in view of the

landmark or the string or the brook. My emotional abyss receded. And a dozen armloads of firewood graced my living space, with potential for dozens more.

My head already knew that problem solving doesn't have to be mathematics to distract, and that activity warms—better than longjohns or sleeping bag. Now my bones understood. The chill had left my hands and toes and spine. A little thrum started in my brain stem.

But depressing cold dampness still permeated camp: through tent to sleeping bag, to flannel sheet, B Blanket, and longjohns. The sleeping bag, rated effective at fifteen degrees, failed me at Fahrenheit thirty-something-and-soggy. And every time I entered the tent, my family stared from their frame at my bedside. Their smiles reproached me.

The nadir again. A person can't sleep through damp chill winter regret. I know; I tried. My drizzling misery transformed to deluge when I stupidly retrieved the little carved wood box from my flute case, and held its pin in my hands. I touched the tiny pearl flower, stroked silver wings. Sank into a black abyss.

Then I got purely sick of it. If one can crawl ferociously, I did so, out of the tent to the fireside with both pin and flute. Not to burn them but to dry them. They were going to mildew like me otherwise. I returned to the tent and turned my family's photo face down.

Somehow that got Karinne Carafe channeling through Elaine Aluminum, the camp coffeepot. "Well, look who found a little backbone," she said. "What else can you do besides just lay down and die? Get out the hot water bottle? Warm up some rocks, like they used to do with bricks in pioneering times?"

Kind of nice to hear that harpy voice again.

I found golfball-sized rocks in Little Brook and put them in the fire. When they were hot, I used a stick to push them into one of my—still muddy—blue towels. I'd burned the back of my hand on the hot wire grate and now the towel started smoldering. I dumped rocks back into the fire, took the towel to the creek, rinsed it, and rolled the hot rocks in again. Carefully.

Steam. Okay, that would work if I ever wanted a sauna. I washed both towels and hung them up. I didn't expect them to dry—this place made dry things wet, not vice versa—but I hoped they'd progress from dripping to camp-damp.

So now, how could I use the hot rocks?

I burned myself again as I pushed them into my frying pan. I scorched the sheet when I left the pan in my sleeping bag.

But my bed was warm when I crawled in later, and the rocks heated the tent after I pulled the pan from the sleeping bag. My hot water bottle, filled with the water always heating on my fire, warmed my toes. Whoa. A free upgrade; practically five-star accommodations.

The next night I burnt my hands again and scorched the sheet. But the third night I got smart enough to heat the rocks in the pan at the edge of the fire, then let them cool for an hour on another, upturned, pan inside the tent. The tent warmed up and a few minutes of hot rocks in my bed while I brushed my teeth provided toasty sleeping comfort. Why hadn't I done this weeks ago?

My flute's pads seemed dry, so I returned it and Grandma's pin to the safety of the now dry tent. Burgundy Blanket dried out, too, and provided comfort again.

But the freeze returned. January ended clear and cold. My coffeepot had a skim of ice every morning. I again crawled back into bed to squeeze shut my eyes, squeeze away despair. The hot rocks seemed like too much bother. Again I thought of death by hanging, death by overdose, death by hypothermia. And again I found little reason to bother with anything much, even suicide.

Then one night I heard a distant screaming, like a critter being tortured. I knew that sound from home: a cougar's cry. I shivered, grabbed Burgundy Blanket, and went back to sleep. The next night, a second tortured sound accompanied the cougar scream. A kind of howling yelp. Cougar getting its dinner; nothing I could do.

Moments later another scream—right outside my camp—stirred me to action. It sounded like the cougar was just outside the windbreak.

"Cougars do attack humans, you know," Elaine Aluminum reminded me. "Get it out of here."

Critter

Fire seemed the best defense, so I threw my headband flashlight on, lit my candle with shaky hand, and rushed from the tent yelling and shouting. I heard a snarl, awfully close by. I had saved a pitchy branch by the fire, and I grabbed it now, buried one end in the firepit coals to set it aflame, then ran around the perimeter of my camp, waving the flaming branch and screaming. I saw the cougar—or maybe shadows—sliding away in the trees. Making more noisy circuits, I evoked a chubby white image of an ancient aborigine dance. *Dance with Fire*, the sequel to *Naked in the Rain.* My improvised ritual ended with the spraying of bear repellent around the perimeter of the campsite. I didn't know if it worked for cougars, but it couldn't hurt.

Using most of my dry wood, I got the fire blazing. All was quiet, except for my heart pounding in my ears. At least I wasn't cold.

I sat by the fire. Time passed. I heard no more from the mountain lion, though I kept imagining rustling in the shadows by the woodpile. "Calm down, Andy," Elaine Aluminum said. "Cougar's gone. Your fire will keep him away." I started drowsing and went back to bed.

Morning came, quiet and cold and clear, with my usual insistent bladder. I made maximum noise going to the latrine, in case I still had kitty company. I figured after *Dance with Fire*, he was boycotting my theater. Two months, two comedies. Too ridiculous to sell.

I filled the coffeepot and went to the woodpile to replenish the stack I'd used last night. Movement! Not my imagination. My gasp made the critter hidden amidst the branches try to jump up, but it only managed a repeat of the twitch that first caught my attention.

"Oh, poor baby." I saw a petite doglike nose and scared eyes. Was it a fox? Coyote? I moved a few pieces of wood to reveal a little creature, its fur matted with blood.

"You're the dinner the cougar was after last night. No wonder he came so close. You're pretty courageous, darting in here with a human. And fire." My voice sounded odd; I realized I hadn't used it for weeks.

The fire had been merely coals when the critter came into camp, I remembered. Critter surely was frantic to get someplace where the cougar wouldn't go. Probably my fire dance terrified it, but it had no options. And probably the dance saved its life. *Murder in Camp*. Glad we skipped that drama.

The critter was panting. Loss of blood—it needed water. I went in search of a bowl. I flapped in circles for a while, like a killdeer trying to lead a dog away from her nest. All that blood panicked me. I stopped, breathed deeply and concentrated on calm. It would take easy, slow movements for Critter to believe I wouldn't harm it.

"Okay. Water first." I talked aloud deliberately now, almost singing, trying to soothe.

No bowl. "I don't want to give you my pot. How could I

sanitize it enough to use again? Find a piece of old wood to hollow out for you? No. You look miserable. You need water soon. And how can you drink when you're flat on your side like that?"

"Those drip water bottles on Sabrina's gerbil cage—we need something like that, don't we, baby? Is there anything in the garbage?"

I poked a hole in an empty foil bag with my knife and went to Little Brook for fresh water. But the water came gushing out; the hole was too big. A second try was no better. Oh lordy, I thought, can I ever help this little guy? A needle, not a knife. Zipper bag? I filled it with water then poked the hole and got a nice small stream when I pushed at it.

To calm Critter I'd been babbling. Or singing. Math songs. Made me think of Holly. All those years ago. My voice, getting warmed up, sounded less like a door on a rusty hinge as I returned to the wood pile.

"Hey, kiddo, it's Dr. Andy with part one of The Cure. Take it easy now. I want to drip water on your nose. I know you're a good kid, but we haven't been properly introduced. I don't think that's a smile. Looks more like a future bite. I'd greatly appreciate your thinking about refreshing water and not about tasty hand. I promise I'm not any more excited than you about sharing a tight place. Easy now. I'll move slowly."

But wait. My new acquaintance had denned up in a tiny area created by shorter branches amid longer ones. Before I approached with water, I needed to move wood away from Critter to open up the space. One slow branch at a time, I got enough of an opening. He made growling noises and thrashed, but he had no place to go and was too weak to even roll onto his belly. I hung a towel across his entryway and gave him a minute to feel hidden again.

As I draped the towel, Critter looked up at me with liquid, slightly bulging brown eyes above dark wet crescents. Critter's name changed to Sly right then.

I'd need hot water later. So while Sly acclimated to his rearranged den, I cut wood into shorter lengths and stirred up the fire, talking or singing the whole time. Finally I returned with the water bag, slowly moved the towel away and eased down to the ground, arm's length from Sly. He wouldn't like my standing over him any better than my students at school did. "Sly, it's OK. You need this water."

I leaned on my left side and slowly moved my right arm over Sly and squeezed. His startled reflex when water hit his nose was a snarl and a lick. He didn't jump much; he still seemed unable to move. But the snarl and lick had marvelous effect. I squeezed more and he licked, tentatively at first and then eagerly. The snarl faded and died. When I moved away to the fire, I left his opening uncovered this time. Maybe he'd watch and get used to me. After breakfast—with coffee—I rounded up everything likely to help doctor him.

"HooRah McGraw, for all the vet supplies I found at home and nearly killed myself toting here. Didn't plan on you, Sly. They were in case *I* got hurt. But I'm gonna do my best for you." What a sweet-looking, undoubtedly vicious, little animal.

"The first thing is to clean you up, Sly. I saw a lot of blood."

This was going to be tricky. I could end up mangled, too.

Voice low, I inched more branches away. My initial impressions were confirmed. Sly was a fox with a beautiful bushy tail, gray coat and a terrible wound along his left side. A small steak appeared to hang off his shoulder, a piece of Sly. A slash along his ribs sagged open. I could see white, cartilage or tendons or bone, in spots on both his shoulder and his ribs.

"Whoa. Sly, this is bad."

I'm sure his eyes would have broadcast "You're telling me!" except they were full of a hundred iterations of "What are you going to do to me? Do humans eat foxes?"

Blood and torn flesh make me go wobbly and faint-headed when it's Sabrina, anybody for that matter, but I do better with animals. Experience helps, and after decades with dogs, cats, chickens, goats, and horses, experience was something I had in abundance.

"I'm no doctor," I told Sly. "Will this shoulder muscle even function? You need four good legs to survive here. Infection—another problem. Boy. That cougar missed your belly by an inch. You'd have been an ex fox for sure, old fella. I hope your other side isn't this bad. I dunno about your chances, but maybe they're better with me than without me."

I gave him more water as I thought about what to do. "I don't think you'll like this much." So much blood. But perhaps that would work in my favor, make him too weak to run. Or attack.

In that hole his wounds were hard to reach. And I didn't care to be trapped if he started acting like, well, like a wild animal. So I'd need to move him.

From behind him I slid a towel, pushing as much under him as I could. From the other side, I used a stick to pull on the towel until I had enough to safely grab its edge, then tugged towel, with him on it, closer to the fire. His teeth flashed; he was no wounded puppy.

I had Betadine, an antiseptic wash often used by vets. Just a little, because it's heavy. "Thought *I'd* need this, Sly." I poured some into a zipper bag and added warm water, leaving the bag open by a centimeter.

With an injured horse, you start a wash near his nose so he can smell that it's not his own blood he feels pouring across his body. But horses are prey; foxes are hunters, so I didn't know if the thought process would be similar.

"Okay, fella. I hope you understand what I'm doing." I flooded the wounds, moving from his nose across his shoulder and along his flank, talking to him all the while. He flinched and snapped, teeth flashing millimeters from my hand. His back feet propelled him at least a foot. I was amazed; he had seemed incapable of movement. But then he collapsed again, perhaps calmer, perhaps just resigned.

I did a second wash the same way. It was when I was trying to pat him dry with the other towel that he got me. The transformation from passive surrender to ferocious attack was instantaneous and astounding. Needle-sharp teeth dug deep into my left hand.

If my earlier crooning had any beneficial effect, I undid it now with my yelp. "Ow! Damn! Geez Louise." I jumped up, and hunched over, holding my left arm. Gripping tight against the hurt, I sagged back to the ground and leaned on the firewood pile. I'm such a wimp; pain makes me woozy. "Sly, I can't afford this. What if it gets infected? Dang. You hurt me, fella."

No blood dripped from between my fingers. Couldn't be all that bad, I thought. He's just a little guy. I moved my hand from the injury and stole a look. It *was* bleeding. That's okay. Cleanses. Two short but deep gashes, one on my wrist, one just above it on my arm.

My self-treatment matched Sly's: flushing with antiseptic and patting dry. "Betadine doesn't hurt, I'm glad to know, Sly. I'd say you bit me out of fear, not pain." I smeared Bag Balm onto my sliced arm, bandaged it, then appraised the situation.

"I guess any wounded scared critter might attack like that. You're dangerous. I *do* get it." I sipped at my coffee for a while. "What if you get me again? What if I get infected? Get a fever? Pass out? Who will fix me?" We glared at each other across the fire pit.

"But I can't just leave you. You're such a little thing, a youngster, I bet. Those sharp teeth might belong to a kid. Kit. I still think I might be able to patch you up." I gave him more water, dripping it as before from a bag well out of tooth-range.

I decided to muzzle Sly, using a strip of flannel. The trick would be getting it on him. I'd learned a relevant bit of physics when geese chased me in my youth: an animal cannot bite you as long as you have a firm grip on the back of his head. With a goose it's easy; one hand around the upper part of the neck does it. I'd try a similar trick to muzzle my little fox.

Holding a strip of flannel between my teeth, I approached him from behind, grabbed a handful of loose flesh at the back of his neck, and pinned his head to the ground. He sure didn't think I was a friend at that point.

His back feet kicked as he tried to push himself away, and his nails dug grooves in the dirt. He snapped and snarled, and I just hung on. Finally, holding his head still with my right hand, I wrapped a loop of flannel around his nose with my left. As his back end spun and struggled, I held him pretty brutally. One end of the flannel strip was between my teeth as I pulled it tight around his nose. I made a second wrap, tied a single knot under his chin, and pulled the ends of the flannel strip behind his ears, securing the muzzle with a slipknot there.

Using another strip of flannel, I tied his back legs together to limit his wriggle power. I thought a minute then did the same to his front legs and tied front to back. My poor little fox had been bulldogged. "Maybe I'll take up rodeo-ing in my next life. If they ever have a foxdogging contest, I'll have a major edge. Foxdogging." I snorted.

Sly didn't answer. He just lay there, his sides heaving. "Well, tough. My sides are heaving, too, Mr. Stallone, and I'll bet my adrenaline matches yours. You bloody well came close to nabbing me again with those teeth."

The struggle had been terrible for him; blood oozed again from his wounds. Oozing, I suspected, because not enough blood was left in his body to spurt.

Hours passed as I did what I could for the little gray fox. I needed a razor to cut away fur to tape him together, but I had to make do with tiny, bad scissors from my manicure kit. After I cut what I could, and rinsed and dried his wounds again, I pulled the hole on his shoulder closed and taped across it in three places. He was going to move and the tape would pull loose, but maybe he'd be healing by then. After slathering on Bag Balm, I laid gauze over the wound. I treated the gash on the ribs the same way. He lay breathing fast, eyes closed, probably hoping the end would be swift.

To help hold the wounds closed, I created a sort of flannel harness over the gauze, around his ribs and across his chest, sewing it together where the chest band met the belly band. "Glad I saved that piece of sheet. And brought the sewing kit. Sure never thought I'd use it this way." The belly band did a better job of holding together the tear along his ribs than the tape did, and the chest strap did a fair job of covering the shoulder wound. I wrapped him round and round with Pet Wrap, a sort of sticky version of an Ace bandage, another vet supplies item I'd thought I might need for myself. "Maybe everything will hold together long enough to heal, Sly. You'll try to chew it off when I remove that muzzle, but hopefully you'll be too stiff and tired to succeed." He was still limp, his breathing fast and shallow.

I had taken a look at his other side as I created the harness, pulling on the towel under him to roll him onto his belly on my lap. He had three parallel shallow scratches there, which I smeared with Bag Balm as I worked, trusting the antiseptic ointment to cleanse, too.

Finally I rolled him onto the towel again and dragged him to his hidey hole. He must have felt safe. Or he was just exhausted. Anyhow, he didn't struggle at all when I removed his restraints and replaced the towel-cover over his space.

By the time I cleaned up, it was mid afternoon. I made a package of hiker stew for myself and set aside another for Sly. Then I refilled his water bag and went to see how he was doing.

He wasn't doing well.

Fox ICU

Sly showed little sign of life, except for the panting. But he licked again at the water I dribbled on his nose. I stayed there beside him for the afternoon, trickling the water every five minutes or so.

At dinner, I ate the package of stew I planned to give Sly. I mixed gravy for him, put it in another bag, and spent the evening dribbling it, alternating with water. He licked at each when I first offered them, then seemed to lose strength and just let it dribble to the ground. I went back every hour, and every hour he took a little sustenance.

As it grew dark, I acclimated him to the flashlight, carefully shining it above his head and not in his eyes as I continued my dribbling care. My throbbing hand kept me awake that night, which was okay. I had a fox to nurse anyway. I continued to give him licks of water and gravy every couple of hours. Faint light was showing in the east when he began whining. I worried because he didn't want water or gravy now. He kept whining.

Finally as early light seeped into camp, I built up the fire, made coffee for myself and gave my hot water bottle to Sly. I remembered giving my arthritic dog half an aspirin to ease her pain. Would a fox tolerate aspirin? And Sly was so small. I tried just a sliver, buried in a bit of warm chicken meat. He gulped it down. Aspirin or warmth worked after a bit; he lay his head back down and slept.

For myself, a Tylenol. I had awakened feeling stiff. Tetanus? The cold water of Little Brook eased the throbbing in my wrist, and the Tylenol helped. I thought of a warm salt water soak, but I had no salt.

Holey Moley. I could be in big trouble. What if I got tetanus and my muscles spasmed and I couldn't walk out for help?

"You're okay. You wake up stiff every morning. And you could be in big trouble a thousand ways. Like if you burned the tent down. Or fell and broke a leg." Reassurance, ala Elaine Aluminum. I applied Bag Balm and tried to let it go.

Some time in the night, Sly had stopped growling at me, so I hoped I wouldn't need the muzzle that lay on the woodpile. He seemed at ease in his hidey-hole, so I took away the bloody, dirty towel hanging over him.

Sly brought better weather. I'd noticed the absence of ice when I put coffee on. Now sun warmed the meadow, though winter briskness still hung in the air.

When Sly next whined, I took him for a walk in the sunshine. It wasn't much of a walk on his part. I made a sling using the remaining strip of flannel sheet, and he teetered and staggered even though I held him up. But he got his limbs moving, gazed around the meadow as though astonished at seeing it again, found a shrub to half lift a leg at, and slumped gratefully down back in the woodpile. Apparently we had a truce. No snapping, no snarling, even when I pushed the walking-sling under him. Therefore no yelping on my part.

But my coffee was too hot and kind of frothy when I spat it out. Rabies?

"Sly will show symptoms of rabies before you do. Geez what a wimp."

Okay, Elaine. I won't worry about rabies yet. Unless … maybe humans get it faster than animals?

I went wood-gathering in the direction of a big downed tree and returned with a thick branch, which I sawed lengthwise. Blade the Knife and I spent most of the rest of the day hollowing the wood to create a bowl for Sly.

I repeated the previous day's routine with frequent squirts of water and gravy from plastic bags, and Sly took a bit more each time. In late afternoon, little gray fox again in the sling, we went for another walk and made it as far as Little Brook. Sly drank for a long time, then found another bush. His kidneys were working.

This time when he lay down, it was on his belly, not flat on his side as before. He ate hiker's stew from his new bowl and later drank water from the same bowl. His bright eyes followed me everywhere for an hour, and then he closed them and slept. No growling. No snapping. My painful hand reminded me that he was a wild animal. But we were getting along.

I began journaling that night, telling the tale of the wounded fox while I waited for Tylenol to suppress the fire in my hand. Were bright eyes a sign of tetanus?

Like a baby's cry, Sly's whine was irresistible. It was deep in the night. His bandages were cool, so probably no major infection was involved. He didn't want more water. I stirred up the fire: I'd warm up his hot water bottle.

In the meantime, his whine was so persistent I needed to act. In desperation I took him for another walk, by moon and flash light. Maybe the stretch would help? Though my night vision was insufficient to take us far, as we came back into the firelight I saw Sly moving a little easier. But he still whined after he lay back down.

I gave him another bit of aspirin in chicken meat, followed with a second course of hot hiker's stew. He ate it all, chased it down with the fresh water I put in his bowl and moved around a bit on his own to get comfortable against the rewarmed water bottle. No more whine. He closed his eyes and looked exactly like the faithful dog on the hearth. Well, faithful dog in a hidey-hole.

My hand wasn't on fire any more, but it ached, and it was stiff. Rabies? I thought I'd try heat, too, and soaked it in warm water. With Tylenol I, too, relaxed. We both slept late the next morning.

All those times caring for Sabrina when she was little and ill. Neil that time with the flu. Poor little Brian, so sick and Sabrina in labor. Ghosts.

"I wonder, Sly. Will I ever hear another 'I love you, Grandma?' Or a gleeful shout when I arrive, or a piping voice ask to come to my house?"

"Why whine, you strange human?" That cat look on Sly's face: half disdainful, half inscrutable. "We are warm, full and healing." Fox, carafe, coffeepot: my world was full of disdainful, inscrutable lecturers.

"Don't you miss your family, Sly? And your den?" Probably not. I supposed male foxes come equipped with hobo mentalities.

Elaine Aluminum spoke up from her place at the edge of the fire. "You need to think like him, not like some transplanted hothouse flower, bare roots throbbing like your wrist at night."

Stinging criticism, that hothouse flower bit. But "transplanted" felt right. Our essence, Neil's and mine, belonged there at our home near Silver Creek. We had worked and traveled widely, but always returned to our welcoming niche. The aura of Sabrina's childhood lingered there where she had found hidden sanctuaries, discussed life with her dog, listened to the creak of her saddle. Goat kids and puppies and foals and joy lingered there in spirit. I sought solace in the big trees when Sabrina wed without us. They comforted me again when Neil died. Pi Tree and her sisters extend mothering arms to us orphans, exhaling oxygen and serenity, saving our lives. Instead of dreaming about bombs, I should have talked to Pi Tree.

"And neither of you worries about how stiff I am. About tetanus," I grumped.

Sly started grooming himself. Elaine steamed.

Nothing changed with Sly's arrival, but also everything changed. Despite the ghosts, I felt like I'd poked my nose over the lip of my miserable black pit, and if the hole was still too deep to crawl out, at least I could see beyond my gloom. Grief and depression became a little less tenacious. I didn't want to die, especially of rabies.

I re-bandaged Sly once, four days after the attack. After that he moved away or rolled into a protective ball, tearing off the little dressing I managed to attach. By then my own bite wounds started itching and felt better if I left them unwrapped, too.

Was itching a symptom of tetanus?

"So be it," I told Sly. "We'll just leave the danged bandages off." I looked, didn't touch; washed my sores, and he licked his. He mended slowly, stronger each day and more fluid in motion. His wounds gaped less, oozed less, developed more lumpy scabs that held promise of scar tissue forming beneath.

If our physical change was linear, slowly upward, my emotional progress was more sinusoidal, moving up as weather improved and as Sly's needs compelled attention, and then down when Sly got better and the weather worse.

Early in the second Sly week, morning ice again crusted the water, and for several days I never shook the chill, despair again lurking around my edges. The weather warmed, my spirits warmed with it, only to be dampened yet again in a downpour, water sliding in a steady sheet from the lower edge of the tarp and dripping through the overlap of tarps onto the fire.

When I went searching for another branch to hold up the center of the tarp and stop the leak, Sly strolled along. He had needed the sling for only three days, though he hadn't gone far until now. As we walked, he kept me company like a cat, saying, "Isn't it nice that we both happen to be going the same direction?" A dog would have said, "Oh, boy, oh, boy, can I come too?" Sly may have been canine, but his attitude was all independent, undomesticated cat.

So the low of that week just wasn't as low as my January abyss. We found the center-stick, propped up the tarp, sat by the fire, and listened to rain rustling on our canopy. A little cocoa, added to my coffee, made the world a better place.

Hot rocks still comforted me on bad days and so did the hot water bottle, which Sly no longer wanted. On chill evenings he transformed to furball, always coiled to the left to protect his wounds, fluffy tail over his nose, ears still on alert.

I spent more time journaling, filling in the gaps since the bombing in Utah, and I started experimenting with camp cooking. Biscuits became standard fare, with gravy and chicken or beef. Sly didn't mind helping with the biscuit failures, hard and burnt as they were. He ate most of several cakes, too, until I found a way to nestle the fry pan in cooling embers in the evening. For breakfast, I had a lovely biscuit-mix cake, sprinkled on top with cinnamon and sweetener. That first success, re-warmed at the edge of the fire while I made coffee for me and stew for Sly, made me decide I might as well keep living for a while.

Time of the Crocus

There came, later in February, another gift from the gods.

The magic wasn't there at first. I crawled from the tent on a cold morning to find frost and fog, the usual chill misery. But as I returned from the latrine, gold tinged the fog on the west side of the meadow, reflecting the awakening sun in the east. By the time I dressed and stirred up the fire under the coffeepot, the day began to glow. So I moved my sitting-log outside the tent compound and settled with oatmeal and coffee to watch.

After a few minutes, Sly joined me, acting in his catlike way as though he really weren't with me. On this incomparable morning, he moved past me and lay in the green grass. Then he watched, too.

Fog wisped in shining tatters against the dark forest to our left. On our right the tinge of gold on fog stretched itself to gleaming consecration all across the meadow. A hummock briefly became a steaming volcano, reinforcing the fog as moisture rose from it to meet the air. As the hummock steamed itself out and the last fog dissolved, I felt some opaque thing within me melt away, too. The world emerged in stunning clarity.

The morning grew warm, and I peeled off my jacket. But a briskness lingered that made me glad for my fuzzy thermal shirt, and the west wind breezed, *I am February, still.* Sly looked my way as I shed clothing. I wanted to apologize: I know, I'm profaning this sanctified morning with my commotion.

Before his gaze slid away, he flashed me a look that said, "You poor human, furless and almost hairless, always fussing about being warm or cool."

I refilled my coffee cup, then learned stillness from Sly. His only movement was an occasional flick of the ear. A robin hopped and harped as it searched for offerings from the earth. A rufous-sided towhee appeared, under brush on the edge of the meadow. Above him another bobbed from branch to branch. Invisible at first, camouflaged by brown feathers in a milieu of brown leaves, juncos emerged to become stars of the show. Rockettes with a dash of *Saturday Night Live*, the little comics bounced their bottoms enthusiastically as they scratched for morsels.

I feared Sly might try for breakfast on the wing, but he seemed as content as I to watch. Eventually, though, and reluctantly, I moved. Unlike young foxes, even non-rabid aging humans get stiff sitting so still in cool morning sunshine. I stirred up some stew for Sly, just to be sure his mind stayed away from bird breakfast. But he had little interest in hiker meals these days, a hopeful sign that he independently pursued his own, unbird, culinary tastes.

Big Stream beckoned me. I hadn't been back since December when I'd carried my last supplies up from the road to its confluence with Little Brook. Now I stashed dried fruit, fishing gear, and sketch pad in my fanny pack to walk back down Little Brook, where I found few traces of my passing.

When I reached Big Stream, instead of turning south toward the road, I went upstream and discovered a spot that would attract hikers on summer weekends, if they knew about it. But for now, there was no sound save swishing of stream, no footprints but mine, no human cacophony.

I sat on a big flat rock beside a wide pool and tried pieces of fruit for bait. Fish were out there; I saw several splashes as they leapt for bugs skimming above the water. My enjoyment of the day was unabated despite catching nothing. Maybe because I caught nothing—I still wasn't hungry enough to murder fish. But my sketch pad caught the lovely scene.

Shivers in my spine told me I was being watched. Here? Wouldn't I have heard something? Conversation or tramping? Where was my knife?

Motionless, I looked for my observer, my eyes searching into dimness of woods and along rocky edges of the stream. My heart reverted to the almost-forgotten banging about in my chest of those December fear-filled days. Finally I saw him and sighed with relief. It was Sly, the fox who never accompanies me but is always there.

"Sly, you old fox, why don't *you* catch a fish?"

My backside hurt after an hour on cold rock. "Dam-Sam. I'm going back to camp."

Maybe it was time to lose some of my edginess. Sure I'd ventured out of my safe camp, but even if I'd seen someone, wouldn't we have swapped fishing stories and gone on our way? Why on earth had I thought of a knife?

I must be old news by now, my face fading from public

memory. And my appearance was changing: I was more weathered, body firmer, bagging pants held up by string, hair growing away from short brown curls to its white, straight, unruly natural state. Maybe I *could* pass myself off as a genuine Mountain Woman, or at least as a true kook.

"What do you think, Sly? If I saw someone, would I run? I don't think so. I'm Beverly Thomas now, seeking an outdoor adventure. I'd howdy them and walk away. Not toward camp."

As I walked back up Little Brook, I wondered if trilliums wouldn't soon be emerging. Crocuses were probably springing up at home in Silver Creek. And, come to think of it, thoughts of home were coming with warm fondness, not despair.

Back at my meadow home, I heated water and took the best bath since my arrival. I heated more water for a double shampoo. Heated water again and boiled underwear. Hung my sleeping bag out, and Burgundy Blanket, too. I contained some of my hair's wildness by combing the top of the back into a tiny ponytail and holding it in place with string.

Sly stared at me. He might be accustomed to my human presence now, but this was strange new behavior. His scrutiny flustered me. Like being caught picking my nose in public. "Mountain Woman can be clean, too, you know, Sly."

He blinked and stretched out from his erect sit onto his belly, ears still on alert.

We ate outside the compound again. Sly returned to his morning spot, and I to mine. He focused on rustling bushes. But I watched the last of the golden sun as it lit the western sky.

A day of sparkling emeralds and diamonds, in morning fog,

in meadow's dew, in stream's reflections. A day of bird symphonies and warbling brook, of earth smell and grass smell, of evergreen aroma and sea breeze scents. Day of warmth blessing my skin, freshness blowing my hair, sun squinting my eyes. Oh, Venus of days, thank you for returning my life to me.

On this day, I felt stirrings of hope.

On this day I began to forgive myself.

On this day I glimpsed truth: the only time given us is this moment. The past is gone. Let go of its failures and even its joys, learn its lessons and move on. Cup your hands and let the cold clear waters of the present run through your fingers.

* * * *

Every Oregon February of my memory held a week of days like this. But oh how I needed this February's gift, the magic after January's anguish. And so Sly and I had our week of warmth and light before winter closed in again. A week that made winter more bearable, clearly finite. If I had seen over the edge of my black pit before, now I crawled out.

Something about the freshness of the light in those days inspired creative activity. I began to find too many things to do. I sketched. I cooked. I watched the birds. After the dark desperate days huddled in my sleeping bag, I understood the power of action. "Holy Moley, Sly. Who knew that too much to do is a blessing?" Well, I knew it now.

I took out my flute, removing Grandma's bird-pin and stashing it back out of sight in the lower bag. I moved my family's picture there, too.

I lifted up my silver flute and played. And played again.

My practice sessions were short at first because I was short-winded. Without sheet music and the informal classical ensemble I'd been playing with, I first practiced old songs, pulling them from the depths of memory after substantial struggle. Then I rediscovered scales. I piped arpeggios representing major chords, minor chords, minor sevenths. I explored how chords are related, made the fifth of one sequence the base chord of the next. All of that was a challenge, but I was proudest of transposing familiar songs to other keys. I spiraled upward. As I became able to sustain arm position and breath control I played for hours, with much more intensity than I had ever accomplished in normal life.

February's brief spring segued into March's misery, but I didn't go there, into the misery. I had too much to do.

Wilderness Diminished

I was running out of food. Terrified or not, I went to Coos Bay Fred Meyer, counting on changed appearance and elapsed time to keep me safe. Bad counting. And I taught math all those years.

I was in Household drooling over a battery-powered gizmo that grinds and perks fresh coffee. But it was too bulky and heavy. I was sadly returning it to the shelf when something raised my hackles, a cold wind down my neck. Like Sly that day at Big Stream. I turned. A round-faced clerk at the check-out counter averted her gaze. *Watching me?* I moved down another aisle. Let my eyes drift her way. She was looking at me again. The prickles on my neck were vivid, dry bits of grass falling into your shirt in a hot hay field. She looked away again. Too carefully. Was I imagining this?

A memory flashed: Neil and me camping, darkness falling, him by the car lighting the lantern and me washing dishes. I kept thinking I saw a bear, felt foolish and didn't mention it until my neck prickled like now. I walked to the car. "Neil, I swear there's a bear over there."

Neil handed me a flashlight. "Where?"

I beamed the light directly into the bear's eyes a few feet away. That big black bear didn't blink, just kept coming toward us. We jumped into the car and the bear eventually left. But it was *not* overactive imagination.

It was not overactive imagination now, either. As I moved to women's wear, I watched Round Face talk to her frizzy haired friend at the next register. My panic grew when Frizzy Hair left her register and moved toward me. To straighten a display. Maybe. I feigned indifference and put something in my cart. Pjs, I think. Frizzy sure paid more attention to me than that display she was organizing.

I wheeled away behind shelves at the back and got rid of the camp stuff in my cart: too many hints about me in there. Frizzy H was with Round Face at the registers again. Heads together, eyes searching. Look, look. At me, at something beside the register. My wanted picture? Natter, natter. Deciding what to do about me? I wished there were more customers. Those clerks weren't busy enough. And my brilliant idea to wear paisley pants, ruffled blouse and retro glasses sucked.

The store was suffocating me. I felt lightheaded. My stomach threatened to give back egg sandwich whose cardboard-and-mud flavor had already disgusted me once. I scolded myself, to keep my feet from running. Nightmares are usually the opposite: you try to run and can't.

I pushed my cart toward a side door near women's wear, tossed in socks, a tote bag. The dressing room door was out of view of my nosy friends so I took a jogging outfit in, pulled it from the hanger, dropped it on the bench as if I'd tried it on, and left the dressing room. Pretending to work a shoe back on, I bent to peek around the corner. Round Face had a phone in her hand. She and Frizzy were craning their necks toward the spot they had last seen me.

I moved to the next clothes-rack over and peered between hangers. Round Face and Frizzy still focused on the other side of the dressing room. I moved to the next rack, speed-browsed and peeked. A thousand racks later, I was out the door.

Subaruth was light years away, across the parking lot by the main door. Now I was in the other nightmare, the one where you can't move. A weekday, too quiet out there, just a couple of senior citizens limping into the store from handicapped spaces. No one chasing after me. I dived into my car, ducked down, reclined the passenger seat, and grabbed stuff from the back. In about thirty seconds I had a red flannel shirt over the white frilly one and the black wig was on my head. I sat up again and looked in the mirror. *Wig is crooked.*

I straightened it, added dark glasses and floppy hat. Spoke sharply: go slow. Go slow.

A police car came in the side access.

My heart raced. Subaruth headed to the main entrance, staying calm.

Frizzy met the policeman at the corner of the store. They scanned both directions.

A light changed and I joined a whole gaggle of cars. Thank gawd.

The clerk was looking all around, but not particularly at me. No flashing police-car lights. Whew.

The roaring in my ears sounded like Multnomah Falls. Too noisy to think. A block down highway 101 I found an espresso drive-through. The folks at Freddy's might look around their parking lot and maybe at traffic, but pay little attention to this line. I hoped. As I waited I pulled a blue denim slash-pocket skirt over my feet, covering the silly green paisley capris. Those clerks could identify horrid paisley, for sure.

I'd escaped. As I waited, anonymous amid another car flock, my breathing regained near normality and the waterfall faded away. I ordered double espresso double chocolate mocha.

I still needed stuff, so I drove an hour inland to Roseburg, a bigger town. Store clerks would be busier there. What had alerted Round Face? I wanted to run back to camp and hide. But you should get right back on a horse when you've been thrown, before you have time to think about it, or you might not ever. Marching right in to the Roseburg Fred Meyer, I found lines at all the check stands, clerks busy. My knees quaked under the denim skirt, and I did not linger over coffee makers. Was that lady looking at me? Groceries took forever. Was my wig slipping? Why was that guy dialing his cell phone? Even sticking strictly to my list, I hyperventilated for two hours in that store.

I kept my planned date with Goodwill: three pairs of jeans, two nondescript skirts, and more flannel shirts all a size smaller than the already smaller ruffled blouse and paisley capris now in the donations bin. I'd tossed my oversize, grimy, worn camp jeans in the trash on the way to town.

After weeks of longing for "real" food, I found the hamburger I got on the way home no better than the breakfast I'd had on the way out. Grease plus cardboard and rubber.

One last stop at a rest area. Hot running water and toilet that flushed. A strange day: Warming up in the car. Being in a car. Cardboard food. People all around, some looking at me.

Two trips in to Little Brook, and half my booty still to go, I collapsed into my new camp chair. A steak, wrapped in four zipper bags, hung with other new groceries in the branches of my pantry tree. Tomorrow. Tomorrow I'd have the strength to bring in the rest of my supplies and enjoy that steak. Tonight I sat in a comfortable chair for the first time in three months and enjoyed the most delicious orange ever grown. I wished for light to read *Time* or the newspaper. The Pope could have died, or the Mob could have acquired nukes, or maybe nobody survived *Survivor*.

After a while, Sly decided my strange new sitting-place wouldn't hurt him and lay by my side in front of the fire. He didn't tolerate petting, but he had an itchy spot just above his tail that tempted him to near domesticity at times. This was one of those times. "Holy Moley, Sly. I had the beejeebers scared out of me this morning. I'm purely wrung out. But tomorrow there'll be some steak scraps for you."

Hot mocha topped off the evening. Something about coffee and chocolate restores fear-depleted endocrine systems. I offered Sly one of my few remaining packets of campers stew. He declined. Sly was doing well on his own.

I managed a short flute practice and placed coffee cake in the coals to bake overnight. Though I'd nearly frozen taking a thorough bath the day before, I reaped the rewards now as I pulled a fresh new sheet over my relatively-clean body and laid recently-washed hair on my new pillow in its crisp new pillowcase. Cleanliness: another concept that had changed.

When I turned over, light speckled through the branches framed in my tent window, and my bladder informed me night had slid by.

And then I had the beejeebers scared out of me again. As I stirred the fire and heated coffee, wondering where Sly was, the branches in my cache tree rustled and rocked. No birds could make so much commotion. Bear? They were still hibernating, weren't they?

A paw reached down and batted at the rope holding my steak. I nearly bolted, but I really wanted that steak. I picked up some rocks and threw them. Wham. Wham. Wham. "Get out of there, critter. That's MINE."

And *Sly* came scrambling down the tree trunk! My knees gave way. Good thing I'd gotten that chair.

Sly scowled, "What the blue blazes is wrong with you? I was about to nab some really tasty breakfast."

Geez Louise. A fox up my tree. I could understand a raccoon or a squirrel. Or a bear. But a fox? I retied the rope so his tasty breakfast dangled farther below the branch, out of reach. He could have scraps. After my dinner.

That morning instead of reading the meadow as usual with Sly at breakfast, I read the newspaper. Nothing much new.

I burned the note I'd left on the front of my journal: If you have discovered this, I'm in jail—please try to deliver this journal to me. Not so irrational, my terror at leaving this safe haven. It took an hour to chronicle my adventure.

After two more trips for the rest of the new supplies, I relaxed with the flute, then got out my new mirror and make-up. How could I change my appearance? I tried some ideas from *Cosmopolitan.* Felt silly but any make-up made a good disguise, very un-Andy.

Idly, I tried putting mascara on my overgrown chin hairs. Maybe my next public appearance could be as Mountain *Man.* Sly cocked his head and agreed.

Elaine thought I was crazy. "Foxes don't talk," she said.

Scraggly bunch of chin hairs. I plucked them.

It was tempting to whack my hair, too. Straight and fine, too short for a pony tail, long enough to be a constant annoyance, it fell over my forehead. Got in my eyes. Tickled my neck. But no. If I pulled it back from a face that was starting to show more bony contours, the Andrea Glass in the newspaper faded away. Next time out, chubby cheeks gone and hair long enough to keep back, I'd be safer.

And then dinner. Reminded me of the restaurant scene in *When Sally Met Harry.* Sally simulates orgasm and the woman at the next table says, "I'll have what she's having." Asparagus, in my case. Steak, and baked potato with sour cream and bacon bits.

I whimpered with perfect pleasure.

UpandDownandUpand

It had started out so lovely, that day early in April, despite my long trek, all my long treks lately, searching for fire wood. Hadn't found much wood, but I found trilliums. White like little doves signifying peace, these three-petaled flowers hid shyly under sagging branches. And again in a mossy niche.

I came to a spot I hadn't taken on because of the brambles, but now I hacked and sawed towards a pile of limbs visible in their midst. My foot caught in a vine and I fell. A long way. I landed headfirst, face and arms stinging from thorns that had ripped across me. My leg hurt; something poking it. My elbow hurt. Untangling hurt, too, thorns gripping fiercely. Finally I got loose. I hadn't chopped any body parts with the hatchet. No broken bones protruded. I supposed I was okay.

Those brambles had hidden quite a view. I was on a bluff high above the road. I could just make out a bit of Subaruth's roof showing through the trees where I had hidden her. The Sixes River bent around behind her. The road was as quiet as the day I'd found Big Creek, as quiet as the day I'd gone out for supplies. No sign of traffic during the time I sat there catching my breath.

Something tickled my face, and when I wiped at it, my hand came away bloody. My arm hurt. I struggled back up the ten-foot bank I'd fallen down, recovering hatchet and saw en route. My inner wimp reeled, but I had to get back to camp and

I might as well drag a branch of firewood with me that half mile.

"Lucky," Elaine Aluminum grumbled. "You could have broken a leg."

"Oh, shut your effen spout. Please."

"You'd of had to crawl a long ways back."

"Gotta have firewood."

"So chop down a damn tree."

"As if that couldn't kill me."

She just steamed. Good thing. I needed hot water. I cleaned and doctored my scratches. I didn't like her insinuations. Not one bit. Because she was right.

But no good alternatives. Cutting down the forest was a bad idea. And it wasn't the forest's fault I had to hide.

I could move my right arm okay, but it sure ached. I'd landed, that arm outstretched, palm first. I wrapped a cold wet towel around my elbow, but that gave me the chills. So I took two Tylenols and warmed up by cutting up the wood I'd dragged in. Or trying to cut it, left-handed, holding the branch by stepping on it or sitting on it, anything but flexing that right arm.

That night I lay awake, arm throbbing. What if I needed a doctor? I got up, filled the hot water bottle, took Tylenol.

As I finally relaxed, I realized my stirrings had interrupted a frog chorus, the sound coming from Little Brook's direction. A sure sign of spring, I thought, broken arm or not.

Yeah, arm probably broken. I'd felt like this before, the other arm, after a cinch had loosened, saddle rolling around to the horse's belly and dumping me on the ground. I'd landed similarly, arm outstretched, and it broke the tip of the bone at my elbow. The doctor had removed the cast after a couple of weeks. "Be careful," he said. "It's barely stuck together, but you'll lose flexibility if you don't move it."

An owl added his soft who-who to the frog chorus as I drifted off thinking he should be saying what-what. A splint for my arm, that's what.

At breakfast Sly and I saw flashes of blue where wildgrass met cattails: promise of a jay family. Juncoes, robins, and towhees hopped in and flew out. Yep, spring.

Instead of heading out right after breakfast to gather wood as usual, I devised a splint for my arm. Sly tired of waiting for me, taking off on whatever mission called him. I found a bent half-inch branch, wrapped it to my arm with an Ace bandage and retrieved Sly's flannel sling to use as Andy, umm Bev, arm sling. The relentless ache subsided.

The previous long, hard wood-gathering days were holidays compared to this one. Left handed sawing. One handed hauling. Tripping, no hand free to catch myself. But that pile I'd unearthed held enough firewood to last for weeks. If I could get it back to camp.

At day's end I found it difficult, too, to hold the flute, difficult to bend fingers around it. Sly came as readily to dissonance as melody, though, and we ate dinner together. In bed with hot water bottle and Tylenol, I drifted off to frog-and-owl concerto.

The next day my foot caught on a vine as I was dragging a

branch to camp. I fell. Crashed onto my face, the splint/sling preventing me from cushioning myself. Good thing for my arm; bad thing for my head. I fell again the next day. And again.

* * * *

By mid-April I'd learned to tuck and roll, but scabs and scratches attested to my up-and-down life. I'd brought in all the wood from the overlook, though, and cleared out briars.

Sly and I spent a day hanging out at Overlook Bank. We gazed down at the silver Sixes River, at the splotches of purple created by wild irises on the bank, at the sage and lavender hues of still-curled Dogwood petals. Beauty epitomized and beauty promised, with flute accompaniment, splint off for the moment.

I saw red-winged blackbirds perched on bare branches, and tree swallows went zinging about for bugs. I especially love swallows: their flight, their glistening pearl breasts and their aerodynamic little bodies. I tried to sketch them, but they were too quick, or I was too slow.

With help from my native herbs book, I discovered wild onions to add to the mint leaves from the bottom end of Camp Meadow drying now on the line at camp. I spotted Camas on Overlook Bank, too. But it has poisonous twins, and I'd moved past suicidal thoughts.

We basked in the sun's warmth, nearly 60 degrees that day. Sly spent an hour up a tree, high on a big branch. I thought his *personality* was catlike, and so was his tree climbing. He embraced the tree with his front legs to skitter up and down.

As light played on that bank, lighting flowers like pieces of art in a gallery, I thought about how I'd stopped enjoying my garden in Silver Creek. Flowers reminded me of weddings, and weddings still made me think of the one I missed. *Pariah, unworthy*. The joy of burgeoning spring had swelled into throttled anger, like the bulge in Mt. St. Helens before she erupted.

But here each discovery of a fresh wildflower, shyly offering up its beauty without obligation, cooled my anger. Lava flowing into the sea. A rift deep in my interior began to heal. I could touch its scar now.

Was it despite the misery: the January cold, the deep ache of carrying wood and water and supplies, the throbbing arm, the hard ground of my nights? Or because of it? Had Sly gotten me away from that awful place? Or was it just nestling with mother earth, bathing in her soft air, feeling her heart beat, listening to her rhythms? Surely, if I had my rune stones here, I'd draw the lovely, rare-for-me Gebo, Partnership. Unity with the Higher Self.

Though still hurt and bewildered by the rebuff of Sabrina's wedding, I felt that, like lava extending an island, my heart reached toward …

Toward what? I was no closer to understanding. I had been wronged. The wrong continued, weddings without families. But until I stirred up my memories, they lay more peacefully in my depths.

That night I realized a frog had taken up residence just behind my tent. The Little Brook choir sang tenor "whee-up whee-uh whee-up," while his baritone solo was "RIB... IT. RIB ...IT."

In the morning I decided to leave the splint off around camp. The arm moved okay, and it sure speeded up food preparation. Coffee and cake for me, leftovers for Sly, breakfast in the meadow. Wild irises made purple spots there, too, and the redwings, the swallows, towhees and robins joined us. Bluejays, too, who at first had been surprised and delighted when I dropped a tasty crumb. Now they were noisy and incensed if I failed to deliver. The rarer bluebirds were shy, and I had to watch carefully to catch their soft blue backs and rusty chests.

* * * *

The thermometer, trophy of my March shopping trip, told most of the story. Median highs were 54 degrees the last two weeks of March, and 57.5 for April. I thought of computing means and standard deviations. Nah. Squaring, adding, and finding square roots took too much time.

One wet morning in late April the dream again haunted me—sobbing sounds, grief for the Whitesons. Sorrow seemed to flow with the rain. Whiteson faces ghosted up with the woodsmoke. Then my family's faces followed. Sabrina. Josh. All the children. Mark. My growing contentment with this place vanished up that same column of smoke. How was I ever going to get those beloved faces back? Light years from here to family, an ocean to cross in a rowboat. No compass. If I could draw a rune, it would advise: "Wait. See a blocked path as opportunity for a new direction." Dam-Sam.

The flute cheered me. Arpeggios in B flat minor.

My new direction could not be toward family. Not yet. But

leaving Camp Meadow would launch that rowboat. Life acquired double purpose: comfort here and leaving here.

I turned again to mirror and make-up, altered appearance. The face reflecting back at me revealed ridges and bones now. More of my flyaway hair stayed in a tiny ponytail. I didn't like the sagging skin, though it might be even worse without my outdoor active life.

Was it gone, whatever those clerks at Freddy's saw to set them gawking? I straightened and darkened the line of my eyebrows, made lips thinner with brown-tone lipstick, and enhanced new facial hollows with a dab of darker foundation. Surprising, the difference.

A week later I could accomplish the look in minutes. So I took my new self to town.

A letter from espionage.com, forwarded to Beverly Thomas from Eugene, awaited in the post office box I had acquired just before *Terror at Fred Meyer* two months earlier. I ripped it open. What new name, social security number and driver's license awaited?

Nothing. Nada. Just a long document, in fractured spelling and horrible grammar. Any pearls at all in there? I'd study it later. Dam-Sam.

Unready to face Frizzy Hair and Round Face, I went to Roseburg again. It felt normal, like any shopping trip. Errands to do. No spotlight shining on me. And that night the second steak-eating moment was as sublime as the first, augmented by green beans done on my new two-burner Coleman stove. Fresh salad. An orange. And I sat at my new roll-up table.

"We'd be completely uptown," I told Sly, "if I'd brought out the candle."

He didn't care. He just wanted steak scraps. On the ground suited him fine.

Elaine huffed. She'd been telling me that it would be more work to carry that stove and propane bottles than it was to haul wood. She doesn't handle being wrong very well.

It rained steadily that night and I again dreamed of a sobbing Whiteson family. Darn rain makes it hard to dispel the vision because the sighing in the trees matches the sighing in the dream. In the morning I stirred up the fire—I was still using a little wood—added cocoa to my coffee, ate my breakfast cake and focused on espionage.com.

Good ideas for a teenager wanting ID for beer, maybe. Search cemeteries, the document said, for someone who would be my age but died as a child. Get a new social security number and driver's license using that name. Yeah sure, if I were 18, but why would a retired person be acquiring a new social security number?

Forget social security death lists, I learned. Even out-of-state numbers will pop up date of birth and *date of death* at DMV, for example. There I'd be with my bare face hanging out.

As I reread in hopes of finding SOMEthing useful, I did. The germ of an idea. The letter said to look up the obituary for that child in the cemetery.

Well, obits do have good information. What about finding someone my mother's age? I'd learn her maiden name, birthdate, family history. Could I assume a daughter's identity?

What about a social security number?

I wasn't social. Not secure. Good at numbers.

How could I survive in civilization? It's so easy in crime novels. How do they do it?

I left it alone for a while. The solar shower I'd bought supposedly got warm even in crummy weather, so I set it up, black bag full of water to warm in the lower meadow. I spent hours retrieving new purchases from the car then finally got to play with my new boombox. Literally play, the flute. That first Peter Paul and Mary tune; what key was it in? I must have replayed it ten times before I realized: the end of the phrase is an F. Key of F? Yep. I played a few bars with them, keeping F in mind. And I tried improvising around the tune using arpeggios like I'd been practicing.

Wow. Cool. Long ways to go with this, but cool.

* * * *

A couple of days later I took a shower. Hadn't been so clean in months. Nor so cold. The water warmed up okay, but somebody forgot to tell the meadow. To take a solar shower, you rinse, turn off the water, soap, rinse again, and dry. Just try soaping and drying in a breezy meadow in May. Invigorating isn't a strong enough word. But ohmygosh: fresh new towel, fresh new pjs, clean sheet, hot chocolate with mint leaves from the meadow, hot water bottle, frog chorus. Bliss.

Now I was anthropomorphizing towels. I loved my new fluffy green one, but the thought of throwing away the old stained, bedraggled, semiprecious blue ones grieved me. Every loop bore witness: muddied when I ran from home, bloodied when I doctored Sly, rinsed in Little Brook, burned by hot rocks, boiled sanitary. And I'd actually used them as bath towels. Full of history, those towels. I almost got tough and tossed them, but realized in time that they were still useful, for muddy after-shower feet. For carrying hot things. So I named them Midnight and Terry.

Sly left for several days, and didn't explain himself when he returned. It was okay. I had heard nothing more of the cougar, and a bigger, healthy Sly could fend for himself. And an entire menage kept me company. Meadowlarks trooped through, and goldfinches wheeled up in congregations from their meetings in the meadow. Hummingbirds visited spring blooms, and so did butterflies: swallowtails, cinnabars, and loverly little blue things. Killdeers looked at me askance and flew away again. "Come back next year. I'll be gone," I called after them. I wished they would stay, with their stick legs, tuxedo chests and slapstick vaudeville antics.

But I had birds and butterflies, the frog chorus, the hoo hoo of an owl, bluejays with their demands, crows that squawked profanities from high places, gulls swept in by occasional winds. And the crosspatch, Elaine Aluminum.

Home on the Hill

From my journal, June 5, Tuesday:

Wild strawberries have ripened. Juicy, sweet little tidbits, they're like my old chocolate cravings. I can't seem to manage anything but to gobble them on sight. Boiled dandelion greens delight me less, but my diet is otherwise short on greens.

My Little Brook home needs some spring housekeeping. Only a month has passed since I went shopping, but I'm going to go out again soon, to buy a few groceries and wash piles of laundry. And I guess I'll buy underwear. And clothes again at Goodwill. I'm lots slimmer; have to keep hitching up my jeans.

* * * *

A few days later my journal notes an uneventful trip. Another little step back to civilization. Maybe toward my family.

One balmy day later in June I left my sleeping bag to air on a bush during my usual vigil at Overlook Bank. Summer might bring visitors. Still, I came here more for ambience than for surveillance. My arm had healed and my quiet life felt like a prolonged camping trip. *Well, duh. It* is *a camping trip.* But enjoyable now, less prisoner in Siberia, more vacationer as in the old days with Neil and Sabrina. On the way to the overlook I'd scared up a band of quail, their topknots bobbing as they tried to decide which way to run. I detoured for strawberries, which decided the quail for the opposite direction.

From behind my branches on Overlook Bank, the road was clearly visible. I couldn't see Big Creek, door to my domain, but I could hear the few cars, and no one ever stopped: The creek was just a splash of water and no access to the Sixes River existed here. Gunshots near the river had alarmed me, but nothing emerged to threaten my space. Except clouds now. Coming fast from the west. I turned and ran for camp. My sleeping bag was going to get soaked.

I'd gotten civilized. Cool but sunny days had prevailed, so I showered with only a hint of ice around my edges. I washed clothes and expected them to dry. I'd laundered everything but the tent in Roseburg. And I aired my bed roll like a good hausfrau with her duvet. I'd even taken the rain fly off the tent.

Big drops were plopping out of a blue-black sky as I ran into camp. I snatched the sleeping bag, tossed it in the tent, and ran for the rain fly just as the deluge began.

There was some hail in it, little BBs bouncing at crazy angles. I got soaked, but I shielded the tent until the rain fly did the job for me. The storm drummed on my tarp. Josh would love it. A breeze flowed through my wind shield and reminded me of January. So did the sleeping bag, just damp enough to be useless.

I knew how to fight this now, though, and I spent the afternoon in damage control. Dry clothes, long johns, wool sweater. Hot rocks, hot mocha. Hot water bottle to bed with me that night.

No comfort for the mind though. The Whitesons ghosted through again. When I awoke my mind was nailed to the second bag on the right: my family mementos, picture and pin.

To go there was to go back to a deep dark hole. Grandkids growing fast without me. Lively, engaging daughter. Fine son-in-law. Terrible wedding. No way back.

I couldn't *not* go there that day. So I wrote down what those mementos represented. Went on for pages, about anger, guilt, grief. I wanted bright curious Josh. I wanted my daughter back. I wanted my husband back. And, while I was at it, Katie, the Lab-Setter who'd shared nearly two decades of our lives. And I didn't just want my daughter; I wanted her to be ten again. I wanted all that full life. Not this silent wet one. I wrote it all down. Black and white so my mind wouldn't have to keep reviewing it.

And then I didn't go there again. Nothing heals when you pick at it.

That afternoon I stayed by the fire and read—newspapers and news magazines from my last trip out. I hadn't missed much, just bitter politics. The Portland *Oregonian* had lots of obituaries. Even with its sparser details, I learned a lot about Rose Whitlock: her maiden name, when she married, where she had spent most of her life. Born in Kansas City the same year as my mother, she had a daughter, Denise Nagle, and grandchildren Darren and Amy Nagle, all of Olympia, Washington. I know more about Denise than about Beverly Thomas. Except social security number. Big problem.

After I fried one side of my brain thinking about ID, I fried the other accompanying a CD. Not to play along, but to jam, riff, scat. Balanced, equally fired cerebral hemispheres. My staid classical group would never recognize this flutist.

Early in July I took the Frizzy Hair test. Went to her town, her store, her checkstand. Round Face still ran the adjacent register. Neither woman glanced at me as I stood in line to buy hot dogs, buns, potato salad, fruit, newspapers, and a cold soda. The cash in my hand shook so hard, it's amazing Frizzy Hair could grab it. Maybe she thought gray-headed people always shake. "Look's like you're planning a picnic," she commented.

"Perfect day for it, don't you think?" *Hah ha, Frizzy Hair, you forgot Paisley Pants. And I'm talking to a* person, *not a fox. Not a coffeepot. Nothing against Sly or Elaine.*

Scary but not foolhardy, this outing. In June in Roseburg my mirror reflection startled me. Who was watching me? Make-up tricks help but mostly my body belongs to a different person. I've twice gone down two sizes in jeans, and all my aches turned into muscles. Denim covers firm flesh now.

I roasted the hot dogs over a snug, smug fire on the beach. Then I walked, in sweater and bare feet, letting the ocean lap at my toes, feeling the ancient sea wind cutting cleanly into me.

The main point of the trip was a library stop to search white pages online. Could I find daughters of any of the women I'd seen in the obits?

Nope, not that day. Either no listing or no address given. But I still liked the idea, getting ID that way. Surely in time I'd have better luck. I was forming a halfway notion of sneaking into a house to get a social security number, perhaps while the family attended the funeral. I'd just need to find tax files.

My thinking was theoretical: I tried not to dwell on the scary aspect of going into a home. I wasn't going to *break* in; I'd look for an open back door or window.

I wondered why going into a strange house seemed so much scarier than crawling over temple fences and creeping to foundation vents to plant bombs. Maybe because staying outside the temples made it feel less like walking into a trap. Maybe because I knew ... I thought ... no one would be there. Or maybe because pyrotechnics, removing a barrier, had an Independence Day feel to it. Until the Whitesons.

At home I shared my leftover hot dogs with Sly. He declined the boiled dandelion greens and the wild strawberries, chilled in Little Brook, served with milk and sweetener. How could he resist? With dessert I read the news, fox by my side. Felt downright normal.

Nearly normal life. I had a shower *and* a tub with separate toilet, as uptown as any estate owner. The tub was the pool on Big Creek. We won't mention the cold water and chill breeze to *Better Homes and Gardens.*

The heating system failed the snob test, too. One large branch, toted from hundreds of yards away, provided about six evenings of flickering low flames invisible even from Little Brook. Low flames because wood was scarce. Low flames because, even though I'd seen no sign of intruders, traffic had increased—to five cars per hour in busy times. Thanks to the green willows cut along Little Brook, my evenings alfresco had a smokey component which, along with bats, birds, repellant and long sleeves, cut mosquito bites down to a million or so.

Once darkness fell, mosquitos left and so did Sly. This night as usual, I got the flute out. I played softly but well, improvising easily now around every track on the CD. I could see more CDs with greater challenge in my future.

* * * *

Median temperatures were 61 in May, 64 in June and 65.5 in July. It drizzled though, a couple of days every few weeks. Rainy nights seemed to bring grandkids to mind. Or the Whitesons. Practicing scales in A flat minor helped, the need for total concentration short-circuiting thoughts that couldn't bring back my old life.

* * * *

In July I took part in an entire conversation. I'd been going out weekly and spent a hot afternoon inland at Tenmile Lake. I swam and then climbed into my new inflatable kayak, stretching out and drifting in a craft that was more inflatable than kayak. As the softly rocking boat cushioned a body amazed at absence of pain, I drifted. Bliss.

I awoke with a start when someone said, "Are you all right?"

"Oh, yes, thanks. I probably looked unconscious out here."

"Well, we weren't sure. Thought we should check. Sorry if we bothered you."

"Not a problem. I'll bet I have a sunburn as it is. I'd have been parboiled if you hadn't awakened me. Thanks."

Heckandgolly. Wow. Dozens of words. Aloud.

I paid for kayak comfort. Despite my subsequent dip into

chilly water, I spent a flaming restless night. Parboiled, the right word. The outing was a good idea, though. The next time I took care to cover myself with a tee shirt and towel.

In August I took up heart-pounding activities again. Not bombing. Not breaking. Just entering. Or trying to.

The funeral was Saturday afternoon. I'd spent a couple of days at a Roseburg campground, researching deaths and daughters and addresses. A couple staying two campsites down from me was happy that I volunteered to help spread the gospel so I marched up to Margaret Olsen's door, armed with *Joy's Bulletins.* No one answered the doorbell. Yep. They were at the funeral.

It was a typical moderate-income neighborhood, sixties-style ranch houses lined up in tidy rows. Not too likely someone would be looking out one of those picture windows on a weekend midday, but feeling conspicuous, I dropped some of the pamphlets, bent to retrieve them ... and look under the doormat for a key. Nothing.

I checked for loose bricks in the planter. Nope. Felt the ledge above the door. Nada. By now a tight band around my gut constricted breathing. I knew *Joy's Bulletin* wouldn't explain this. Letting myself through the side gate, I looked for unlocked windows. No luck. In my past I had a sliding door I could push open when I locked myself out, but either this patio door was more secure or I had lost the hang of it. Dam-Sam.

I sure hoped that neighbors were too busy to observe the bizarre proselytizer.

I returned to the front to leave a flyer in the door. Maybe

that would mislead anyone checking on me. Pulling off sweaty plastic gloves and managing not to run, I got to the car and drove a few blocks then parked again, turned the air conditioner on full blast, and breathed.

As I drove home, I realized it could be done. I could find a name and enough information. I'd looked at weeks' worth of papers to locate an appropriate person and her address, and then couldn't get into her house. But, I remembered, a cop friend told me once that one in four houses are left unlocked and vulnerable to break-in. Just a matter of time. And luck in remaining unobserved. Luck in avoiding heart failure. If I could find tax files, I could get everything I needed from the first page of a 1040. No one would know I had been there. I'd disturb nothing, steal nothing. Except identity.

I wanted a staid, indoor existence soon. Normalcy, except without normal family. I had to believe family would come.

Back home with my new bird book I listened for the shy wren's gurgling song from the forest and its "chick-chick" scolding from nearby brush. I saw branches moving near the source of the song, but not the wrens. I learned how chickadees cling upside down to branches to get seeds and insects, and I watched their acrobatics with amusement. Josh would love this. Crows harassed me from the treetops. I hoped Sly didn't eat my meadow co-tenants. I suppose he did, actually, but he was discreet about it. Sly, The Godfather.

* * * *

The weather turned so beautiful I just kept lazing in the sun. I went out a dozen times with the kayak, swimming at Buck Creek and Sunshine Bar and Tenmile Lake.

Now it was September and I wasn't understanding the conversation around me in the checkout line. People were talking about running down stairs and jumping off buildings and towers collapsing. I picked up a paper and puzzled over headlines about "twin towers," and "cleanup," with accompanying pictures of rubble. Clearly, I couldn't just ask the next guy in line, but back issues at the library told me the story. I returned home in shock.

"Such a terrible event," I told Sly.

"Building fragments look a lot like your temples," Elaine Aluminum butted in.

"All those lives," I said.

"Thousands. Not two. Makes a difference, I guess," Elaine said.

"Intent should matter, too."

"This might divert the Feds," she perked. "Raises so many problems for them. Makes Andrea's sins seem small."

"Could I return home?" The thought sprang from my heart like a deer from captivity.

Sly looked at me with his usual, "What are you talking about?" Though it's just the wary look of a predator who could become prey in an instant, a fox seems wise like an owl.

"Yep. You're right, Sly. I can't go home: maybe they won't have time to look for me, but they'll come ask questions if I show up." I wished I hadn't had the thought at all. It was a sorry thing to see joy flee like that same released deer.

Sly cocked an eyebrow at me. And Elaine hissed.

"Nope. I'm not staying here. I can't go home, but I can go indoors. Same plan as before. But this terrible event does mean the spotlight will switch to others."

I didn't go. Not then. Little Brook's safety held me. The comfort of warm days and froggy nights held me. I had table, chair, stove, shower, frequent steaks, and Sly and Elaine for company. And my flute. October passed. No rain. It hit 80 one day.

A bit of rain. Crisp nights. Winter? Sunshine returned.

The change was abrupt. One cold morning fog lay on the meadow like a benediction. My secret world compressed to a 20-foot capsule floating in white space. Trees hid in the mists and emerged again with changing breezes. Light filtered from somewhere high in the heavens, making clear that benediction would not turn to curse. Yet.

"What next, Sly?" I could leave him now. He merely dropped by from time to time to visit and perhaps stay for a few scraps—his version of a social cup of tea. I had told him I'd be going. When? The fog forced the question.

But still I lingered. November. And two chilly, rainy days. I awoke to a skim of ice on my water containers.

That did it. I had to leave this safe haven. The alternative was another cold, wet, hopeless winter. I'd miss Little Brook's faithful gurgle. And Sly, though I saw him now once a week at best. Silly the way I seemed to be rowing upstream with reluctance to leave a place where gloom had pulled me down like some mythic whirlpool.

I supposed I'd be living in Subaruth for a while, so my immediate problem was damp stuff. Thankfully, the fringe of ice came with blue sky. I tore down most of the wind shield. "That'll get me breezin' on outta here," I told Elaine. But she just huffed. No sense of humor, that coffeepot.

The shield's small branches created a hot drying fire. Made two trips to the car that day, with table, chair, campstove and boombox. The support posts of my former wind shield held heat overnight, so most of my clothes and linens were dry enough to carry out the next morning. I went on into town to grab a salad and create disguises at Goodwill. Andrea was going to pop up at ATMs and grab some of her retirement income.

Sly showed up in response to steak smells. He looked like a wild fox should. Only a ripple in the hair along his left side hinted of his near-death experience. He walked, ran, and climbed trees with complete ease. I thought he would have a normal life without me. But I would miss his sage companionship, and I sure hoped nobody else would cook a steak nearby.

Moving out was easier than moving in. Downhill trail, now established even if hidden, helped. My fitness helped. Empty food bags helped. On the third moving day I carried out garbage, duffel bags, tarps, the solar shower.

My last evening meal was typical camp fare: potatoes, gravy and foil-package chicken. The next morning, while the early mists were still on the meadow, I savored coffee and breakfast cake, cleaned up, and dismantled my fireplace. The sun came out and dried my tent while I took rocks back to Little Brook, filled in the firepit and latrine and rolled up my sleeping bag.

The site of my home over the last eleven months looked trampled. No one had found it so far; perhaps no one ever would. A good thing. I wanted no signs of my passing. Contrarily, a bad thing. I wished for a permanent memorial to my pioneering here. Surviving such cold and despair merited recognition.

I looked at Sly. He had turned up, seemed to know he was saying good-bye. "You're my memorial, I guess, Sly." His very life marked my presence here. That would have to do.

That and humming "Pomp and Circumstance" to myself as I took a last look at the bands of sunlight woven through trees at the edge of the meadow and then trod one more time down the path beside Little Brook.

Part II Finding Kate

In From the Cold

I drove south on Highway 101 for most of the day. I'd probably go to Portland but first I wanted to access cash where Andrea's tracks wouldn't lead to me.

In the restroom of a park in the redwoods halfway between Eureka and Ukiah, I changed clothes, trying to temporarily look like Andrea Glass for the cameras at ATMs, figuring there would be some sort of surveillance connected to my account. Because I wanted Andrea to disappear quickly after the transaction, I created three layers; jeans that would have been tight on Andrea but were now three sizes too big, over a big man's heavy quilted coveralls, over khaki shorts with a plain white tee shirt. I'd been practicing so I knew I could kick off shoes and step out of the coveralls in 23 seconds. I could pull jeans off with the coveralls, and the bulky parka slid off fast. Total time less than a minute.

At Rohnert Park I parked at Sonoma State University, put on dark glasses, a curly brown wig that looked like a longer version of the last Andrea Glass hairdo, and topped it off with a cap.

Flinging my backpack across a shoulder, I shook off anxiety as though it were water and I a fox. I headed across the parking lot toward the lights. Yep. An ATM was in the student union. I spotted its camera lens to the left and up, so I tilted my cap to run visual interference, the camera showing, I hoped, brown curls, cap, glasses, and a chin tucked into a parka.

Twenty dollar bills spat out at me with indifference. In less than a minute I was finished, folding the bills, receipt and card into my backpack as I walked to the bathroom just down the hall. In the stall, in another minute, I was down to tee shirt and khakis, my own long gray braided hair, and flip flops. I strolled out with my outer layers in the backpack, except that I carried the most recognizable items—cap and parka—in an opaque plastic bag which landed in the back of a pickup parked at the other end of the same lot where Subaruth awaited me.

So far, so good. I needed to repeat that trick a couple more times.

I dressed up again in a park restroom in Petaluma: a big floppy blue denim hat, denim peasant skirt and navy knit poncho, legs and sleeves of coveralls rolled up out of sight. Parking on a dark edge of Safeway's parking lot in Napa, I went in to buy fresh fruit, then stopped at the ATM.

My card spun back to me! "Transaction denied" flashed on the screen.

Too much? I revised $2000 to $1000 like earlier. "Transaction denied."

Geez Louise.

Snatching my card, I strode out, shedding my outer layer in the darkness of the parking lot. I ditched my poncho and hat in another pickup and fled north to Redding.

The motel felt safe. I looked very different after two minutes with make-up. I parked amid a slew of other cars at the back before I registered as Bev Thomas, giving a license plate number I had just spotted on the freeway.

What a blissful night. Ah, the shower. Clean new clothes. Food prepared by someone else, not over a campfire and not from a drive-through. A bed. Swinging feet from bed *down* to the ground. Hot running water. TV, but it made too much noise.

I awoke at four in the morning feeling suffocated. I'd dreamt about the look on the clerk's face when I paid cash. He wanted a credit card. I told him I had given up credit cards until I got out of debt, and I argued that he could quit worrying about my running up phone charges by taking the phone from my room. But that look on his face. I should have paid better attention to it. Disbelief. Skepticism. A what-kind-of-con-are-you-pulling look.

By 4:20 I had dressed, thrown my things in my bag, dropped the room key in the overnight drop box, and gotten a few deep breaths in the parking lot before Subaruth and I made swift tracks out of there. Ten miles south I used a pay phone at a gas station to call the 800 number on my Andrea Glass debit card, and then I learned about my daily limit. A freeze had been placed on my account because I'd exceeded my limit and also had 'unusual activity.'

"Please," I said after providing my (real) social security number and mother's maiden name, "allow runs of large withdrawals. I'm buying arts and crafts, and sometimes sellers aren't set up for credit cards. You won't freeze my account again, will you? It's a little embarrassing to say oops, I guess I can't buy this after all."

When the bass voice agreed to $2000 per day, I flew back to my car. After having awakened with hot ghosts' breath down my neck, I now burned with anxiety. All that ID stuff I'd provided. I was so out in the open. I didn't quit sweating for a hundred miles. Subaruth was hot and airless. In November. Even when I rolled down windows, the air was snatched away from me. Nothing to breathe.

Maybe they're too busy with 9/11 to pay attention to me, I thought. But wouldn't a hound or two awaken with the whiff of Andrea Glass again?

The ATM double header I managed that night in Sacramento, however, felt sweetly vengeful. In a new costume I withdrew maximum cash at 11:50 p.m. and again across town half an hour later. Nyah nyah nyah nanana. I made thirty minutes equal two days. No problems.

With enough cash for months if I lived lightly, Andrea could disappear again. But first I dropped a note to Sabrina. I was leaving Sacramento; a postmark from there wouldn't expose me. What to say to Sabrina? She must be terribly worried by now. I'd been a *person of interest.* I'd bet the Feds had contacted her. They'd know I'd sold Winnie, probably knew I'd been home, probably noticed the surveillance stuff on the driveway. Probably Bruce, my trustee, had rented the place out. Sabrina would not understand any of this. Mostly because it was not understandable.

I had composed a long note in my head, but nothing sounded right, and I was in a panic to leave. So I just said, "Dearest Sabrina, I'm OK, or will be when I get my head on straight. I love you and Mark and the kids, and I miss you so much. Mom" My only possible plea to her, I thought, was insanity.

I drove to Roseburg that day. Beverly Thomas spent nearly a week in the same KOA campground as during the summer, studying the obituaries and the phone book each day. The trapped feeling of the motel in Redding didn't recur; I was 500 miles and several days away from Andrea Glass.

I'd almost become Mountain Woman, most comfortable when unenclosed. Except sleeping on hard ground or hard cargo space had lost its charm. And hot camp showers felt as miraculous as the one at the motel, and I was glad to warm up in my car or in a restaurant or at the library. My sleeping bag felt damp one uncomfortable evening, so I ran it through the dryer the next day. Such luxuries.

Three daughters in the obits seemed like good possibilities, but only one was listed in the phone book. During the funeral I went to her door with a clipboard and phony consumer survey, forswearing my brief career in proselytizing. No one was home but again I found no way in.

So many dead ends. I went back to a name and address from my summer snooping, and watched that house. Saturday, husband and wife left, came back with grocery bags. Sunday they left at 9:30, returned just after noon. Monday they left at 7:30, returned at 5:30. The same on Tuesday. Finally,

Wednesday at 9 am, confident everyone had gone to work, I knocked on the door with poll in hand. I was checking for a key in the umbrella stand when I heard the lock turn from inside.

"What are you doing?" The ancient, stooped woman at the door glared upward at me and simultaneously looked down her droopy bulbous nose. I had straightened from the umbrella stand; she must have looked through the window beside the door before she opened it.

I looked down at her five-foot collapsing-pear figure. Her glare belonged to a seven foot giant. "Oh. Sorry! I dropped my pen in there."

"What?" She cupped her ear.

"I think I dropped my pen. No. Wait. Here it is."

"What about a sloppy den? What do you know about my den?"

I pantomimed. "My pen. I thought I dropped it." I had begun to sweat, bodily denial of an outdoor temperature in the mid-thirties.

"Well, what are you doing here anyways?"

"I'm Agnes Wilson. I'm conducting a poll for the NSR Corporation. Could I have a moment of your time?"

She thought I was Phyllis Dillman, selling bowls. She didn't want any. What kind of bowl sells for a dime, anyway? The glare continued unabated.

"Ma'am, I apologize for intruding on your busy day. Clearly my voice is in the wrong range for you. I won't bother you any further. Have a good day." I was backpedaling down the steps and up the walk away from this old bit of dynamite. Once I reached the sidewalk I was in flight mode *again!* speed walking to my car, parked down the street and around the corner.

I drove randomly for half an hour. For the first ten minutes I wiped my sweaty face and caught my breath. For the second ten minutes I laughed. Finally, I assured myself that henceforth I would stick to houses where I knew they'd be attending a funeral. Even lethal grandmas should be gone, attending the service.

Phew.

Back at the campground I packed up. I liked the idea of a small town, people more likely to leave a door unlocked or a key under a brick. But there weren't enough deaths in Roseburg of women who would be old enough to be my mother, whose maiden name was given in the obituary, and who had at least one daughter living locally, whose name was also given in the paper.

So I headed north. Portland, I thought.

* * * *

Some unknown urge stopped me in Eugene, not Portland, and made me check the bulletin board in the student union. "Room available through fall quarter," I saw. Hmm. The notice had been there a month, but I called anyway.

One of the four students who shared the house had dropped out. In January another friend would move in. Would I be interested in such a short arrangement?

Well, maybe. I went over to look.

"So how much do you party?" I was talking to a kid named Steve.

"You won't see a party. We've had a couple, but it's almost exam time and we're all trying to maintain scholarships here."

"And you think you can live with a grandmother for a few weeks?"

"The only problem might be girlfriends/ boyfriends. Sometimes people stay overnight, but we don't get in each other's way. Sleeping arrangements involve the person's own bedroom, and meals are individual responsibility, too."

Compared to Little Brook, the drafty, battered craftsman house felt snug. Living with kids would quickly become tiresome, I thought, but I'd be leaving in a few weeks. I'd have my own bedroom, sharing a bathroom with Michelle. She had stuff strung out all over in there, but I no longer needed much room. Running water, hot shower, hip-high bed—for this I could wade through a few bits of drying underwear.

I might have hesitated if I'd known how noisy Michelle could be. When squeaking springs, progressed to 'thump-thump' of bed legs, I blushed in the darkness. I felt as though I were peeking at them through the keyhole. The *oh-oh-oh*s and *yes-yes-yes*es were even more unnerving. This could be why the other roommate had gone home. Never mind. I could turn up the CD player. And buy ear plugs.

Returning to civilization was otherwise far easier than I'd expected. No recurrence of the Redding-motel claustrophobia. My personalized space, new geometric-patterned comforter, burgundy sheets and navy microfiber blanket generated calm. Maybe that motel panic was simple awareness of vulnerability in a public place. But that look on the clerk's face. Maybe he called someone. Maybe the law was the hot breath I felt on my neck that morning.

*   *   *   *

Seeking coffee, Ian came into the kitchen one evening a week after I moved in—my new coffeemaker and I had been much appreciated—and muttered as he poured. "The P value represents the probability that random samples of identical groups could vary by as much as observed. The P value represents the probability that random samples of identical groups could vary by as much as observed. The P value represents..."

"You don't understand P values."

"No shit, Dick Tracy. I can't find *anyone* in class who does understand, and the midterm is tomorrow."

"What's your major, Ian?" I casually refolded the early edition of tomorrow's *Oregonian* from the obituaries to the crossword and took another sip from my own big mug of coffee.

"Business. This damn stats class is a requirement."

"And there are probably hundreds of business majors, maybe even a thousand, here at U of O?"

"I suppose so." Ian blew on his coffee as though he were extinguishing all statistics.

"And I'll bet there are about as many architecture students?"

"Probably. Why?"

"Suppose I hoped to show that architecture students are smarter than business students, and I selected a random sample of a hundred each and gave them an IQ test. If it came out 120 average for business students and 121 for architecture students, would I have proved it?" I wrote bus. 120, arch. 121 on the margin of the crossword page.

"No way, Dude. One point difference?" He leaned up against the green tile countertop and crossed his bare feet. "That doesn't prove anything. You might have picked the smartest architechies for your sample."

"It was a random sample."

"Exactly. Random means the groups won't match perfectly."

"So you're putting the P value at about 98%, I'd say. You're saying it's extremely likely to get that small a difference in random sampling of equal groups."

"Oh!" He slid into a chair across from me at the big round oak table.

"Suppose the IQ scores were 120 business and 130 architecture?" I made a new column on my paper.

"Well, I'd have to think maybe architecture students *are* smarter."

"And if it were 115 business to 135 architecture?"

"Okay." He sipped and exhaled with that breathy *aahhh* of a contented coffee drinker. "Are you a genius at math AND java?"

"Well, the coffee machine and the beans get the credit for your caffeine, but I do know a little about stats."

"So." He was thinking hard. "A difference of one IQ point is pretty likely in sampling when the groups really aren't any different. 'Pretty likely' equates to a high percentage." He took my newspaper, wrote P = .98 by the 120 and 121.

I nodded.

"And," he continued, "a bigger difference is less likely in the sampling process. You could happen accidentally to get a few very bright kids, or a few very dumb ones in the other group, causing a point or two difference in averages. To make ten points difference you'd have to catch mostly dumber ones from one group and mostly smarter ones from the other for your sample. Twenty points? That would be just about impossible if you were sampling blind."

"But it *could* happen," I reminded him.

"Yeah. About once in a million years."

"Which would make the P value..."

"Really, really small. Like maybe .0001. So when the P value is that small, the difference is so unlikely that you decide the groups *aren't* the same. One really is smarter than the other." He gleefully wrote P<.001 on my newspaper, tossed down my pen, and jumped up. "You're a genius, Bev. I get it."

"Go explain it to a couple of your classmates, and you'll understand for life."

* * * *

And that's what led me to the tutor business. Next thing I knew, Michelle was asking for help in calculus and Steve wanted me to explain matrices for econ. I didn't understand the econ, but I could explain matrix operations.

Then friends wanted help, and we set up an hourly rate. They were delighted because they could split the cost between them, and I was happy to earn some cash to delay the time when I needed to go ATMing as Andrea Glass again. I got so busy tutoring (cash only, please), my fees covered my rent for the month I was there.

As I was inventing a new lifestyle, I made sure it incorporated lots of veggies and lots of walking. Being a fugitive provided great incentive to maintain my new slim profile. I was no longer on the Little Brook weight-loss plan: escape regular temptations, eat sparingly of mediocre food, burn calories by nearly freezing, and exercise lots. I could see the ads. *New weight loss program! Plus our special formula for eliminating life's biggest annoyances* (bomb them)! *Now only $99.95!*

Michelle's scale showed I had lost over seventy-five pounds, and the house's mirrors told me again that I was hardly recognizable. Maybe even Sabrina wouldn't know me. No, she'd recognize my voice.

An important part of this life involved reading the Eugene *Register Guard* and Portland *Oregonian* every morning with my coffee. I took promising obits with me to the university library to check the Salem *Statesman* and Roseburg *News-Review* and look up phone numbers. With obits from that many papers I found one or two addresses almost every day. I traveled, sometimes two hundred miles, with my phony survey, met many locked doors, but found no more warrior grandmas.

I told my housemates I was hunting for a permanent place for my daughter, who would be returning to the Eugene area in January, and that explained my presence in the house as well as my all-day absences. I talked about the places I had tried to enter as though they were local houses the realtor had shown me.

Tuesday evenings belonged to a jazz bar just off campus: jam night. After I sat in on one, I got invited to improvise with several regular performers. Who knew you could get tips for having so much fun? I wanted to never leave.

Tutoring occupied most other evenings. At the end of one session Ruth, Michelle's friend, started talking about her troubles with her boyfriend. These kids didn't want grandma-advice, but it seemed like Ruth was letting herself be dominated by a jerk. So I lingered, trying to help Michelle reinforce Ruth's backbone. The conversation went in circles until Michelle brought out a little book and a small gray bag of stones. I recognized it immediately, but it always seemed better to act ignorant about my former life.

Ruth didn't know about runes at all. "What the heck," she said.

Michelle explained. "Each stone has a carving on it. You need to roll them all around in your hands. Think about your problems with Blake. Take the one that comes to your palm."

"Woo-de-woo," Ruth said.

I'd thought that myself. Except darned if those runes didn't always seem true.

"Your stone will only pull up things you already know about yourself," Michelle said. "It doesn't foretell the future or anything like that. It just helps you get in touch with your Self. Capital S, *Self*."

So Ruth drew one, *Kano* reversed, and we read its meaning from the little book. "Darkening … friendship dying … face that death or lose opportunity … don't be seduced by old ways." Maybe if Ruth couldn't hear us, she could hear the stone.

Michelle drew one for herself, too, and after we had talked about it she had me draw one. I got *Isa*, stone of cold and ice. Michelle read about winter, retreat, things moving with glacial slowness.

Tell me something I don't know, I thought. A year of *Isa*, literal cold and figurative ice carving out my heart. And could a glacier ever move back, back to the arms of family? I returned the stone. "I dunno," I said. "Doesn't seem to relate to me."

Fortunately Michelle and Ruth were wrapped up in their own problems. I went out for my usual evening walk. Three miles that night, to dispel the shadow of the stone.

* * * *

Isa or not, I had some luck on the thirteenth day of my search. I found a key in Sherwood, buried in the soil of the brick planter beside the front door. No one answered when I rang the bell. I unlocked the door and replaced the key in the planter.

I went in, re-locking the door behind me. I'd entered a small foyer, kitchen and dining on the right, living room straight ahead. A fast tour assured me no one was home: Everyone at the funeral, as I'd hoped. No dogs, no electronic surveillance blinking its red light. I found den and bedrooms to the left of the entry. My most likely spot. A second round told me more. The door in the utility room to the far right off the kitchen led to the garage and another door allowed passage from garage to side yard. French doors opened from the living room to a patio in back. The backyard was fenced but had unlocked gates on both sides. All the ways out were past living areas.

Kitchen cabinets showed me nothing of interest. Living room shelves held good classics, current titles, impressive biographies and world histories. Stiff books with crisp pages.

Okay. I'd glance at the bedrooms before a thorough search in the den.

I found twin beds, suitcases, nothing much in the dresser. The next room held an old-fashioned dressing table. Queen bed. Clothes, jewelry, make-up in the bureau drawers. Husband and wife. Some boxes on the closet shelves. I'd check them if I didn't find anything in the den. Hall closets held towels, bedding, coats, and games.

A photo collage in the hallway portrayed white people, my color. A gray-haired couple in the middle, my age. So far so good.

But I should have gone straight to the den. The desk there had the file I needed. Last year's taxes. I had it in my hand when I heard the key in the lock.

Finding Myself

Too early. Funeral just started. Too late for me to run. They were coming in the front door. I'd have to pass there to get out.

From the den closet I heard them talking. Two ladies. They went to the kitchen. I couldn't duck out. The hall was clearly in view from there.

Squeaky Voice went in and out of the house bringing food. I left the closet, listened from behind the den door. *Come ON, Ms. In-Charge. Go help Squeaky carry some of that stuff.*

My chance to run didn't materialize. The subject of coats came up, and I ducked out of sight again. The loveseat in the den, they decided. *Oh lord, what if they check the closet?*

"Leave the den door open," Ms. In-Charge said, turning on the light. "We'll send people here to put their things down. It's just family: purses will be okay, too."

Little did they know. Just family, them, and me.

Stuffed at a half stoop amid coats, boxes and garment bags, I had the old suffocated sensation, in the pond again under the raft. Naked again, hiding in freezing woods. Trapped again by a fallen tree. This time, one part of my brain shouted that air wasn't making it to my lungs. The other side said, "Geez LOUISE. We've done this routine, already." My throat muscles pulled and strained at the lump of air that seemed unavailable, trapped in a balloon pushing at my jugular.

The calm guy in my head said, "Just cool it. They're going to hear all that gasping." And Neanderthal Mind said, "I gotta breathe. I'm dying here." In retrospect, it sounded kind of like the duet in *Music Man* where they sing different things together. Only there were two people. And it was romantic.

Family. They expected family. No strangers. I couldn't mingle then leave. How was I going to get out of here? Go away now, ladies.

As I suspected I wasn't dying. I tiptoed out and opened the den window a few inches for air. If no one noticed and closed it, perhaps I could survive in the closet. The ladies were busy setting up: food in the dining room, drinks in the living area. Please go home, I thought, just leave your comfort food for the mourners.

Nope. No luck.

Probably this room had been designed as a bedroom, my hideaway a typical older-home clothes closet: long, narrow, sliding doors. Now that I was breathing again, I made myself a hidey hole—*hey, hey, Sly*—behind garment bags on the side they couldn't open because I had stuffed a stretched-out hanger in its track. I sat curled in the corner.

Hidey-hole is Sly's thing, not mine, and I again visualized clawing my way out. This *can't breathe* sensation: much too familiar, like the waitress who calls me 'honey.' Har har. I rocked forward, moved the hanger out of the track, and rolled my door open a few inches.

Better. Air. Light. I could hear the ladies, clattering dishes, moving between kitchen and living room, and I could read the file folder I'd carried to the closet when they arrived. Might as well get the information I came for—and paid for, not in Euros but in beaucoup fright.

Katherine M. McGuire, the daughter's name from the obit. Social security number 813-52-8411, married to Paul D, social security number 903-26-3840. Moderate income. She's a bookkeeper. He's an RV sales manager. Mortgage interest expense. Tiny interest income from US Bank, tiny dividends from Merrill Lynch. Credit for elderly care. They were helping pay nursing home expenses for Dorothea Bennett. Her mom, who just died.

I took notes. I wanted to take nothing, to leave no trace, to have no one suspect anyone had entered the house. I'd been careless once already: the ladies had tch-tched over footprints in the living room and about having to wipe them up. My footprints, after I'd checked exits from the back yard.

Ah, yes. The State return had birth years. She's five years younger than me. Might have to get some of that wrinkle remover cream. Here's W-2s. They both work for Travel World.

Katherine's place of birth? Birthday? The obit for Dorothea said the Bennetts first settled in Kirby, Illinois. Guess I'll have to look in Kirby newspaper archives, I thought, maybe even go to Illinois.

The ladies were chattering away. So I crawled out of the hidey hole to put the tax return back where I had found it. I felt exposed, had trouble breathing again, but I took a minute to look at the other files. "Dorothea," "Katherine," and "Family Tree" looked promising. I scooted with them back to the closet.

A dark day: December, 3:30. Funeral would be over soon.

Squeaky and In-charge never left. Feeling invisible in my unlit space, I watched through a half-inch slit as people came, walked into the den, left coats, went out. I saw that I couldn't pass as great-aunt Lois, go mingle, leave. My denim skirt was clearly out of place; everyone dressed in better, darker clothing. And everyone knew everyone else. I lacked the panache for such a ploy, anyway. Home, sweet closet.

I crouched in that narrow space for five more hours listening to them in the living room, talking about what a wonderful person Dorothea was. They must have been drinking away their sorrow out there, because it got very loud.

I wanted a nap. No. I wanted *out.* Weren't they tired? Why didn't they go? Eventually I went back to my reading material. The disorganized folders held everything from school projects to web genealogy searches, but finally I found "Katherine Miriam Bennett, June 18, 1944." Later I discovered an unofficial birth certificate from St. John's Hospital, in Kirby, Illinois. With that information I could get an official certificate through Illinois Department of Records.

Dorothea's folder had great pictures, taken in the twenties. If that was Dorothea, she was quite a flapper.

I ventured out of my space again to return the files. Then back to sit in my corner. And sit some more. I wiggled my toes. I stood. Or rather, I hunched. My feet went to sleep. I hunch-marched in place. I sat again.

Eventually the guests straggled in for their coats. Then I heard the first two ladies load up their stuff.

No wraps remained on the loveseat, but the den light was still on and voices still came from the living room. Three ladies and a man, I thought. My bladder had moved beyond urgency to pain. The bathroom was across the hall. Taunting me. Geez Louise. What do I do? Pee in the closet? Wet my pants? Thinking about it made it worse. I gritted my teeth and hung on.

I stood up again. My butt was numb. The clock on the desk said 10:30. When Katherine McGuire came to turn off the den light, I got a look at her through my slit. She matched the photo in the hall and a picture I had seen on the living room mantel, so I knew her swollen eyes were blue. Pear shape, gray-brown hair, top of her head reached the top of the shelf by the door. Shorter than I, I thought. Wide mouth and oversize fleshy nose. I thought I could pass for her at DMV. Maybe lie about my height.

Another two hours. Bathroom noises. Running water. I had to plug my ears. Who knew a full bladder could be so painful? Some cowboy once told me something about peeing in a boot, but this closet held no boots. High heels, inadequate.

Talking in the guest room: two women. Katherine and Paul in the big bedroom. Finally quiet, except sobbing next door. At last, silence.

I slid the closet door open. *So loud.* No one stirred. Stepped out, closed the door. *So noisy.* No one stirred.

I took the few steps to the door of the den. Snoring in the master bedroom, soft breathing in the guest room. Was Katherine asleep? Snoring, a deep rumble, was probably Paul.

I stood a few minutes. Quiet.

The bathroom, so close, so inaccessible. I deserved a Guinness Book of Records award.

I stole down the hallway, away from the bedrooms, toward freedom. *Front door?*

No. Noisy to unlock. Can't relock it.

The French doors were farthest from bedrooms. I eased the lock open. Maybe they'd think they forgot to lock them, put the lapse down to grief. The rearrangement in the den closet might worry them, too. Maybe they'd search a bit. But they'd find nothing missing.

"Emily, is that you?" The door had scraped a little as I opened it. If Katherine had been sleeping, it was lightly.

"Katherine, what is it?" Emily sounded drowsy and a little cross.

"Were you in the living room? I thought I heard something out there."

"Kathy, try to sleep. It's OK for people to move around," Paul rumbled.

There was more discussion, but I was outside by then. I think the talking covered up the scraping noise as I shut the door. Cold rain.

Around the corner I flew, through the gate and along the front fence. A light came on, shining from the peak of the garage. I moved fast down the street to my left and knelt in the shadows two doors down. Paul had come to the door, was saying, "...motion detector..."

Subaruth was half a block away, around the corner to the

right. Past that bright light. *Oh lord I need to pee.* It was half a mile to a cross street that would allow me to circle and avoid passing the McGuire house. *They're stirred up in there now.* They'd all gone back inside, but they might watch for a while from the living room. I headed for th+e cross street, bladder jarring. Cold.

They might call the police. I had no idea what I'd tell anyone wanting to know why I was out walking after midnight. Insomnia? Watch for lights, be ready to duck into shadows. Five more minutes. Almost to the car.

Yes. I made it. Didn't wet my pants. I drove a mile to the main highway, found a gas station. The need to urinate had been as painful as fingers jammed in a door, relief as wonderful as if the door had opened, acute pain gone, lingering ache.

Whoa-hoe. I got out. I got what I needed.

Adrenaline got me fifty miles down the freeway, but there was no way I could make it back to Eugene. Once the scare left me, so did all my starch.

I found a Walmart in Salem and pulled off with the RVers to sleep in the back of Subaruth. Fifty-one weeks ago I did that the first time, on a stormy December night on Oregon's south coast as I ran from home and family. No sleeping bag this time, but my coat kept me warm.

And then the next morning as I drove through downtown in the early dimness, I saw street people starting to stir and had the idea that led to a second usable alias.

Homeless

I had remembered a novel in which the hero, to get ID, terrorized a guy drunk in a gutter. Terrorizing folks is not my style and I already had just spent hours in a closet to get a good identity. But a second identity was appealing: a driver's license to tide me over until I got Katherine's, and perhaps something to fall back on if trouble arose. And if I'm rotten at terrorizing someone, I'm not too bad at persuasion. I only needed to meet the right person.

To pursue my flash of inspiration I parked again and changed into some Little Brook clothing still in the car: warm and scruffy. The mirror in Freddy's ladies room reflected a homeless type with untamed hair and sleepless puffy eyes. I felt appropriately smelly. I hid a little cash and my car key in my shoe and caught a city bus downtown.

Under the bridge by the park, I watched wintry drizzle. I paced and tucked my hands into my armpits to warm them. Paced some more. Leaned up against a wall beside two fellows who sat aimlessly on a concrete abutment. "Anywhere to warm up around here?" I asked.

After I'd told my newly invented woeful tale, they coached me on homelessness. "You can ride free buses between West Salem and the State Buildings. They're warm," John told me. "The driver will kick you off after a while. What you want to do is alternate. Get off in West Salem. Go to the grocery store and look for free samples. Ride to the bus mall and hang out a while. Check here at the park every couple of hours. People hand out food sometimes. Go over to the Union Gospel Mission if you don't mind preaching."

"That's mostly for the men," Bill added. "They got a place for the ladies up on River Road. You can sleep there."

"Is that what you do at night? Go to the Mission?"

"Nah," John answered. "We got a spot over by the river. We stay there unless it gets too cold, or we get rained out. Or copped out."

Well, you learn something every day.

I followed John and Bill's suggestions, rode the bus, found free samples at the grocery store, ate soup and a sandwich at the park. Met Marie, a shaggy bus-rider like me. Too young for my purposes, but she told me more about the shelter.

I caught bus #48 then walked several blocks west, like Marie told me, to a big gray house on the corner. Three steps up from the sidewalk. Teeny yard. Big door with an oval window.

"Maybe last night in the closet was a warning. Maybe you'd better quit this crap." Elaine Aluminum. Neither weeks of silence nor her current invisibility had diminished her scolding tone. "Go back to your car and drive to Eugene and count yourself lucky you didn't get arrested."

Worst that could happen here is they'd throw me out. I rang the bell.

"Yes? Can I help you?" Medium build, short ash-blond hair,

blue striped shirt under blue cardigan, blue cotton slacks, white running shoes. Kind blue eyes beneath the wrinkled brow. "My name is Julia," she added.

"Oh. I hope so. I hope you can help me, I mean. I'm sorry, standing here like a fool. My name's Bev. I'm outta luck, outta money. They told me you might put me up for a day or two."

Julia waved me into a small foyer. Stairs led upward on the left, living room showed behind French doors on the right.

"You're in need, looking for a bed?"

"Yes, please, and food if possible. And a bath. Just until I can contact my sister in Spokane. I spent my last money for a bus ticket there, and now I can't get hold of her. Darryl won't find me here. Please, can I stay? I haven't slept for two days."

"Well," Julia said, "God has guided you here, and committed our hands to help. I do need you to provide some information first."

"I'm not gonna fill out my full name or anything. I'm scared Darryl will find me."

"Won't he find you at your sister's if you go there?"

"Yeah, but the jerk is a coward. A mean drunk, a lazy bum, but a coward. Darryl's real good at picking fights with women and children. Walt's a big guy. He's done his share of logging, and he doesn't back down. I'll be safe with Walt around." Boy, as soon as I got by myself, I'd better write down all those names: Darryl, husband; Walt, brother-in-law, former logger.

"You'll be okay, Bev. I need some information for our records—our sponsors want to know what we've done with their contributions—but it stays here, in our files. Only summaries get reported and published. Please just fill out this form." She led me to a small desk and chair at the back of the foyer, partially under the stairs. "Do you have a driver's license?"

I shook my head. "Snuck some money from Darryl's wallet into my pocket and ran. Didn't have time to go looking up my purse."

"If you're here a while, you can go to DMV and get a copy of your license."

I nodded, picked up a pencil, and filled out her form.

Name: *Beverly Baker.* Beverly, I thought, so I keep my aliases straight and answer to the right name. Baker so they can't find any version of me.

Social security number: Each of my three personas contributed a part.

Address: *in transition.*

There was a half page to answer "why are you here?"

When my husband got drunk again, I ran as soon as I could get ahold of a little cash. He's a nice guy—if he isn't drinking—but he drinks more and more and gets worse and worse. I just got rid of the brooses from the last toot. I still got the scar from where he stabbed me with a barbacue fork. I glanced down at Sly's bite mark. *And I got a broken rib last year and a broken arm. There healed now. I try to be Ms. Sweetness and Light but I never know what will set him off. Allmost anything lately. I don't got any idea what he'll do now I run away from him. I'm on my way to Spokane. I'll be save enough there, but first I got to get ahold of my sister.*

Julia didn't read my fiction right then. I hoped she'd get busy, stay busy, ask few questions. Upstairs, she showed me a bed, the showers, and provided soap, towels, toothbrush.

Dinner was at 5:00, and when I came downstairs at 4:00 after my shower, people were already gathering. All waited in the numb manner of the homeless and the terminally ill. Several young women had the terrible haggard look that made me think of meth. At a corner table a sad-faced girl with a black eye and swollen lip worked on a jigsaw puzzle with her two children. The kids made me think of Emma and McKenzie, and my heart clutched.

I grabbed a place at the table beside the worn white woman with gray hair, average height and faded eyes that might be described as blue—as mine were. Janet provided newcomer advice in that distant but helpful manner I'd noticed all day. "Say 'Amen!' a lot during the service," she said. "That way they'll go easier on you if you need to stay longer."

"What about skipping chapel? This 'Amen, Brother' stuff makes me nervous."

"If you want to be throwed out on the street on your butt, skip chapel."

"OK. Gotcha. What else do I need to know?"

"Keep quiet. Don't drink, don't do drugs. Not in here. Go sit in the lounge and read the Bible."

"How long you been doin' this?"

Her rambling story involved alcohol, drugs, and a guy who "thought he was clever and ended up in the slammer, three to five for burglary." Janet's life resembled an out-of-control train ride. "Can't stay here much longer," she added. "Unless a job comes up in their thrift shop, my time's about up."

All right. "Can you keep quiet about somethin'? Do you have a driver's license?" She started to reach into her back pocket, and I snatched at her arm. "No. Don't get it out now."

She gave me a carefully frozen-in-neutral look when I leaned in to suggest meeting at McDonald's the next day so I could tell her about my "brilliant idea that might help us both out."

"My old man was full of brilliant ideas," she grumbled, "and they always brought trouble. But I guess if you got the cash, it can't do no harm to go eat a burger. Or maybe some fries? I got a bad hunger for some hot, crunchy fries."

* * * *

"You gotta be kidding," Janet muttered between bites. "Why would I give you my ID? Why do you even want it? My luck, you'll use it to sell meth or crack or somethin."

I shouldn't have bought her food first. Instead of making her mellow, it culminated all her dreams, complete with fries. Why should she bargain with me if she already had everything she ever wanted? "Janet, I admit to being naive about selling meth, but I'm really pretty sure it doesn't require ID."

Her eyebrows shot up. Oops. Street people don't use words like *naive*.

I tried again. "I got stupid six years ago when I hooked up with Darryl. Had good jobs. Lost 'em because the car wouldn't start or I had a shiner or the jealous idiot called me at work every ten minutes. I can go back to accounting, but I can't use my name. Darryl said he'd kill me if I left. But I'll be fine if I can stop running from him."

"You're nuts. You think I carry my birth certificate around with me? What'll I do without my license? Why should I trust you? You coulda stayed at a MO-tel last night. You lied to Julia. You'd take my stuff and run."

"Janet, would you come look at the little apartment I put a deposit on for you? I'd pay six months on it—you'd get through the winter with no worries about them kicking you out of the shelter."

She saw the place, and I could tell she liked it. An easy walk from downtown hangouts or a bus stop, it had probably started as one of those '40s motor courts, eight little brick look-alike cottages lined up in two rows along a center court. We walked into a homey, cozy niche with one bedroom, a bath, a living-dining area, and a small kitchen.

But she balked. "I dunno. I just don't think I should let go of my ID. I *need* my driver's license. How do I know you'll go ahead and pay rent? What'll ya do to my good name?"

What good name? "How could I hurt it? You could have a decent credit rating in the end."

"You won't be able to get a credit card in my name, believe me."

"Well, how can I possibly hurt your record?"

"If I hand you my license, what do I use for ID?"

"You'll have the apartment to stay in while you go to DMV and apply for a new license to replace the one that fell in the river."

"*You* get the new license. I can't jump through all those hoops. I *need* my license."

"OK. That might work. Let me try. I'd have to look like your picture."

"That ain't hard. Everybody looks alike on the damn things anyway."

She didn't say yes, exactly, but we went into the bathroom and parted my hair to match her photo. Not bad if I stuffed something around my gums to create a bony effect. I practiced her signature. She had a couple of things that might pass as ID: a Social Security card and a card admitting her to Union Gospel Mission.

Then she looked hard at me. "Every time I ignore my gut-instinct I get in trouble."

"But I'm bailing you out of trouble."

"My gut right now is telling me you're not giving me the whole story."

Oh, shit…

"But also that you're as harmless as you look." She didn't smile, but the crow's feet at the corners of her eyes deepened. "And that you sure as hell wouldn't manage very well on your own on the streets."

"Now if you could just let me have some of that intuition of yours along with the ID…"

"So if you paid some of the rent here up front…"

Oh, *yes*. I was nodding like a fool.

"…and I go with you while you use my ID to get your license…"

"You can't do that. They'll see you and know I'm not you."

"I'll wait across the street and, believe me, I'll be watching the door, so don't you try to sneak off."

"No, no, I have no intention of sneaking off."

"If something goes wrong, I could claim you stole my wallet."

Could I count on her not revealing this exchange? Still, her name could get me out of town.

I paid first and last month's rent and the cleaning deposit. Janet needed furniture, so we stopped at thrift shops on the way to DMV. By the third store, we were like a couple of teenagers shopping for a prom dress though the bed, recliner, and card table with chairs probably cost less all together than a formal gown. The shop would deliver after they closed.

In the bathroom of a mini-mart we experimented with the gauze I'd just bought, stuffing it between my gums and cheeks until my face approximated her pronounced bones.

"More would be better," Janet said.

"Until I opened my mouth and it all popped out."

"You've aged some, Janet."

"Age happens. Close enough?"

She nodded and I headed to DMV. As promised, she waited across the street.

It bothers me some that I'm getting so calm about deceit.

When we compared the new photo on my/her license to her old one, she said, "I was right. Them pictures all look the same."

At the bus stop she said, "That apartment doesn't have any dishes or towels or bedding. And what'll I eat?"

I wondered if she would just run me dry, asking for more and more.

We took the bus to Fred Meyer's north. "What keeps you on the streets anyway, Janet?" I asked.

"Booze. I'm OK at the mission. It's a little scary being on my own."

"Do you have any income at all?"

"Yeah, Social Security. It's due soon, on the tenth. I sober up by about the twentieth and go back to the mission. Or not, in the summer. But they had a *serious discussion* with me the last time I came back there. I've got to either stay and work for them or forget it."

"Seems like a crummy life."

"Yeah, but by the time the tenth rolls around, I've got such a *thirst.* 'One drink,' I say. It's like potato chips. You can't have just one."

"I kind of understand. I'm that way about coffee. And chocolate. Have you tried AA?"

"I've tried everything."

Poor lady. Just like all my diets, until the Little Brook Method finally worked. The trip to Freddy's to get her supplies reminded me of my forays from the wilderness. On the way back to her apartment, we completed our arrangement.

"So you need four month's rent yet." I might have to lose her, go dig out the last of my cash from under Subaruth's spare tire. Or worse, turn into Andrea Glass and go to an ATM.

"Three. That furniture cost you a month's rent, easy."

"Okay." I could manage that. "That'll leave me enough to travel on. Gets you a warm winter. "

The expectant look on her face slowed me down. "Now wait a minute. I'm not handing you cash. I understand about your thirst. Cash brings it on. You'll drink it all up then need more. You'd sell your ID again, or tell about me for a price."

"Maybe you could just pay the manager in advance."

I did that and created an escrow account for her utilities. "Okay," I told her. "I hope I can get myself set up this well. Someplace far away." True statement. "If I can keep passing as you, we could do this again next fall." Another true statement. She was a decent soul. And she'd given me her full name, parents' names, birthdates, everything. "Can you get meals at the shelter?" We hadn't carried much food from Freddy's.

"Yeah, or at Union Gospel Mission downtown, or the park. I'm a good walker. What if I need to get ahold of you? What about next winter?"

"You ever use e-mail?"

Janet nodded. "No problem. I get online at the library."

"Well, where I'm headed is a secret, even from me. But I check my e-mail." I gave her Bev's Yahoo address. "Ever had a passport?" I thought to ask as I left.

"You gotta be kidding. What would I do with a passport?"

"I was just wondering. It might come in handy," I said. "So long, Janet Martin."

"Bye, Janet Martin," she replied.

I picked up my car at Freddy's south then bought six boxes

of nonperishable food. I didn't want Janet to see Subaruth, so I dropped everything at the manager's.

* * * *

I (Bev) stayed in Eugene two more weeks until the end of fall term, life as usual except I got Janet's birth certificate. Drove to Portland to Oregon Records office, showed her driver's license and was done. Took maybe half an hour. I had an identity. For as long as Janet kept the secret.

As for Katherine McGuire, I sent to Illinois for her birth certificate. Next, Kate would obtain a driver's license—in another state where the real Kathy wouldn't pop up on DMV computers.

Maybe I could develop split personalities to go with all the names. Temple toppler, Andrea; fox mender, Bev; math nerd, Janet; musician, Kate; tutor, I dunno who. No more closets for additional identities. No no no.

I bought little Christmas gifts for my roommates. And I spent a lovely day in Discovery and MindWare stores, grandchildren on my mind. I bought origami instructions and paper for fussy Laurie, now nine. For Brian, eight, a kit to construct a solar car—I figured Laurie wouldn't boss him about that. Six-year old Josh The Inquisitive got a wonderful biology set with a microscope, slides, magnifying glass, bug specimens, and a little book of investigations. For Emma, four, and McKenzie, eighteen months, I found a schoolhouse that opened up to reveal children, teacher, and desks. I added crayons and paper, things they might work with if they were in the school. Picking out stuff for the kids gave me half my

Christmas joy back. The other half, watching them open their gifts, MIA.

For myself, I got a car like Brian's.

* * * *

The day I left Eugene I sent Sabrina an e-mail from the library and mailed the gifts. I was leaving tracks, but leaving town, too.

I wrote the message in my mind for days. What I wanted was a hug. There is nothing you can say, really, to a family you deserted a year ago. But I tried.

> **From:** Andrea Glass <andrea_glass@marioncollege.edu>
> **Date:** Mon, Dec 17, 2001 10:18:31 AM US/Pacific
> **To:** Sabrina Severson <theseversons@aok.com>
> **Subject:** It's me
>
> Oh dear daughter, what can I say to excuse the worry I'm sure I have caused you? A huge emotional crisis hit me from nowhere. I went into solitude away from civilization, post offices, phones, computers. I'm better now but not okay yet. I'll keep you posted whenever I can. But I'll still be mostly secluded. People make me even more nuts. I can't emerge, really, for a while.
> Much love, Mom

Would I ever emerge again? I wondered.

Gathering

Much as I wanted my family, I'd settle for some immediate goals: cash, a holiday at Priest Lake in northern Idaho, more cash—a year's worth of Andrea's benefits in Janet's account. Then a move to a state with minimal scrutiny for a driver's license for Kate. In 2001 Arizona looked good.

If any holds were placed on Andrea's bank account, all of us—Andrea, Janet and Katherine—were in trouble, because we were out of cash. But no, five days, five ATM stops. Proceeds deposited in Janet Martin's account. Janet Martin, me. To mislead any hounds sniffing for my scent, I'd looped south on my way north to Idaho.

I thought I kept cool through all the Andrea ATM appearances. Until the nightmare: Low Voice. Low Voice from the day of my flight from shower into woods. Low Voice with his long stride, his pressed and belted raincoat, and his strength made explicit by broad shoulders and calm speech. In the dream he stepped out from behind a pillar just as cash slid from the automatic teller. And there I was, with Andrea's card and Andrea's appearance and Andrea's complete inability to outrun this man's long legs and towering strength and secure self-possession. I awoke in shock, unrested. The dream repeated the next night. And the next.

I remembered childhood forest-fire nightmares. Mom helped me confront the fear, to plan to survive the flames: Find a lake, get under water, breathe through a reed straw.

Where was my mom now? How could I escape the Low Voice inferno?

He might catch me. It could happen.

I'd deny everything, I decided. I'd hinted at a nervous breakdown to Sabrina. Could I build on that? Guilt feelings, not from bombing but from identifying with bombers? Such an internal tangle I couldn't function? Close enough to truth, come to think about it.

Confronting fear worked again and the Low-Voice dream ceased. But danger didn't. Were they watching Andrea's withdrawals? Looking for patterns, timing, location, appearance?

My safety lay in being unpredictable and unrecognizable. Thousands of ATMs, one Low Voice. My procedure became as elaborate as the mating ritual of a Mongolian ring-necked ptarmigan. If there is such a critter.

Like Susanville. I arrived in town in early afternoon, parked my car around the corner a block away, and walked to the bank to investigate. Sidewalk ATM. Would late-day sun glare into the camera? Nope. Dang. It faced north.

ATM camera lens was in the usual spot, upper left. I stayed out of range. Who knows; maybe motion sensors were in there. I located the card slot, screen and input buttons then ducked around back.

Voila. The drive-up window there closed at 6:00, with only a tall fence and windowless back walls otherwise. I had a place to change clothes.

Clothes: one part charade and one part chagrin, like being the only one in costume at the ball. In Susanville on the bottom I'd look masculine, with chinos, white shirt, tie, wool sports coat, and fabric briefcase. I'd hide my braid inside the shirt. To be Andrea on top, I'd wear jeans, blue parka, brown curly wig, and a plaid deer-hunter cap with ear flaps. Everyone I passed dressed similarly—well, maybe not the wig—bundled up against the cold.

When I returned to the bank after dinner, the little mag light made sense on the dark street. It also accidentally blinded the camera, I hoped, as I read the screen, punched the buttons, got my cash.

Around in back, I shucked off clothes fast and stuffed them in the briefcase. *Cold.* What would I say if someone came back there? Why would anyone want to?

Barreling back to Subaruth through the freezing, dark side street, I passed a pickup in a driveway. So glad for so many pickups in this world. Kind of a run-down house, family could probably use the extra parka and hunter cap. A few miles down the road I quit shivering and my stomach untwisted.

Either the procedure worked, or nobody cared.

My travel routines involved setting a pattern then breaking it. First, south toward Las Vegas: Eugene, Susanville, Reno (another 11:50 pm / 12:10 am double header), Carson City (midday), Hawthorne (very early). ATMing completed, and about to leave Nevada, I let Andrea Glass show once more. E-mail, even receiving it, leaves traces. Traces, if I've done it right, that point nowhere. I did a 180 toward Idaho.

* * * *

From: Sabrina Severson <theseversons@aok.com>
Date: Mon, Dec 17, 2001 4:01:56 PM US/Pacific
To: Andrea Glass <andrea_glass@marioncollege.edu>
Subject: Is it really you?

Mom! Dang! I spent the morning not knowing whether to laugh, cry, or scream. If Josh ran away from home, and I didn't know if he was ok, and then I found out he was safe, I'd react the same way I have with you. I wanted to hug you and I wanted to punch you.

Is it really you? Where have you been? Your two notes kept me from deciding you were dead in a ravine somewhere. Are you OK? What's this "emotional crisis" stuff? You, the rational one?

Love ya,
Sabrina

From: Sabrina Severson <theseversons@aok.com>
Date: Wed, Dec 19, 2001 9:13:05 AM US/Pacific
To: Andrea Glass <andrea_glass@marioncollege.edu>
Subject: Is it really you?

Mom, we got your package today, postmarked Eugene. Are you there? Can't we get together? We heard you sold your RV in Albany last winter, and that you were in Eugene then too. Have you been so close and not come to see us? The kids really miss you and so do Mark and I.

Why don't you come here for Christmas, spend Christmas Eve and Christmas Day at least? You can't stay at your place. Bruce Douglas showed us your letter asking him to rent it out. Mike sold your car. He said you signed over the title.

This is SO not like you. I'm still not sure that David person didn't kidnap you, force you to do all this. Are you even really alive?
Please come see us here. Let the kids know they still have a grandma.
Love, Sabrina

* * * *

Well, what could I say? I couldn't go show her I'm alive. Did Low Voice tell her about my selling Winnie?

I turned north, toward my Idaho retreat.

* * * *

I couldn't stay awake. Nevada had been great—a casino in every town; an ATM in every casino, plentiful bathrooms for Andy / Bev changes, low lighting; preoccupied people paying no attention to me But I wanted to be far from Nevada, far from Andy Glass transactions, before I registered at a motel, Janet Martin or not.

Fading fast, I pulled into a big parking lot at a Winnemucca casino and parked on the leeward side of an RV. I was okay in Subaruth in my sleeping bag, with both car and RV sheltering me from icy blasts. Even with temperatures in the teens, I was warmer than at Little Brook. I did wish for a shower after four Nevada nights.

The RV woke me at noon as it pulled away. It was still Friday; I had until Sunday to go a thousand miles to the lodge at Priest Lake.

I freshened up in a casino restroom and had lunch, then looked at the jumble in Subaruth. Five days and ten costumes: what a mess. What if someone wondered about camping gear, coffeemakers, wigs, weird glasses?

An hour later...she still overflowed with stuff but at least I'd organized it. And at least I had hidden Andy wig and ID in the tent bag on the floor under folded-down back seats.

For days my nerves had been zapping and bouncing like downed power lines. Sagebrush hills alternating with sagebrush flats through gray Nevada into gray Oregon diluted the electric blue of my mental landscape. I began to feel safe again.

Snow that sounded more like sleet pelted the car but blew

away, off the road. My gray milieu was turning to black as I drove through Basque. I'd read about this place. Shepherds lived here a century ago, in underground houses to escape burning summers and glacial winters. Escape. Underground. I could relate. Basque was now dark cold, deserted. Deserted desert.

At the end of my stay at Little Brook, I had mentally prepared myself to be Bev Thomas, and in Eugene I answered readily to Bev. But now I needed to think of myself as Janet Martin to match my new driver's license, birth certificate, and bank debit card. *Hello. I'm Janet Martin.* I talked to myself, Janet, through the sage, past the desert, and then back into sage. I intended to register Janet in a motel now, but I seemed to have this expanse to myself. No motels. No rest areas. A pullout strewn with toilet paper. Uncanny. Har har. Another night in Subaruth.

Saturday was better; breakfast and fresh coffee in Nampa, an early lunch, finally out of the sagebrush at McCall, and, at last, a stopover as Janet Martin in a motel in Lewiston.

"I'm back in the sage here," I wrote in my journal, "but that's okay. I took two showers. And I swam. I'm revitalized. I'm planning another ATM run next week after Priest Lake. For tonight—a wonderful real bed, a small old motel room, no foreboding, just being Janet. "

Mending

I registered at Blue Mountain Lodge in the late afternoon of Sunday, December 23, and arranged for a cross-country ski tour the next day. I went to get my skis and tried out the equipment in the ebbing light. Cross-country skis are surprisingly different from downhill skis. How do you move the skis around when your heels aren't attached?

Between dark and dinner, I settled into my room. I put flute and four used-book-store paperbacks on the low table beside an overstuffed, deep-forest-green love seat. Above moss carpet, huge windows framed glittering bits of light from cabins along the lake. Earlier I had hardly noticed the room's welcoming ambience, so demanding were these windows: brilliant snow, green-black trees, silver lake, and blue sky behind more white and silver, the Selkirk Mountains. This isn't Little Brook anymore, Toto.

I lit a fire in the fireplace then composed a history for Janet. I needed to keep my lies simple, so her childhood was just like Andrea Glass's. But she married after her first year of college, raised a daughter, worked in the office of the local high school. She has lost her husband and feels a need for complete change of scene. Easy lies.

After dinner in the lodge, I took my flute to the lounge, found a table in the corner, ordered a glass of Chardonnay, and gazed around. A slight blond fellow played show tunes at the piano bar. His playing was casual, easy, without effort or enthusiasm. An older couple chatted with him as he played, put cash in his tip jar, called him Tom. A young couple smooched at a back table. A foursome told tales and laughed. Four others appeared to be related, the older couple her parents maybe.

When I'd finished my wine, I thought *Why not?* and, picking up my flute, went to the piano. Tom glanced up at me, then looked quizzically at my flute case.

"Think it's quiet enough tonight for me to try a song with you?" I figured he'd be comfortable agreeing to one song, and more would follow if he liked it.

"Do you have something in mind?" he asked.

"Not really. I've been working on jamming along with whatever. "

"Well, hell." He sat up a bit. "Let's see what happens."

Four hours later another dozen people had drifted in from the dining room, both our tip cups were overflowing, and we had gone from old show tunes to "Phantom of the Opera" to unfamiliar classical jazz to "Dark Side of the Moon." I worried a little about all the people, but lighting was low in there and I was playing unlike anything Andy had ever done. Same instrument, but there are many flute players.

"I'm going to have to call it a night," I eventually declared. "I've had more wine and more brain strain than my system can handle."

"Wow, what fun," Tom replied. "Are you going to be around here a while?"

"Couple days."

"Let's do this again tomorrow night."

"You're going to be here on Christmas Eve?"

"Yeah. Seven to eleven. I was dreading it, but you'd make it fun."

"Wow. Okay. If I don't kill myself cross-country skiing tomorrow, you've got a date."

* * * *

When snow piles deep onto ancient trees, the profound silence is more than absence of noise. It's alpha waves, a meditation. Enlightenment. Understanding. Even the teenagers among us on our ski tour respected the prayer of the forest, all of us slipping silently past. No wonder they call it Priest Lake. A place of contemplation, a place of grace.

Fortunately the going was easy there. But after the trees, we climbed for an hour up an open slope, and that's when I had all the trouble. Profundity became profanity.

Trying to herringbone, pointing skis outward and tromping, I fell exactly one buzillion times. My dang heel wasn't attached, my skis flopped, caught in the heavy snow, twisted and tripped me. Or I slid backwards, the backs of my skis crossed and tripped me. Or my skis didn't change directions with my body and tripped me. Snow piled up on my skis and I fell. On a short downhill I slid out of the track and fell.

Once I was down, with sticks protruding from my feet in both directions, I couldn't move a heel under my butt to get upright. As I struggled to push myself up with my poles, my skis slipped forward and again I fell. Weightless powder pinned me down; insubstantial white froth betrayed me, my hands punching deeper into snow when I intended to push myself up. I was so flushed with effort, I didn't much mind the snow down my neck and up under my jacket.

Two teenagers, Will and Carrie, dropped back to help.

"Geez LahWHEEZ." I had found yet another way to tangle up.

"Ohoh, Carrie. Cover your ears. Out of control cussing on the pristine hillside."

They offered to help me up, but I waved them away. "Got to figure this out myself."

"You'll figure how to avoid falling," Will told me. "Nobody can get up in this stuff." Bless that kid. I'd been feeling like such a relic.

My "get up technique" evolved: Flop around and point skis sideways to the slope in a long shallow trough in the snow. Then roll on my back, lift skis high to get momentum, and slam them into the depression, cartwheeling upright. I nearly kept tumbling, but stopped myself with the poles. The kids applauded.

"You know how cross country skiing is like a beach in Hawaii?" I asked them.

"Not a clue," Carrie said.

"Flip flops. Har har."

"Maybe we should just leave her alone," Carrie told Will as they tromped to smooth out my hole in the snow so the next skiers wouldn't break legs. "Bad skiing is forgivable, but I'm not so sure about bad puns." They stuck with me, though, good kids to the end.

Once I could get up, I quit falling. "How fair is that?"

"Well, we can take turns tripping you up, if it will make you feel better," Carrie said.

We had the worst of the climb behind us when Susan, the kids' mom teased, "That hour climb takes twenty minutes if you skip the sliding backwards part, Janet."

I grinned back at her because by then I'd been functioning pretty well. I even started thinking about buying my own skis as we glided along the top of the world to an overlook where Ellie, our guide, suggested lunch. We dusted snow from various stumps and rocks and, with the lake glistening below, made quick work of the most delicious ham sandwiches ever created. I turned to Susan's husband, Greg. "What do you folks do when you're not putting up with clumsy skiers?"

"I teach economics at Washington State in Pullman, and Susan is a history professor. We've been coming here since the kids were babies. Actually, Susan first came when *she* was a baby. Her family has a cabin another five miles up the lake, but it's miserable there in the winter, so we come to the lodge most Christmases."

A good thing about my just-widowed story is that people understand when you don't talk much about yourself. Susan and Greg had been in the bar with her parents the night before, and we talked awhile about flute and improvising. During the wonderful long gentle downhill back to the lodge, Greg explained how economics utilizes matrix algebra. So that's what Steve's econ class was about, I thought.

After a nap I started Scottoline's *Final Appeal* then joined

Susan, Greg, Will and Carrie for an intimate Christmas Eve dinner in the lounge. Had a nervous moment.

"Where did you acquire all that math?" Greg was thinking about our discussion of matrices as we skied back to the lodge.

Oh, oh. Told them I'd finished just one year of college. "Thought I'd be a math major, took calculus and linear algebra that year before I married … Wayne." *Boy, almost forgot my "husband's" name.* I jumped up; Tom was already at the piano. "Good talking to you. Will, Carrie, thanks for sticking with me today. Music calls. Enjoy…"

So dinner hour segued to Christmas Eve. Candles, conversation, melody. Hours passed. Tom and I got tips for having fun. Greg and Susan lingered late. "See you tomorrow. Merry Christmas."

My thoughts flew to my family as I fell asleep that night. Family faces lingered on my interior screen in the morning. Not Janet's fake family. Mine. Sabrina and Mark. Laurie and Brian. Josh. Emma and McKenzie. So distant. I hoped they would like my gifts.

I shook away those images, lit a fire in the fireplace, put on my robe, and went downstairs where I discovered a hot waffle iron, batter and almost-frozen strawberries. Hot chocolate *and* coffee. Then, back in my room, feet up in front of the fire, breakfast on my lap, I thought about Christmas a year ago: weeping, freezing, struggling with my wind-guard.

I moved to the window with my coffee to gaze at lake and mountains and sky. I grieved for the Whitesons, dead somehow in that temple. They shouldn't have been there, my mind shouted, but Karinne Carafe's voice floated across the lake to me, "*You* shouldn't have been there! You should have swallowed your loss and moved on."

My family. The Whitesons. Holly. Sly. Neil. My ghosts paraded to an unsung dirge.

The flute pulled me back. I improvised with Christmas tunes playing on an FM station.

And my solar toy car, the one I'd bought for myself. I built it, read for a while, then went downstairs.

Will liked the car. He examined its little motor and rubber-band drive mechanism. He covered the photoelectric cells with a napkin to see how long the car would keep running.

I put a discarded bow on it. "Merry Christmas, Will." I held out the cheery little gadget. "This is a good way for me to thank you for your support on the trail. Share this with Carrie."

"Oh, no, I didn't want to take your car from you. It's just that it's so cute."

"I got to put it together this morning. Now I want you to have it, Will."

"Well, thanks." He gave me that little smile, eyes wrinkling, lips curving up at the edges, that people reserve for taking the pot at poker.

Everybody, hosts and guests, prepared the table and dined together. Talk drifted through music, math, life at the lake, the year gone by—2001. So many grieving for loved ones lost on 9/11.

"I hope we bring those terrorists to justice," Ellie, yesterday's ski guide, said.

Murmurs of agreement. I risked my question: "What is a terrorist, exactly?"

Bemused looks came my way. Silence. Finally a lanky fellow on the other side of the table said, "You can't *not* know what a terrorist is."

"Well, of course we know the guys flying the jets into the twin towers were terrorists. But they're dead. We talk about getting the terrorists, but where are they? Who are they?"

"Good question," Susan said. "In this country eco-terrorists," her hands made quote marks around *terrorists*, "burn down forestry buildings."

"People release animals from labs," Carrie added.

"They bomb Mormon temples," Greg said, "protesting … secrecy?"

Close. Thank you Greg, I thought.

` "Terrorist crap," Lanky Guy said. "Put 'em all in a damn dungeon."

"Well," Ellie said. "I guess I was thinking of people who kill people for no reason."

"Sorry. Sorry." I waved an imaginary white flag. "It's confusing. Shades of gray. On Christmas I might better ask if you ever ski across the lake?"

The group seemed happy to return conversation to recreation and the mundane.

Some of us skied again, along the lake to work off a little of the indolent day. But then we undid the exercise, mingling over fondue and a dessert buffet before heading off to our rooms, many of us with a carafe of wine. I finished *Final Appeal* that evening and started *Risk* by Dick Francis the next morning.

Annendag Jule, my family calls it, the day after Christmas, play with toys day. At Priest Lake we skied. I had the hang of it now, tromping up this day's long hill like a pro after another meditation through trees. Our lunch vista allowed us to see bits of the upper lake and the narrow passage to it. Through the cold clear air we heard foxes yipping north of us. I talked with Susan and Greg about books, about improvising on flute, about where to buy skis, about anything but math. Or terrorism. Or family.

Tom joined us for dinner, then he and I again entertained each other. We noodled around on one piece for half an hour. He played the tune, I vamped. He got me going on melody and he vamped. Then we were off to the next phrase. Somehow, the patrons loved it, too. Maybe because Tom and I were having so much fun. Fun evolved into mystical experience as we became greater than the sum of our parts.

* * * *

Andrea Glass could never have had this Priest Lake experience. She couldn't have completed the ski trip, would never even try it. She couldn't have made music with Tom. Some deep impediment made her antsy, angry, and forlorn, made her itch to go bombing, made her unable to shrug off that left-out-of-the-wedding sensibility. But silence and trees, mountains and joy, music and conversation all tugged against the pull of Andrea's long deep black hole.

Still, Janet's promises: "I'll write when I have my winter address," were lies. Janet was an unreliable persona. Another sorrow. I liked Tom, and Susan and Greg, and Carrie and Will.

Soon I'd become Kate McGuire. I'd spend the next several months in Arizona, because it was warm and an easy place to get a driver's license. Then Colorado, or Montana, The Rockies, I thought. Love the mountains. Only I needed immediate ATMing, for the substantial bankroll required to live in civilization.

Collecting

I wandered for ten days. Beats forty years in the desert, I guess. As I drove, mind drifting to Christmas conversation, terrorists and me, I discussed justice with Karinne Carafe. "Really, what's the point of prison?" Not wanting to be sent there may have biased my viewpoint.

"Oooh. Oooh. Easy question. You put bad guys in prison so good guys will be safe."

"Consider my case. Society pays three times if I go to prison. Once when I destroyed a temple. Once to pay my upkeep in jail. And once by keeping me unproductive. Maybe they could send me to Africa in the Peace Corps or something."

"So the US sends felons *and* banned pesticides to third world countries? Clever, Janet."

"Like that woman … drove a getaway car for some anarchist group in the seventies. Led an upstanding life for twenty years. Turned herself in. They put her in jail, left her young daughter without a mom. Who benefits from that?"

"Society. You can't penalize only some people, sometimes. And people need closure."

"*Closure* means revenge."

Silence. Just tires humming. Guess I won *that* argument.

* * * *

From: Sabrina Severson <theseversons@aok.com>
Date: Sun, Dec 23, 2001 2:01:51 PM US/Pacific
To: Andrea Glass <andrea_glass@marioncollege.edu>
Subject: holiday

Mom, We haven't heard from you. I hope it wasn't just some random radiation from outer space that somehow looked like an email from you. Guess not, the packages are real enough. Just want you to know we're still holding a place for you on Christmas Eve and Christmas Day. Any time you want.
We love you,
S.

From: Sabrina Severson <theseversons@aok.com>
Date: Wed, Dec 26, 2001 11:56:13 AM US/Pacific
To: Andrea Glass <andrea_glass@marioncollege.edu>
Subject: it's you!

Well, Mom, it was definitely you. The gifts are SO you. Thanks. Though we would have preferred our mom / grandma. Please don't disappear again. We worried so much, called Uncle Al and all the cousins when we heard your RV was sold. We wondered if you'd been kidnapped or what …
S.

From: Andrea Glass <andrea_glass@marioncollege.edu>
Date: Fri., Dec 28, 2001 4:34 PM US/Mountain
To: Sabrina Severson <theseversons@aok.com>
Subject: It's me

Please, please, dear Sabrina, don't worry about me. I tried to let you know I'm okay, held hostage only by my own distress. I can access e-mail more often now, but it'll be irregular. I miss you hugely. I'm still working through some things, though, and it needs distance, not close-up. It's cheaper than a shrink, but probably more painful . . .

How did you know I sold the RV? What have been the big events for you since I've been gone? Did the kids like their gifts?

Much love,
Mom

* * * *

I hit ATMs in Sandpoint, Butte, Denver, another midnight double in Minneapolis. My account was still functioning. *Hurrah.* By St. Louis, I was tired and the city large so I decided to stay for three withdrawals. I drove around to check out ATMs, got cash from one, then used Janet's debit card to register at a motel. With all the people at motels here, surely the presence of both Janet and Andy wouldn't be noticed. Just to keep Subaruth totally out of the picture, I took city buses to get to a second ATM the next day. The third day in St. Louis, I took another bus to another ATM and learned what a fool I'd been to stop over like that.

After my withdrawal, I came around the corner from the side street where I had just changed to my bottom layer, a wool skirt of brown tweed with matching jacket over a creamy wool sweater. Pearls, tam, panty hose, loafers. Very professional.

Low Voice was standing there! Low Voice, from my nightmares, as straight and composed as I remembered.

Don't stop. Don't run. Don't notice him. Geez, is the game up? Just like that? If I ran, my head told my feet, he'd catch me in three steps. I kept walking, got to the bus stop. He was approaching. I recognized the athletic stride, the blond hair, the big shoulders, the self-containment. *Run! Don't Run! Run!* I snugged up the reins on myself: he was merely a random stranger walking to my same bus stop. My heart pounded as though I had indeed been running, Low Voice close behind.

I glanced at him, shifted my weight to my other leg, looked at my watch. When he spoke, his baritone rang a bell from that last day at home.

"Excuse me, ma'am. I'm trying to find this person, and I think she was just here. Have you seen her?" He held a picture in his hand of me minutes before at the ATM.

The panicked part of my mind watched emergency-calm slip onto my shoulders. As with an injured child or a wounded animal, my close encounter with Low Voice evoked a cool, steady response. I might collapse later, but for now I studied the photo he showed me.

My gawd. Stay cool. I had done well: with the light behind me, the dark picture revealed floppy hat, dark glasses, and plaid shirt, now residing in the canopy of yet another pickup. The curly hair was at the bottom of the Macy's bag I carried.

I stood fast, hiding my quaking knees. I hoped. What had he asked? Had I seen her? "No. I don't think so. Hard to tell from the picture." *He is so tall.* I had to tilt my head back or talk to a big four-hole button on the pressed, belted blue raincoat.

"Here's another picture. Older one. Ring any bells?"

I looked at my Andrea-self. I remembered the moment, taken with Sabrina on Independence Day. You could see bits of the parade in the background. Sabrina had been clipped out, the picture enlarged.

"Noooo, I don't think I've seen that person. But I just got here from Macy's." The bus pulled up. "I honestly don't pay much attention to other people when I'm walking down the street. She could be around here and I just didn't notice. Got to catch the bus. Good luck with your search." And I was out of there. I fled up the bus steps.

All these adrenaline rushes can't be good for my heart. I am a senior citizen, after all. I sat on the left side of the bus, away from Low Voice, who still stood on the sidewalk, looking around, looking forlorn. Looking formidable. Startling blue eyes …

After half a dozen stops, I sat back in my seat and took deep breaths. I guess I was breathing before then, too, or somebody would be picking me up from the floor. Gradually my heart quit its tappity tap. The spinning sensation left my brain. I looked around. No stares, no sideways glances, no one studiously ignoring me.

Oh my gawd. Ohmygawdohmygawd. That was much too close. But he didn't recognize me. He … did … not … RECOGNIZE … me. Ohmygawd.

I spotted a restaurant as the bus passed a mall, so I got off and walked back to eat lunch there. Sat down, started writing on my napkin. So many questions zipping through my brain. Maybe writing them would slow them down a little.

How did Low Voice get there so fast? How did he get the ATM photo? Did he come from inside the bank? Is he hunting me full time? Still? Am I his total focus? Does he have help? Are there other agents I haven't noticed?

I concentrated on the menu and then people-watched, encouraging my mind into the kind of drift from which best ideas come. Could Low Voice be following me?

Following? From the motel … No. He wouldn't be asking about Andrea on the street if he knew where I'm staying. He must have been close when I went through the ATM. Was he watching from the bank or a building nearby?

Maybe he followed Andrea's withdrawals to St. Louis. And if *I* was looking for me, I'd ask around, see who had seen me.

So, say he came to St. Louis because of my ATM transactions, then stayed to see where I would show up again. He'd know there was at least a chance I'd do a repeat in St. Louis, though all my previous repeats have been midnight doubles.

I made seven withdrawals in seven days. Logic would tell him that I was on a run. Run for your money, Andy. Har har. So even if he didn't expect me to appear again in St. Louis, he might stay there until I showed up somewhere.

He had to have been within minutes of the bank where I'd just gone. Coincidence? Are there motels close? Local FBI office? How far away was yesterday's ATM? Maybe he's just staying close to my trail. He ran into Janet, talked to Janet.

I didn't want him to see either Janet or Andrea again. I picked up a curling iron and a sable rinse at a drug store in the mall then caught a bus. Just a rinse; I'm fond of my long silver hair.

At the motel I arranged to drop my keys very early the next morning then went into my bathroom. Silver braid became brunette curls. Hoping I looked different enough from the person Low Voice saw by the bank, I went with Subaruth to learn what we could about him.

We started at the ATM I'd used yesterday. We circled, found a Marriott, backtracked, worked it out: ten minutes from that ATM to a hotel. And *three blocks* from Marriott to *today's* ATM. Different street, strange town, didn't realize how close the ATMs were. Dum-dum-dum-dumb! He waited for me to make mistakes. I obliged him.

I figured Low Voice, drawn to St. Louis by my activities, stayed at the Marriott, near my last ATM action. Then maybe somebody called him when I withdrew cash today. I suppose it's possible to have a photo profile that a computer could identify, sending out an alert. Well, no. They don't need a profile. They'd pick up on me the minute I insert my card. Then Low Voice could access my picture electronically. He'd had plenty of time to get from the Marriott to the bank while I finished the transaction and changed costumes. Speedy change of appearance—and pure luck—had saved me.

Far across town I drove through another ATM and deposited the proceeds of Andrea's withdrawals into Janet's account. Piles of cash would *not* help her cause.

At 5:30 the next morning Andy made a withdrawal in Perryville, about 100 miles south of St. Louis and just off Interstate 55. Anyone plotting my activities from Minneapolis would see an arrow pointing to Memphis. From Perryville, though, I headed west, through Farmington to Jefferson City, getting to Kansas City and Interstate 70 around 1 p.m. I spent the night in a rest area in the middle of Kansas, went to an ATM in Denver early the next afternoon, then checked my e-mail.

* * * *

From: Sabrina Severson <theseversons@aok.com>
Date: Wed, Jan 2, 2002 10:34:38 AM US/Pacific
To: Andrea Glass <andrea_glass@marioncollege.edu>
Subject: Now I understand infinity

Mom, I never understood about infinity and different orders of infinity and all. I just thought of it as where the number line runs off the edge of the paper. Now I have an infinite number of questions for you and an infinite answer to your question about what has gone on in the last year.

The easy answer first. The kids LOVED your gifts, and their other grandparents were a little jealous because the kids kept going back to the things you sent. Laurie made such beautiful birds. Brian happily worked on his car, Josh is funny as anything with his microscope and magnifying glass, and the little ones play school every morning. YOU SHOULD BE HERE TO SEE IT!

I guess I know now that you are okay. I was so afraid you had been kidnapped, or worse, by that David guy. The kids kept asking where you were and when you'd be back. I made excuses, and I hope they didn't pick up my fears—or tears. I guess it must be important, or you wouldn't have gone like that, but I really wish you could show up, in person, to reassure us all.

You need to be here to take care of things, too. The FBI started asking about you last December. We told them what you told us, that you went to New Mexico, probably Chama. There's one guy, Matt Sheridan, who keeps coming back. Within a few days he told us you couldn't be in New Mexico, that you had sold your RV in Junction City. From then on I don't know if he believed anything we said, even though I fell apart on him, and even though he's LDS and knows we are, too. He wants to talk to you about the temple bombings, Mom, and your being gone from home every time, and being in Provo at the time of the last one. He's asking why you didn't go to Chama, and about a warm house when they first went in, and some kind of crazy alarm system, and a missing computer hard drive. I probably said more than I'm supposed to. For sure, you picked a bad time to run away. I don't want to whine, but I AM a little stressed.
Love,
Sabrina

* * * *

I skipped a hundred miles north to Cheyenne for a 1 a.m. withdrawal. A map on a wall somewhere might have five stickpins matching my eastbound cash-gathering, then another four southbound. What would Low Voice make of my sudden jump back west to Denver then Cheyenne? Maybe he'd guess I was looping northwest, back to Sandpoint? Or Oregon?

So I went northeast to the little crossroads town of Bridgeport, Nebraska for one more withdrawal. I found an internet cafe and googled Matt Sheridan. Sheridan, if it's the right one, used to play basketball, BYU. The kid in the sports pages looked a lot like Low Voice. Who hopefully had given up if he'd been trying to anticipate my moves.

Whatever. Andrea sent one more e-mail and dropped off the Low Voice radar. I'm sorry, Sabrina. So sorry. I'm still a fugitive.

Matthew Sheridan

From: Sabrina Severson <theseversons@aok.com>
Subject: Fw: Understanding
Date: Sat, Jan 5, 2002 1:30:41 PM US/Pacific
To: Matthew Sheridan <m_sheridan@fbi.us.gov>

Mr. Sheridan:

You asked me to let you know what I hear from my mother. Maybe this e-mail explains a few things. I received it yesterday. It's just like her, definitely from her. As I told you, I feared she'd been kidnapped or worse, but this e-mail is authentic. I still don't understand her leaving that way, but I'm convinced she knows nothing that could help your investigation. I always knew if she was able she would immediately report anything suspicious, but her seeing something would have been a huge coincidence. Kids and dogs love her. She made up songs for her math classes to help them remember formulas. She wouldn't know a bomb unless it blew up in her face.

Sabrina Severson
|
--------- Forwarded Message
From: **Andrea Glass <andrea_glass@marioncollege.edu>**
Date: Fri., Jan 4, 2002 10:43:21 AM US/Central
To: Sabrina Severson <theseversons@aok.com>

Dear Sabrina,

I'm so sorry I've caused you distress. Please tell Mr. Sheridan that you aren't responsible for me. Rather than difficult children, you have a difficult parent.

David and I stopped in Provo so he could show me Utah's beautiful red canyons. But his family had an emergency, and he had to go. My coming unglued had nothing to do with him. I just used him as an excuse.

I can't talk to my own daughter: how could I talk to a stranger from the FBI? I'm among a buzillion people with no fondness for temples after being excluded from our children's weddings. Half the buzillion were probably not home when bombings occurred. Like me, those folks know nothing about bombs and could not help an investigation. Many people have alarm systems, especially people alone in isolated places. Couldn't tell you about a warm house, unless the sun was shining in the south windows. Computer crashed; I've got to replace its guts. Sure seems like Mr. Sheridan would have better things to do. Do I remember a Sheridan, an athlete, maybe?

Probably I won't be in contact for a while. I won't be kidnapped, mad or in trouble. I just will be out of cyber space again, possibly for months.

Maybe your God put me here to challenge your ability to forgive and have charity. Please, for me, try. You're in my heart and my hippocampus. All my senses remember you. And the kids and Mark.

Love,
Mom

* * * *

Matt had considered deleting the bloody message unread. With hundreds of e-mails, hundreds of voice messages, and stacks of snail mail, mostly related to his big insurance fraud case, he was tired of Andrea Glass. Two weeks chasing her in circles. Enough. His current worries involved companies depriving people, right now, of necessary care. Temple destruction still stung his Mormon sensibilities if he thought about it, but it had gone back-burner. Ms. Glass probably didn't know anything anyway.

How many insurance employees knew about company delaying-denying tactics? What customers had been defrauded? Was he investigating a bad company or a bad industry? News about these fraudulent insurance policies would break any day, and looking like an incompetent fool was not his favorite occupation. Fortunately Wayne had kept up with things.

The guy was a little hard to work with sometimes. Or, Matt wondered, maybe it was Matt who was hard to work with, tending to issue orders when he was in a time crunch—often. Wayne was willing to work the soles off his shoes to help, but was no flunky, drawing the line at brusk orders from a man fifteen years his junior. Wayne had a point. Experience trumps BYU or Quantico. Wayne had field experience, and he was good.

So Matt was glad when he showed up at lunch time, sandwiches from Sally's Deli in hand. Hot meatballs, cool head, cold facts. Good combination.

"When did you get in?" Wayne asked, setting milk and sandwiches on the side table.

"I flew into D.C. last night and got to the office at 6:30 this morning. Look at this pile. I had almost gotten caught up and then that ridiculous woman led me in more circles. Two weeks turning myself around like a silly dog trying to get the right position for a nap."

"Well, if you got any sleep, you're ahead of the rest of us."

"My sleep balance sheet is in the black, but my fact balance is bleeding red."

"I'll get you caught up. Maybe you can do that Sheridan trick and see something we've missed. First —what happened to your bombing witness?"

"It's just like before, one withdrawal after another. Only

they were farther apart, clear across the country, eastbound. I figured after Minneapolis, I'd get ahead of her by going to Chicago. So she shows up in St. Louis, twice. I go there, figuring I'd be a few hundred miles from wherever she shows up next—which was right down the street. I'm not kidding, Wayne. Up a couple of floors with a good breeze, I could've spat on the woman."

"What did she have to say?"

"I was there so fast. How did she even get her card out of the machine by then? Nobody was there. Nobody! A couple of people in the bank, one on the street, and nobody saw her."

"Maybe you should deactivate her card."

"I have no real basis, and at least I get a glimpse of her when she withdraws money."

"Some glimpse. I never saw anybody take so many bad pictures."

Matt chewed on his sandwich. "Then she loops back west and disappears. Mrs. Severson got another e-mail on Saturday, which she forwarded to me. Got it this morning."

"What is Andrea going to do with all that money?"

"Yes, my worry exactly. Another bomb? Is she the supplier? Is she headed out of the country? I should have gotten back for this insurance case, but I wanted to catch up to her."

"It's just me and you on that case, too. Everybody is nuts, chasing down "jihadists." Mexicans, Italians, Turks, even Asians. Anybody with black hair is a jihadist these days. Including Greek Orthodox priests."

"We're the only ones working the insurance case?"

"The folks who aren't chasing terrorists—they foiled at least two other plots, by the way—are busy chasing down intelligence on Iraq."

"Iraq? Iraq! Why that on top of all the other stuff?"

"You got me. Request came from high up, maybe even the Oval Office."

"If it's just us on this insurance thing, we'd better get busy. Help me catch up, okay?"

"First, while we're talking about Andrea, let me see that e-mail from her daughter."

Matt printed a copy and refreshed water bottles while Wayne scanned it.

"Well, she explained some stuff, maybe. What's this about you being an athlete?"

"I played basketball, for BYU. The pros got interested in me. I was in the news some."

"Would Andrea Glass know that?"

"I haven't done much thinking about it. I've been trying to wade through my other mail. Why would she ask? Maybe she googled me." Matt googled himself as Wayne looked over his shoulder. "Yep. There I am."

"Still, why ask? Check if she had the right Matthew Sheridan? See what you look like?"

"Could she have seen me? Everybody who sees me asks about sports. I should go under cover as a hoops pro."

"If she saw you, wouldn't you have seen her, too?"

"Where could I have been that close? St. Louis? Her e-mail was after that."

"St. Louis or the Coos Bay store, or the Seattle airport, or the motel in Redding. Maybe that mall in Salt Lake City, though those reports weren't very credible."

"Mrs. Severson's house?" Matt turned to the computer to list their ideas. He had to put this aside, but his subconscious might tell him something when he reviewed the list later. "Maybe even Mrs. Glass's house."

"Yeah. You were so sure she was there. I was pissed that you'd left me sitting in the rain. Figured the most I'd see was a coyote. I'm thinking now that you were right."

"In the woods? Barn? No, that was too far away. She sure wasn't in the house."

"What about St. Louis?" Wayne brainstormed well. "Who did you see there?"

"I talked to the tellers, two customers and one woman on the street outside."

"Have you got those sketches? The ones the artists did of how Andrea could look with changed appearance?"

"Right here." Matt studied them again and handed them over to Wayne.

"What about the bank customers? That woman on the street? Could any of them be her?"

"The customers were an old balding guy and a woman in her twenties. The lady on the street was ten years younger than Mrs. Glass. She looked like a runner, or a dancer."

Wayne picked up Ms. Glass's ATM photo. "Could any of them have been this person?"

"*Anybody* could be that person. *I* could be that person. The bald guy—put a wig on his head and a hat. He might have stolen her bank card. He might be an accomplice."

Wayne laid out artist sketches, the maybe-Andreas, and compared each to her ATM photo. "You're right. You match this photo better than any of the sketches do."

"She doesn't want to talk to us. She's smart. She figured out the ATM cameras."

"So maybe she shaved her head and was the bald guy in the bank."

Wayne was exploring an interesting avenue that Matt had not thought about. "The person at the ATM is not bald. Look at the photo. Curly hair sticking out from the sides of the cap. That could be a wig, but … No. The guy in the bank had no place to hide a wig."

"What about the other two people you saw?"

"Well, the female customer is out. Clearly too young. The woman on the street?" Matt gazed out the window, down Pennsylvania Avenue. "She was the right height. I stood next to her and she came up to my chin. Close to the right age, but younger than any of these sketches. Very cool. Incredibly cool if it was her. She stood right there, looked at the ATM picture, and calmly told me she had not seen that person. She even complained about its being a bad photo. I really can't think that elegant lady could be the same as the slouched figure in the photo."

"Nevertheless," Wayne suggested, "go over to Quantico on your way home and get them to sketch the Woman on the Street while she's still fresh in your mind. The Bald Man, too."

Matt nodded as he gathered photo and sketches. "Now, where do I start, with all the insurance data flooding my desk? It'll take weeks to sort through, and we don't have weeks."

Becoming Kate

Before Subaruth and I got to Arizona, we stopped for a little online scouting. Tucson, we decided. It looked like housing was cheaper there than in Phoenix. Tucson had an inexpensive campground nearby, a good temporary place. Its community college and university offered potential for tutoring. Because of its high elevation, blazing spring temperatures would cool a bit at night. Ergo Tucson.

My current ambition was to stay warm this winter and to become Kate McGuire. In 2002 Arizona was an easy place to get a driver's license.

Freezer to fire for me: low temperatures in southern Arizona equal highs at Little Brook. Maybe fire was okay. Isa's chill threatened again. I was alone, my Eugene and Idaho friendships ephemeral. But maybe fire wasn't okay: Isa's frozen steppes or Arizona burning deserts, literally just a matter of degree. Barren is barren. Even Arizona's people seemed barren, shallow WASP country-clubbers, khaki people in white pants. An easy driver's license, yes. *Joie de vivre*? Unlikely.

By lantern light in my camp twenty miles north and a thousand feet up from Tucson, I drew a rune stone. *Wunjo*: a fruit-bearing symbol signifying the end of travail. A flicker of hope there, but the stone was reversed, meaning that things would be slow in coming to fruition. My gawd. Hadn't enough sad and empty time gone by?

Exhausted after irregular hours and long days of driving, I slept late and showered long. But I got to Pima Community College before noon on Tuesday, a week after New Year's Day, and signed up for a class on creating web pages that would begin next Monday.

"Provide an address and pay fees within ten days, Kate," the registrar explained, "get your photo ID, and you're all set for class and to use the library and computer lab."

Photo ID. Kate. Yes.

PCC and U Arizona bulletin boards had no appealing housing offers. Okay. My own place this time. I ate brunch, read apartment ads, then asked a quiet woman at the next table.

She eliminated several of my circled ads. "Too many parties around here. Near the university is good; some kid stuff, but professors, too."

I drove around all afternoon with a Tucson map, getting lost, getting frustrated by one-way streets, getting too far from campus. I found some dilapidated adobes, some places on noisy streets, some that looked unkempt, but at the end of the day I'd seen half a dozen that looked plausible from outside. Most advertised a separate, common-use clubhouse, perhaps handy for tutoring. Even with grandma types, one-on-one in an apartment can look bad.

An owl talked back as I played flute after dinner at my mountain campsite, and Isa's chill subsided. I studied the Arizona driver's manual by lantern light, and amended Kate's back story: When her husband died, Kate moved to San Francisco near her daughter's family, and didn't drive or need a license there.

* * * *

On my second day in Tucson I found a small apartment, downstairs in a stucco two-story complex in the university district. It was a bit worn around the edges, but it had all the amenities: light switches, running water, fridge. I did worry about the ancient air conditioner but perhaps the first floor would stay cool. Rent was nearly as low as Janet Martin's in Salem, so I took it despite a ten day wait until the place was available

"I hope cash is all right," I told the manager. "I don't have a bank account set up yet. And do you think I could go ahead and use the clubhouse if I'm tutoring?"

"Cash is always fine. So is tutoring. After you complete these reference forms."

Aaack. Dam-Sam. References, addresses. Time. I needed time. I looked at my watch. "I. Umm. I ... Can I take those forms and bring them back this afternoon? I'm already going to be late. I have ... um ... an appointment with my ... um ... advisor over at Pima CC."

He nodded and handed me the forms. I sped out. At the city library, utilizing Map Quest and the yellow pages, I found an apartment building in what looked like a pleasant part of San Francisco. Aha. My "previous residence!" I used its address and phone number, reversing a couple of digits. The Tucson manager seemed happy to have one "mature" tenant, so maybe he wouldn't check. I hoped.

It worked. I dropped off the forms, paid in cash, signed the rental agreement, and shook hands with a happy guy who handed over clubhouse keys. Apartment keys would follow ASAP, he told me.

As long as I seemed to be on a roll, I joined an athletic club a few blocks from the apartment, and got Kate's first photo ID. One more piece of ID for DMV, one more way to stay trim.

At home in my mountain campground I practiced flute and studied the DMV manual.

On Thursday, with address and cash in hand, I completed enrollment at PCC, acquiring another photo ID and access to the computer lab. On Friday Katherine McGuire went to DMV for her driver's license.

I handed the clerk Kate's two photo IDs and the birth certificate which had arrived in the mail before I left Oregon.

"May I have your previous license?" he asked.

"I lived in San Francisco. Haven't needed a license for years."

"How did you get here without a license?"

"My friend Judy drove me in my car. Her husband picked her up. Oh, and I need Arizona plates, too."

I held my breath. No questions about another Katherine McGuire. They gave me the test. I passed.

I had it. I had Kate's ID. It represented safety. Shelter. And separation. Ahh, Josh, when will I see you again?

I had just enough time Friday afternoon to place a math

tutoring ad, giving my new cell phone number My flute and I went that evening to check on the night life. Didn't find much.

After class on Monday I opened a checking account for Kate. I didn't want this account to show up on original-Katherine's credit report, so instead of Katherine McGuire's social security number I used a similar one I'd found in the social security death lists.

If I could just access Andy's funds, my life would be free of fear. It was like a ship wreck, I supposed. Get safe first. Find some flotsam to climb onto. Then find a way home.

I couldn't figure out the ringing in my backpack at first. A phone ringing. For me. My first tutee, as it turned out.

Becca's mom, Ann Harrison, greeted me at her door with, "She's been crying. Finals are in two weeks. Her teacher helps her every day after school, but Becca says the more help she gets the dumber she feels."

"Well, I think I can help, but I don't do miracles. Two weeks isn't much time."

"I know," Ann said. "We tried. She had another tutor, a smart college student who did her best—but Becca just got more frustrated."

So Becca and I sat at the dining table and I made up a mini exam "to see where you are in preparing for the final." Twenty questions, should have taken five or ten minutes. I watched her struggle for half an hour.

I found Ann and arranged for more time, no charge, then went back to flush-faced Becca who was still writing and erasing and sighing. "Becca, enough. I didn't mean to give you such a huge task."

"Okay. Just give me a minute." She scribbled a bit more and handed me her paper. Many answers. Some questions had two. "I think it's 3a, but it might be 12 + a" kinds of answers. Three correct out of twenty. I thought I'd given her five "gift" questions, easy ones.

"So you have -3 + -5 = 8. Does that mean that if you lose 3 yards in one football play and then you lose 5 more in the next play, you have a *gain* of 8 yards?"

"No, if you lose twice, you've just lost a bunch. How could it be a gain?" She tucked a stray bit of coffee-brown hair behind her ear.

"Well, look at your answer to number four. Did you mean it to be *positive* eight?"

"Yes. Two negatives make a positive."

Oh geez. Good rule, wrong place. "We have work to do, Becca. Only your first three answers are right."

"Nuh-uhhh. What's wrong with number four?"

"Two negatives make a negative when you add."

"Nuh - uh! Mrs. Anderson keeps changing the rules on me. You can't do that, too."

"I'm not changing rules. There are just different ones for adding and for multiplying."

"What about number twelve? I worked and worked on that one. I *know* it's right!"

Oh geez. "You've said that x = 63. If x is that big, wouldn't it be pretty unlikely for three x's plus 12 to equal 27?"

Tears were welling. "Why do three x's plus twelve have to equal twenty-seven?"

"Because that's what the problem asks. See? $3x + 12 = 27$."

"I did the problem. Look! Three times twelve is thirty-six. Add twenty-seven and you get sixty-three."

Oh geez. No clue that the symbols on the page have the meaning I just gave them.

"I'm going to flunk! My answers are *always* wrong. Some dumb different reason every time. I can't do this crap. Why do I care what stupid x is anyway? I *hate* this class. My friend Karen just goes out the back door and has a smoke that period. I might as well go with her." She swiped at the tears that were now rolling down her cheeks. Water and fire coexisted in green eyes. Flecks of brown there.

"Oh wow, Becca. You're right: It's going to be an uphill climb. It'll be hard. You can do it, though. I know you can. But don't go out and get lung cancer. That won't solve a thing."

Her pencil slammed to the table and rebounded onto the floor. "Well, I'm going to flunk. I might as well be doing something fun if I'm going to flunk anyway." She jumped up, tipping her chair over, ready to flee.

"We *do* need to try to buy you some time. And I agree: It hardly pays to be in class if they just seem to be talking Greek."

"You better believe it!" She stood agape, flight canceled.

She's amazed that I agree, I thought. "Let me see what I can do. Let's be up front about it, though, not skulking around blackening your lungs."

Becca went upstairs to change clothes to go for a run. I

went back to the kitchen to talk to her mom.

"She has a list of algebra rules" I told Ann, "and no concept of when to use them or why. I'll work with her, but she's like a westerner lost in Beijing. She has a street map and a destination, but everything is written in symbols she doesn't understand."

Ann Harrison's eyes tightened, and she stood very straight. "Are you saying Becca should just give up? Do you think she's not smart enough?"

"No. Not at all. Though, confused as she is, she feels pretty dumb right now."

"So what *do* you suggest?"

I sipped at the coffee she'd provided. "Do you think her teacher might agree to an incomplete this semester? Or to change her grade after second semester if she improves? After all, second semester depends on understanding first semester."

"Maybe. Mrs. Anderson is very kind. She's spent hours helping Becca."

"If Becca and I start over, I could show her algebra from another perspective. We'd move at her speed. Becca is perfectly bright, but she got off on the wrong foot, she has too much practice doing things the wrong way, and now she's angry, discouraged, and panicked."

"Boy, that's the truth."

Mrs. Anderson was to agree. Becca could work on other classes in the library during math class and focus on algebra with me after school until she caught up. And Becca, Ann, and Mrs. Anderson all ended up sending more students my way.

Flutist Kate

That first Friday night, wandering with my flute, I found a lot happening but nowhere to sit in. I was looking for Tom, I guess, and a repeat of that transcendent Priest Lake experience, but I didn't find him. The combos were well-established and carefully rehearsed.

"Wednesday is jam night," a classmate told me on Monday. Sure enough—there was a professor, Sam, playing keyboard at Beanos Coffee House who said, "Comeon, comeon" to me. I didn't recognize the song he was playing—he was more current than I—but I started noodling with it a bit, and then a tall brunette in a pony tail abruptly pulled up a chair and pulled out a guitar. "I'm Meredith," she said, "this is the night I get a baby sitter, and I make the most of it, what key are you in?

A couple of songs later, Randy, obviously another regular joined in on mandolin and harmonica. The three of them sang, good harmony, and we were sounding all right.

"I'm thinking I'm gonna like Tucson," I said.

"Good gosh," Meredith said. "It's ten o'clock. I've got to get two kids off to school in the morning then sound halfway coherent at a district court hearing."

"You're an attorney?"

"Yep. Just one more tune, okay?"

At 10:30 I said, "Can we try 'Bridge Over Troubled Water?'"

At 11:00 Sam said, "I've got to go. Haven't prepared my lecture for tomorrow, but can we do 'Ain't No Sunshine' first?" Then Randy mentioned some reading he hadn't done for a seminar at UA, but started fiddling around with 'You are My Sunshine,' and we all picked that up, until finally at midnight we packed our instruments away. "Next Wednesday," somebody said, and we all nodded.

But on my second Tucson weekend Isa, the ice, was upon me as I moved my few things into the apartment. Tucson was warm, but I was cold, my aloneness palpable. Glacial detritus, my life. I wanted Josh. All the kids. Sabrina.

Friday night I huddled in my new apartment.

Saturday evening I threw down the book I hadn't succeeded in reading and steamed in the shower for a while. Too early for pjs, so I donned clean jeans and pink tee shirt, and walked out the door. Turned back to get my flute. What the heck. It was a little flute. Portable.

I found crowds of people out on this Martin Luther King weekend. Mostly kids, though.

On my third stop, at Cassandra's, I nearly turned and walked out again, but I decided to be polite and have one drink. The din was awful. The band consisted of five *loud* guys, three on electric guitars, one on drums, and one getting unimaginable noise out of a keyboard. All five screamed into mikes.

Who would think that the band would take a break right then, when I was barely halfway into my drink? Or that their table was right behind mine? Or that the drummer would look at me and do a double-take: "Hey! Weren't you playing flute at the coffeehouse on Wednesday?"

I nodded.

"Ryan Palmer." He shook my hand. "I liked what you were doing, fitting right into anybody's tune. I thought flutists always needed sheet music and practice."

"Well, thanks. I sure was having fun." Wish he didn't shout about it. Probably deaf from all their noise.

"Comeon over here. I want the band to meet you." He pulled out my chair and took my arm like a classical gentleman might. Classical gentleman with backwards cap and wild long hair. "Guys, I want you to meet Kate. It is Kate, right?"

I nodded. The other four appeared puzzled. Why would they want to meet this gray headed gramma? I shared their bemusement.

"Kate kicks ass on flute. She was at Beanos the other night. Great improv. Kate, meet Ray over in the corner with his sweetie, Lauren. That's Andrew, lead singer. Charlie plays keyboard. And Mac plays bass."

Oh. One of the noisy guitars is actually bass. Gotta quit thinking a bass is a big thing that sits on the floor. I nodded at them. "Pleased to meet you. You fellows really put out the sound."

"I imagine we'd be a little hard to improvise around." Andrew's smile was an attempt to be polite, but I felt older than dirt.

I wasn't dead yet. "Oh, I'm sure I could manage." Why did I say *that*?

Ryan's voice rose over my thought. "So give it a try. You have your flute here, Kate. I saw its case on your table. Whadaya say, guys?"

I started backing away. "No, no. No. Nah. You have a coordinated thing going here. I'll get in your way." And you'll all drown me out anyway.

"Comeon, Kate." Andrew's smile felt smirky. "Give it a shot. One tune. What's to lose?"

Gawd. He was so young, so innocently patronizing. That tone doomed me, along with the three Black Russians I'd consumed over the last couple of hours. What the hell. I'd brought my flute because I wanted to play. And noisy didn't make it not music.

"Okay, Andrew. We'll try one number. Just put me on a stool at the back, so nobody expects something special from me."

Then it happened again: no way we were going to stop at one. "Just like potato chips," Mac said.

Wow. It was fun. Five students from U of A in torn jeans, grungy shirts and long hair. All jumping and dancing, gyrating and falling to their knees except for Ryan, whose drums more-or-less held him down. With one gray-haired gramma, neatly dressed, sitting quietly on a stool playing flute. For some reason it worked. A flute riff in a pause, a long low fifth—or maybe a minor seventh—beneath the noise, interesting back-and-forth with Mac on bass.

"They liked you, Kate," Ryan told me.

The place was closing down. After 2 am, I realized.

"We divided the cup six ways instead of five," he said, "and still came out ahead."

I must have been okay. I got over fifty dollars.

"Well heckandgolly," I said. "The three-day weekend, I suppose."

Then the manager came up, handed everybody two fifty-dollar bills, didn't hesitate when he got to me.

"Dam-Sam."

"See?" Ryan grinned. "Nobody clings to his cash like Cass…."

"Cash Cass," Andrew said.

"… but even he knows you're keeping 'em here. They keep buying drinks, and I betcha he comes out ahead even after cutting you in." Ryan was so proud, you'd think he'd invented me himself.

I kept playing with *The Ruffians*. Tips kept coming and Cass began handing us each *three* fifties. Isa waned.

I briefly collaborated with another group, *Classique,* a lot like Andrea's Oregon group: violin, cello, bass and piano. The kind of bass that sits on the floor. I met them through Sam, the professor at Beanos, *Classique's* pianist. They were good, but they took themselves awfully seriously. And they performed before big audiences in the UA auditorium.

They invited me to perform with them, but I begged off. Too much attention for a fugitive. A lot of people saw me at

Cassandra's but they were busy flirting and drinking, not paying all that much attention to the flutist at the back of the dimly lit stage.

"I'm flattered," I told *Classique,* "but I'm not going to be in town long." I managed to not run to the exit.

Being Kate

The steps to the coed's apartment were by my door, so I had seen her several times, though never with tears dripping off her chin. As usual, she wore a white U of A sweatshirt, desert boots and olive-drab shorts, which hung on her bony hips, her fleshless knees on display. What with all the salt water pouring down her cheeks, I couldn't tell whether she had her usual scrubbed look, but the pony tail was in place. If you call that much stray hair *in place*. Her book bag threatened to overwhelm her as it hung from shoulders that belonged in a "before" photo of a body building ad.

Maybe, if I hadn't spent a lifetime with kids, I could have ignored the futile wipe of arm across sopping face and the three part snuffle: phnnnh, hhha, huh.

"Only thing I know causes that much distress," I said, "is a handsome devil."

"Phnnhh, hhha, huh. Phnnh, hhha, huh."

"Better come on in to my place." I had my key in the lock. "Probably easier to tell this story to someone you don't know. We can go sit on the patio."

"Phnnhh, hhha, huh. Phnnh, hhha, huh."

"You keep shaking your head like that, you're going to splatter water all over the walls just like my old black lab used to do."

That won me a rueful smile. "No. I can't hhha hha bother

you. You hha don't even know me. Hhha. I need to go pull hhha myself together."

"Now listen. I'm older than you. Could you guess it?"

She gave me another small smile.

"And I've learned, in my venerable years, that things always sound ten times worse when you're talking to yourself. Come on in. I'll get some ice water."

So she came in.

"Dump that backpack here on this chair." I had a green canvas camp chair by the door for drop-or-grab items. "Every time I see you I wonder whether gravity will win and you'll end up on your back kicking your legs like an upended potato bug."

"It *is* pretty heavy." I had startled the sobs right out of her.

"Coffee or ice water?"

"Water, please."

"Coffee for me." I turned on the pot. "Do me a favor. Take a couple of bowls, these Grapenuts, and bananas out to the patio. I'm starving." I had just returned from the gym for breakfast, and my rumbling stomach had no sympathy for tears.

While she was out, I put a wet hand towel in the freezer and poured a carafe of ice water with lemon. When she came back, I handed her the water, milk and a box of Kleenex. "You can take this out, too. Give me a minute until the coffee perks. Gotta have my morning fix."

When I joined her with my coffee, she had found a spot in the jumble: tables and chairs, poker chips and plastic cups left over from yesterday's study sessions. I handed her the chilled towel. "Here's an eye cooler. As opposed to wine cooler."

"Ah. That's nice. My face feels like someone poured hot wax on it."

"My family eats when they're blue." I handed her the cereal. "Also when they're happy, or bored, or anxious. Of course we all weigh six hundred pounds. But I can't see where a bowl of Grapenuts would do you any harm."

To my surprise, she meekly poured a substantial bowlful, slicing banana over it, adding milk and digging in. Gives her time to regroup, I thought.

She gave me a slanted, guilty look. "I shouldn't be imposing on you like this. I always see you heading out midmorning, for a ten o'clock class, I imagine."

"It's okay. Today is Friday. My computer class meets at ten on Mondays and Wednesdays. I keep in the habit and go to the lab at the same time the other days. Tuesdays and Thursdays I do homework. I just use Fridays for personal projects. I'm Kate, by the way."

"Tara. Tara the Stupid."

"Stupid? With that backpack full of books? Although, come to think of it, it *is* kind of dumb to carry so much stuff all the time." I smiled at her

"It's smart, actually. I always have supplies handy and I'm getting in my weight training." Tara managed a smile in return.

"Yeah, okay. I'm paying out both time and money for my exercise." Weight training, my arse. You can't weight train and be that skinny.

We munched our Grapenuts.

I asked. "So who's this handsome devil?"

She described Bob as a combination of Adonis, Einstein, and Joe Montana. If it was the guy I had seen headed down her stairs, he was more Jeremy of *Zits* cartoon. Skinny, slumped, rumpled, uninspired.

"And," she finished, "he doesn't call or come by or return my calls. He's avoiding me; he's never in the coffee shop or library where we used to meet."

"You dated him a long time?"

She shrugged. "*Dated* might be the wrong word. One movie. But we hung out together constantly since we met in September. We talked. Studied. Laughed."

""… he spent the night," I added.

She reddened. "A few times. Then he just disappeared. I feel so dumb."

"Your first major love interest?"

She nodded again, looking down at her empty bowl.

I passed her more Grapenuts. "Well, I know of a woman who wanted a powerful, charismatic man. She was careful *not* to sleep with him because she had observed him flitting from one affair to another. She got him; he married her. And then he beheaded her."

Her head jerked up and so did her eyebrows.

"Ann Boleyn and Henry VIII. I guess I'm saying, 'cheer up; it could be worse.'"

I can't spell her next comment. She sounded like a horse who'd spotted a coyote.

I tried again. "So, Tara, you were in love. He was in lust."

She bit her lip. "I'm still in love. What am I going to do?

How can I at least talk to him?"

"What would you do if you weren't that interested in someone who clearly was getting stuck on you?"

Her mouth did that tighten-down curl that precedes major grief. "Is that what happened?"

I jumped in fast. "What's your major, Tara?"

"Microbiology." The lip uncurled a bit with her puzzlement at my shift of topic.

"Then I know you can do this math problem." I posed a situation ending with: "Suppose you meet five men. What's the probability that at least one connection results in a promising relationship?"

"Ohmygosh. Binomial probability theorem, isn't it?"

"Yep. One method, anyway. Hang on. I'll get some paper and a calculator." Wonderful math. Disconnects emotions every time.

So we worked it out. There was better than a 67% chance that at least one of the five held promise, compared to only 20% if you just meet one person.

"So I'd say that you just haven't met enough men. Now tell me this. If 80% of those tentative matches fail, how does one side let the other know?"

"I guess you tell them outright, 'I'm just not that interested.' Or you say no to dates, avoid meeting … Oh."

"It takes a lot of nerve to tell someone you're not interested. Honest but hurtful."

"Well, you sure shouldn't sleep with them," she huffed.

For a while Tara contemplated her ice water and I my

coffee. She was still visualizing her Adonis, I supposed. A baby breeze put a chill in the blue, cool day and stirred us from our inertia.

"It's time for me to go, but thank you so much, Kate. You were right; it would have seemed even worse if I'd been alone."

"What are you doing this evening, Tara? How do you feel about getting outandabout a bit? Maybe moving toward that 67% chance?"

"Oh. I just want to hole up."

"I play flute, just joined up with a totally obnoxious group. I don't see how you could mope in all that din. And you could practice bacchanalia."

"What?"

"Debauchery. Partying. Or at least Looking At The Opposite Sex."

"Yeah, right. With my puffed up eyes. "

In the end, I talked her into it.

We spent the afternoon on an upgrade. Tara 2.0. A lovely long-sleeved powder blue, scooped neck, knit top from Goodwill and a flared black skirt with a tendency to cling to her legs. Her black sandals polished up nicely. Wresting control of her flyaway hair was tough, but with mousse and some combs, we managed it. Her scraggly ponytail with loose hair everywhere converted to a smooth bun and a couple of curled tendrils. We darkened her eyebrows, emphasized her lovely blue eyes with mascara on the long lashes, and put a touch of color on her cheeks. Emaciated student metamorphosed into elegant ballerina.

Turned out she had studied ballet for eight years. She moved with lithe, natural grace, the black skirt fluid about her legs. At Cassandra's every time she strode to the restroom or went to the bar for more ginger ale, another male gravitated to her corner. Some were attached to other friends, male and female, but Tara nearly got herself up to that 67% in one evening. Her shyness didn't matter: the band made too much noise for conversation, anyway.

She sought me out at the break. "Don't worry about getting me home. Some of us are going to make the rounds."

"Is there a designated driver?" I sounded like a mother hen. Felt like one, too.

"We're walking."

"But you do have cab money?"

"Kate, I'm 21 years old. I left my mom in Flagstaff."

"I'm sorry, Tara. I just feel responsible. I brought you here, and you haven't become a Woman of the World quite yet."

"I know. Thanks. I'll take care."

"That's all I ask. Have fun. Turn your porch light off when you get home, and I'll do the same. Call me if you get into any sticky situations."

She was off. Confidence, not cosmetics, defined her makeover. Maybe my wunjo rune blessed her moment, because I saw her spirit blossom. My own spirit warmed too.

I never revealed the irony, that I'd developed make-up expertise sixty years into my life as a female. Camp Little Brook Beauty School.

Educating Kate

Tara came by the next afternoon, back to olive shorts and emaciated appearance. In the face of approaching clouds, she helped me clear the patio.

"What are you doing with poker chips" she wondered. "Looks like Texas hold ‘em out here, not math tutoring."

"It’s a technique I have for solving linear equations. Blue and red poker chips for positive and negative numbers, blue and red plastic cups for variables." Becca and her friends hadn’t even realized they were solving equations. They’d be amazed when they saw the connection.

"Maybe I could come by and watch sometime. I can’t imagine how that works."

"Yeah. I’d enjoy that. You might help the kids, too, once you see what I’m doing."

How could I plump out those bones? Not with my carrot sticks and yogurt. I remembered biscuit mix. "I’m making us a cake, Tara, a campfire recipe. So if it doesn’t come out right, we’ll build a fire on the patio and try again, OK?"

"Whadda you doing? Trying to fatten me up?"

"Yep. I can’t get that potato bug image out of my mind. You undone by your own backpack."

"Pthhhb."

"Are you sure you shouldn’t major in zoology? You keep

reminding me of a critter. A horse just now. A black lab yesterday. A potato bug all the time."

"Boy, if I need my ego built up, I'll just be sure to come here."

I looked at her seriously. "How are you doing?" Isa, the glacier, moves slowly. "Distress like yours yesterday doesn't simply vanish."

"I woke up sad again, but I won't drown myself in the toilet or anything."

"Moving up to bathtub drowning?"

She sighed, leaning her skinny hips against the counter. "No, I'm okay. I just had pinned too many hopes on Bob."

"Who is actually pretty hopeless, I suspect. How was the group you met last night?"

"I had fun with them. Doug is a good dancer. We kind of monopolized the floor at Johnny Jumps."

"Did you end up with just him?"

"No. It was the six of us, but the other four got too drunk, and that's mostly what drove Doug and me to the dance floor. Which was a good thing, I guess, because he was enjoying himself as much as I was by then."

"Is it a surprise that Doug was having a good time?" I put the cake in the oven and started rinsing dishes. Rain ticked briefly against the window.

"Turns out that he just got dumped by a girl he'd dated since October. The group took him out to try to cheer him up."

"So, two dumpees melting the dance floor at Johnny Jumps."

"He ended up being the cheer-er. I was the cheer-ee."

"I bet he had a good time, too. You looked lovely last night, and you move with wonderful grace. Very unpotatobug."

"My Tucson Mama," she smiled.

The cake came out fine. Milk for her, coffee for me. "Tomorrow do you want to go cross-country skiing with me?"

"Nah, Kate. I skied at home, Flagstaff," she said, "but I don't think you'll find snow between there and, I dunno, Chile?"

"The Santa Catalina Mountains, just an hour away. I signed up with an outdoor club. I'm picking up rental skis this afternoon."

She went, she skied, she chattered. The girl's off-button was as ineffectual as her on-button had been at first. Good-company chatter, though: her parents, her enthusiasm for biology, her love of ballet until it gobbled up her time. She drew me out, too. I told her my fabricated family story. She wanted to see pictures. Oh-oh. "I'll do the rest of my unpacking tomorrow and show them to you next week." I'd find pictures on the web, go buy a photo frame.

I told Tara about beautiful mathematics, its lovely patterns reflecting life's patterns. "People never admit they can't read, so why is it okay if they can't do math? Both math and reading can be learned, both enrich life, and the lack of either puts you at major disadvantage."

"I guessed you were a mathnut." She said it like *Grapenut.* "How many people would give you a probability problem when you're dying of a broken heart?"

I started to tell her about flute playing, too, but I couldn't talk. At that point we were headed uphill on skis, at 8100 feet elevation. I began gasping after about three steps. Then the snow stuck to my skis. I didn't fall this trip. Good thing. I'd have lain there until the snow melted. My lungs whistled for more oxygen. The skis weighed a million pounds. I was carrying all the snow on the mountain. But not far.

Someone in the group saved me, with wax for sticky wet stuff. I considered fainting at his feet, but he clearly already wondered what such an ancient specimen was doing out on skis.

Half an hour later I still wasn't talking much, but I began to enjoy our setting. We had started the morning in arid cactus country, and now we were in snow dotted with the green of pine and juniper. I would have tried harder to memorize the scene if I had known that in a year the entire mountaintop would burn up, including much of the town of Summerhaven, with its log chalets and tree-lined walkways.

On the way down the hill, I did explain about the flute. "I've had a couple of rough patches. One when my husband died." Close enough to truth. "More recently, my grandkids got involved in school and their Mormon church activities." Close enough again. "I felt extraneous, like the seventy-seventh trombone, until I started working on flute improvisations."

We set a pattern that weekend, clubbing on Friday nights and doing something physical on Sundays. Talking about everything. Almost. We explored the desert museum, local artist colonies, and a winery. But I soon longed for a bit of Little

Brook life, and Tara shared the longing if not the fugitive experience. So we sought the smell of wood smoke, the brilliance of light, the depth of night, the tiny intensity of stars found far from the crowds. Cold and damp, ala Little Brook, I'm happily deprived of, but before Little Brook I'd forgotten the immediacy of Mother Earth, her zen influence, *carpe diem*, that exists rarely behind the barricades of civilization. Behind the barricades of my anger.

* * * *

Tara came by my place as usual on a Friday to go to Cassandra's. "Hurrah, Friday night finally arrived," she said as she walked in.

"Yeah," I said.

"I'm all packed for tomorrow. Hiking boots, shorts, sleeping bag. Thought we might take eggs and bacon for breakfast, so I stopped by the store."

"Yeah?" I said.

"And I have maps. And I printed off some interesting stuff about the Apaches from the internet. I can read to you as you drive."

"Yeah," I said.

"Well, geez, Kate. Such enthusiasm! What's wrong?"

Oh-oh. Nothing I could tell her. Dead end after dead end in the computer lab. Trying to find an offshore bank where Andrea could send her monthly retirement checks. Where Kate could get them, unseen. I felt really really *really* cranky because this was the umpteenth futile Friday online. *Offshore banks*, no problem. Trustworthy offshore banks, another story. They all wanted money, all promised secrecy and security, all seemed likely to take my money and run.

"I'm sorry," I told Tara. "I had a frustrating day in the computer lab trying to work out the term project for class."

"Oh? What are you thinking of doing?"

"Some sort of website for tutoring." I was also working on a site featuring complaints about temples. Couldn't talk about that either. Tutoring, the default discussion. "I need to use as many bells and whistles from class as I can."

"Well, Kate, hmmm. Maybe a top ten thing? Ten reasons to love math? Ten reasons for getting help?"

Bless her, she wanted to help. And she succeeded in cheering me up as we headed out for Cassandra's, getting me thinking about the class project, though conversation quickly shifted to Ryan the drummer.

A cute couple, Ryan and Tara. Jeremy-of-Zits and Doug the Dancer had faded away. Ryan beamed when Tara came in to sit at a front table, her head bobbing to his beat. Tara had drawn the rune *Mannaz* last weekend, *Mannaz* representing Self and rectification, tilling one's field to prepare for planting. I could see the tilling in her calm appreciation of Ryan.

On Saturday our drive south to camp in the Chiricahua Mountains passed in a flash as Tara read her research on Cochise:

Lieutenant Bascom, just out of West Point, had wanted to rescue a white boy kidnapped by Apaches. Cochise was a friendly woodcutter for Apache Station, but Bascom saw only that he was Apache. Invited to meet with Bascom, Cochise brought his wife and friends. Bascom seized them all and imprisoned them, because he didn't understand the independence of various Apache groups, so didn't believe Cochise when he said he know nothing about the kidnapping.

Cochise escaped, but he was wounded and very angry. He took white hostages and offered an exchange for his still-captive group. Bascom refused. Eventually Cochise's wife and children were released, but things escalated, Apaches were killed, whites were killed. The captured white boy grew to adulthood as a member of the Coyotero Apaches who had seized him. Cochise and his band stayed angry and attacked from their mountain fortresses. Of the thirty-thousand white settlers in the territory, twenty thousand died or fled. All because Bascom misunderstood and distrusted a friendly woodcutter. Because Bascom was ignorant of Apache culture.

I'd felt hostage to a small version of this cultural deafness, the Mormon church my Lieutenant Bascom, unable to understand my truth.

Tara had parallel thoughts, I learned that night, but in naked daylight, we discussed other, less personal parallels. "I can almost blink and see Cochise's warriors splitting up and vanishing in these rocks and ravines," she commented

. "This place and its history," I said, "makes Afghanistan easier to understand."

"The mountain hideaways?"

"Yes. And wild and independent warlords. And failure to understand a culture."

In our tent that night Tara pulled on a sweatshirt in the high chill darkness. "Afghanistan, Arizona, scary resemblance. The same mistakes. The failure to listen, to hear truth. Sort of what happened with my brother."

"I didn't know you have a brother, Tara."

"We haven't talked for four years."

"Do you never see him? Or just hate him?"

"We were always so close. He was my handsome big brother, always sticking up for me. He carried me all the way home once when I sprained my ankle, half a mile at least. I weighed over a hundred pounds by then."

"So what happened?"

"A misunderstanding. Like Bascom and Cochise."

"So did your brother take hostages? Or did you?"

"I guess I did. I was the Bascom, not believing Curt."

"Tara. You can't leave me hanging like this."

"Oh, Kate. It's so hard to talk about. It was all because of this girl, Sherry Johnson, in my health class. She asks me to have Curt set her up with a guy his age that Sherry has a crush on. Sherry is really popular, so I want to help. I talk to Curt, and he says he doesn't even know the guy. So I go back and tell Sherry that, and she gets really mad."

"Why?"

"She didn't believe me. She was yelling at me. I wanted her to like me. Maybe I could be popular like her."

"So what did you do?"

"I went back to Curt, but he was adamant. 'I don't know the guy, Tara,' he said. 'I can't march up to him out of the blue and suggest he ask out some girl I don't know either.'"

"The guy was just one of what, 500? in Curt's class?"

"Yeah, but I couldn't see it. So I think Curt is 'a selfish son of a bitch,' like Sherry says. I say the same terrible stuff to him that Sherry said. Curt and I don't talk like that, so it's really hurtful. 'I thought we cared about each other better than that,' he said."

"So you lost twice. No new popular girlfriend. And no trusty brother friend."

"It's the brother friend that's the big loss. All because I didn't listen to Curt. I love him so much. He has always treated me like Sir Raleigh treated Queen Elizabeth."

Well, I was listening. Amidst tears flooding my face, amidst my own heartache. I don't cry. Despite moonlight filtering through junipers and relieving the blackness of the tent, we lay in shadows, so Tara didn't see me wiping my eyes.

Outside the high desert hummed. Crickets, I thought. Frogs off in the distance, maybe down by the creek. Squeaks, soft gurglings, unfamiliar sounds to a rainforest dweller. Then some yips up on the bluff. Foxes, maybe.

I kept breathing, no sobs. Managed, "He'll forgive you, Tara. But you have to ask."

Disconnected. We humans can get so bloody disconnected.

High Finance

It wasn't all loss. Music, Tara's blossoming, Becca's growing fondness for algebra.

I mostly managed to not think about Sabrina, Josh, all the kids. I had packed and unpacked their picture without looking at it. Ever. Not the faces, the eyes, the smiles. Grandma's bird pin lay wrapped in its tissue far from view. Kate's fake family, images from the internet, occupied the empty space on my dresser.

There should have been pictures on my dresser of the new family I was acquiring without realizing it. Tara. Becca. The band and the jammers.

Obsession with finance filled my every free moment. My tutoring and fluting income met basic needs: food, rent, utilities. If I had car troubles, though, or health troubles, or if Oregon Janet needed more assistance, or music and tutor patrons left—as they would during vacations—Andrea would have to go ATMing again. A wealth of retirement income was accumulating in her bank account. Like Russian roulette, though. Too close, Low Voice at that St. Louis bank.

Friday after Friday I traced web threads linked to offshore banking. Different countries had different regulations. Or no regulation. Was that web site more than sticky fabrications? Had I found a real business establishment? Or con artists? Who could I ask? I felt like a fly hanging in the internet web. After each search I left the computer lab in despair or rage or frustration.

I worried, too, about my basic Andrea Glass account. The Feds were looking for me: they might freeze my funds. I had to hope this was just two a.m. nerves. Nothing illegal about retirement income after all, and Andrea Glass had been convicted of no crime. I'd sleep better, though, if I could silently siphon that money to Kate McGuire.

On Monday of President's Day in February, alone in PCC's computer lab, I found Micheloud & Cie, internet brokers. For a fee they would connect me to a bank then drop out of the picture, just as a realtor would after helping me find a home/bank. Micheloud & Cie's site suggested either traveling to the bank or doing transactions on the internet. I felt reassured by the implication of a real brick and mortar edifice somewhere.

By early March I was beginning to see my way. Andrea Glass would transfer funds from her US account to her Swiss one, then to Janet Martin's Swiss account, an invisible move because, unless it's criminal activity, Swiss law prohibits disclosure of banking transactions. Finally Kate would access Janet's account with no visible link to Andrea. I hoped. I thought of setting up a Swiss account for Kate, too, but Swiss accounts require a passport and the other Katherine might already have one.

I thought I'd gotten over the mountain, but like the bear in the song, I saw another mountain. International law, protecting against criminal activity, required me to document the source of Andrea's funds. Geez Louise.

How could Andrea contact Bruce, her trustee, to get bank statements showing automatic deposits of retirement income?

The web again provided an answer: a mail-drop, a service in Copenhagen that removed my outer envelope, so Bruce got mail from Andrea postmarked Denmark. He mailed the statements back to Andrea Glass in Copenhagen and this "open-minded, private service" forwarded it to Kate in Tucson. Tah-dah.

Then another mountain: Janet needed a passport to open her Swiss account. Her application required information about her husband.

Talk to her in person, I decided. Get it straight.

I flew to Oregon during spring break.

Airplanes terrify fugitives.

Getting off the plane scared me most. My nightmare starring Low Voice became more of a daymare: visions of federal marshals waiting as I walk up the ramp from plane to airport. No place to run. Or hide. Only one route off a plane, single file. I tend to get claustrophobic even in easier situations.

As the plane descended for a stopover in Sacramento, my seat mate noticed my tension.

"Haven't done much flying?"

"I just can't get used to falling out of the sky." Glib, my untruths these days.

She responded with the usual stuff about air resistance and

air flow over the top of the wings and the gentle bump on landing. I gritted my teeth and hung on like any nervous flier. We landed, taxied, and still I gritted my teeth. *Say something*, I thought. "Sorry. Takes me a while to quit thinking I'm gonna die. I just want out of this flying casket."

I joined the can't-wait crowd pushing off the plane. Demons nipped at my heels as I sped up the ramp, joining a family of four and emerging with them at the top.

No cool-eyed, trench coated Feds awaited. No Low Voice. No Matt Sheridan.

I used the forty minute stopover to dash to a print shop with internet. In five minutes I printed my e-mails, paid, and hopped back in the cab. I ran to my gate and down the ramp just before they closed it.

* * * *

From: Sabrina Severson <theseversons@aok.com>
Date: Mon., Jan 7, 2002 10:24:06 AM US/Pacific
To: Andrea Glass <andrea_glass@marioncollege.edu>
Subject: Understanding

Well, Mom, I have to admit I'm getting a little pissed. You're right. I do have a difficult parent. The kids don't understand why you're not in their lives. I don't understand why you're not in their lives. I don't understand why you're so hostile to the LDS church. I wish you'd clear things up with the FBI.

|

When Matt comes back, I'll give him your email address. Until you surfaced last month, I didn't know you were using it, or if you could.

|

You said you'd be away from email for a while, so I suppose that means you've evaporated from our lives again, but not from our hearts, Mom. Cut it out, will ya?
Love,
Sabrina

From: Sabrina Severson <theseversons@aok.com>
Date: Thur, Jan 10, 2002 10:24:06 AM US/Pacific
To: Andrea Glass <andrea_glass@marioncollege.edu>
Subject: Understanding

Mom, I forwarded your last email to Matt. It explained a lot, but you'll still probably hear from him. His phone number is 1-800-555-1010 ext 50314. He asked me to ask you to call.
|
Yes, you might have heard of him. He played basketball for BYU for three years. He was the starting forward and lead point maker. Why?
Love,
Sabrina

* * * *

Aha! I'd found Low Voice when I googled Matt Sheridan .

* * * *

From: Matthew Sheridan <m_sheridan@fbi.us.gov>
Date: Fri., Jan 11, 2002 8:32:02 AM US/Pacific
To: Andrea Glass <andrea_glass@marioncollege.edu>
Subject: questions

Dear Ms. Glass:
Your daughter, Sabrina Severson, provided me with this e-mail address. I've been looking for you because we have some questions regarding the bombings of LDS temples. We have cause to believe you might know something about them. Could you please report to a local FBI office, or to any police or sheriff office? You also could call 1-800-555-1010 ext 50314 to arrange an interview.

Thank you for your cooperation.
Sincerely,
Matthew K. Sheridan, Agent
Federal Bureau of Investigation
401 Capitol Mall
Washington, DC 00103

* * * *

From: Janet Martin <jmmonsta@yahoo.com>
Date: Thur, Feb. 14, 2002 3:54:44 PM US/Pacific
To: Jane Doe <mountainwoman@yahoo.com>
Subject: Hiya

Just thought Id let you know Im doing OK. Thought of you today on Valentines Day, here we are two wemen, same name both hiding out from our husbands. Im doing good apartment is fine even staying sobber. Told nobody about our deal.
Janet

Revisiting Janet

Another bout of terror awaited in the skies above Portland. The effects of panic have shortened my life by at least a decade.

Fear is not rational, so rational arguments don't overcome it. I knew that Janet Martin's name should not be suspect. I knew that the FBI had plenty of terrorist concerns to keep it busy. No one was photographing my eyes to match them against Andrea Glass. There was absolutely no reason to think Low Voice might have been alerted to my flight.

Terror returned, nonetheless, as we began our descent. Claustrophobic terror, worse than that night in Kathy McGuire's closet. Another gauntlet-ramp awaited. When the fasten-seat-belts sign went on, I thought about the Law of Sines. Proof begins … how? Unit circle? Draw a generic triangle? And an altitude. Then what? What next?

Fields and river and freeway rushed by below us. Runway, the plane touching, our bodies thrusting forward. Taxiing forever, waiting in the hot, airless plane forever. Walking with a crowd, the group moving fast, too fast, toward my doom.

But again I was safe. Breathing like a woman who had just taken off her girdle, I, Janet, picked up a rental car and headed to Salem. Once my adrenaline mists cleared, I noticed the Oregon mist, the lovely silver day. At just before noon here, the temperature was 55, the air cool and moist. When I left

Phoenix, the early morning was already hot and dry and likely to get into the 80s for the third day in a row. Weather that had been a misery for Andrea as she tried to stay warm in the wilderness was hard to beat for normal living. I feared discovery here, but surely I could return to the northwest. Somewhere.

* * * *

Oregon Janet wasn't at her apartment. I left a note, hoped she hadn't fallen off the wagon since her e-mail, and went to the far end of town to open a Janet Martin post office box, an address for my Janet-passport.

I, Janet, found a room at a Best Western off Mission Street with a Denny's next door. Andy had once loved Denny's.

At least their coffee was okay.

For Andy's Swiss account—and later for Janet's—since I couldn't identify myself in person there at the Swiss bank, I needed a document called an *apostille*, which certifies that I match my passport. Back in my room, I called notaries at four local banks before finding someone who understood about apostilles. Of course, I had to appear as Andy, with Andrea's passport, to get it. So I donned the old persona again.

More fear. Space closed in. My heart did calisthenics. Again. As I hurried out of the bank, precious gold seal in hand, I checked my watch. Checked again. It must have stopped. Surely I had been in there hours, not minutes.

After finding a quiet street to revert to Janet, I added Andrea's apostille to a big manilla envelope containing the records Bruce had provided via Copenhagen and mailed everything off to Switzerland. That should take care of Andy's offshore account. Janet's to go, one more mountain. Her passport first.

Oregon Janet was home. "Hey, Janet!" she said.

"Hey, Janet, yourself. You are looking really good. Staying on the wagon. That's fantastic."

"Saw your note on the door. You need more information. Comeon in. Hope I've got it."

"I'd buy you dinner if you could dredge up some husband memories." I had decided not to tell her about the passport; she had worried enough about a driver's license.

"Oh, ugh. That might cost you. Steak and lobster, maybe."

"Janet, you've been so great. You're worth steak and lobster *and* an extension on your apartment. With your information I could get cash for that."

"Well. So far none of it has bit me, but I sure wonder sometimes." She pulled out a chair at the little table we'd bought, poured me a cup of coffee. "Are you serious about dinner?"

"Yep. You name the place."

"Okay, let me change my clothes. You're lookin' nice, silky blue shirt and spiffy slacks. I'll just be a minute."

She emerged looking spiffy herself in a pink cotton sweater and soft sage skirt with pink flowing through like spring in Paris. We went to Red Lobster, but when Janet saw the lobsters swimming around in the tank by the entrance, she didn't want anything to do with eating one of them. Turned out she'd never had steak and lobster. It was just her idea of a "high fallutin' meal." Looking spiffy, pleasant ambience, steak and crab … she was almost dancing, to some private tune. No wine; she'd been sober for three months.

"How did you hold off the thirst?"

"I dunno exactly. I like living this way, and I can manage it, I think, if I stay away from the booze. I handed my January social security check over to the manager to pay another month's rent and used the leftover for grocery shopping. Stayed away from the beer aisle. Have to concentrate even when I go for milk, to stay away from the beer aisle."

"Well, that's really impressive."

"Then the next month I bought some clothes, had my hair done. Lots better than going on a toot, but now I've got some change settin' in my drawer, and I think about it a lot."

"One day at a time, they say. Why don't you open up a savings account, someplace that's a little hard to get to?"

"I didn't know if I could get a bank account, what with you havin' my license."

She didn't want to take my word that there wouldn't be trouble, so I agreed to drive her to a bank the next morning.

"You come, we'll be in trouble together, at least," she said.

Mostly I steered dinner conversation away from me, but I did share that I was living out of state and that I entertained myself by playing the flute.

"Wish I had sumpin like that. I get kinda bored. I'd have an easier time stayin' outta trouble if I had a good hobby."

"Do you sew or quilt or crochet?"

"Nah. I get sick of projects, never get them finished."

"Or sing? Or draw? Or watch birds?"

"I usta draw a lot and paint. Mostly draw, though. I dunno what I'd draw now. The teacher always set up stuff for us and we'd pick a part of it to sketch."

"Just draw what you know."

"What do I know?"

Poverty. Hopelessness. "Can you draw people?"

"Yeah. It's just a matter of reworking the eyes until they set right. Getting proportions, just like drawing anything."

"Then why don't you draw despair? You have the feel of it from your days on the street."

"What?"

"Go down to the park. Draw guys sleeping on the bench. Or heads hanging while they wait for the Christians to come by with lunch. Or the kid on a skateboard behind the guy with a bottle."

She gazed into the distance. Perhaps she was looking into her past. "Women with dirty kids trying to find a place for the night."

"You could make sketches, just sitting back in the corner at the Mission or at the park. Then redo them at home in comfort." I really wanted Janet to 'stay outta trouble.' Partly because her trouble might turn into mine and partly because I liked her. I suggested that after we open the bank account, we go to the art store.

She nodded. "I'd like a small sketchpad and a big one. Some pencils, a sharpener and an eraser. I think I could afford that much."

"In the interest of our business partnership, I could afford that much. If you'll send me a sketch."

"I can't send you nothin'. You don't give me any address."

"It might be hard to mail anyway. Just save it for me. I'll be back."

Over dessert she gave me the information I needed for the passport application. She'd had no contact with her husband for years, but easily recalled their wedding date, his birthday, birthplace and mother's maiden name. She had never seen any point in divorcing the guy but wanted nothing to do with him. "He's probably still in jail," she said, "or in jail again. But if he isn't, no way he's comin' to mooch offa me."

* * * *

Before we met the next morning, I had "Janet's" passport photos taken and mailed the application. We found her new bank: she'd need a bus transfer and a walk to get there.

As I paid another month's rent, I got copies of electricity bills showing her name and address. That would establish her US residency when I set up her Swiss bank account. Janet carefully didn't ask questions.

In Portland I, Andy, sent e-mails then visited an ATM. I was doing okay financially, but I might as well get more of my money while I was in a place I'd soon be leaving.

More terror. Another safe landing. By 11:00 p.m. Mountain Standard Time, I was back in Phoenix, safely inside Kate McGuire's skin again. No more Andrea appearances. Ever. I hoped. Except for e-mails.

* * * *

From: Andrea Glass <andrea_glass@marioncollege.edu>
Date: Wed, Mar 20, 2002 4:20:40 PM US/Pacific
To: Matthew Sheridan <m_sheridan@fbi.us.gov>
Subject: questions

Mr. Sheridan, What would you like to know? Do I need an attorney?
Andrea Glass

From: Andrea Glass <andrea_glass@marioncollege.edu>
Date: Wed, Mar 20, 2002 4:25:25 PM US/Pacific
To: Sabrina Severson <theseversons@aok.com>
Subject: hello

Hello, dear Sabrina,

You sure have the right to be angry. My behavior is inexcusable, I know, but I can't seem to help it. Perhaps someday you can get past it and we'll be friends again. I'm just letting you know I'm okay, and I'm thinking of you and Mark and the kids.
Love,
Mom
|
ps Mr. Sheridan contacted me. I've emailed him back.

Red Rock Mysticism

When my plane from Portland landed in Phoenix, I detoured, away from Tucson. I was following the promise of the rune book, that detours are often opportunities. Before I'd left for Oregon I'd cast stones: *Wunjo* again, upright this time. Joy, light piercing the clouds. No surprise. I could feel the coming shift. Then *Raido*, a journey toward self-healing, self-change and completeness. Yep. I'd begun the psychic journey in fragrant mountain blackness, Tara there with me. All the questions. How do we get so divided? Did Cochise's band share our ache at being pushed away from what we treasure and whom we love? Do the Afghanis? The Mormons? Does Tara's brother? Sabrina? Of certain or uncertain faith, in different mountains, we're all under the same stars.

Raido was reversed, so my journey would be full of detours. Of course. Faith baffles me so. How can people believe things they have no way of knowing? Believe enough to take momentous action, like denying family a marriage celebration?

Belief, certainty, drew me to Sedona: certainty of red rock buttes, promises of enlightenment, rumors of vortexes. Near certainty of a gazillion gravel-brained people. I arrived at Oak Creek campground north of Sedona Thursday morning at three. Moonlight reflected from rocky cliffs, and a few stars glittered in the bits of sky visible between black trees. Enough light to find a soft spot and lay out my sleeping bag on a ground-cloth. I slept to the creek's muttering accompaniment. Sleeping bag in a sleeping bag. Har har.

When I awoke, I set up my tent, paid my camping fees, and headed to town. I wandered through shops until I found the Wisdom Canyon Tour Company. After signing on for a twenty-four hour trip starting the next morning—vortexes and sacred walks and a sweat lodge—I watched other people enlist. What brings them here, I wondered. What do they seek? What did Sabrina seek?

I saw people wearing soft shirts in watercolor tones, sandy suede laced boots, and pressed, belted, pocketed khaki hiking shorts. My scruffy jeans didn't match. I saw well-manicured hands, smelled subtle scents—sage and sandalwood—heard quiet voices like those at intermission of a ballet. I wondered if they, and my daughter and all the Lutherans and Baptists and Bahais and Unitarians, expected to solve the mysteries of life and death. Could they change watercolor hues to black and white?

After an hour I left; I'd inferred something of these wisdom-seekers' lives, nothing of their drives. Tomorrow. Tomorrow I'd observe and ponder.

Like its visitors, Sedona is enigma. Red boulders and mesas are strewn about as though a toddler giant had been playing with pattern blocks. I had the afternoon to wander over scenic roadways and hike along trails to surprising monoliths.

And up, over the Mogollon Rim, oh lordy. My body's fear-poisons, from bank transactions and airplane flights, tumbled away like rushing white water as I walked through the high heady aroma of cedar along the creek. Refreshed by winter rains, the forest mat sprang beneath my feet. Old trees, ancient rocks, frothing water. Serenity.

Good thing, because the following day would drain all my resources.

We set out from Sedona at nine Friday morning. No breakfast. "Better not to pollute this spiritual experience with lumps of food in your belly," they'd told us. Nine of us piled into an old GMC van, and conversation moved from introductions to how they didn't usually eat breakfast anyway. I listened—especially to stomach rumbles that seemed more honest than words—and I nodded a lot, trying to be a neutral presence.

We went up Oak Creek Canyon. The brochures say vortexes abound in Sedona, and Oak Creek Canyon is just a hotbed of these power spots that "bring our emotional and spiritual bodies in alignment with the heartbeat of the planet." The Jimmy went off-road near my campground, twisting and winding until I lost all sense of direction. When the rutted road gave way to a narrow trail, we got out of the car. Mules with packsaddles waited in corrals. I saw my sleeping bag carted off to be loaded on a big long-eared gray guy. There went my last hope for a snack, the power bars stashed too far into the bag to retrieve unobtrusively.

This place was red-rock oven, still set on early-morning preheat, but not to be confused with yesterday's cool balm. We walked up the trail a half mile or so, and sat in a circle beneath a towering red boulder where our guide, NanHeToh, gently unwrapped a burlap cloth, exposing a little pile of wheat sprigs. She handed a few stems to each of us.

"Sort carefully," she said, "for the most perfect, golden kernels. Select a dozen grains as your holy gift." As we sorted she taught us chants for blessing and peace. After we had folded our grains in a bit of muslin, NanHeToh sat cross legged, her skirt wrapped about her legs and talked about our souls reaching harmonic convergence with earth's vibrational frequency.

I watched my fellow travelers and smiled and nodded with them.

"… sevenfold aspects of the trinity," NanHeToh said.

Seven times trinity. Twenty-one. I thought about my discomfort there on the rocky, dusty, hard ground. Hot, sun beating on stone.

"… spiritual and mindal realities manifest themselves," NanHeToh said. "… seven chakras, …reiki. Medicine wheel. Urantian star-seed corps of destiny. Mayan Hunab Ku …"

I was getting so thirsty. Don't we get water up here?

"… activation of vortexes and lines. Crystal grid system, energy grid. Hexagram, pentagram, triads."

I nodded. Lines, pentagons, hexagons. Something close to my reality.

"Vortexes …"

Shouldn't it be *vortices*? Like *indices?* I nodded. Wisely, I hoped.

"… openings, perhaps, into another dimension..."

Well that's baloney. We don't need any openings to get up off the floor—two dimensions — and change a light bulb—third dimension. Maybe sticking our finger in the socket … not the energy grid she's talking about . . .

Then we walked, two miles at least, uphill, uphill, to a deep gorge that opened abruptly below us, gray rock giving way to pink and then red in the depths of the canyon.

A second guide, Chalexon, mystically appeared, wearing a blue tunic over buckskin-colored pants, and assured us we were experiencing one of the most powerful vortexes of the world, a place where "the breath of the earth blows away all dissonance." He pointed around us at low misshapen junipers. "The stronger the energy, the more the trees demonstrate an axial twist."

Twisted, all right. Were we getting twisted the same way? We cast our wheat into the winds of the canyon and chanted our newly learned ritual songs.

Undeniably I felt compelling vertigo, as if I might pitch right over the edge, following my grains of wheat into cool drafts along the creek far below. Vertigo was less spiritual phenomenon, I thought, than effect of the heat, the uphill trek here, the cool drafts of air, and an abrupt drop-off, all combined with thirst and vague hunger pangs. They had told us not to eat breakfast; they didn't feed us. Did they intend this dizziness?

Again we walked. We sweated. We walked some more. My calves burned. Salt ran in my eyes. We wound up a narrow, dusty red trail, over rocks, between boulders. I focused on the skyline, doggedly placing one foot after the other, dragging myself up, up to the top of the rise only to behold more red dirt uphill trail ahead. Bear over the mountain again. The sun rose past its zenith and began its descent into the west. I longed for descent for myself, but flat was the best I got. Boy, I'd *really* hate this tour in July. Chalexon disappeared but Wildwind made mystical appearances along our path. A duplicate of NanHeToh, in long straight hair, ankle-length full skirt, Indian beads, and moccasins, Wildwind came with an earthen jug of water. We knelt and held out our cupped hands, into which NanHeToh and Wildwind poured "cool, pure, spiritual fluid of life, water from a sacred spring." Each time I got a couple of little sips as half of the precious stuff ran out between my fingers. I wanted to weep at the loss. I licked at my palms. I was still so dry my lips stuck to my teeth.

Water from a sacred spring? Nuh-uh. Not up here. Lead us to it, ladies. I wonder where they've parked the truck with the bottled water. Chalexon is probably driving. What would they do if I followed Wildwind the Jug Lady, found her truck, and drank everything up?

But I had signed up for this trip to try to understand how people find enlightenment, find meaning in the maze we all wander through, find a way so right one can forsake family on her most important day.

I supposed the guides wouldn't let us perish of thirst. Think of the lawsuits.

At last we came to a low structure, built of branches and covered in blankets, at the edge of a creek. It was approximately round, waist high, smaller than my tent.

"The sweat lodge," Wildwind said. "Here we will build an enormous fire. Here we will heat stones, and when dark falls, we will go into the lodge and cleanse ourselves of the poisons of civilization. Here we will return to purity of spirit and become one with Mother Earth."

Here we at last can sink down into a shaded spot. Here we finally will drink all the water we want. Water from earthen jugs, not from the stream. "You have not sufficiently adapted to Life with Mother Earth," NanHeToh told us.

Yeah. If we got sick from creek water, more lawsuits. The guides did allow us to cool our faces and hands and feet in the stream. A reprieve between heat and heat. Laverne, a friend back in Andy's life, had described her sweat lodge experience. She knew she would die in there, she said. She didn't leave, though. And she didn't die.

I thought I'd last about five minutes. Heat and steam and nine of us in that little hut.

"The rocks are wise Grandfathers," Wildwind said. "For us they will glow red as they did in their formation, lava pouring down to us. We will let their wisdom suffuse through us along with their heat, for they have been long on the face of the earth, and they know its ways."

Trees are wise, but rocks? "Dumb as a rock, dumb as a rock," my mind chanted.

"... into the womb of Mother Earth ... the Grandfathers bring the presence of Father Sun ... fire and earth and water ... pull out thoughts and feelings that have been stagnating in us..."

An enormous stack of firewood lay alongside the sweat lodge. Our sleeping bags were piled behind the lodge, the jugs of wonderful water cooled in the creek, and the mules that had brought everything were tied on a high-line on the opposite bank. Brent, the fourth guide who brought the mules, had readied the site for us.

Brent? A guide named Brent? NanHeToh, Chalexon, Wildwind — and *Brent?* The only one of the four with black hair, mocha skin, and high cheekbones, and his name was Brent?

After dark, far beyond hunger, we changed into the shifts and sarongs they furnished us then filed past a blazing fire to crawl into the lodge after Chalexon. We moved clockwise around the interior to sit facing a central pit. This dark crowded space would normally roil up my claustrophobia, molten like those grandfathers in their original form. But for the moment, tired hungry lethargy prevailed.

Brent handed in the first glowing grandfather on a shovel. Chalexon picked it up with a pair of antlers and placed it in the fire pit. Three more stones were brought the same way, and then Brent closed the flap of the entrance. I saw, for a last brief moment, boots and legs and glimmers of the fire outside and then all that was left to see were glowing red rocks, reflecting on shiny faces around the pit.

Chalexon beat slowly on a hand-drum and led us in chants. Then a dipper, held in a disembodied hand, hovered over the pit, and all was gone but glimpses of red grandfathers through swirling whiteness more felt than seen. Four times I heard the hiss of water pouring on those hot rocks. Steam filled the lodge, pushed through the flimsy shift, forced itself on me, held its hot wet hand over my mouth and closed my nostrils.

Claustrophobia. Trapped. In airplanes. In Kathy McGuire's closet. Behind a downed tree. Under a raft. Out. Oh god let me out.

I didn't scream. I found that if I leaned my head down to the sod floor of the lodge, there was a chance I could keep breathing.

Forget people-watching. Faces obscured. Concentration gone. Thought obliterated. We sank into private interiors. Some muttered chants. Then silence.

Something … something about burning branches and bundles of sage on the hot rocks.

Whatever.

I remained silent. I didn't shriek: *Let me out of here. Open up that flap. I'm dying here.*

The flap did open eventually, letting in cool mountain night air. Sweet air. Precious air. I had lasted through the "round." Completing our circuit around the firepit, we crawled out the door one by one. I didn't claw my way over anyone.

Outside at last, I poured myself on the cool ground, breathing great deep gulps.

In no time I heard Chalexon say, "We've been separated from Mother Earth for twenty minutes. We'll stay out here another ten minutes before we go back for the second round."

Nuh-uh, I thought. Another ten years and I won't be going back in there. I'd avoided radiating my cynicism but now I was radiating heat like a Grandfather. I got up and walked toward the stream and coolness. Empathy be damned.

"No, no," Wildwind said. "You mustn't go in there until you emerge the last time from the womb of Mother Earth."

"I'm very sorry," I replied. "I am a weak child. I cannot return there." I turned toward the pool I had noticed that afternoon. Would the water start boiling as I waded in?

"No, wait. Don't immerse yourself. Not yet," Brent told me. "The contrast is too great. Too much of a shock." He led me to a rock where I could sit with my feet in the water.

I watched the rest of the group follow Chalexon back into the sweat lodge. How could they? Brent handed in four more rocks from the blazing fire and tied down the entrance flap. I felt like I had just watched mass suicide.

I splashed water on my face and neck. Quietly, quietly. If I'd heard cool water splashing when I was in that heat, I'd have run shrieking out.

Brent came over. "Go into the pool from the top end," he whispered. "Slowly. I'll bring you a towel."

Cooling off mutated to shaking cold. I waded out, rhythmic tremors shuddering through my body, and found my clothes. I returned, clean and dry at last, but seizures of cold still shook me. I was surprised to see people already stumbling, steamed and blanched, from the lodge again. Brent waved me away from the fire, pointing to the pile of sleeping bags.

He joined me a moment later with a little penlight. "We'll find yours and you can crawl in for a while." He was whispering, his light shielded from the group.

"They finished fast this time. The last round must be lots shorter than the first."

"Same amount of time as the first one, but time lengthens in there. The shamans think it's like putting time under a magnifying glass. Helps you see each little part of it."

"Will they be going in the water now?"

"No. There are two more rounds. I have to go back in a couple of minutes to help with the rocks and flap again."

I was speechless. *Two more rounds.*

"Here's your bag. You're Kate, right? I'd appreciate your rolling it out here. Less moving around is better for the other participants."

"You must think I'm a terrible wimp."

"You didn't see me going in there did you?"

"No. And your name is Brent. The only Native American in the crowd, not going in the lodge, WASP name, what's with that?"

"My wife is Norwegian and she doesn't like lutefisk. I'm Indian and I don't like sweats. It's legal." He stood. "I've got to go help again. It's rocky here but you can at least warm up."

I paid over two hundred dollars for this: exhaustion, thirst, hunger, fire, ice, and incoherent chants? I gazed at the stars, brilliant in the black sky, and listened to foxes yipping in the distance. I sent a silent message of simple goodwill and affection to Sly via those foxes.

My friend Laverne had said she resigned herself to life ending in that hot breathless lodge. Melodramatic, I'd thought. Now her fear seemed entirely sane. Do people die up here?

Does death bring meaning to life?

That power bar in the depths of my sleeping bag? Nothing ever tasted finer.

I awoke to find naked people all around me, drying off, getting into their own clothes. They, too, had taken "cleansing baths" in the stream.

Cleansing baths? What kind of baths aren't cleansing?

Shifts and sarongs lay in heaps by the edge of the water, white blotches in the moonlight, the wisdom-seekers evidently too parboiled or too frozen to care about nudity.

Brent, Wildwind and NanHeToh bustled around, picking up towels and sweat clothing, and setting up a "feast."

"Smoked salmon, berries, and plenty of pure water tonight," Wildwind announced. "You can warm by the fire, feast and share your thoughts."

I listened as the seekers talked about their ghosts: bad bosses, freeways, teenagers, obligations, no time, no time, no time.

"I thought about joining you each time I came out," Max, who sat beside me, confided. He was trying to comfort me for my wimpiness, I supposed. "Each time, I thought I could manage one more round and went back in. Then we were done. I felt completely drained—but like an engine drained of dirty oil. A good kind of drained."

"Well, kudos to you," I told him. "I really don't think I can venture that close to death ever again. All those mules over there wouldn't have been able to drag me back in."

We all retrieved sleeping bags and crawled in, forming

another circle around a fire. Talk continued, confessional sorts of things, people-never-die-wishing-they'd-spent-more-time-at-work sorts of things. Great spirit, earth and sky, sun and moon sorts of things.

Trying to make sense of their lives, I supposed, to find meaning in daily struggles, their emotions triggered by exhaustion and fueled by chants. But wasn't meaningless ritual replacing meaningless void in daily life? Why did this group seem so pleased with their awful experience? Because they'd paid two hundred dollars?

The next morning we again sat around the campfire, huddled in blankets provided by the tour, and ate coyote breakfast: beef stew with tortillas.

"Such a renewal," Steve said.

"I do feel cleansed," Max said.

"I'll come here every year to be reborn like this."

"This is truly the way to find god."

"Everyone should have this experience," Julie added.

They sounded like my daughter when she became a Mormon. Like the Rajneeshees probably did. Like the Waco group, like the jungle Kool-Aid group. I suppose like every fervent religious group in the universe. Or unfervent ones. Even Unitarians sound like this sometimes. They've come searching for Truth and have merely flung Rationality into the abyss, like wheat into the canyon.

I held my silence, reconciled myself to the insolvable problem. At least this group did no harm. They created no temples, locked no one out of life's rituals.

Aftermystics

Two weeks later in desert darkness, Tara started giggling when I told her about my thirst and the water jugs. She kept giggling all the way through coyote breakfast, the return jeep ride, and my decision not to buy agate talismans at twenty dollars each. "I saw the same stones all over the ground when I was out on my own," I finished. "So what were those tourists looking for? Were the guides pure cynics or what?"

Tara's old soul spoke up. "They were looking for something inside themselves."

"Couldn't they have found it just as well on their patios back in Santa Clara?"

"Maybe not. When people buy into The Rush … hurry to make yourself noticed in a career … hurry to get the nicest house possible … hurry to get the kids on track for Stanford … I think it's like being in rush hour traffic. Hard to change lanes."

I rolled onto my stomach, put my chin on my hands, and spoke into the tent floor. "So they toss away their money and their logic?"

"Maybe everybody got a good deal. My anthropology prof. says all peoples need myth and ritual. In Sedona they satisfied that need and you satisfied your curiosity."

"Myth?" I understood the need for ritual, having been excluded from a major one.

"Have you ever participated in a discussion group after a ballet? Better yet, after a play? "

"Sure."

"Well, don't you talk about the meaning of events? He did this because she did that, which caused . . . ta da da da dada. We do that all the time in my lit class."

"Yeah." Where on earth was Tara headed with this? "You analyze events and relationships."

"As though they were true!" Tara popped upright and sat in her sleeping bag, arms around knees. "It's totally irrelevant whether the people of the story existed, and the events happened, because it's the truth beneath the story, the truth revealed by the story, that's the point."

"Oh. Wow."

Rustling nightlife complemented our silence. Foxes yipped somewhere in the distance.

"So casting wheat into a vortex ..." I wondered.

"A ritual. Gets at the truth about losing things, I suppose. Losing only to a universe that's connected somehow. The wheat left your hands but not your world. Maybe precious things will be returned to you on the same currents that took your wheat."

"And Max," I said. "Max told me he was drained after the sweat lodge, but it was a good drained, like draining a car's dirty oil."

"Well, yeah, sweating out emotional salts with the physical ones... Curt and I needed a sweat lodge." At least Tara had apologized to her brother and the two were talking again.

Foxes sang into the night.

Tara replied. "We really need myth about a heroic protector of the earth, a protector of a connected universe. If we loved that story, we'd emulate its hero, become better protectors of the earth ourselves."

"If we went out regularly to cast wheat into the wind," I said.

"We'd become more aware of wind and wheat and the earth forces we've lost track of in our cities. Maybe we'd go pull up our weeds instead of poisoning them and the earth. Maybe we'd conserve earth's limited resources."

Maybe Tara was only echoing her environmental science prof. Still, it needed some thought.

I could expel my prejudices about gravel-brained Sedona sojourners. "But people come away from trips like mine thinking they have seen Great Meaning. The Way."

Tara sighed. "I dunno. I just have this feeling that Great Meaning has many … faces. Maybe it looks like Mother Earth. Or like Stern Father. Thundering. Zen-like and quiet. All connected. All separate …"

"Yeah, but people who say they have seen Great Meaning …"

"Have seen It. One side of it. It's a revelation to them, and they cling to it."

"Tara, how old are you? Three thousand-how-much? I think you see things through crystal while the rest of us swim in milk. I sit at your feet."

"Oh, cut it out, Kate. Who saw what was going on in my love life? And with Curt?"

"But clinging to one vision ..." I couldn't leave this alone. "You know, I grew up looking daily at the west side of Mt. Hood. The first time I saw it from the east, I wanted to weep. That wasn't my mountain!"

I felt Tara's nod in the darkness.

"But, Tara. The gloaters. The excluders. My-side-or-else." I bit my lip, didn't mention temples.

"They *are* irritating. They can be dangerous: They cause wars, jihads, inquisitions. Bascom probably gloated; he probably thought Cochise was heathen. But in Sedona ..."

"Yeah. I hope I didn't invade their space."

In our silence I heard the yipping again. "Foxes," I said.

"Haven't you noticed? They started right after we set up camp. Like we've taken their territory."

"It's from Sly. I know it." I remembered the Sedona foxes yipping near the sweat lodge.

"What?"

I told Tara a little about Sly. Not Andy's story, just that I'd been camping and nursed a wounded fox back to health. And developed a bond.

"So you'd better go answer your foxmail."

I pulled a sweatshirt over my pjs, got into my walking shoes, then crawled out to tramp into starlit space. At the top of a rise, I looked back at our tent, so small in this wide expanse. Then I sat cross-legged beside a towering organ-pipe cactus and gazed into a desert full of rustlings. A beat of wings. "Tell Sly I hear him. I appreciate the benediction." Was I singing to foxes or chanting? "I'm catching on to things." I thought a moment. "I think he has news, but I don't understand foxspeak."

People need myth, Tara said. Even simple ones like George Washington and the cherry tree, I supposed. Sabrina had found her myth, so compelling for her she could forsake friends and family on her momentous day. I didn't know how to forgive the myth for that.

What was Tara's myth? Ecology? More than that, something closer to Sedona but without delusion. What was my myth? Who knew? Sly, maybe. That wise creature.

"One more moon," I yipped. "Tell Sly I'll come after one more full moon." That surprised me. I hadn't known I was planning such a trip.

When I returned to my sleeping bag, I thought long about attachments and leavings. Neil. My family. Sly and Holly. Becca. Tara. Her brother.

Tara rustled around in her bedroll. I turned on my side and wadded the pillow under my neck. "Ryan is keeping you busy these days." Bright kid, her drummer, physics major, sociable, outgoing. Hard combination to beat.

"Yeah. I really like him."

"I'm so glad. But probably you'll have less time to wander with me."

"Oh, I don't think …"

"We both are in transition, headed elsewhere. I'm so glad for your friendship. And I hope we'll always have a bond …"

"It won't be much of one if I hit you with a tire iron for talking so much. We're still on for that early hike tomorrow before it heats up, aren't we?"

Bless her. Hits me square between the eyes with my own attitude. "Yeah, you're right. I'll shut up. But it is only 10:30, I went foxtalking, and we've developed a complete new world philosophy. G'night."

"Old world philosophy. Nothing is new under the sun. 'Night."

* * * *

"Wow," Tara said. "You're about a million miles away." She fell into step with me as we swung into the apartment complex.

"Oh! … Hi, Tara … Yeah, I've been thinking about … umm … about that website I'm designing for my class. Remember that top ten list idea? Dead end." I'd really been thinking about how to develop my secret website, Templetopple.com. It had been on my mind ever since I fled, since talk-show discussion about why anyone would bomb a temple. That Priest Lake conversation about terrorism.

People didn't know that you couldn't go to your own kid's wedding. I wanted a little understanding in return for my months of misery, but how to state my case without making an insane rant of it? Or was it just insane, period?

Anyway, I'd taken the computer class for two reasons: to get some picture ID and to learn how to set up websites. Of course Templetopple was secret. My class project was Mathville, a tutoring site. Now I wrenched my thoughts from Templetopple to Mathville and Tara's suggestions.

"So what isn't working?" she asked now.

"I just think kids need to feel that with help they can succeed. I dunno. A top ten list of why they should like math seems full of things they hate, that remind them of their failures. And it doesn't seem to lend itself to the graphics tricks we've learned."

"Maybe a confused student, a door opening?" she suggested. "Student turns, smiling and confident?"

We sketched it out at my tutor table: a sad kid with a test paper dripping in red ink walks through the opening door, solves equations using my poker chip strategy and ends waving an A paper at her mom. On the blackboard, it says, "Open doors to mathematics."

Becca was happy to model for me. My first Tucson tutee was an enthusiastic algebra nerd now. She called herself Rebecca A. Harrison. Her middle name was Marie, but *A* stands for *algebra*, she told me. She no longer needed help, but often stopped by during math table, usually to share a new number pattern. After Tara took pictures for the web site, we talked about powers of (x+y) and genetics, enlightened by Becca's pattern du jour, Pascal's Triangle.

Tara's idea worked for the templetopple site, in reverse. Joyous faces first—a wedding—then a door closes. Slams, with great audio effect. Gray heads bow, shoulders sag. We zoom in to see a posted notice: "Nonmembers prohibited." It seemed to capture the essence of my gripe.

I added a shape, perhaps a wedding cake, perhaps topped with a bride and groom, on the left of the home screen. Then from the right a round-bellied little guy with spiky hair and a black mask runs across with a black bomb and puts it below the cake-shape that now has an angel on top and might be a temple.

He backs up, laying out a fuse, and strikes a match. "Boom," says the entire screen. Then we see the cake/temple again, on its side with "Wrong Policy, Wrong Reaction: Two Wrongs don't make a Rite," printed below. Links on the left included the official Mormon explanation of temples, a they-shouldn't-do-that site with unhappy reactions to temple weddings, a they-shouldn't-do-that Jewish site with unhappy reactions to proxy baptisms, a they-shouldn't-do-that site focused on limited population growth. I saved it on my own disk, to download somewhere else, somewhere safe.

* * * *

April passed quickly. My tutoring hands filled with end-of-semester panic. I didn't get out as much for Wednesday jams, but Friday nights with the *Ruffians* continued, for fun and for profit. No more camping trips in the heat. Tara fell totally for Ryan. Bright, gangly kids sharing joy and, I gathered, broiling sex.

Broiling in Tucson is redundant. To cool off we went tubing on the Salt River out of Phoenix. Ryan remained the easy, affable guy who got me involved in *Ruffians*, and the three of us shrieked down the river. I did worry about getting singed in their personal flame.

College classes ended in early May. Tara was off to summer work involving dance at the Grand Canyon, and Ryan had a high-paying summer job in construction near his family's home in San Jose. One band member graduated, and so *Ruffians* was now a disband.

My high-school tutees still faced finals. The apartment was

hot, so I began sleeping where my Tucson life had begun, in a campground at 7000 feet elevation. Coolness, outdoors, fresh food, good books, no fear, no hiding.

"What's with all the foxes yipping around here?" the camp manager asked me one evening. "I come here every spring, and I've never heard foxes like this."

"I dunno. I'm new to Arizona. But I think they might be friends of a friend." That comment got me a skittish sideways glance, but I didn't explain, just went back to working on an A-minor seventh combination.

Little Brook and Sly stayed on my mind, though. He'd be expecting me if there really was a foxmail service. Bizarre, the way I kept hearing the fox world view.

ReOregonizing

Perhaps Andrea has a lesbian relationship with her alias Janet. Andrea provides all of Janet's income, according to the application for Janet's Swiss bank account. I used the words *significant other* on the application, figuring that the Swiss carefully don't inquire. It worked. Micheloud & Cie responded that they needed only Janet's apostille to set up her account. Another reason to head to Oregon again. I left my stuff stacked by the front door—a month remained on my lease.

In Palm Springs I found an internet cafe and uploaded *Templetopple.geocities,* a generic free site associated with generic free e-mail, impossible to link to me. Unlikely, too, I thought as I drove west, to be discovered, tucked away in the labyrinth of the web. At least it was out there.

I waited a day, found another cafe in Sacramento, and checked my e-mail.

* * * *

From: Matthew Sheridan <m_sheridan@fbi.us.gov>
Date: Thur, Mar 21 2002 4:24:52 PM US/Eastern
To: Andrea Glass <andrea_glass@marioncollege.edu>
Subject: questions

Dear Ms. Glass:
We request an in-person meeting soon. Only you can decide if you need an attorney. Please report to a local FBI office, or to the police or sheriff wherever you are, or call 1-800-555-1010 ext 50314 to arrange an interview.

Thank you for your cooperation.
Matthew K. Sheridan, Agent

* * * *

Similar e-mails were dated April 4 and April 18. In May Sabrina weighed in.

* * * *

From: Sabrina Severson <theseversons@aok.com>
Date: Thurs, May 2, 2002 10:24:06 AM US/Pacific
To: Andrea Glass <andrea_glass@marioncollege.edu>
Subject: FBI

Mom, Matt Sheridan is getting pretty onerous. He wants to talk to you. Maybe he believes us, that we don't know where you are. I feel like the longer you put off contacting him, the harder it will be to talk to him. I wish you would do it; just show up, tell him in person what you've said all along and go on your way. Can't be that bad. While you're at it, wish you'd come talk to us, too.
Love,
Sabrina

From: Matthew Sheridan <m_sheridan@fbi.us.gov>
Date: Fri, May 3, 2002 11:01:20 AM US/Central
To: Andrea Glass <andrea_glass@marioncollege.edu>
Subject: questions

Dear Ms. Glass:
Your daughter tells us you are irregularly in receipt of e-mail, so we assume that is why we have not had a response to our multiple requests for a meeting. Please get in touch immediately upon your receipt of this message. We have some questions regarding the bombings of Mormon temples and what you might know about them. Please report to a local FBI office, or to the police or sheriff wherever you are, or call 1-800-555-1010 ext 50314 to arrange an interview.

Thank you for your cooperation.
Matthew K. Sheridan, Agent

* * * *

Yes, Sabrina, I too wish I'd come talk to you. And yes, onerous was right. Sheridan wanted to talk to me as badly as I wanted to avoid him. I'd be confronting FBI *and* Mormonism. What a combination.

I responded to Sheridan after miles of thought, and I still wondered if I should have said something else. Or not replied at all.

> **Reply From:** Andrea Glass <andrea_glass@marioncollege.edu>
> **Date:** Wed, May 22, 2002 6:08:28 PM US/Pacific
> **To:** Matthew Sheridan <m_sheridan@fbi.us.gov>
> **Subject:** questions
>
> Dear Mr. Sheridan:
> I've been in seclusion, largely because of a delayed reaction to incidents arising from Mormon temple policies, and I'm simply emotionally incapable of discussing this with you at the moment. It doesn't matter—I know nothing that would help you. This copy of an e-mail to Sabrina tells all I know:
>
> I can't talk to my own daughter: how could I talk to a stranger from the FBI? I'm among a buzillion people with no fondness for temples after being excluded from our children's weddings. Half the buzillion were probably not home when bombings occurred. Like me, those folks know nothing about bombs and will be unable to help the investigation.
> I found some informative websites: leavinglds.netscsape.net and lonelywed.yahooweb.com.
>
> Andrea Glass.

* * * *

No, I thought. Don't provide my site. Not just a day after I'd set it up. I wondered about my reply to Sabrina, too. Maybe it would anger more than reassure.

*   *   *   *

From: Andrea Glass <andrea_glass@marioncollege.edu>
Date: Wed, May 22, 2002 6:22:46 PM US/Pacific
To: Sabrina Severson <theseversons@aok.com>
Subject: hello

Hello, Sabrina,

I've just seen a bunch of e-mails from Mr. Sheridan. I've e-mailed him back, but I don't suppose it will help much. I'm just not ready to talk to anyone, much less him. I'm OK, miss you. Hugs to all the family.
Love,
Mom

*   *   *   *

Subaruth and I arrived in Salem and found Janet's passport waiting in her post office box. To get Janet's apostille I went to a different bank and notary than I had used as Andrea. Even though Andrea didn't get involved this time, my calm surprised me. Once I dropped the apostille in the mail, everything was in place to channel money from Andrea to Kate. I just had to wait a few days for international mail and, I assumed, a few days for Swiss bureaucracy. Meanwhile I drove south and west.

Hiking in to Little Brook hadn't gotten easier. Either the trail had grown over or I'd forgotten its brushiness after Arizona's sparse growth. In two exhausting trips I managed to haul enough for a couple of days. The tent in the same spot as before didn't lure Sly into camp. Neither did the abbreviated version of a firepit.

I arrived on Friday afternoon. Foxes yipped in the night.

Sly? On Saturday I hiked, lolled about, read, and played flute. I had a prickly Sly feeling when I put down the flute, but didn't see him anywhere. Foxes sang again that night. On Sunday I went out for groceries, including a nice T-bone. Just as I turned it over on the fire, the prickly feeling made me look across the meadow. There he was, sitting perfectly still at the far edge.

"Sly, you clever fellow. It's me. And it's steak. Your favorite."

I watched him obliquely as I sat with T-bone, baked potato and my coffee. He came to the edge of camp, lying twenty feet from me, ears up, eyes intense. He looked beautiful. I was glad for his shyness with me. He'd be even more cautious around other people.

"Doesn't look like you had any trouble getting along without me, Sly." I wished he was a tail wagger. I was going to have to get myself a dog. Hadn't had one since Neil died, long overdue, possible if I found the right living space now that I'd quit travel-bombing and fleeing. "I got your messages. Did you get mine?"

When I finished dinner, I walked slowly west with scraps; Sly was south of me. When I, too, was twenty feet from the fire, I turned, took a few slow, slow steps toward Sly, put down the scraps and retreated to my place in camp.

He stood, then flowed over to the food. Beautiful is an insufficient word. His coat gleamed silver over burnished copper in the late-day sun. He moved like something liquid. I could see no sign of his scars, no stiffness, no slowness. I felt an inner glow that matched the sheen of his coat. This fox was alive, a new fox, because of me, and I was so glad.

Sly ate the smaller scraps, but picked up one big piece of fat and the bone and carried them off. First he, then his tail, disappeared into the little bushes at the far edge of the meadow.

The stars emerged, faint dots transforming to brilliance. Then the faithful freshening northwest evening breeze pulled me back to attending my fire. As I thought about the beautiful fox who had just breezed in and out of my life again, I thought too about my family, from whose life I'd been blown. Like Sly, I had become a new person. If Andy ever returned home, she'd be more Kate. My family would have changed, too. No way I could ever go back. Not to the way it was. But whether I was Kate or Janet or Andy or NanHeTo, I missed them.

Maybe I could stalk them. Go to their church? No. Can't fade into the crowd in small Mormon-style gatherings. Volunteer in their classrooms? Josh would be in second grade … Ah-ah-ah-ah! No!

Stay away forever? No. No, there must be another option

A bat swooped close. There were several, I realized. Thank you, bats. Let's be in the moment: bats feasting on insects, me feasting on lovely night, lovely frog songs. Joyous yipping silenced the frogs. More fox talk.

In the morning I felt those fox-alert prickles again as I put coffee on. Boy, I thought, I don't have anything to feed him this morning. I looked across the meadow and stopped, amazed. There were two tall foxes and three short ones. Sly stood and moved a few feet closer. The others sat like rocks.

"You Sly fellow. You've got a lady. And little ones. Is that what the foxmail message was? What a lovely family. I heard you all singing last night. My flute doesn't come close to your beautiful medley."

Should I get something to feed them today? I wondered. But if I feed them, they might lose their reservations about people. As if to confirm my thought, the family stood and moved together off into the brush.

Oh, wow.

They visited three more times in my remaining five days, each time staying well back in the meadow. I succumbed to temptation the next time I went out for groceries, buying five rawhide bones. When I put them in the usual scraps spot, Sly carried them one by one into the woods. The kids would probably get only his scent by the time they had the bones. I ate another steak, and Sly again came for scraps, carrying away the bigger ones.

Then he must have thought his family had enough of people. Kind of like humans deciding their kids shouldn't watch any more TV. They sang to me in the evenings, but didn't come back to camp. I followed their musical sets with my flute, tunes Sly hadn't heard before.

With joy for my fox family, with sorrow at their absence, with greater sorrow at my separateness, I again left Little Brook, again at loose ends and unsure of my destination, again determined to forge a life, to redeem my sins, to somehow reconnect with my family.

* * * *

From: Matthew Sheridan <m_sheridan@fbi.us.gov>
Date: Thur, May 23, 2002 8:42:27 US/Eastern
To: Andrea Glass <andrea_glass@marioncollege.edu>
Subject: questions

Dear Ms. Glass:

I must insist on a face to face interview. If you don't come in, we will have to issue a warrant to require this meeting. Please report to a local FBI office, or to the police or sheriff wherever you are, or call 1-800-555-1010 ext 50314 to arrange an interview.

Thank you for your cooperation.
Matthew K. Sheridan, Agent

Part III Finding Montana

Erik

His tent was pitched in the best site in the campground on Lolo Pass. I eyed his setup when I arrived. I hoped he'd be leaving and I could claim the spot, beside the river, away from the road, close to the water pump and far from the privy. But no luck.

As I was out for my after-dinner stroll, I saw him seated in front of his campfire, one foot propped on the cool edge of the cement firepit, playing guitar. I'd heard him singing before I got there, but now he was hunched over trying to work out the next bit. *Ta-ta, ta-ta tum*, I thought. *Key of F.* I was headed back to my camp anyway, so I got my flute, and played the phrase. The strumming-humming stopped and I played the bit again, pitching it an octave higher so he could hear it more clearly.

"Yeah, I think that's it!" he called. "Could you and your flute come over to play? Coffee's on."

Coffee. I tucked my flute under my arm and grabbed my chair and empty cup. I hoped his gray hair meant he wasn't too young for me; the thought surprised me as I strode two sites down to his place. I held out my cup as I sat down. "Alms for the poor? I haven't gotten my fire going yet, need caffeine."

"There's a price." He pulled the pot off the fire and poured. "Please play that bit again."

So I did. Twice with sips of perfect coffee between. He was with me the second time, and then I was with him for the entire melody. "Today, travel far," replaced "ta-ta, ta-ta tum." It was a haunting "Greensleeves" sort of song, one I'd never heard.

"I like the song. Where did you get it?"

"Made it up today. How did you know the missing piece?"

"I dunno. Heard you getting to it a couple of times as I walked by, and my brain just went 'ta-ta, ta-ta tum.' I went to get my flute because I can't sing."

"Well, you do a passable ta-ta, ta-ta tum, but your flute is more than passable. Perfect for this song, I think."

"Yeah. Nothing does a haunting melody quite like flute. It's a wonderful, memorable melody. Wish I'd thought of it myself."

"Well, thanks ... I'm Erik Mathieson." He pronounced it Mat HEE Son, the Norwegian way, and reached across the fire to shake my hand. As he unfolded from his chair, I noticed how he just went up and up. Six-foot-three, I guessed. Six-foot-two of legs.

"Kate McGuire," I responded. And then something made me take on the up-down tones of a Scandinavian accent. "I vunder if ya come from da olt country."

"Begorry, you've got a name from across the sea yerself, lass."

And that fast I was friends with a bearded giant, possessor of best campsite and creator of songs. A man with a coffee pot within arm's reach. This could be love.

Now Erik poured me more coffee, and we found much in common besides the music. I stuck with my Kate story, family now in California, kids too busy to appreciate a hovering gramma, the move to Arizona, and the decision to try Montana because I'd seen its beauty on previous visits.

He had moved away from his Vermont family a couple of years earlier. "If I was nearby, they needed something. Moving broke the 'lean on Dad' habit."

"Without even a patch?"

Erik laughed. "They don't make Dad-patches the way they used to. The kids are fine, busy. If I went back now, they'd have trouble fitting me in."

Blue eyes. Like the blue in the plaid Pendleton shirt. Abundant salt-and-pepper hair, matching beard, neatly trimmed. Good. I don't like big bushy beards. Bushy eyebrows are okay. Wonderful long lean legs. Kind of soft in the midsection. No ring. He's big, not fierce. More like an oversize koala than a grizzly. He was telling me he was a retired teacher …

Like me

… of English, in Vermont. And he'd been tutoring

Like me

in Missoula. But now music increasingly took up his time

Like me

and he had gone on a one-man retreat for the summer to create songs that were uniquely his.

"I put my stuff in storage in Missoula." I told Erik. "I like university towns: lots going on and good for tutoring. I'll look for an apartment and get to work, maybe in early October." No way I'd throw away money for rent in good weather, I didn't add.

Erik tossed a log on the fire. "I can tell you who to contact at University of Montana if you want to work in their tutoring center."

"Thanks, but I think I'll start independently. I had good luck in Arizona that way." And I wouldn't have anyone checking my past.

"Why did you leave?"

"Too hot. My friend Judy talked me into going there, but she travels a lot. I spent most of the summer wandering, myself, and I can tell you it doesn't get any prettier than here. Rivers, forests, mountains. Green."

Erik lived in a boarding house but had shopped around, so I asked him about apartments.

"I like the Heritage House," he said. "It's a nicely refurbished old hotel with a game room, gym and lounge on the first floor. The apartments must have been created out of two or three hotel rooms; most have living, bedroom and kitchen areas."

"Okay, I'll take a look at it. Would you play some of your other songs? Maybe let me noodle along?"

The magic of music led us from one song to another. Time flew. His stuff seemed really extraordinary. Lovely melodies, catchy rhythms, lyrics ranging from grandpa love to political satire. With ashes cooling and stars out, we finally quit and I walked back to my camp.

* * * *

I stopped by his fire again the next evening, but he was cross. A different person. His eyes were the gray of November skies that night, brewing up a storm behind wire rim glasses. He'd been working all day on another new song, wasn't satisfied, didn't know why, didn't want to talk about it.

"When you get it worked out, maybe you could bring it by my camp."

"I'd like to do that. Just not tonight."

I rarely stopped by his camp after that and spent non-Erik evenings as I had all summer, reading, flute playing, or reviewing math proofs. But Erik came to my fire with a new song at random times. He was good company when he wasn't preoccupied.

"Have you spent the entire summer here?" I asked him one evening.

"Since early June. Took a week to go back and visit my kids in Vermont at the end of spring semester. This is a great place to work. Gets me outdoors. I can go hiking when I'm completely stuck. Saves rent."

Like me. "And what will you do with the new songs?"

"I'm part of a band. We stay busy, performing in Missoula, at Flathead Lake, in Bozeman, Billings. Spokane. Occasionally places like the Roseland in Portland."

"Wow! The Roseland. I *thought* you were good. Did you entertain in Vermont?"

"No. It's something that developed here, after I retired and escaped the family."

Like me. "Yeah. Kind of the same for me on the flute. Except I would hate big-time stuff."

"Why? Haven't you felt the electric charge from hundreds of pairs of hands applauding?"

"Electricity scares me. I'd be one of those people who throw up before every performance. Why does anyone suffer through that?" *And how can you hide in such limelight?*

Besides running through new songs, we spent some evenings on old favorites. Erik liked Everly Brothers and used "All I Have To Do Is Dream" to persuade me out of my singing shyness, patiently teaching me harmony. I began to learn not to stray out of my part into his. His blue-eyed persona was a good encourager, and when my voice did stray, he just laughed, stopped playing for a moment, said "hmmm," in the note I needed. When I hit it right, he would say "hmmm," down a fifth from my note, and we'd "hmmm, hmmm, hmmm" a while until I was nice and solid. Finally I didn't feel too foolish singing. Still I mostly played flute, and let him sing.

One cranky morning I persuaded Erik to hike to the hot springs. His stormy tension evaporated in the soothing waters, and he talked about life in Vermont, his three children, his five grandchildren, and his wife, taken too soon by cancer.

I told Kate's widow tale, but also true stories about Neil and Sabrina, goats, horses, and pi tree. I mentioned a recent week at Elk Lake near Bend.

I didn't mention Mormon weddings and avoided discussion of banks, especially Swiss ones. But I did finally have a safe pipeline to Andrea's funds. As a test I'd written a hundred-dollar check from Andy's stateside account to the Swiss one, transferred it to Janet's Swiss account, thence to Kate. My money didn't disappear offshore. The FBI didn't react. And Kate withdrew fifty dollars—as Kate, no costumes—using an ATM in Bend. Now half of Andy's funds were in the Swiss account after many thousand-dollar transactions, each small enough, I hoped, to escape attention. *Yes.* I had solved the financial piece. Unless someone froze Andrea's Oregon account.

Erik was waiting. What had he asked? "How I'd spent the summer?"

"Mostly wandering. I told about Rocky-mountain ramblings, Bend and the Cascade lakes, my inflatable kayak. "And some medical stuff I'd put off. Vision, dental, all that." Now that I had money.

"I'd better do that, myself. You forget about it when you leave your regular doctor."

"Exactly. I even needed to treat my car to some checkups. But I spent most of the beautiful summer in the Rockies, south to north: Chama, Durango, Estes Park. Camped for a week on the Yellowstone, and another week at Flathead Lake. Went through Fort Collins."

Holly's family had lived in Fort Collins. She'd been on my mind so much I went by an elementary school and tried to imagine her there. Years ago, now.

* * * *

After Erik folded up his camp for another visit in Vermont, I stayed on, went back to playing Andy-style classical stuff. I really liked jamming best, but you can't jam alone.

Considering Montana, I drew the rune *Algiz*, Protection.

New opportunities and challenges, my rune-guide said, and a mirror to use in my battle with my Self. Considering Erik, I drew *Eihwaz*, Defense. Obstacles, the guidebook said, not to stop me, but to delay me to my benefit. I should wait for the spring, the oracle counseled, wait for the fruit to ripen. Try to foresee consequences. But, it says, once a decision is clear, the doing will be effortless.

Wait, wait, wait. For what? Would Erik delay me? Would the ripening fruit be a return to my family? How? Would I always be Kate? Back to my family, I begged, back to the fulcrum on which I balance my life.

Missoula

Camp got cold in September. I'd done cold. No thanks. Heritage House, the apartments Erik had mentioned, suited me fine.

On the wall behind my garage-sale-new couch, I hung Janet's small sketch, a few lines depicting a mother sitting at a long trestle table with a child at her side and another in her lap. Their posture said it all: *We have no hope.* I had the drawing mounted in pale gray with a charcoal frame, and looked at it every time I sat in the living area.

I'd visited Janet again before I left Oregon. Oh, her drawings. Stubble-faced men in wrinkled shirts sitting knees up, back to the wall, holding bottles of whiskey thinly disguised as bags-of-something. Tired-faced women holding silent children. Gloomy faces waiting in a row for lunch. Economy of line, economy of spirit. I took the still-sober Janet around with her portfolio of those soft aching drawings, and fifteen now hung in various galleries.

One less Oregon worry, Janet, but other worries moved into place. Sabrina. I was afraid to use my Marion College e-mail address after Matt Sheridan's threat to issue a warrant to find and question me. Could I use my Copenhagen mail drop? I kept in touch that way with Bruce, my trustee, so my monthly draws didn't alarm him, or leave him short of funds for home business. But connect that with Sabrina—and therefore Matt Sheridan? The thought made the "1812 Overture" play in my head, the cannon booming a warning.

So I hadn't contacted Sabrina since that Sheridan message.

Maybe it was silly, but I obsessed about the Biscuit Fire, raging south of Little Brook. Though firefighters seemed to be succeeding in keeping it away from my little fox, wouldn't he be threatened by new prey driven into his range? But what did I think I was going to do? Dash in and snatch him from the flames? Stand guard at his den?

So I stayed put, worried, pushed good Sly-vibes his way and went on with a life of tutoring and jamming.

I had found students, by advertising and by word of mouth, as in Tucson. Study tables and private tutor sessions took up much of my days and enabled me to stash most of Andrea's retirement income in Kate's new account in Missoula.

I jammed on Tuesday nights at Miss Ooula's with a group of regulars reminiscent of Beano's in Tucson. Guitar, bass, piano.

When I called Erik to let him know that Heritage House had worked well for me, I didn't even need to close my eyes to picture him, clearly in gray-eyed funk mode again, trying to adapt his new songs to the other two members of the *Songsters Three*. I didn't know how Doug and Al contended with him while he was *in extremis,* but I didn't belong in the picture. So I wished him luck and hung up.

Somehow the *Songsters* got Erik's new stuff worked out. In

October he invited me to a performance, their second one with new material. Al told me later that Erik had been an almost unbearable bundle of unsheathed nerves until the first performance went well. Not a surprise.

By November four of us, the three songsters and I, had a standing two a.m. date after nearby performances to mellow over wine and pinochle in the game room at Heritage House. I was a regular groupie, never tired of listening to them perform. Erik's melodies bore no resemblance to their gray-eyed creator, but alternated between joyous and haunting with some lovely minor sevenths that kept me listening for more. As he played mandolin, Doug sang close harmony with Erik, and Al's acoustic bass provided both rhythm and counterpoint.

Erik, the calm blue-eyed version, said, "Bring your flute to Thursday rehearsals." Doug and Al nodded politely over their pinochle hands.

I would have loved to agree; I missed those summer fireside musical rambles, and I think no sound yet invented beats flute with acoustic guitar. With Doug's mandolin and Al's bass anchoring the sound—well, *sublime* would be the word that fits. But their big venues just didn't suit a fugitive. The Thursday night jam at Miss Ooula's would have to do as my musical outlet.

"No," I said, "if I go to rehearsal, there are two possible outcomes. You'll like the flute or you won't. If you don't, everybody will be disgusted at wasting their time. If you do, you'll ask me to join you. And, I'm telling you, a big concert for me is like the glass elevator at the Space Needle for a person with acrophobia. Besides, *Songsters Four* just doesn't have the right ring to it. Whose bid is it?"

We had that conversation about four thousand times.

Eventually there came a Thursday evening in early December when Erik and I met musically again. *The Songsters* didn't need to rehearse; they had a week's break before the start of a regular gig at the Mountain Inn. So we two had salmon steaks at my place and then went down to Heritage House's lounge to play where we wouldn't disturb neighbors.

When we came back to my apartment, I said, "If you'll stir up the fire, Erik, I'll put my flute away and make coffee for a cup of Irish."

"Sounds wonderful. I'll put my guitar away, too."

"No, leave it out. It's quiet and I'd love to have you play a bit more."

"After that session we just had downstairs? My hands are going to fall off, Kate."'

"OK. Enough fun for one night, I guess." I took the guitar case from the closet, handed it to Erik, and headed for the kitchen. After I put coffee on I started cleaning my instrument at the counter separating me from the tiny living area. "I don't know when I've had such a good time."

It had been so much fun, I didn't want it to end. I was glad Erik had agreed to a nightcap. He leaned the guitar in its case by the door and began tending the banked fire in the woodstove. As he picked up a chunk of wood from its carrier he said, "I'd forgotten the amazing way you wrap flute harmony around whatever I play. You tell me you've never played professionally, but that's hard to believe. Where did you learn those tricks?"

Coffee burbled as I put my flute in its case. "It's the usual long story, Erik. About a really crummy period in my life when the flute saved me. That and a little fox."

"What?" He stood gazing at me, wood forgotten in his big hand.

"I'm mixing these Irish coffees the way I like them. Good strong coffee, good strong whiskey, dollop of vanilla, dollop of cream. Does that sound OK to you?"

"Yeah, delicious. What did you say about a flute and a fox?"

"You open the draft on the stove with a little handle under that flap on the right side." Smoke was boiling out of the open door.

"Oh. Yeah. OK. I guess holding onto the wood doesn't heat the place much, does it?" He opened the draft, put in wood, stirred the fire.

I came around the counter and handed him his mug as he straightened his long frame. "Well, if you want a little more of something, just help yourself. Everything's on the counter except the cream—top shelf of the fridge."

"Mmmm. Perfect drink to cap a perfect evening. Now I'd love to hear how you became such a virtuoso." Satisfied that the wood was catching, Erik shut the stove door and settled beside me on the sofa in front of the fire.

The overstuffed relic on which we made ourselves comfortable was a mark of decadence for me, despite my clumsy mending of three tears in its burgundy mohair fabric. No sitting on the ground, no stiff camp chair. Getting the heavy thing to my second floor apartment had been a triumph involving a Montana pickup, a teenager, a free tutoring lesson, and an aching back.

"Practice provides great emotional release." After avoiding so many of Erik's questions, I thought I could answer this so-called virtuoso one. "I don't know if a man's mind gets all gooped up like a woman's does. You said you went through a bad time when Elene died and then again when your kids started leaning on you for the littlest things. Did you get so you couldn't think through anything? Or did you just go hit a punching bag or something?"

"Playing guitar saved me. I guess that's what you're saying about the flute. I formed an ensemble with a couple of guys there in Burlington, and we learned a new song every week. Practice Sunday and Thursday nights. Sometimes I didn't know if I'd make it till then."

I kicked off my shoes, leaned my back against the arm of the sofa and put my feet up on the cushions. "The thing about playing scales is that it's repetitious enough to do even when your mind is stuck in bubble gum. But once I mastered a scale and the arpeggios that went with it, it got mechanical, and I was back in the ooze again, merely playing scales in the muck."

Erik pulled my feet to his lap. If he felt my inward jump, he didn't betray it. "What had you so down?"

"So I started doing connected scales: C, F and G first. I thought about things like minor sevenths connecting to the fourth. I spent months. Then I went to A, D and E. That was tough. All those sharps. From there I worked on the other combinations that guitars use a lot. Then I jammed—with a CD."

"Guitar combinations—because you just knew we'd get together?"

"Because I really hoped something like that would happen. I have always loved the resonance between guitar and flute."

Erik nodded. "Resonance is good." He seemed to be off the subject of my depression and Sly and he was massaging my cold feet.

I relaxed. "Pull off my socks, would you? I'll give you a week to quit that."

He did pull off my socks, and he didn't stop the massage. "Do you purr?"

"Rrrr. Rrrrrrr. Rrr."

"Blue is the color of my true love's feet…"

Erik sang, so I sang back. Tentatively. "In the winter when it snows…"

Then he joined me, "In the winter when it snows, that's the time, that's the time, I love the best."

"All right, Kate. You're getting the harmony thing down really well."

"I'll never be comfortable with voice like I am with flute."

"Come to *Songsters'* tomorrow afternoon." They planned to spend a couple of hours staying in shape and fiddling with ideas. "You don't have to sing. Just bring your flute. They'll love you. If flute and guitar are good, think how it will be with mandolin and bass added in."

"No. No, no, I just can't, Erik."

"You're too good to stay hidden downstairs, playing for whoever wanders in, or even jamming at Miss Ooula's."

"That was enough of a crowd for me tonight. There must have been a dozen people hanging 'round by the time we quit."

"Well, they sure didn't seem to intimidate you."

"My mistake." I didn't mean to say it aloud.

"What?"

"Are you a light bulb? You've said about a hundred *whats* tonight."

"Come on, Kate."

"Oh, Erik, I'm so flattered by your encouragement. But the *Songsters Three* play at some big venues. I couldn't handle that. And if they start rehearsing with me, they're going to be angry at both of us if they can't extend that into performance."

"I'll tell them it's strictly a trial basis on both sides, and that, if you join us, it'll just be for the Mountain Inn gig."

"You are persistent."

"Please?"

I sighed. "I have to admit it's tempting. But let me get used to the idea for a few days."

"OK. If you'll let me take the braid out of your hair."

"What does *that* have to do with flute or guitar or ensembles?"

"Absolutely nothing."

I laughed, reclaimed my feet and got up. "I'll go get a brush and make a couple more coffees on the way."

"Can you make mine hot chocolate? I have to be a responsible working senior citizen tomorrow. Do you have any cocoa? I'm likely to be wired all night with this coffee."

"Whiskey counteracts caffeine."

"Baloney. For you, maybe." Erik stretched himself upward from the couch and ambled over to lean elbows on the counter. "For me, caffeine is caffeine and wired is wired. My tutees have trouble with complete sentences even when I'm coherent enough to help. Of course, if you want to be wired *with* me all night..."

"Hot chocolate it is, Erik. With a bit of cream and a splash of creme de menthe. That's an even better caffeine antidote than whiskey."

He asked for the bathroom. It was off the bedroom, so I picked up my brush on the way back from showing him.

"You're good at ignoring stuff," he said as he rejoined me on the sofa.

"What do you mean?" I handed him his cocoa.

"Well, like my telling you that there is no antidote to caffeine in Erik World and your putting in creme de menthe as an antidote."

"You know what mathematicians do? They ignore stuff all the time. If there are too many variables, they just say, 'Let's consider A, B, and C.' And they put aside D through Z, act as if they don't exist."

"Kate McGuire, mathematician extraordinaire." He clinked his mug against mine in a toast.

"I'm just a tutor, Erik. But I've studied my prey."

"Am I your prey, too? I notice you studying me a lot."

"Yeah. I'm out to get you and all your wealth."

"And I yours. Skøl." We clinked cups again and sipped. Then he put his mug on the end table and took the hairbrush from my hand. "How about turning around and letting me at that braid?"

"All right. But I gotta warn you, Erik. My hair won't fall flowing into your hands. Shimmering and rippling and all that. Forty years ago it might have. Now it's been around too long. It's fine and thin and limp." But he already had undone my hair.

"It's so wavy."

"Just a clever ruse on my part. The braid kinks it." I set my Irish on the floor.

"Your hair is lovely, Katie. Like the rest of you."

"Umpff."

"You are so locked up, pulled tight sometimes, just like your braid. How do you do it?"

"Divide it into three strands. Pull the left one between the other two, then the right one between the other two. You have to tug a little. Ouch. Not that much."

"I'll find the combination, Kate. I'll find a way to unlock my mysterious flutist." He tugged on my hair, pulling me back.

Ohmygosh. He's kissing me. I'm kissing back. I flew upright from the sofa. "Buck."

"What?"

"Buck, buck," I said.

"Katie, what are you…"

I don't know what strings pulled me to tuck my hands into my armpits, flap my elbows and chicken-dance. "Buck buck buck BUH UH BUH Uh Uh. Bu UCK Uck. BAWK BAWK ba

AWK. AWK." I could feel my loose hair flying with my loose self.

Erik sat still on the couch, but his inner rooster said, "Well, Rrk rrk. Rrk a Rrk RRK to you, too."

I'd already lost it and now I exponentially lost it. I snorted. Then I laughed. Laughed louder. Shrieked with laughter.

Erik laughed a bit with me. "Shhhh. If you're afraid the flute will disturb the neighbors, what will this do? Shh, Katie. Do I call the men with the white jackets now?"

"You know, there just is NO critter as dumb as a chicken. Nor as hysterical. Totally emotionally unbalanced."

"*You*, on the other hand…"

"If I could talk chicken I'd ask whether 'bu BUCK BUCK bu bu bu BUCK,'" I flapped again, "means 'an EGG EGG; oh my gawd an EGG,' or 'oh OW OUCH; geez Louise OW!'"

There was silence.

"Erik, I'm sorry. I've been so unfair to you. You've got to go. It might be Pandora's Box you're trying to unlock."

"Is Pandora's box full of chickens?" Erik stood, took my elbows, my chicken wings, into his big hands.

"Must be. Full of many many other ugly, stupid, mean things, too."

"There's nothing mean or ugly or…"

"I've got to do some pacing and some thinking, Erik. Can I buy you dinner tomorrow after your rehearsal? If we're going to move forward… If we're going to move anywhere… I've got to tell you some stuff. I've got to sort it out. If I can tell you. If you want anything to do with me then. I'm so sorry. Tomorrow night? Casey's? Please say yes. Forgive me for tonight. Don't forget your guitar. You've got to go, Erik, before I really do go cackling off on my broom."

"Are you all right? I'm afraid to leave you."

"I'll be all right. Say yes to dinner?"

"Yes, of course, Katie. Goodnight. See you tomorrow evening. Can I call you in the morning, to be sure you're OK?"

"I'll be OK. Goodnight, Eric. See you at Casey's at seven." To the closed door after he left, I added, "If I don't cut and run."

Andrea Revisited

Erik arrived at Casey's at about a quarter to seven and found me at our usual booth in a quiet back corner. "I thought I was early. Been here long?" He slid onto the bench opposite me.

"Just long enough for a couple of sips." I waved my glass. "It was get my butt here or run away. To Newport Bay. Just to stay in rhyme. Har har."

"I half expected you not to show up. You were so…"

"Berserk. I know. Did rehearsal go OK?"

A waitress came, asking Erik if he wanted a drink. A tension-interlude.

"What do you have, Kate?"

"Chardonnay. Would you like a mixed drink? Irish coffee? I'm buying."

"No, but a beer sounds good. How about a Henry's?"

The waitress left. Our unease returned.

Say something, Andy. Kate. "So how was rehearsal?"

"Just great. We're working on a new piece, something Doug wrote. I kept hearing your flute. It would be so perfect in that song."

"Buck buck."

"Oh no. Katie, don't go nuts on me here."

"It's OK, Erik. Relax. I rarely go nuts in private and never in public. I wish I hadn't mentioned the band, though."

"I know I made you edgy by begging you to join us, but I didn't think that was why you…"

"It was the band *and* your kiss. The kiss is maybe the easiest part to explain."

"Then please do. I've been so worried."

"Oh, gawd. What you don't know about me…"

"So start with what's easy, Katie. Please start. I couldn't sleep last night."

"Even without that second Irish coffee."

"Yeah."

The waitress returned with the beer and her order pad. Neither of us had looked at the menu, but we knew Casey's pretty well.

"Stew and cornbread for me," I said. "And coffee."

Erik ordered the same, no coffee. Then he just leaned back, looked at me, and waited.

"Neil died a decade ago. No romance in my life. My libido was gone, and I hadn't missed it. And it's like dancing. Don't do it for a while and you're not sure you can. What are the steps? Can you catch the rhythm?"

"*That* set you off? Kate, it's been years for me, too, but I knew what I was missing."

"All that tension. The huffing and puffing."

"Ah, Katie. I bet you huffed and puffed with the best of them."

"That was another person. All my body cells have replaced themselves since then."

"You kissed me back for a moment."

"Yeah. I noticed."

"It's a long ways from kisses to huff 'n puff."

"Not in my experience."

"Katie. It's too soon to say 'I *love* you' with big soft eyes and violins and flowers in the background, but… I feel so good when we're together."

"Me too."

"I don't go around kissing women."

"I was pretty sure you didn't. That's part of what scared me."

"I'll not push you. Can I hold your hand, though?"

I reached my hand across the table. I thought my hands were large, but not compared to his. "I wear a size large glove. What on earth size is yours?"

"I dunno. Twenty-seven? I shop at specialty stores for big men. I just try things on until I don't rip them."

It felt good to laugh. "You know, I have no trouble visualizing you doing exactly that." And then I felt Erik waiting again. Eyes: blue. Brows: squeezed together.

So I stumbled onward. "And the rest of what I have to tell you. You may not want… We'll have to start over. Or go nowhere at all…"

"No. Whatever it is, I've seen enough of you … But what, Kate? What!"

I reclaimed my hand, reached into my bag and pulled out newspaper clippings for Erik. "This will tell you."

"I remember the story," he said, skimming the articles. "It was in the news a couple of years ago. This woman disappeared.

They thought she had something to do with bombing Mormon temples. What does this have to do with …" He looked up. I had put on my big round glasses and Andy wig. "Oh my gawd."

"You see the resemblance?"

"You're Andrea Glass?"

I snatched off the wig and glasses and darted a look around nearby tables. "Shhhh!"

More quietly, "You're Andrea Glass?"

"Yep."

"You're sure?"

Yep, I was sure.

"I mean…I can't believe it… It's just wig and glasses. With them *I* could look like this picture.

I handed them to him. He put them on and preened. Put one hand behind his head. Fluttered his puny eyelashes.

"Nope." I had to grin. A lovely short reprieve. "Maybe without the beard …"

I looked at the waitress, who had just come with our dinner. "Pretty cute, don't you think?"

"Different anyway," she said. "Can I get you anything else?" Ms. Professional.

"No," we said. "We're fine. This is good. Thanks."

Get it done. Maybe the worst had passed. "I'm Andrea Glass, Erik."

"But…"

"I'm—Andrea is hiding. It began with a tent in the hills above the southern Oregon coast, hauling supplies, hauling wood, freezing, eating hiker meals. I adopted a wounded fox.

That photo is me all right, minus a a gazillion pounds and the dye job. Longer hair, new muscle tone, different glasses, different clothes. Same brain cells. It's me."

"Holy cow."

"I got so cold out there, so lonely and depressed. Missed my family. Hated myself for killing those people. I can't bear to think about that."

"You *killed* somebody?" Eyes: gray. Brows: still scrunched.

"Not on purpose. It's in the article. A couple was in the temple when I…*we* bombed it. The Whitesons. I saw it on TV before I left civilization." *We* bombed it, I'd said. I supposed that even Erik should think I was just one of a…a gang.

"There's something…"

"I, ah, *we* were so careful to plan times when no one would be there. What were they doing there? Why didn't … we see a car or anything?"

"It seems to me something…"

"Anyway, it scared me and I ran. And quit bombing … having anything to do with bombing."

"Bombing. Bombing! Why, Kate? Damn. You're not even Kate. Andrea. Who the hell *are* you, anyway." Eyes: even grayer. Erik in a funk, the music isn't right.

I played with my spoon, balanced it on the edge of my glass. Tried it upside down. Minutes passed. Or eons. "Maybe I'm *not* Andrea any more. It sounds odd to hear you call me that. Please call me Kate. I need to stay Kate. Until I can figure out another option. I'd like to figure out another option, see my grandkids… Erik, you're such a good person. I don't know if there's any chance of your understanding what Andrea did. But could you promise me twenty-four hours warning? If you need to turn me in?"

"I dunno. I guess I don't know you at all. You really had a part in those bombings?

"I helped demolish three temples. I don't want to tell you much more than that. If you don't know, you won't have to lie if you're questioned about it."

"Can you tell me why? Help me understand this, Kate."

"I'll try." My voice was coming out high and thin. Eyes wet. I don't cry. "And I set up a website. No sense knocking down temples if no one understood why. It's http…"

"Kate, this is Erik. Don't send me to a website. Tell me."

"Yeah. Later. When you've gone home and started wondering again, look at it. And maybe there are some things I can't say…"

"You just aren't a hater. I can't believe Andrea was a hater either." Eyes: unreadable. Brow: knotted.

"It's hate of a principle, a mind set. Not of people."

"Why? What did they ever do to you? How could you be part of bombing … anything?"

So after a deep breath, I launched into my history. Sabrina married so young, the celebration denied us. That took a long time. Erik couldn't believe that the church would neither allow us in nor approve a ceremony outside.

"Surely you could have reasoned with them."

"I objected left and right and upside down. Read the damn brochure Sabrina gave us. Wrote letters to the Big Kahuna. The

Mormon authorities. So some elders, a local group, came to our place ..."

"To explain to you?"

"I guess so. They said, 'You can't go in the temple. Happens all the time. Why all the fuss?' Made Neil madder than he already was." Sonny gun. Don't cry. Dohncry.

"How long ago was this, Kate?"

"Ten years, I guess. Phnnuh Huh." Damn.

"It still brings on those tears?"

I could only nod. Erik handed me his handkerchief and suggested another drink. The fuss with that gave me a moment. I dipped the handkerchief in ice water to cool my eyes. Erik wondered if I wanted a restroom break. At least my stupid weeping diffused his anger.

"If I go there, I might run out the back."

"Well then, stay put. I don't want to lose you, Kate."

"Knowing what you know?"

"I don't get it yet. I. do. not. get. it. I do know you—you have brightened my life. I'm not ready to return to dreary."

"Oh, Erik." My cheek settled into my palm, an elbow on the table. "Thank you. But ..."

"Oh, geez. More tears ..."

"Poor Erik. If it's not insane cackling, it's tears."

"Tears are bad. Insanity is worse. I really worried if you had a return ticket from whatever flight you'd taken to the Mad Hatter's."

"I was terrified. Of telling you. Of recalling the pain. Of remembering the dreary eons. Neil's strokes, my retiring to care for him."

"What?"

That took us another long time. Was it coincidence, strokes following disappointment like that? Couldn't I have, at least, continued in the teaching career I loved? "Why not bomb your daughter? Her car or something. She made those choices. Temples? "

Good thing Casey's wasn't busy, because that took a while, too.

"Those big, elaborate...*edifices*, for special occasions," I said. "Rigid cold marble things. The rigid cold dogma they stand for. All the other parents being hurt by sanctimonious bullies. The earth being hurt by belief in big families. Dead people being baptized by proxy in those temples. All the men being priests, all the women being child bearers." Oh-oh. I was ranting. And I wasn't saying this right. Wasn't getting to the hurt.

"So you went to the bomb store at the mall one day? Kate."

"Not that straightforward. Both Neil and I tried to forget it. But when my guy was gone, I had just a big hole left. Full of rage."

"Were you trying to get even?"

"That self-righteous sonofabitch. Bishop, probably. S.o.b. - bishop."

Erik's eyebrows shot up.

"Mormon bishops are a dime-a-dozen. If you go to church and tithe, you're a bishop. If you're male, of course."

"Sons-a-bitches are pretty common, too?"

"We'd asked to witness our only child's wedding. The pompous sophomoric rednecked bastard wondered what our problem was. 'Couples get married in the temple. Mormons only,' he said. 'Outsiders wouldn't understand.'

"Shit. We understood our child leaving our hearth, our protection. Embarking on a new life. In a ceremony excluding us. What had we done? Held the wrong beliefs."

The waitress came and cleared dishes. We ordered coffee. Erik's eyes were still gray, but he took my hand.

* * * *

"You know … I understand now—the Balkans, the Middle East, even Ireland all those years ago," I said. You want to get their attention, show them the pain. Still, I was only thinking about it, imagining …"

"Then the next thing you know…?"

"*Kerblam*! That first temple … They sort of puff up, then crumple. But when people were killed…"

"Yeah, gosh. What was that…"

"I absolutely wanted to not hurt people. I … we were really careful to pick times when nobody would be around."

"Something. Later. A hoax?"

"I dunno. Real rubble. Real funeral, on TV. Then I vamoosed. De-part-ted."

"Geez. I can't remember. Maybe I'll look it up online."

"I was horrified. And then I panicked for myself, too. They'd really search for … the culprits, now. I'd be lucky to get life in prison."

"So you ran."

I nodded. "Another kind of prison. I'm cut off from family forever, maybe. I was in total isolation for a year."

"Seems like you did to yourself worse than …"

"I know. Poetic justice. I was mad because I missed a ceremony. Now I'm missing their lives. But, Erik. It wasn't just the ceremony. "

"Yeah. You don't agree with their tenets. That's the way the world is getting to be. If you disagree, blow something up." He let go my hand, leaned back.

"Sometimes you just can't get people's attention. In grad school there was an activist group, some of them wanting to do anything big and noisy, because folks just didn't listen. What about those guys in 1776, going on about liberty or death? We so venerate them."

"What about those guys on 9/11 going on about the Great Satan? We so revile them."

Erik and I looked at one another across a growing distance, Erik anchored, me adrift, flotsam in a violent flood.

"Bombing. Oh, man, Kate. This is something to digest, you know. It isn't going down real well. All that destruction. Poetic justice, bullshit. Face a judge." His eyes were beyond gray. Steel. In a blizzard.

"I was wrong, Erik. But those … *saints*, they call themselves, all the damage *they've* caused. Who brings them to justice? At least *I've* stopped. Even the itch is gone."

"Their figurative demolition goes to some figurative court, Kate."

"Oh, Erik, please. Please tell me you'd give me twenty-four hours warning if you decide to report this?"

He got the head-rubbing, butt-wriggling jitters. "Good gawd, Kate. I gotta get out of here. This is all … It's too much."

I dug in my purse. "I'm buying, remember?"

"Yeah. And I can't. Buy it. Maybe I will. Gimme time. Quiet—time." He stood, focused on me again for a moment. "Thanks for dinner. For truth."

Outside, white and weary, we faced one another again. "It's hard to think," Erik said. "No sleep last night."

"Didn't do so well myself. I paced, thought about how to tell you, paced thought about running away …"

"I've gotta go home, Kate. Got my own pacing to do. My brain is just noise. Static."

"You can't promise me twenty-four hours, can you?"

"What the hell?"

"Warning. Before you report me."

"Don't know who I'd call at eight at night, even if I wanted to. All I can tell you right now is that I've got to do some hard thinking. With luck get some sleep."

"I was afraid. Your reaction. It's who you are. The response of an honest man."

"Well, my gawd. Katie. Blowing up big sacred places."

"Goodbye, Erik. Rest well, if you can." I'd wrapped my emotions tight, like wire on a bale of hay. Cut the wire, the bale sprongs apart.

"Good night. Just so much to sort out …" He wandered into the darkness.

Erik Decides

By one the next morning Subaruth was stuffed and the apartment nearly empty. I decided to leave bed, sofa, and my folding tables. They required a trailer, which is just a tad hard to acquire in the middle of the night.

I'd drawn *Odin*, the unknowable, the blank rune. Death of life as you now know it, the oracle said. I guessed I'd revert to Janet. I'd get money on the way out of town, didn't suppose I could keep using the Kate McGuire account I'd so triumphantly established. Didn't know where I was going. Supposed I had it all to redo: the obits, stealing another social security number, another closet, trapped. Another identity, another Swiss account. No family, no friends. No Erik, no Tara. Hearts really do hurt, the muscle strained.

I balanced a big box of kitchen stuff to take to the car, parked for hours in a thirty minute spot out front. Midnight, nobody cares about parking spots. I swung out of my apartment and nearly sent the box crashing down. Somebody there! With a box, too. Not jumping like mine.

"Kate. Don't go. I'm so sorry."

An eternity of juggling and gasping. "Erik. What the hell ..."

"I came to my senses, tried to call ..."

"You called? Who? FBI? Cops?" Should I drop the bloody box and run?

"Nobody. I tried to call you, is all. I realized you said goodbye and I'd left you with no options …"

"What's with the box?"

"It's from your car. You don't need to go anywhere, Kate. I haven't called anyone. I won't call anyone. You're safe here."

"Oh. But …"

"Can I come in, Katie? I promise you're okay. I promise no one will come pounding on your door. I didn't knock either. I just waited. I was afraid I'd spook you."

"You did spook me. What's the probability that I'd open my door in the middle of the night to find someone standing out here in the hall?"

"Can I come in? This isn't the best place to talk."

My pulse was still pounding, fright to flight. But I needed my purse, so I backed up into the apartment. Erik followed me, put his box down, took mine and stacked it atop his. He stood between me and escape, taking off cap, coat, and scarf, laying them on the boxes. I watched his gaze go from empty bookshelf to bare kitchen counter to the missing throw rug at his feet.

"I was almost too late. You've about emptied the apartment."

"Just the fridge to do. A bit from the bathroom. One more trip after this one."

"I saw your car was loaded."

"Say it one more time? That you haven't called anyone?" My voice sounded like it had squeezed through a narrow space. Which it had.

Erik took my shoulders and guided me backwards until I sat on the sofa. Then he sat on the floor in front of me, picked up my left foot, pulled off my shoe, and started rubbing. He'd already learned that will get him everywhere. The end, the beginning, the Odin stone had said.

"Okay." His earnest look touched me. "I screwed up and you're ready to run. Listen carefully, please. You said yourself that I'm an honest man. I'm as honest as I've ever been in my life when I say that I've told *no one* about our conversation tonight, about Andrea Glass. Nothing. Nada. Not a peep. I tried to call to tell you."

I relaxed an iota. "I heard the phone. Couldn't bear to talk."

"I was afraid you were gone. I must've hit 70 getting here. It's snowing. Getting slick. I was scared."

I put my shoe back on, and we brought some boxes back in from the car and parked properly. Our coats were wet so I draped them on the kitchen counter. "They'll dry there by the air vent. Wow. I'm fading fast."

"Good," Erik said. "That must mean the adrenaline rush has gone, and you haven't." He picked up one box. "Come on. I'll help you make your bed again."

I started pulling bedding out of its box. I found the mattress pad and sheet and separated them.

"Hasty packing, Elskede," Erik said.

El-who, I wondered. "At least it's more or less in reverse order. Bedspread and pillows went in first."

I looked at Erik when we'd finished making the bed. "Sneaky, Erik. That's one way to get into a girl's bedroom."

"Yeah. I read about it in *Playboy*. Technique number seventeen. Scare the starch right out of the girl, so she packs up and runs. Then allay her fears, help her with the bed ..."

I gave him a shove. It didn't help. He sprawled onto the comforter. Blue circles, burgundy squares and rumpled Erik.

"And then tell her something that will make her want to thump you. She'll literally push you into her bed."

"You know," I sat beside him, "if you want to mess with a dead body ... what's that called?"

"Necrophilia."

"Well, if that's your preference, you've got one at your mercy. A dead body."

Erik got up. "Do you have pjs or something in the suitcase?" I nodded; he grabbed the bag, tossed it to me and went into the living room, closing the bedroom door behind him. I heard him puttering out there as I undressed.

Then he knocked on the bedroom door. "Can I come in? There is something important I haven't told you yet."

I threw open the door, toothbrush still in my mouth. "What important?"

"No, nothing to scare you. Good news." He looked at me, distracted. "Where did you find such scruffy pajamas?"

"Bought them specially to impress you. If you want scruffy, you should have seen the longjohns I wore night and day for months in the wilderness."

"That's OK. Flannel with Snoopy and all those fuzz-pills—suits me fine."

I went to the bathroom and finished cleaning my teeth. "I'm exhausted."

Erik pulled aside the covers, motioned me into bed. "I'm harmless tonight, I promise, but I do want to tell you. It's good news. Then I'll go."

"Oh, lie down here. It's a big enough bed. Pull off your shoes. I don't want you getting in a wreck because you fell asleep on the way home."

"The neighbors. In the morning …" But he sat on the bed. "You didn't kill anybody."

"Yeah I did. The Whitesons. The funeral was on TV." I tossed his shoes into the corner.

"It was a hoax, Kate."

"No. It was on the news for days." By now I was snuggled under the covers, and I pulled them around my ears.

"It was a hoax. Fooled everyone, including reporters and investigators, for more than days. Weeks. There was a big article on it in the LA Times. I just found it again on the web."

I sat upright. "The Whitesons weren't killed?"

"Never even existed, Katie."

"What? What! I saw their pictures. The funeral. Why would they … How …?"

"A group in Utah noticed the pattern: bombs planted when no one would be around. They wanted action. Maybe if someone were killed, the bombers would panic and reveal themselves. Maybe the investigation would ramp up."

"It worked on me." Somehow I was on my feet. Pacing. Again. "Oh, my gosh. I shouldn't have run. No, maybe I had to anyway. Investigators came to my house … The trick worked on the investigators then, too. But how … there had to be bodies …"

"This group was good. In the articles I read about the 'Whitesons,' they still hadn't figured out what real people were involved, but 'rescue workers' found 'body parts' that turned out to be beefsteak, a 'crime lab technician' identified 'two different people,' a 'dentist' provided the 'Whitesons' dental records' for the 'technician' to 'match and identify.' In addition they had a whole cast of 'family members.'"

"A hoax. I kept wondering how someone could have been there. How did they catch on?"

"A reporter. He couldn't find any history on the Whitesons."

"Wow. A reporter who investigates." I plopped down again.

"This guy had no suspicions. He only wanted a freelance sympathy article on the Whitesons, and 'the family' avoided talking to him. Then the answers he did get, to simple questions like number of kids, profession … He kept hearing different things."

"Holey moley. Hohhhhh Leeee Mohhhhhh Leeeeeeeee."

"So maybe you're a little safer than you thought. You're certainly not the villain you thought …"

"Geez Louise. My brain's zinging."

"Crackle. Pop."

"Okay." I stuck out my lower lip, blew at the hair hanging in my eyes. We were both sitting on the bed now, leaning against the pillows, feet up. It felt like a train was pulling away from the station, and I was simultaneously on the train and running to catch it. "How safe am I? There's still the bombing."

"Well, no deaths: no death-penalty, I assume."

"So ninety-nine degrees of horror instead of a hundred."

"They suspected you were involved, I guess?"

I explained about returning home in secret, packing for the wilderness. "And just the day that I was leaving anyway, they came. I barely evaded them. Even in my panic I knew I was in a hilarious scene. It was December, cold and raining. I jumped out of the shower, grabbed a towel and my clothes and ran into the woods by my house, naked as a belch in Boston. Soapy wet hair, muddy feet, damp towels, didn't dare move while they were so close. Fortunately the brush is dense in Oregon."

"You *barely* evaded them!"

"Yeah. Har har. It was a miracle they didn't spot the muddy trail going up into the woods."

"So maybe they were insurance salesmen. Missionaries maybe, just wanting you to become a Mormon."

"No. I heard them talking. Something about my daughter telling them I wasn't home. And then one of them left to get a search warrant."

"Oh oh."

I told Erik about hearing on the radio that I was a 'person of interest' and about seeing Low Voice again in St. Louis at the ATM. And about the e-mail from Matt Sheridan, who was probably Low Voice. "The e-mail said they—the FBI—want to talk to me about the bombings. If I didn't come in they'd issue a warrant for me."

"Did they? Issue a warrant?"

"I suppose so. I haven't opened e-mail since."

"Wow. Lots to figure out. Will you tell me the whole story from the beginning? How does a nude woman escape from the woods?"

"Pfffft. Sounds like a puzzle I used to give my students. How far can a nude woman go *into* the woods?"

"I dunno."

"Halfway." I relented and explained. "If she goes more than that ..."

"She's less than halfway from the other side. Okay, funny. But what students?"

"I'm a retired math teacher."

"Kate Andrea Glass McGuire. You have a *lot* to tell me."

"Ohmygosh. Yes. Yes yes. It's a long story. You deserve to hear it. Just not now." My secondary adrenaline burst had faded. I was unstarched, un-ironed, almost unconscious. "If I weren't already sitting in this bed, I'd be reduced to a puddle somewhere."

"Yeah, me too."

"Huge news, though, about the Whitesons. Woke me up for a while. When my brain restarts, I need to think about what it means. I've needed to think about what to do next, anyway. But thanks. For coming. For telling me. For. Everything."

"If you let me, tomorrow, maybe I can help you work through it all."

"Yes. Wonderful. Please. Are you comfortable?"

"Can you tolerate my smelly self?"

"If you were smelly, I'm not sure I'd notice." I was murmuring into my pillow.

Erik went into the bathroom. I wriggled and stretched under the covers, then pulled blankets aside for him as he crawled in. Tee shirt and boxers.

"Tell me one more time." I sounded like a 78 rpm record playing at 33. Low, slurred, and drawn out. "Doesn't a man of integrity report his bomber friend?"

"How could it show integrity to hurt someone I care about?"

"A criminal someone. If you change your mind, you'll still give me twenty-four hours?"

"More than that, *elskede*. I'm flattered at the credit for honesty, but I'm not a black-and-white person. What you did was wrong, but I also think you've been … hoisted by your own petard. I promise I will *not* report you. Maybe *you* should report—stay anonymous—maybe stop more damage. Whoever you helped with those bombs …"

"No. No. It won't help. Nobody …" I was mumbling. So tired. So much to explain. Or not. He was holding my hand. When did that happen?

"The others? Maybe plea bargain? Help catch them?"

"I can't think about it any more tonight. My alligator brain is in charge. Fear from telling you. Two traumatic days. Dredging up two years' trauma. Two decades?"

"Oh, Katie. I'm sorry. Will you let me try to help? Think about options?"

"For tonight, Mr. White Knight, if you could just hang on

to me, keep me from flying into insanity…"

"Err a err er err."

His rooster call answering my chicken-panic. Good guy. So glad he came back.

Blizzard

The next morning I came out of the bedroom sniffing. "I smell coffee. It's been a buzillion years since I woke up to the smell of coffee. Ummmm."

"I found dishes, coffee maker, coffee. I don't know if I've put things in the right place."

"Will you marry me?"

"Absolutely." He grinned.

"Though … I dunno. You look fuzzy in the morning."

"That's because you don't have your glasses on."

I patted my face with my hands. "Ohmygawd. Clearly I'm still not right, even after that wonderful sleep. I haven't touched feet to floor without my glasses for … for *two* buzillion years at least."

By the time I returned, glasses on, Erik had set the table.

"You still look fuzzy."

"I don't have my greasy kid stuff here. I'm nervous about the neighbors. They're going to see how fuzzy I look."

"Only people our age worry about what the neighbors think."

"So? Don't people our age count? Several of them were downstairs listening to us the other night."

"Yeah. You're right. Borrow my maroon stocking cap. People will see a UM fan, won't see hair. But later. Now, let's have bacon and eggs and French toast and steak and eggs and . . ."

"Anxiety makes you hungry, huh?"

"That and moving all my stuff in the middle of the night. Let's definitely have fruit and French toast. Maybe some bacon. And read the paper for a while."

"I have a special talent for flipping pancakes."

"Okay. I'll mix up batter, defrost some of my frozen berries. You flip pancakes, I'll go get the paper downstairs. We'll eat and read the comics and drink coffee. We'll pretend for a while that we're normal."

"It's a plan."

"After that, could you help me unpack the rest from my car?"

"Okay." He looked out the window. "It kept coming down while we slept, obviously. Good thing I've got my snow tires on."

Over his shoulder I saw a white quilt spread everywhere. "Cold weather, great excuse to sit by the fire. More Irish coffees—it'll be after noon by then—while you see if you can straighten out my life."

"And catch up. You're still hanging out in the nude in the rain in my head."

"However much you can tolerate. I wasn't kidding. It *is* a long story."

"With adventure? Drama?"

I handed him the bowl of pancake batter I had mixed. "Yep. Something between a soap opera, an adventure story, and Dick

Tracy. Or maybe the Pink Panther. I'll be right back with the paper."

I had awakened wondering whether to tell Erik there was no gang, no one to turn in. No one to plea bargain about. Or should he remain unaware of the details? He'd be a lousy liar if he were questioned. Of course, I thought I was a lousy liar two years ago when this strange migration began. Maybe I could describe a loosely knit group, people who didn't know each other, communicating online, faces concealed on the job?

Nah. I could hear Erik's disbelief: trust people you never met? To properly conduct illegal activity? What if someone was an informant? What if someone didn't show: no bomb, or no timer, or no lookout?

The more I told Erik, the greater my jeopardy. But he'd offered to help. I liked him. I'd jumped into ten-foot deep seas by telling him anything. If telling all put me in ten-*mile* deep seas, so what?

Besides, he'd never forgive more dissembling.

* * * *

"I want to hear about Sabrina, when she was little," Erik said over pancakes, "and—what's his name? Your real guy? Ned?"

"Neil." It was so the right place to begin. I talked about goats and horses and dogs. About 4-H. About clearing brush and improving the house. About what a good kid Sabrina was, what a good rider, how she communicated with the animals, doctored them when they were hurt. About her finding the "monster," a catfish in the creek. About our travels. About teaching, me in math trying to increase confidence, Neil in history trying to shake complacency.

Amazing how good those memories felt, no injured edge.

Erik left to shower and de-fuzz and found me unloading boxes when he returned. He starting putting books back on the shelf.

I didn't know what I'd done to deserve this blue-eyed kind giant with the mellow voice.

"Were Neil and Sabrina close?" he asked.

"Oh yes. What a pair." I described the little tow head and a dark graying one bent over a piece of tack, adjusting it just so. An adolescent and her dad getting all teary-eyed over the beautiful Bill of Rights. A young woman working with her best mentor on her valedictory speech. The joy on his face. "Smart girl, Sabrina. Whatever led her to this foreign faith? College should be a place to grow, but she seemed to get narrower."

"Still, it seems like a stretch to think her wedding and his strokes are connected."

"Yeah. Who knows? 'Correlation is not causation,' as the stats people say. But emotional well-being does affect physical well-being. We do know that. And, real or not, they're connected in my head. In my bones."

"How did he react when he learned about it?"

"You know, we liked Mark; that part was fine. When they told us they were getting married, we were both happy. Excited. Then the temple came up. 'Oh. But you can find a way for us to be a part of it, right?' I said.

"And Sabrina tried. She talked to somebody. Another

bishop, I guess. And called us. 'The temple ritual is so sacred. Any other ceremony would defile it,' she said.

"Neil, on the extension, reacted. Emphatic words. The curly phone cord connected me. But I was disconnected, trying to breathe, vision gone. Pressing receiver to ear with aching arm. Hearing static, noise. He came roaring round to see if I was still there. Where else would I be?"

"So what did you do?"

"We went camping. Couldn't stand to sit at home. Had a lovely trip, lost track of the days, almost. We were at Mt. Robson that day."

"Neil seemed to be okay?"

"We both seemed to be okay. We didn't talk about it: what was there to say? But I was teetering, couldn't get my balance. And Neil's first stroke hit within a year. Blanked out on his feet in front of thirty ninth-graders. Right in the middle of describing the horror of the U.S. civil war, no words would come. For months his words refused to come. He had to give up teaching." Not so great, these memories. These memories hurt.

"He lived for a while?"

"Four years. I was busy, trying to be there for Neil, trying to make the most of the days left to us. We traveled in Winnie a lot. On the road ... you didn't notice the ragged hole ...."

"When he died is when you . . ."

"Oh, Erik. I just fell into darkness. I grieved for Neil, I grieved for everything, for Katie O'Flanagan that sixteen-year-old lab-setter I was telling you about, for Sabrina's lost childhood, for Smudge, the sorrel quarter horse mare who hauled us and pulled lariat-loads of brush and pounded on the door with a foreleg if we were weekend-slow at giving her breakfast. I grieved for my mother, for President Kennedy. I played Shostokovitch, Bartok, anything dissonant at top volume. Nothing helped. Nothing."

Erik was just nodding. He knew. Losing his Elena to cancer had been no easier. "The difference," he said, "was that I had no focus for my own rage. Just the gods."

"When you've been destroyed, you don't want anything left whole. Nothing that had anything to do with the devastation."

It got easier then, the telling. We could laugh at some of it: *Naked in the Rain, Dance with Fire, Closet Dweller*, even my encounter with Matt Sheridan at the St. Louis bank. Erik found my story of rescue by fox and flute compelling, too. So as light faded that afternoon, order reigned in the apartment and in Erik's hair. He'd heard most of my story. All truth. His eyes stayed blue and his understanding was like Bag Balm on ripped flesh.

When I told him that, he tipped his head back and his joyful baritone laugh rumbled from somewhere deep. "As a poet, you'd better not give up your day job," he said.

Then we looked out and realized we were in the midst of a blizzard. We could hardly see the street from my window.

"Let's have dinner right here, before the electricity goes out," I suggested. "I have the makings for spaghetti." I got out sauce, noodles and a couple of pots. Eric found an onion and started chopping. We were wonderfully comfortable together, and before long we were seated by the window with our dinner.

"So are you content being Kate McGuire?"

"Well, definitely an upgrade, Life 3.0 compared to a couple of years ago. The glitch is my family. And health insurance. What if I'm badly hurt? But it's my family I can't bear to think about."

"Do you still miss them like you did at first?"

"It's a different kind of missing." Chewing spaghetti bought me time for chewing on the thought. My answer had surprised me. "I had to put them out of my mind to survive. I'll never get them back, truly. They've grown and changed. I've changed, too. But I can still get nuts, thinking about never seeing them again."

"Which is what will happen if you keep hiding."

"But it also makes me crazy to think of coming out. I finally feel safe. Usually."

"I know. 'Buck, buck.' Poor hysterical chicken lurking just below the Placid Kate surface." Erik got up, got some paper and a pen from my bookshelf. "How much would we risk setting you off again if we list your options?"

"Well, let's start with staying here, staying Kate McGuire …"

He wrote that on the first piece of paper. Then he made two columns, labeled "pros" and "cons."

"Yes, Erik. I like that way of thinking. Dispassionate. Are you a closet mathematician?"

"No, this is English teacher mode. So we have *safe* on the one side, and on the other, *health insurance* and *FAMILY*. Big capital letters." He wrote as he spoke. Then his pen lifted and so did his eyebrow. I figured he was trying to gauge my buck-off probability. I didn't know either, whether I had sanity firmly in place. "Let's think about insurance," he said, "the easy issue first."

It didn't take long. People aged sixty-something should have it. Andrea does, with payments deducted monthly from her checking account. If she uses the policy, she gets caught.

"So, buy a policy for Kate McGuire."

"The real Katherine McGuire probably already has one."

"Oofta!" Next to *insurance*, Erik wrote, "Andy can't use. Kate can't buy." *FAMILY* provoked a mercifully brief discussion. "Kate can't see them. Minimal communication, maybe," he wrote. Then he added question marks. "Maybe we're not creative enough."

"Nope. Unsolvable problems, Erik. I've spent two years going round in circles. I can't risk seeing the family. I can't risk buying insurance. At least I'm probably healthier after roughing it for a year."

"You were lucky: a bite and a broken arm. What if the cougar had attacked you? What if you'd broken your back? Ruptured your spleen?"

"Or now, a car wreck or shingles or an abscessed tooth?"

We didn't know what to do about insurance. Or family.

The electricity went out. We lit a candle, finished our dinner, and cleaned up the kitchen. "Maybe your family wouldn't recognize you now?"

Dang. The guy was persistent. "Oh, Erik. I solved so many

problems just to be Kate McGuire in Montana. My head hurts. Let's go downstairs and do a little music."

Erik took the candle back over to the table. "I can't finish these lists in the dark, anyway, but let's brainstorm for just a few more minutes."

I so didn't want to think about it. I groaned.

"Come on, Mathematician Problem-Solver Extraordinaire." Erik softened his challenge with a smile and took my hand. "Maybe you could go back to Oregon as Kate McGuire, volunteer in your grandkids' school or something." His nose four inches from a new page, he wrote carefully, "Oregon as Kate." He made two columns for pros and cons as before.

"That would solve the miss-the-family problem. But I think they'd recognize me, at least by the first time I opened my mouth. Write that when we have light, Erik. We'll remember."

He took another sheet of paper. "You could surrender." He snatched a fourth sheet. "You could confess to being part of a group—just a hanger-on." Yet another page, "Or you could go home as Andy, deny any involvement."

"You should have been a psychologist, Erik. You're good. Whipped right on by that 'surrender' option."

"Well, we'll probably rule it out fast. It does need research though—sentencing guidelines, possibility of suspended sentence, plea bargaining, that sort of thing."

"All the terrorism stuff now, Erik. And being part of a gang doesn't hold together. I thought that through this morning. And …"

He read my tension correctly. "Okay, we'll write all that

down when it's light. Like you said, let's go do some music."

It was pleasant downstairs, an overstuffed living area with fireplace. Erik persuaded me to work on a couple of the *Songster* tunes that we had played by the campfire and again Thursday night, B.C., Before Confession. But now Erik was thinking how the other *Songsters* might interact: First verse, all of us. Second verse, mandolin and bass only. Third verse, flute and bass only. Fourth verse, all of us. He was talking me into this.

Our playing again attracted an audience. With no one going anywhere in the storm, we provided a good diversion. The manager came out with a pot of hot cider, and a young woman asked if she could sit in with her cello. Somehow her joining us evaporated the last of the fear lurking in my innards. We forgot the audience and just made music.

When we got back to the apartment, Erik closed his eyes and took a slow deep breath. "I think all the emotional toxins have dissipated..."

"From the apartment *and* our bloodstreams, I hope."

We relit the candles—tranquil cranberry scent—then stirred up the fire and fixed more Irish. I was making a believer of Eric. He was so relaxed, it wouldn't keep him awake at all.

We drew a rune. *Uruz*, the wild ox. Strength. But reversed. Opportunity disguised as loss, the oracle said. Seek among the ashes for new perspective, new strength.

At the window with our coffees, we watched midnight snow slanting sideways into headlight beams of occasional passing vehicles. Erik turned, took the cup from my hands, and put it on the table with his own. When he folded me into his big, warm embrace, it felt like coming home. Like walking into Grandma's kitchen, hot apple pie on a cold day. His kiss, a natural extension of the tenderness he had shown me all day, evoked neither bucking nor squawking. He tasted like Irish coffee and Old Spice.

Then we discovered all systems were go. All my systems. Erik, after my Thursday panic, was carefully restrained. In fact, foreplay became fiveplay which turned into gazillion-play. Enough thoughtfulness already. Finally I slid away from him.

"Kate? … Kate?"

By the time he got to "what's wrong, Kate?" I had flown from the bedroom, across the short space of the living area in the all together darkness and grabbed a butter knife.

I laughed, flapped, buck-buck-danced back to him and held the knife to his neck. "Make your moves or die," I said.

"Rape!" he chortled and filled that need, too.

As he did again in the thin light of December morning. And again at noon, shower interrupted, plans for lunch at Casey's changed.

Finally, over peanut butter sandwiches in mid-afternoon, we worked a bit more on Erik's brainstorm lists for my future. He added another page called "Marry Erik." In cold afternoon objectivity, we decided to research prison terms and realized Kate couldn't marry Erik: she was already married. And if Andy married Erik, she'd spend her honeymoon—or her life—in jail.

We had another false start for Casey's, taking two tries at a shower before we succeeded. Finally, with electricity on, snow stopped and roads passable, we drove to the restaurant and annihilated oversized steak dinners. We decided I would go to Vermont with Erik to visit his family for Christmas. From Vermont, I would contact my attorney and try to get some advice. I'd call my family, too, and see how quickly they recognized my voice.

I waited in the car while Erik picked up clothes and shaving kit at his place. We had until the next afternoon before the world, aka tutor clients, would intervene.

Us

Eventually I understood. It's not about REconnecting. It's about connecting. Sometimes we outdistance our pasts. Like eggs in pancake batter, the past is essential but no longer recognizable. Erik was my now. Is my now.

We formed *Songsters Four*. Believe it or not, the hardest part of that transition was for Erik. In our first performance together I was going to play in just a couple of songs which we had carefully rehearsed. But the crowd wanted more flute. I knew I could do it. Doug and Al knew I could do it. Erik was a plan-ahead and rehearse rehearse rehearse guy. He relented. The hasty plan was for me to take the lead in the third verse, but in the middle of that I forgot the tune and started riffing around. Doug saved me, picking up my part on his mandolin. Erik's face had turned an interesting shade of grey-blue white. I steeled myself, waiting for the crash as he fainted, but he recovered. During our "short break" Erik gasped and sputtered and the guys laughed until they too were hyperventilating. Doug threw in a few extra licks at the end of the next set, just to see Erik's reaction. Then in another performance Al did it. More random riffs here and there. Finally Erik did it to them—during a rehearsal. Now all four of us can bounce around a melody. Three of us think that makes our show less wooden. One of us tolerates it, believing we worked out the best possible variation during rehearsal.

In Vermont that Christmas I was the one needing to improvise. I met some open arms, some reservations, some lingering sorrow for a lovely mom/grandma taken from them young. I blended myself into the background and let them talk about old friends, old times. But when we went to bed on Christmas Eve I curled into a tight cold ball, a stranger here. Estranged from Sabrina, my own grandchildren, Mark. My family so far away. The little girls wouldn't know me at all, a person from half their lifetimes ago. I flipped onto my belly. Weren't there several ways to prove the Pythagorean theorem? The a+b square and what else?

Erik got up. Shuffled around. "Kate, come back. Come away from Oregon and back here to Vermont. This may not be the time, but I have something I want to share with you."

I turned my head, cracked open one eye. He'd lit a candle. And his hands held a gift box.

"Oh, Erik, I hate opening gifts early. I love suspense, the surprise."

"This might be too much surprise. There's a second box downstairs that you can wonder about. This is about the two of us."

"What? Birth control pills, maybe. Believe me …" Now I was sitting up.

"C'mon, Kate. Help me out here." He sounded nervous.

Oh - oh. What? What, what ...

He climbed behind me, my back against his belly, his arms

and legs around me. Then he handed me the box, about the size of a box of chocolate covered cherries. It didn't look dangerous. "Please open it now, Katie."

So I did. Inside the chocolate-cherry box there were no candies. Just another smaller box. Jewelry.

He's nervous. Surely not a ring. We ruled out 'Marry Erik.' But what else would make him so nervous?

"Katie, you're killing me here. Will you open the bloody thing?"

It was a ring. A marquis-cut garnet obviously set to overlap a second ring. A smaller sapphire was on each side. He had noticed my partiality for blue and burgundy. It was lovely. And unique. And clearly an engagement ring. I gazed at it for a long time.

Erik let out a breath. He must have been holding it. "Is that a 'no,' Katie? It feels like 'no.'"

"Ohmygosh, Erik." I slid myself to look upside-down at his face. "I can't imagine anything nicer than spending the rest of my life with you. But … But you know it's impossible."

"Katie, if you would wear this ring, it would make me so proud. I want it to mean you'll stick with me. Not that we'll have a particular ceremony at some prescribed time, but that we'll care for one another. Look out for each other. For better or for worse."

I was silent. Stricken. Tears started sliding. I nearly gave myself two black eyes swiping at them. "Erik. It could be so one-sided if things don't work out. If I go to prison. Or have to stay hidden. All take and no give on my part."

"I want this ring to mean we're hoping for the best but prepared for the worst. No, actually, that together we'll strive to avoid the worst. Will you wear it, Katie?" His voice was fading from soft to nearly inaudible.

"Well, let me make a couple of things perfectly clear. First, it's a bright, beautiful concept. I love every minute I spend with you, and I'd like to spend all the minutes possible with you. Second, it's a wonderful ring. Extraordinary." I tilted the box and watched the light reflect from the stones. "I'd wear it with pride, both because of itself and because of the wonderful thing it represents between us." I took a deep breath.

"There's a 'but' in there. I hear it coming. Deny it, Katie. Hitch up to my wagon. Lumber through life with me. Go with the music."

I couldn't think of a reason not to. He could improvise. Why shouldn't I? I liked the man, I loved the man. I felt warm and safe with the man. I had the hots for the man. No 'buts.' I held up my left hand, and he slid the ring on my finger.

"Perfect fit," I said. "Is that why I couldn't find my turquoise ring last week?"

"Yep. My artist friend up on Pinecrest Road created this one."

"I love it. The colors. The cut. Unique. Special."

"Like you. Andy or Kate—just one special you." Erik's baritone was like wind in trees, a river talking to itself on its way to destiny.

"I love the colors. I love you. I'm just afraid there's

something about this that is a bad idea, Erik. But I can't figure out what."

And so I wore his ring. I was still Kate, with Kate's problems, but we forgot those. For a while.

* * * *

It was March, almost spring break, when Erik caught me crying. I didn't expect him but his last tutor client canceled. So he came home early and discovered me in the terrible blues.

"You've kinda been off your game lately," he said. "You'd better fess up."

"I don' cry. I *hade* crying. Makes my eyes hurd, nose stuff ub, head ache. Nothing geds any bedder; my body jus' ends ub feeling lousy, too."

"So, Elskede, you've been suddenly hit with a virus-from-nowhere that gave you red eyes and a stuffy nose?"

"No dammid. I've been crying. But I *hade* it." I'd been putting his books on the new bookshelves we'd bought for the den, and I slammed three more from box to shelf.

He kissed each sorry eye and moved to the door. "Do you want coffee or Irish coffee?"

"Oh, yes. Coffee. Give me whiskey when I'm in this stade and I really get pidiful."

You do so much so right, Erik Mathieson. I tried to wipe at my eyes while he was gone, but swelling doesn't wipe off. My face felt like I'd taken a long swim in an acid bath.

He came back with a cup for each of us, went to the couch, sat, and patted the place beside him. When I joined him, he handed me my cup, set his on the shelf, pulled my feet on his lap, and started rubbing. *Deja vu.* It was the same sofa, same picture hanging behind it, maybe even the same coffee cups as when he first chipped away at my reserve and sent me flying off into the chicken dance. Only now I was wearing his ring, and we were living together in a lovely rambling old house we had found in Missoula a couple of months earlier.

He remembered, too. "Rrr a uhrrr a uhrrr?" Those beautiful blue eyes.

"No, thank gawd. Now I know I can depend on you, Erik. I can tell you stuff."

"So tell me, already. What happened? A week ago, I'll bet."

"The thing is, it's an unsolvable problem. Maybe I should write it up in a math journal. Math nerds love unsolvable problems."

"Katie, I guess it's good you're not 'buck-buck-bucking,' but you *are* e-e-evading."

I sighed. All this talk, just like shoveling chicken shit. Same stink in a new place. What golden egg was Erik looking for anyway? "It's the same old story, Erik. I have a better life with you. Life 4.0, vastly improved over previous editions. But I really, really, *really* miss my family. I read my e-mail while we were doing that Spokane gig. Sabrina had her baby. Named him Benjamin." I'd created a new e-mail account, an occasional electronic connection that only pushed my lonely key.

"Warm little sweet-smelling baby nestled under your chin," Erik said. "The thought even makes me blue."

My breath hiccuped. "Yeah. And older brothers and sisters that need a little snuggle themselves. Laurie and Brian probably think they're too old for such stuff. I'll bet they're playing assistant mommy and daddy. But Josh. And Emma and McKenzie, though I guess I'd be no help to them. They wouldn't remember me at all."

"That Josh. Shouting the moment he heard your voice when you called." I had phoned during a stopover on the way home after Christmas. "He sure remembers you. You'd think you were on speakerphone the way I heard him shouting."

I smiled, hearing it replay in my mind. "Mom. Dad. Mom. Come quick! It's Gramma! Gramma's on the phone. Quick. Come quick!"

I nearly wept, hearing him in my mind. I remembered how Erik and I had just sat and rocked for a very long time there at that airport phone.

"Have I ever shown you the proof that the square root of two is irrational?" I asked.

I can't write Erik's response, somewhere between a snort, a groan, and a volcanic eruption. "No. Nope. Uh-uh. No way," he said. "You stay right there and drink your coffee. I'll be back in a minute. You're not going to keep dodging *this* problem."

"It's unsolvable," I said to his back as he headed down the hallway.

I sipped my coffee as directed and got to thinking about whether there was a sound equidistant from *snort*, *groan*, and *eruption*. Three sounds, three emotions, three words. Like a triangle. Then I started wondering if I remembered how to construct the circle around a triangle whose vertices were S (for snort), G (groan), and E. The center of that circle is equidistant from the three points of the triangle. Is it the angle bisectors? Boy, I was forgetting way too much math.

Ignoring Erik's instructions to stay put, I grabbed my coffee and headed to our office. We now had a den, a music room—aka dining room—*and* an office.

Erik was there, scrabbling through the drawers of his desk.

"Here I am," I told him. I sat down and got paper from my bottom left desk drawer and a ruler and compass (the kind that draws circles) from the top center. I had constructed large triangle SGE and had begun some angle bisectors when Erik found what he was looking for and interrupted.

It was the list of options for Kate/Andy, begun during that December blizzard.

You are *so* from Mars, Erik, I thought. Gotta problem, gotta solve it. I like problem solving, too. When solutions exist. Leave it; just commiserate, Erik.

He wheeled his chair beside mine and began flipping through his pages. "Okay. 'Marry Erik.' That should be an option. It requires you to be Andrea, though."

I glanced over, nodded, bisected another angle.

"Also on the table: 'Go to Oregon as Andy, deny everything.' We can toss 'Surrender' and 'Confess to being part of a group.' We know that now." He wadded two sheets and threw them into the trash.

True. On the way home from Vermont, before I'd called Sabrina's house, I'd phoned my (Andy's) old attorney. "I look so guilty. I have no alibis," I told Ralph.

"Surely we can establish reasonable doubt."

"If we can't?"

"Massive property damage. Possible hate crimes. 'Terrist' fears. With luck, life. Less if they decided you were just an accessory. Thirty years, maybe."

"Oh, shit." Thirty years, life, same thing when you're sixty-something.

So yep, no confession for this soul. I nodded again. "Dang," I said. "It isn't angle bisectors. I should be able to prove this but I'm not thinking very well."

"Katie. Put down that damned contraption." Gray eyes. "You've got to help me here. It's your life. I want to share it and I don't want it to be miserable."

"I'm terrified, Erik. These circles are keeping me sane. It *is* my life, and I could lose it. All of it. You. Sabrina. The music. Tutoring. Everything. It scares me silly."

"Yeah. Well…you can't keep avoiding… Just give me a couple of your brain cells on this." He rattled the papers in his hands. Shuffled them. "It won't get any better here. You won't see that new baby. Maybe you could, if we thought it out."

I nodded and drew another triangle on the back of my paper. I started constructing perpendicular bisectors.

"We got a good start on it in December, Katie. Then Christmas … your bad-news attorney. Finding this place…work… *Songsters.* Now it's almost spring. Minus a grandbaby."

Maybe perpendicular bisectors was right. The sides of the triangle need to be chords of the circle.

He waved two sheets of paper. Stuck them under my nose. I

couldn't see my triangle. "Two options, Kate. You're currently on Plan A." He shook one of the papers. "'Stay here, stay Kate.' I don't like it. No family, no insurance, no marry-Erik, no play-with-the-band."

Songsters was playing in Boise in June, two nights, probably a thousand people each night. Scary. *Songsters Three*. Not me. Not there. "I can't play with the band if I'm in jail." I pulled out my paper and made two more arcs. "Might be able to marry you but it wouldn't be such a hot marriage, me in prison, you here." Our relationship had, in fact, remained quite hot. His current gray eyes notwithstanding.

"Well, I'm throwing away this page, too. We know all about it. I don't like it." And out went Plan A. "That leaves 'Go back to Oregon as Andy, claim you didn't do it.'"

"Buck, buck," I muttered.

He pulled out the rune stones and I drew three. Overall was Isa. Cold.

"No shit, Dick Tracy," I said. "It's the icy hand of fear."

The second stone, representing my challenge, was Odin. The blank stone. The Great Unknown. "Well, duh," I said.

But the third stone, representing action, was Raido: journey, communication, reunion. Well. I didn't have to read the handbook on that one either.

And Them

At first it was joint glimmer-dreaming, not quite asleep. "Suppose you told Sheridan you're innocent. You knew nothing about bombings. You say you just ran because …"

"Because I'd felt such empathy with that gang."

"…and no, you don't know who they are."

"I know nothing about them or bomb-making. But I felt so TERRIBLE."

"You shared their anger at the church …"

"… and that anger had gotten people killed, I thought."

"You felt responsible."

"Yeah."

And then the light was streaming in through the windows and we'd realize we'd fallen asleep in the middle of our plotting. Like me when I first contemplated bombing temples.

We spent months researching. What could Sheridan know? We read old news reports. We read every line of my journals. We read theories on the web. The only evidence against me seemed to be my proximity to the bombings. And by hiding I'd cast more suspicion my way. That was it. Absolutely. Wasn't it?

We spent more months in rehearsal. What would Sheridan say? How to answer? How might he try to trap me? How could I respond? We rehearsed at breakfast. We rehearsed any time we were alone. We rehearsed on the way to Tara and Ryan's July wedding.

"Why did you run if you weren't guilty?" Erik asked from behind the wheel of his Jeep.

"I *looked* guilty."

"...and felt guilty," Erik prompted.

"Oh goddamn. Shit. Sonofabitch!"

Erik was staring at me, amazed. I don't cuss. I don't cry. Here I was, doing both.

"Watch out!" I yelled.

The ugly curl of my mouth, my language, the tears straggling through my wrinkles nearly shocked Erik's Jeep into parting company with Uncle Sam's I-15. If only he'd crashed, maybe he'd give up this effen plan to get Andrea's life back.

"I'll take the next exit," he said after we quit fishtailing. Erik doesn't drive like that. "I dunno what scared me worse—the car off the edge or you off the edge."

By the time we pulled into a rest area, my emotions appeared to be in hand. But my jittery coffee cup betrayed truth: I wasn't in the same galaxy as okay-ness.

"So I thought we planned to just keep rehearsing possible scenarios with Mr. Sheridan?" Erik was so puzzled, was trying so hard, was so repulsive.

"On run-through number one-gazillion you told me I sounded too rehearsed. Now, run-through number one-gazillion-one, you correct me when it's not exactly as rehearsed. I can't do this, Erik."

"I'm sorry... It's so important..."

"No. It's not important. I'm not doing it. I can't."

"You can't tolerate life without Sabrina."

"Maybe I'll just have to see her from my jail cell."

"And me?"

"And you." I thought about giving back his ring. Why did I wear the ring of someone so bloody obnoxious? I toyed with it.

Erik read the thought. "No, please, Kate. That ring suits you. It's yours no matter what. It's not what's causing your distress." He sounded calm but his face was white.

Why did he even like me? Why did he want me to keep wearing this damn ring? How could I possibly drive another five hundred miles with this obsessive idiot?

He turned back toward the car. "If you stay here, you'll only get hot and hungry. I'm going to Tara's wedding. You're going to Tara's wedding. I won't talk about Matt Sheridan until you bring it up."

I heard hurt leaking through his measured tones like sap oozing from a wounded tree. I'm such a shit. Or he's such a shit. I followed him to the car. He played the recording of Arthur Miller's *The Crucible* for the next two hundred miles. He's the shit. Sure, the play was in next semester's curriculum, but trial probably lay in my own future, and I didn't want to hear about it.

* * * *

Erik and I serenaded Tara and Ryan's rehearsal dinner, and then she came to sit beside me. We were barely into the what-have-you-been-doing conversation and hardly past the let-me-see-the-ring ritual when Guru Tara emerged.

"So do you love him or hate him?"

I sighed. "Yes."

"He seems like a good person. Your soul twin, even."

"He is a good person. But obsessive. About *Songster* rehearsal. About… He's asking me to do something, for my own sake, that scares me. Worse than that sweat lodge."

"He knows about that hidden thing of yours, then."

I nodded. It hardly surprised me that Tara knew I had a *hidden thing.*

"Move to his side of the mountain, Kate. He's strong. He'll support you if you let him."

I nodded again. She was right, of course. Half my misery came from fear of losing Erik, and fear would fulfill itself if I kept pushing him away.

"I think you should take Erik to meet Sly," Tara added. "Sly introduced his own family to you, after all. Ryan and I have been hearing a lot from the foxtalk network lately."

"We planned to visit there next, but I suppose it will work only if Erik and I start actually talking to each other again."

It was Tara's turn to nod.

And so when the dancing started, I went to Erik, took his hand, led him to the floor, and he had to hold me. "Matt Sheridan," I said, tipping my head back to see his eyes.

It's an astonishing thing to watch tension dissipate from the face of someone you love. Little, nearly invisible lines smooth themselves out, and a malevolent presence makes itself evident by its departure. And, in Erik's case, grey eyes turn blue. I still didn't know how they do that. "I think I like Tara a lot," he said and pulled me closer.

We left the party early.

* * * *

Then the what-ifs. "What if…" we'd say as we drove from Tara's wedding to see Sly—who came, alone this time, and thrilled Erik. "What if…" all the way back to Missoula. "What if…" as we sat in the den with our Irish coffees. We'd work it out, then we'd rehearse. No TV, no pinochle. We tutored, played with *Songsters* and engaged in what-ifs.

* * * *

I'd never have done it, gone to Oregon that November Friday, met with Sabrina, met with Matt Sheridan, if not for Erik. I was terrified. He reassured. I was terrified. He reassured. I was terrified …

Sabrina: She's a loving daughter, but I had scared her, hurt her, puzzled her. My defense was an attack on her faith. As a good Mormon she believed in forgiveness, and she gave it her best. The two older kids were distant. So was their dad. But Josh, his exuberant personality only slightly subdued, greeted me at the door by throwing his arms around me at hip height. "Oh, Gramma, I've been waiting and waiting. I thought you'd never get here." The baby was like all babies, warm and fragrant, wailing at a stranger's touch, but settling in on my third try. The little girls, infants when I left, warmed to me slowly, as children do with well-intentioned strangers. Four out of eight. Not too bad.

Matt Sheridan: We met at Sabrina's house the next day in as comfortable a place as possible for this uncomfortable exchange. Yep. Sheridan was the guy I had been visualizing, the man I had seen at my house and at the ATM in Missouri.

And the guy watching us at the hotel, linebacker build, permanent black shadow on his chin, polished loafers with tassels? I'd asked him about magazines on the lobby tables after we noticed him always there. Squeaky Voice. From behind my house on the day I fled.

Sheridan started mildly enough: no I wasn't a suspect, just might have witnessed something helpful.

But then:

"Why were you in Provo? Your family thought you were in Idaho."

"Some guy at McCall, a couple of spaces down, got talking about Utah's red rock country in the snow, how spectacular it is. So I drove down."

"Why did you rent a car?"

"Bad roads, bad conditions for an RV."

"Please explain why you returned it at 3 a.m. Monday."

"I drank too much coffee."

"I beg your pardon?"

"I had decided to go back to McCall that day. Only I got reading. When I realized it was two in the morning and I was buzzing from caffeine, I had the choice between staying awake and driving, or staying awake and going nowhere. And I figured I'd avoid the commuter traffic."

And later:

"You heard that a temple had been bombed and people killed. You didn't have anything to do with it. You didn't see anything. You didn't hear anything that made you the least suspicious. Yet you ran away like a fugitive?"

I shrugged. "I do stuff like that. Go for the sake of going. Is that a crime?"

"Who is David, the fellow you were going to New Mexico with?"

"A nonexistent handsome devil made it easier to explain my leaving."

"I'm sure you can see how puzzling your behavior was. Why did you hide?"

"I went by that temple and saw only a barrier that divides families when they should unite. And I wished destruction would rain down on it. A couple of days later it was gone and two people died. It felt like my fault."

"You thought your wish caused people to die?"

"I dunno. In the glare of logic it makes no sense. In my gut …"

"You didn't have anything to do with that bomb?"

"No. Except to wish it." There. The lie. Which I had grown to believe. Almost.

He kept asking that question, in different ways "Let's go back to your running…Why did you hide?…How can you feel guilty for something you had no part in?…"

I lost it finally. "Dammit! I have a goddam emotional crisis, and it gets dissected by the Feds." I was on my feet without any memory of standing up. "The friggin church brought it on, and I can't even see it through without a hassle from the effen LDS-FBI." I don't swear, and the big O on Sabrina's mouth mirrored my own internal astonishment. This wasn't part of our script. Erik's foot moved under the table to nervously tap mine, but you can't stop a racing horse mid-stride. "Yes, I effen ran. You're making a bloody federal case out of my running from my own demons."

Matt Sheridan's hands gripped each other with vein-popping intensity. "You somehow blame the Church of Jesus Christ of Latter Day Saints for getting bombed. You somehow segue into personal crisis, despite sympathy with bombers. I don't understand. Perhaps you could sit down and draw a picture for a poor simple-minded man."

I sat down. Not that I wanted to. I wanted to do some B-movie karate chops and inflict maximum harm. I started to pull my braid over my head to look for split ends. I remembered Andy's bleepen wig just in time and bit a rough edge off a fingernail instead. Poor simple-minded man, my ass. I should have spent more time with Sly. Maybe some wily fox would have rubbed off on me, and I'd be more evenly matched here. Should have rehearsed more with Erik. Should have stayed in Montana. Should maybe just shoot myself.

"Wold you like hot cider, anyone?" Sabrina hovered. Not an easy task with a baby in her arms and a toddler underfoot.

"I *want* a friggin cup of coffee!" Kah-wham. Karate chop one. Innocent victim down.

Benjamin started crying. McKenzie stared at me, eyes wide, mouth open, body rigid. Sabrina jiggled Ben and headed out of the room. McKenzie stared.

"I'm sorry. I'm sorry, McKenzie." I leaned toward her, didn't pick her up. "I turned from Gramma into Big Bad Wolf, and I know you don't have coffee here, and I attacked the wrong people, and I do that once every zillion years when I get really, really, *really* frustrated. Please go tell your mom that Gramma's about to cry, too, for being so stupid."

"Mom says you shouldn't ever say that word, Gramma."

What word. I'd said a whole bunch of words.

"She says that *stupid* can hurt people a lot." And McKenzie turned to find her mom.

* * * *

Sheridan waited. He had asked why I ran away. He wanted an answer. As opposed to a tirade.

I turned my water glass on the table. Watched as the glass rotated faster than the ice. Sighed. "There's probably a psychological term for it. The feeling of guilt when something you wish for … More than wish for. Cheer on. Root for, like a freshman girl at a pep assembly…"

Sabrina was back. Both kids must have gone down for a nap. That was quick. I'd rather have had her away. Probably should have arranged to meet Sheridan someplace else. But coming here felt way less scary.

I talked to a spot on the table, along the line where the leaf and the table joined. "When it comes about, you rejoice. And then it has terrible consequences. Someone killed. Oh. Shit. You wonder what kind of human being you are. You wonder *who* you are. What is your justification for breathing in and breathing out? And it takes a long time to accept that you didn't bring it on by wishing it."

"Why would you feel that way?" The edge had left Matt Sheridan, and he was looking at his own spot on the table.

"Wanting to destroy a beautiful, holy place?"

"An institution that shuts a family off from a ceremony as important as a wedding…no, no, don't dismiss this," I added as he got a 'cryin' out loud, not *this* again' look on his face. "Do you have children?" I asked.

He nodded.

"Do you have a daughter?"

"Two," he said.

Of course. He's Mormon. "Can you tell me you have never thought about seeing your daughter, lovely in a white gown, kneeling at an altar and uniting herself with some promising young handsome fellow?"

The look on his face answered me.

"Now picture that happening and you're not there, forbidden to take part."

* * * *

It seemed to be over early that afternoon, and we spent time with the family. But that night Matt Sheridan was waiting in the hall in front of our hotel room. More questions. He tried to pressure me into talking to him then.

I protested, late hour, exhaustion. Finally, "No." Erik spoke for me as he held my sweaty hand. "If you have some reason to arrest her, we have no choice, but I think that's not the case. Furthermore, this conversation is getting adversarial; she needs her attorney present."

"You don't need an attorney, Ms. Glass. I have just a couple more questions. I didn't want to see those little kids upset again."

He had a point. And so did Erik. My heart steadied and my brain rebooted. "I'll be down—just tell me where—in the morning, with my attorney. But I won't be able to reach him until his office opens. Say ten o'clock, if he's available."

* * * *

Matt Sheridan started with the same questions. Nick Merrill, a sharp young trial attorney recommended by my long-term guy, said, "Mr. Sheridan, Ms. Glass described yesterday's conversation. These are old questions. If you have new ones, ask them. If you have some specific charges, arrest her. Otherwise, we're leaving."

Bless him.

Sheridan was using the word *evidence* now. Evidence I'd been near the L.A. bombing, too. Evidence that I'd left the RV and rented a car, done things my family didn't know about.

"You have hooey, not evidence," Nick said. "My client travels often. When she comes across the possibility of an interesting experience, she goes there. At home she focuses on family, not endless details of her wanderings."

Sheridan still wanted to know what I was doing in L.A. The family thought I'd gone to Mexico.

All on script: Went to Nogales for shopping and dining. Swung over to San Diego, butterfly exhibit. Then L.A. while I was close. What had happened to Grandpa's possessions, his paintings? His house completely emptied. Dad couldn't find out. Neither did I.

"Why did you rent a car?" Sheridan asked.

"Are you kidding? L.A. in a car is bad. Tooling around in an RV is insane."

"Let's talk about bomb residue in your rental car…"

Oh, shit. Not on script. But how?

"…purchases of plastics components in Nogales…"

Oh, double shit.

"…matching residue at the bomb site."

"Is this the same forensics that found the human remains there?" Nick asked.

There was a deep flush on Matt's face. Sabrina had said the FBI had been embarrassed by that hoax. Sheridan in particular, I bet. Maybe Nick didn't know he just delivered a body blow.

Deny, deny, deny, Erik had advised. "Mr. Sheridan, I have no idea what you're talking about, except that I have visited Nogales, as you know. I shopped, went to dinner. Why would I buy plastic? Plastic what? Too much plastic in my house already."

"Do you have credit card records of those plastics purchases?" Nick asked Sheridan.

No, he sure didn't. I always paid cash.

"Mr. Sheridan," I said, "I can only tell you one more time that I don't know any bombers. I don't know about bombs. Empathy with bombers does not leave residue." A little later Sheridan said, "We have an eyewitness report of a woman matching your description, in a car identical to your rental car, waiting outside the temple gates the night of the L.A. bombing."

"Well," Nick began, waving an arm at me like an outfielder

signaling *I've got this one.* "What color was that rental car?"

"White."

"What make?"

"Toyota Camry."

"Anything special? Mag wheels? Flags flying on the antenna, dents in the fender?"

"No, but bits of carpet from your Winnebago were found at the site, too, Ms. Glass. Must have caught in the Velcro closures of the backpack left on site. The backpack the bombers used to carry the bomb."

I sat back. Sheridan's questions and Nick's points of order about evidence—where was it, when could we see it—became just so much background noise. Credit card purchases in Nogales? Absolutely false. A lady sitting in a white Toyota? Not me. Bomb residue? Maybe, but probably not. And carpet fibers? "I'd like to confer in private with Mr. Merrill, please," I said.

We stood outside the Sheriff's office as traffic on busy Commercial Street lumbered by. "Nick, are the Feds allowed to just make stuff up? Claim they have evidence that is nonexistent?"

Nick's shoulders relaxed a bit. "No," he said. "Not allowed but sometimes they do it anyway. You know, to get a suspect to talk."

"Well, Nick," I said. "Those Winnebagos came standard with a textured brown carpet. Only thing is, Neil and I tore it up ten years before any bomb went off. Replaced it with vinyl. Easier to keep up."

Nick's eyes gleamed. "C'mon," he said. We turned and went

back in. Nick took charge. He referred to some rule about misleading witnesses. Or suspects, which was it? And did Sheridan really want to subject the person who saw the lady in the Toyota to the kind of cross-examination Nick would conduct? Wasn't it dark? Weren't there thousands of similar cars in L.A.? How far away were you? Were you standing there or just driving by? If Sheridan was going to arrest me, he, Nick, wanted to see the evidence. Otherwise it was time to let me go.

Sheridan said no no no, of course I could go.

How is it that people signal doubt? The tilt of the chin, the downward arc of mouth, a raised eyebrow, a spine curving toward the back of the chair. Who knows, maybe I'd convinced him. More likely he was giving up for lack of concrete evidence.

Whatever. I'd take it. Walking out of there felt like flying. Gliding.

With my Andrea / Kate transformations, it wasn't too hard to slip out from under Squeaky Voice's nose, reconnect with Erik in Vegas, and catch the second leg back to Missoula.

That was one long weekend.

Afterwords

In January, after ten weeks' silence from Matt Sheridan, Erik and I bravely invited my family to a *Songsters Four* concert on a Friday night at the Roseland in Portland. I'd already shed first my bulk, then my wig on previous visits, but they knew nothing about Kate McGuire. We told them we would meet them there, but not that we *were* the *Songsters.*

When the lights came up, I couldn't see the audience. But I'd spotted them from backstage and so I winked in that general direction. Sure enough Josh's voice came piping,

"It's Gramma! On stage! On the stool with the flute. Look. It's Gramma!"

I spoke into my mike. "Ladies and gentlemen, it's Gramma Songster on flute, Erik doing vocals and guitar, Doug mandolin and vocals, Al bass and vocals. And down in the audience, its my grandson Josh with his brothers and sisters, mom, and dad. I pulled a fast one on them. They knew I was working out of state, but not that I had become a *Songster.* So let's hear it for Josh." Over the applause I continued, "And Emma, McKenzie, Laurie, and Brian. And their Dad, Mark. And the best daughter ever, Sabrina."

Afterwards they played our CD again and again, deciding on their favorite songs. My name on the disc was Andrea Kate.

"Wow. I didn't know you were famous, Gramma," my

favorite eight-year old commented. They wanted another concert, which we delivered at their house on Monday.

Erik and I drove home the other way, up Meacham Hill into the Blues. And we were content.

* * * *

In February at the Mountain Inn in Missoula I became Andrea Katherine Mathieson. The memory of it glows as warm as the fire in the big stone fireplace of the lodge's great room. Firelight and candle light and the light of our joy reflected soft against polished log walls, against the burgundy velvet of granddaughters' dresses, against the wine glasses and silver ice buckets.

We had fourteen attendants: our kids and grandkids. It's a wonder there was anyone left in the audience, but in fact, the room was packed: our *Songsters* collaborators and fans, Montana students, Becca—my favorite Arizona student—and her mom and dad, Tara and Ryan, her brother Curt and his wife, Arizona jammers, Montana jammers. I thought of the others, missing links because of who I was: the Eugene roommates, the company at Priest Lake. I thought of Sly, a fragile link because of who he was. And of Janet Martin. Erik and I had found her comfortable, busy and sober, but I couldn't tell her much. Not if I wanted her identity for my just-in-case persona.

I had found a knit dress to match the garnets in my ring. It had a soft scooped neck, three-quarter push-up sleeves and a skirt that fell in gentle waves from my hips to my ankles. My usual braid gave way to a French roll, and I had matching flowers in my hair and in my hands: blue irises, burgundy roses and white baby's breath. Grandma's silvery bird pin sat on my shoulder as it had when I'd married Neil. As it had not for Sabrina.

Erik was handsome in light gray slacks and sapphire blue jacket, and the smile on his face matched the light in his blue eyes as I came, a proud grandson at each side, down the stairs from the balcony and across the room toward him.

Three of us got married. Andrea and Erik and Kate. No matter. All three had supporters. I felt opulent in friends and family.

We had a short ceremony and a long party, and our lives stretched forward from there. Though we of course planned Oregon time, Missoula would be our home now, with one more move before us, to a house of wood and windows in the hills just outside of town. Grandkids would spend summers, Harry the hairy red dog would guard us fiercely, band would rehearse in the sun room, and the coffee pot would always be on.

We'd heard no more from Matt Sheridan. But had he really disappeared from my life? Kate Mathieson tucked away Kate McGuire's identity along with Janet's. Perhaps I would never need them again, but their shadows lingered.

And, too… "Something vital is missing for Brian and Laurie," I told Erik. "Sabrina gives me these sideways glances every now and then. It does hurt not to be able to completely reconnect to them. Or to the land where I had such deep roots once."

"Don't I—and *Songsters*—make up for that?"

"Yes. No. I dunno."

"Staunch ambiguity again."

"Without you, I'd be without hope. With you…well, it's like a piece of burgundy satin, rich with sheen that seems to come from within. Life 5.0. Upgraded again. But there's some rips and tears."

"We'll mend them, Elskede."

"Just maybe those bombs started discussions somewhere." I said. "Maybe some prophet will see it in my light. Have the revelation I'd hoped for."

"You might have been equally effective holding up a protest sign along the freeway," Erik pointed out.

I could only nod, because by then I was kissing him back.

Book Group?
Some issues worth discussing . . .

Is it wrong that Andrea "got away with it?" Andrea says, "Society doesn't need prisons. Punishment happens." And "Society pays three times if I go to prison" - the cost of the crime itself, the cost of prison, the cost of an unproductive life. Who benefits from jailing a mother for a crime committed 20 years earlier? What the difference between *justice* and *revenge*?

What is a terrorist, exactly? Was Andrea one? Would it change your answer if she'd actually killed the Whitesons? Is a random shooter - in a school, theater, church - a terrorist? Was Timothy McVey, the Oklahoma bomber? What about bombers of abortion clinics? The shooter at Norway's political summer camp?

Kate and Tara find a connection between their own dilemmas, the Apache wars, Afganistan. Are they right that cultural deafness is the root of wars, both personal and civic? Always? Sometimes? Never?

What about Kate's experience at Sedona and later in the desert with Tara? "How can people believe things they have no way of knowing? Believe enough to take momentous action, like denying family a marriage celebration?" Is the search for Truth equivalent to flinging Rationality into the abyss? Do we all need myth and ritual? Is it the story or the truth beneath it that is important? Does closing the temple to outsiders protect the story? The truth? Do we see only one side of the Mountain, and is that the same as cultural deafness?

Barbara K Freeman lives in western Oregon where she has taught math, raised a daughter and other critters, pulled tansy and scratched at poison oak. She has bombed no temples. Her dog howls when she tries to play sax. During her teaching years her literary accomplishments were limited to works like "2b or not 2b," but now she has written numerous short fiction pieces, has garnered third place in the 2007 Creative Nonfiction Competition at the Baltimore Review and is working on a second novel, *Circle*.

Visit her website at: www.barbarakfreeman.com.

Made in the USA
Charleston, SC
01 October 2012